Breach of Promise

N.T.
LB
CW

Also by James Scott Bell

Deadlock
Deadlock audio and ebook

Breach of Promise

James Scott Bell

GRAND RAPIDS, MICHIGAN 49530 USA

ZONDERVAN™

Breach of Promise
Copyright © 2004 by James Scott Bell

Requests for information should be addressed to:
Zondervan, *Grand Rapids, Michigan 49530*

Library of Congress Cataloging-in-Publication Data

Bell, James Scott.
Breach of promise / James Scott Bell.— 1st ed.
p. cm.
ISBN 0-310-24387-4
1. Fathers and daughters—Fiction. 2. Custody of children—Fiction. 3. Divorce—Fiction. 4. Actors—Fiction. I. Title.
PS3552.E5158 B74 2004
813'.54—dc22

2003022154

All Scripture quotations, unless otherwise indicated, are taken from the *Holy Bible: New International Version*®. NIV®. Copyright © 1973, 1978, 1984 by International Bible Society. Used by permission of Zondervan. All rights reserved.

The website addresses recommended throughout this book are offered as a resource to you. These websites are not intended in any way to be or imply an endorsement on the part of Zondervan, nor do we vouch for their content for the life of this book.

All rights reserved. No part of this publication may be reproduced, stored in a retrieval system, or transmitted in any form or by any means—electronic, mechanical, photocopy, recording, or any other—except for brief quotations in printed reviews, without the prior permission of the publisher.

Interior design by Michelle Espinoza

Printed in the United States of America

04 05 06 07 08 09 10 /❖ DC/ 10 9 8 7 6 5 4 3 2 1

For Allegra

I have walked through many lives,
some of them my own,
and I am not who I was . . .

—Stanley Kunitz, *The Layers*

Breach of Promise

Moon Dance

– 1 –

Halfway through *Twister*, when Helen Hunt was about to run down another relentless force of nature, I turned to Paula and said, "Please don't do it."

"Shh." Paula put her finger to her lips. She was really into the movie.

I hadn't been able to concentrate on the film since the first tornado. In fact, I felt like a tornado was churning inside me, destroying all my fixtures, and I knew I had to get Paula's answer.

"I really mean it, Paula."

I saw her turn toward me, her face reflected in the glow of the movie screen.

"Why are you talking about it now, Mark?"

"I can't stop thinking about it."

"We already talked it out."

"You talked. I went along."

A *shush* issued from in front of us, like a snake hiss.

"Can't this wait?" Paula whispered.

"No." I surprised myself at my own insistence.

"We're coming back to see this," Paula said emphatically, then got up and started for the exit. I followed her out.

The bright lights of the lobby and the smell of popcorn—that odd theater smell, somewhere between fresh popped and yesterday's laundry—hit me. So did Paula Montgomery's glare.

"Do you think," Paula said—her hands were in front of her, palm to palm, fingers pointing at my chest like a spear—"that this is an easy decision for me?"

"No, of course not." I was only vaguely aware of the old couple shuffling into the theater next door, showing the Tom Cruise movie *Mission: Impossible.*

"Then why bring it up again?" Paula said. Her eyes suddenly filled with tears. They gathered on her lower lids like rain on lily pads. I hugged her, burying my face in her midnight hair, which smelled like honey and cinnamon. Her shampoo. Which I loved.

"I'm sorry, baby," I said. *Baby.* "But I want it. I want our baby."

"Please. Mark."

"And I want to marry you, Paulie. I do."

She pushed me away and cursed at me. The old couple stopped in the maw of the theater doors and the woman's mouth dropped open. Paula turned and ran away.

I found her crying at Pretzels Plus in the heart of the mall. I hardly knew how to approach her. There was a big, fat pretzel lying under the glass, dotted with chunks of salt. Another twister, of a sort. Everything was twisted now.

It wasn't fair to spring this on her in the middle of a movie. She had struggled hard with the decision. I knew that. I knew pregnancy wasn't good for her career. Not at this point. She'd have to be written off the soap if they couldn't get her pregnant in the story. Maybe she could sue them, like that one actress who sued Aaron Spelling. But Paula didn't want to sue. She wanted a career. And hers was just starting to take off. She'd gotten a cover on *Soap Times.* "Up and Coming Vixens" was the title of the article.

Abortion was the logical thing. I had accepted it. For about a day.

But it gnawed at me until I had to say something. I didn't want her to do it. But not wanting that probably meant I had lost Paula Montgomery for good.

"I'm sorry," I said.

Paula was leaning against the yellow tile wall next to the pretzel glass. "All right," she said, her voice a thin reed.

I touched her shoulder. "All right what?"

"I'll marry you," she said.

Half my heart filled with new life.

"And the baby?" I said.

She looked at me, eyes red and wet. "Do you know what this is going to mean?"

"No," I said.

"Well, you better learn." She hit me in the shoulder as hard as she could, then threw her arms around my neck and held me like I was now her tether to earth.

One would have thought that a Christian wedding would have pleased all concerned, especially Paula's Bostonian matriarch mother, Erica. After all, I was "doing the right thing" by marrying Paula. But Erica the Red, as I called her only to myself, did not like me. Never had. Not good enough for her daughter. I had the feeling no one ever would be.

The Christian part of the wedding was Erica's choice, too (Paula's father, Franklin, had died two years before). I was not a Christian yet. I worshiped at the altar of Brando and James Dean. My view of Jesus was that he would be a good role to play if Steven Spielberg or Antonio Troncatti directed me in it.

Paula was not a Christian, either. She had some sort of Buddhist leanings. But we both enjoyed the pomp and circumstance that attended us in the big church in Hollywood. The Presbyterians might have been a mystery to me, but they sure had themselves a good land deal and a wonderful architect.

And Paula Montgomery was stunning in her wedding dress. I couldn't believe she was walking toward me.

We had met at a party a year and a half before, thrown by my crazy friend Roland. Roland was a gifted jazz musician by night and a writer of jingles by day. He could sit at the piano and create an ad line for any product you cared to name, right on the spot. He was doing just that when Paula walked in the door.

And knocked me out. As she did maybe half a dozen other guys there. She had hair the color of a Malibu night and violet eyes that ran on their own electricity. I had to do a lot of broken field running to get to her. But I finally managed to get her out to the balcony for some air—sweetening the deal by snagging a bowl of peanut M&M's—and I had the chance to work my magic.

Which she didn't fall for. After my few, fumbling attempts at charming small talk, she looked me in the eye and said, "Why don't you put a hold on the fluff and just tell me what you're passionate about?"

Her eyes were not just hypnotic, they were intelligent. I told her I loved acting, old movies, and baseball.

She smiled, and my heart pounded for mercy inside my chest. "Me, too."

I was so in love my mouth refused to work. I'm sure she thought I was a babbling idiot.

So the next night, when I called to ask her out (I practically assaulted Roland for her phone number), the *Yes* I heard from her was a shock on the order of holding a winning lottery ticket.

I took her to Micelli's, where working actors liked to eat. It gave hope.

"Too bad LA is not a theater town," Paula remarked at dinner. "I'd love to do Rosalind someday."

She was a serious actress, in other words. Shakespeare was not something a lot of young actors attempted anymore. It's scary to do the Bard, but also the best feeling when you carry it off.

"I'll do Orlando," I offered.

She laughed and said, "It's a deal."

I fell more deeply in love. It was like Shakespeare had written the scene for us, in modern lingo. I promised myself we would do *As You Like It* someday. As husband and wife.

And now I was marrying her. When it came time to promise to love, honor, and all the rest, I said *I do* with more intense joy than anything I'd felt before in my life. And then she promised the same. It was too much like a dream.

The nightmare was still five years away.

Throughout her pregnancy, Paula continued to act on the soap. Her character was having an affair with the respected town doctor, who was pressuring her to have an abortion. I wanted to go into the TV and slug the guy. It felt good to want to do that.

Paula did have her moments of disquiet about the upcoming birth. I was often not very helpful.

Once, after our Bradley natural birth class, we went to Ralph's Market to pick up a few items. I grabbed a straw from the deli counter and then went to the produce section and selected a big, ripe cantaloupe. I took the items over to Paula.

"See," I said. "All you have to do is pass this—" I held up the cantaloupe—"through this—" the straw. "It's easy!"

"Shut UP!"

– 2 –

When Paula went into labor, I was auditioning for "young father" on a Lucky Charms commercial. It was not a cause of great celebration in my heart. I was twenty-nine and not ready to be listed as "young father" on the casting sheets in town. My agent had not told me she approved the change. I found out when I walked into the audition with my headshots and the C girl said, "You need to update these." I looked too young in them.

So when the call from the hospital came on the cell phone, I did not hang around. I was about to become "young father" in real life. How could Lucky Charms compete with that?

Paula was in labor for eight hours. It was not smooth sailing. There were times when this beautiful woman took on the face of Lucifer's less attractive sister, glaring at me with knives, because I was responsible for *getting her into this*.

When I told her I had given up a Lucky Charms spot to be here with her she said, "Get me *drugs*."

They gave her an intravenous injection of Demerol, which at least softened her back into the beautiful wife I knew. And she was beautiful, even without makeup, even with sweaty strands of ebony hair stuck to her forehead like wet string.

We knew we were going to have a girl, and we had decided to name her Madeleine Erica Gillen. The Erica, of course, was for Paula's mother. I didn't fight her on that, because one does not do battle with the Montgomerys and survive.

The Madeleine, though, was my idea, something I just hit on one day, reading through a baby name book. For me it had a classic quality to it, but also suggested just a little bit the madness that I felt for Paula. As in madly in love. As in the woman of my dreams.

The Demerol did not last, and finally an anesthesiologist gave Paula an epidural with a needle the length of California.

That's what I remember most, up until the time Madeleine's head slid out, followed by the rest of her, into the hands of Dr. Malverse Martin.

I began to believe in God at that moment.

The next few years passed like a montage in a family movie, complete with musical score. The bad scenes—the tensions, the arguments, the pressures, the finances, the auditions, the juggling of two careers and one baby—these ended up on the cutting room floor of my mind. I kept the good shots on the front of the reel:

The baths. Maddie's skin so soft and my thumbs nearly the length of her tiny head.

My skill as a diaper changer. How I could wad a used Pampers up into a ball of almost impossible density.

Holding Maddie all night in a recliner, because she was so stuffy with a cold she could not breathe when lying flat.

Bringing her to Paula for midnight feedings.

The early, fuzzy sprouts of Maddie's hair.

Her first word, *Dada,* which really upset Paula. Her third word, *Kaka,* which to her meant *cookie,* and cracked me up completely.

The big day we bought Maddie her own potty, and she decided it would be a bed for her bear. Much discussion ensued.

When she was three, we announced we were taking her to Disneyland. Even at that age, a child in Los Angeles knows what Disneyland is. It seeps into their heads while they sleep. When we told her, her blue eyes got huge and she said, "My heart is beautiful!"

I still can't think of a better way to express happiness than that.

And then the time we were watching *It's a Wonderful Life* on TV one Christmas. Maddie was four. Donna Reed and Jimmy Stewart started singing "Buffalo Gals" as they were walking home from the high school dance. I glanced at Maddie and she seemed mesmerized.

Aaaaannnd dance by the light of the moon.

Jimmy and Donna, singing.

Maddie looked at me then. "Can we do that?" she asked. Paula was on the phone in the kitchen. I alone had to field this one and knew from experience that Maddie's questions sometimes threw a bolo around my head.

"Do what, honey?"

"Dance by the guy in the moon?"

"By the light of the moon."

"Whatever, Daddy."

"You bet we can."

"Now?"

It was one of those things you don't stop and analyze. I think God implants a certain instinct in fathers (who are somewhat slow on the uptake) that tells them to heed their children without extensive cross-examination.

"Sure," I said. I lifted her off the couch—she in her soft cotton PJs with rabbits and me in my cutoffs and Dodger T-shirt—and went to the kitchen to tell Paula we were going up on the roof of the building. Paula, phone at her ear, put her finger in the air, telling me to be quiet.

I carried Maddie up to the roof.

The moon was almost full. It seemed huge. It cast a glow over the hills, where million-dollar homes gawked somewhat incredulously at the apartment buildings below. The kind of homes I dreamed of living in, with Paula and Maddie and a big, fat $20 million contract to star in the next Ridley Scott movie.

But tonight I did not care that I was on an apartment building roof. Maddie had her warm arms around my neck, and I held her and swayed, swayed, swayed. Time went completely away as we danced by the light of the moon.

Bad Things

– 1 –

I can pinpoint the start of the bad things.

The three of us were dining at Maddie's favorite restaurant, Flookey's. This was an establishment on Ventura Boulevard serving a selection of hot dogs and chips. It had an outdoor patio. Maddie liked to eat outside so she could say hi to all the people.

At five she was already networking. She'd make it in this town for sure.

Paula's cell rang and she picked up. I half watched Paula and half did a hand game with Maddie.

After thirty seconds Paula looked as if her mother had died. She was silent, her face draining of color in the fashion of an old ghost movie. Just before I asked what was wrong, her face transformed into an incandescent smile. Then the tears came.

She said something and put the phone down.

"That was Phyl," she said. Phyl was Paula's agent.

"Good news?"

"Look at me, honey," she said. How could I not? She was in the grip of something. She put her hand on my arm and with her other hand grabbed Maddie's fingers.

"Antonio Troncatti wants me for his next film," she said.

The name, the news, hit me like a rolled-up *Variety* across the face. Antonio Troncatti was the director of the moment, the new anointed one. A thirty-five-year-old Italian whose first movie had been nominated for Best Foreign Film. His next project had been for TriStar, a portrait of Napoleon starring Sean Penn. It was a huge international hit. That caught everyone by surprise because it did not contain the action elements usually required for big foreign box office.

The rumor now was he was in preproduction on a major thriller to be shot mostly in Europe. And every actor in Hollywood wanted to work with him.

"Wow," I said in a half whisper.

"Wow!" Maddie screeched. She had no idea who Antonio Troncatti was, of course. She just wanted to be part of the fun.

"I can't believe this," Paula said, her voice and face otherworldly.

"How did he happen—"

"To pick me? Phyl says he wanted an unknown for the role, but a certain look. I guess I have it."

"What about—" I nodded my head toward Maddie.

"What do you mean?" Paula said. I could tell I'd just deflated her a little.

"I mean, are you going to be in Europe, shooting?"

"I don't know, Mark," she said sharply. "I don't know anything yet. Can't you just be happy for me right now?"

I recovered quickly. "Yeah. Sure. Of course. You're going to be a big star. You hear that, Maddie? Mommy's going to be a big star!"

"My heart is beautiful!" Maddie said.

But my heart was not beautiful. To be perfectly frank, I was envious. Acting couples are that way. It's a competitive business, and when your spouse gets the big break you have been hoping for yourself, it's one of those good news/bad news things.

I have to admit that, when we got married, I thought I was the real actor in the family. Paula was on a soap. Not a bad thing. The money is good, the work steady. But it's like the minor leagues of media. I never wanted to be on a soap, just in films or a solid TV series.

My unspoken plans were for me to get into feature films, starring roles, and Paula to follow along afterward. Maybe make her big splash in one of my own movies.

Call it male pride. Ego soufflé. That's the way it was.

Paula could sense it, too, on the drive home. She gets quiet when she's upset, and a little line forms in the flesh between her eyebrows. I call it the John Gruden line, after the Tampa Bay football coach whose sneer is now legendary among followers of the game.

Maddie, happy in her car seat in the back of the Accord, looking at a picture book, ignored us.

"When's it supposed to start?" I asked.

"I don't know any of that yet." Paula looked straight ahead. "Phyl will fill me in."

"Phyl you in? I get it."

Paula did not see the humor. Neither did I. I had done standup comedy for a while, on open mike nights, and I knew when a joke was lame. That was lame.

"Troncatti," I said.

"What's Troncatti?" Maddie asked from the rear.

"An Italian pasta," I said. "You make it with Alfredo sauce."

"Daddy's joking, honey." Paula turned around, protecting her child from the bad jokes of the driver. "Antonio Troncatti is a famous moviemaker. Mommy's going to be in his movie."

"With sauce?" my daughter said.

"Good call!" I slapped the steering wheel. "Alfredo sauce and pretentious dialogue."

Paula spun around to look at me. "What are you doing?"

"What?"

"Why are you putting him down like that?"

"I'm just joking."

"It's not funny."

Maddie said, "Not funny, Daddy."

"Look at your book," I told Maddie. "Mommy and Daddy are talking."

"Talk, talk, talk," Maddie said.

We drove in silence along Ventura. It was crowded tonight, and I hit every red light. Each one was like a little slap in the face.

Finally, I said, "Look, I'm sorry. All right? I want you to succeed. I really do. This is great news. I just feel, I don't know—"

"Jealous?"

"Honest? A little."

Paula put her hand on my arm. Her hand was hot. "Mark, you're a great actor. I really think that. I think you should be getting your break soon. I want it to happen for you. I know it will."

Back at the apartment I waited until Maddie was asleep before stirring up some hot chocolate for Paula and me. I took it to her with a big swirl of whipped cream on the top. She was watching a movie in the living room—*All About Eve*, one of her all-time favorites. She smiled as she took it and gave me the first sip.

"You know, I like being a man," I said.

"And why is that?"

"Because when I retain water, it's in a canteen."

"Oh please."

"And a phone conversation takes thirty seconds, max."

"Very funny."

"But the thing I like most about it?"

She looked at me.

"I get to be married to you."

Two weeks later I had a knock-down-drag-out with Paula. She had officially signed on to do the film with Troncatti. There was still a part of me that hoped something would go wrong. Film cancelled. Change of mind on the casting. Selfish, I know, but I couldn't help feeling it.

When the contract was signed, the reality was like a refrigerator dropping on my foot. Paula was going to be doing interviews, preproduction promotion, media stuff. She had a hundred other things to do trying to get ready to go. One night in the apartment, she asked me to help her go over her list, see if she'd forgotten anything.

"Yeah," I said. "Maddie."

She gave me her signature roll of the eyeballs, which only ticked me off.

"I mean it," I said. "You're going to be in Europe for what? Four months?"

"Give or take," she said.

"And when are you going to see your daughter?"

"Mark," she said, pulling off her glasses—they were black-framed and she never wore them in public, but when she pulled them off she seemed like my fifth-grade teacher about to chastise me—"four months is not a big deal."

"To you maybe, but what about Maddie?"

"Bring her over."

"Right. And meanwhile I quit auditioning."

"What's wrong with that?"

The way she said it entered my pores like an arctic wind. She might as well have said, *Your career isn't exactly taking off, like mine, and you haven't had a paying gig in eight months, so how can it be wrong to have you fly over where I'll be making myself into a legend?*

"That's just like you all of a sudden," I said. "You're the center of the universe now."

"Maybe I am. Maybe it's my time."

"You sound like George Segal in *Look Who's Talking.*"

"Huh?"

"When he cheats on Kirstie Alley and tells her, 'I'm going through a selfish phase.'"

"That is so mean."

"Comparing you to George Segal?" I can be nasty when I want to be.

"You don't want me to succeed, do you?"

At that precise moment I was not sure if I did. I could feel her star ascending like it was launched by some heavenly Cape Canaveral, while I sat here back on earth, a boulder in Death Valley.

I did want her to succeed. Part of me was so proud of her. She was going to become a major star, I had always believed that. And she was *my wife.* I never felt so good as when I walked into a party with Paula on my arm. Everyone would stop what they were doing and just stare—at her—and then they'd look over at me, thinking *Who is that lucky guy?*

But I also didn't want her to go away. And I yelled at her about it.

Paula yelled back. She had a good, strong voice. Great for theater work.

My voice is stronger, however, and I used it. Paula got so mad she started to cry and took off one of her shoes and threw it at me as hard as she could. She missed and I laughed. (To this day I am sorry about that. It was a cruel and ugly thing to do, and I did it because I wanted to *win.* That was all that mattered.)

And then Maddie came into the kitchen where World War III was commencing.

"Guys!" Maddie said emphatically, "this is not what you do!"

We looked at Maddie. I looked at Paula. Paula looked at me. Then Paula started to laugh. And I started to laugh. Maddie put her hands on her hips and said, "This is not funny."

– 2 –

"Mark, I've been thinking."

Paula and I were in bed. I'd just finished getting Maddie settled by letting her read Dr. Seuss to me. I chose *Marvin K. Mooney Will You Please Go Now!* All the way through I was thinking about Paula. She would be going soon.

"Good," I said. "A woman who thinks is very sexy."

"Not about that."

"Can I change your way of thinking?"

"Will you listen?"

"I'm listening." I folded my hands on my stomach and looked at the ceiling. It had a brown water spot in the corner. Funny, but I hadn't noticed it before. Did it come after the last rains?

"It's about you and Maddie."

"What about me and Maddie?"

"I think maybe we can work something out while I'm gone. To help."

"Help?"

"You know."

I got up on one elbow, looked at Paula. "No, I don't know."

Paula sighed. "About taking care of her."

"What, you're saying I can't handle the job?"

"You said so yourself."

"When?"

"When you were bagging on me going to Europe. All that about your career suffering."

"What are you, an elephant? Never forget?"

"It was three days ago. It's not like last year."

"Why are you bringing this up now?"

"Duh, because I'm about to leave."

"Forget about it. We went through this."

"No, you went through this."

"Then you said okay."

"When did I say okay?"

"When you didn't say anything. That was a silent okay."

She shook her head. "This is starting to sound like a bad Seinfeld script. I'm telling you I've got an idea. You want to hear it, or do you want to bat around lines?"

With a hand to her shoulder, I said, "Or something else?"

She pulled away from me. "Stop it. I'm serious. I've been talking to Mom and she's willing to come out here."

The dreaded *M* word. "You want your mother to come out here for the entire time you're shooting?"

"She says she doesn't mind. She'll lease a house."

"A *house?*"

"That's not a problem."

"I guess not. But I've got a problem."

"Mark, you—"

"No." I rolled off the bed. My feet hit the floor like asphalt pounders. "I don't want your mom taking care of Maddie."

"It's only to help, while you're—"

"It won't stay just helping. Your mom will try to take more and more—"

"Maddie will still live here."

"Well, thank you."

"This is for Maddie."

"You don't think I can do this? Take care of my own daughter by myself?"

When Paula didn't say anything I got mad. "I don't want your mom within five states of this apartment."

Paula got up, so she could face me. Fighter to fighter. "That is so unfair. She is Maddie's grandmother."

"And about as fond of me as, what? A rash? A festering boil?"

"Stop."

"That's what she thinks."

"You won't give her a chance."

I pounded my chest with an open hand. King Kong. "What chance has she ever given me? Huh? She thinks her precious daughter got hooked up with a loser!"

Before Paula could say anything we heard a pounding on the wall, coming from Maddie's room. And then her voice, muffled but emphatic: "Hey, some people are trying to sleep around here."

Now that *should* have been funny. Coming from a five-year-old with perfect timing. But I didn't so much as smile. Neither did Paula. We let a chill settle between us, silent and misty.

"Paula?"

"What."

"Don't worry about Maddie and me."

She did not reply.

"Hey," I said.

"What now?"

"Remember when we went to see *Doctor Zhivago*? At the Dome?"

"Yes."

"Remember the part where Lara's leaving the hospital? After Zhivago's fallen in love with her? And the cart pulls out and watching it go, you can see on his face he thinks he'll never see her again?"

"Yes."

"And he walks back in and that yellow flower is starting to die—"

"I remember, yes. What about it?"

"That's how I feel right now."

I felt the bed move, and then she was up against me, her breath on my face. "Dope, this isn't a movie. I'm just shooting one, okay?"

"Don't make me go to Russia looking for you."

"Deal," she said.

– 3 –

And then, sooner than I could imagine, it was time for Paula to go make her movie. We—Maddie and I—did not take Paula to the airport. The studio sent a driver around. For some reason that made me feel like a forgotten man. But I kept a smile on my face, for Maddie's sake.

Paula kissed and hugged us. Maddie cried a little, but tried to be brave. Paula promised to phone her a lot.

The last thing Paula said to me, after a final kiss, was, "Be good."

In a morbid, ugly, horror movie sort of way, that *is* funny.

After Paula left, Maddie was very clingy. She had hold of my jeans and wouldn't let go. I walked around the apartment with this five-year-old growth on my leg.

"Don't go away, Daddy," Maddie kept saying.

"No, cupcake," I said. "I'm here. I just have to go to a meeting this afternoon."

"No!"

"Honey, it's for my work. Mrs. Williams is going to watch you."

She pulled my jeans hard. "No! I wanna go with you."

"It'll be boring. I'm going to have to wait around and—"

"I can color."

How could I argue with that? We packed up a couple of her coloring books—SpongeBob SquarePants and Powerpuff Girls—and hopped in my Accord for the ride to CBS on Radford.

The gate guard, a skinny old guy in a dark jacket (even though it must have been ninety outside), gave Maddie a scowl as I checked in.

"She's not on the list," the guard said, looking at his clipboard like it was incriminating evidence.

Before I could open my mouth, Maddie said, "That's my daddy!" She had a look on her face that was not to be trifled with.

I smiled sheepishly at the guard. Who broke out into a toothy grin. "Go on," he said. Maddie the charmer had done it again.

My audition was in a production office next to Studio C. In the reception area, in between potted plants and ostentatious urns, sat about half a dozen guys roughly my age.

The competition.

I recognized one of the guys from my acting class, Steve Monet (pronounced like the painter). He gave me a half smile and wave, the kind that said, *I know you're up for this, old buddy, but I sure hope you drool during the reading.*

The receptionist handed me my "sides," the two pages of dialogue I would be reading in order to land this national spot for Colgate. I sat in the one empty chair, put Maddie on the floor in front of me, and started reading the lines.

"That's pretty desperate," Steve said.

"Huh?"

"Bringing your little girl to the audition. Going for the sympathy factor?"

"Funny." I went back to my sides.

"I mean, you really going to bring her in with you?"

"She wanted to come with me."

"Oh. That's right."

"That's right *what?*"

"I read about Paula. She's doing the Troncatti film."

"Yeah."

"Making you Mr. Mom?"

"Something like that. Hey." I held up the pages, a signal that I needed to get back to business.

"Troncatti's a wild man," Steve said. His half smile slid from one side of his face to the other.

That was too much. He was playing with my head, I was sure, because he wanted me to flub the audition. But his ploy worked. My mind created a picture of Paula and Troncatti, laughing it up on the set, having a good old time. Too good?

Snap out of it. This is Paula's break. Yours is coming. Read the lines.

"What's the kid's name?" Steve asked.

"You mind?" I said. "I want to get ready."

"Take it easy, man."

Maddie looked at him. "My name is Madeleine Erica Gillen and I'm five years old."

"Whoa," Steve said, throwing up his hands in mock surrender.

Maddie went back to coloring Powerpuff Girls.

When my turn came to read, Maddie wanted to go in with me. I got a cold eye from the casting director, a man, and a tepid smile from the producer, a woman.

"Nice touch," the producer said.

I read my lines to the camera and got the traditional "We'll call you" from the casting director. It sounded like a door closing and being locked from the inside.

Actors are paranoid, but then again, everyone is out to get us.

– 4 –

I wouldn't be Oprah's first pick as the model of fatherhood.

My own parents met dropping acid in San Francisco in 1968. Mom got pregnant, and I guess the two of them decided this was *groovy*. They were never officially married, though I think someone chanted at them one night as they sat on a bed of flower petals and bayed at the moon.

I was born into a commune outside Santa Cruz, one the cops broke up not long after my birth. I was not the cause of the dispersal. A thriving marijuana field maintained by my dad (who had taken to calling himself Kalifornia) was the real reason.

Dad ended up doing some time in a California prison, by the way. I think I wrote to him once. He never answered.

Mom, whose real name was Estelle Gillen but who preferred to be called Rainbow, returned with me to her mother's home in Chatsworth, a suburb of Los Angeles. My early memories are of my grandmother, Joyce Gillen, a widow who worked reception at Hughes Aircraft. Even when I was six or seven, I saw her as the mother figure in my life.

Mom was trying to come back from her years as a brain-fried flower child. She hooked up with another man, a guy named Barza who ran a Harley shop in Canoga Park. Mom, in photographs from the time, is very beautiful in a natural sort of way. I suppose she thought he was the epitome of *groovy*. That must have been the reason why she announced one day, to me and Gram, that she was taking off for a ride across the country, "like in *Easy Rider*."

Someone should have mentioned that *Easy Rider* didn't turn out so good for the guys on the bikes.

We got the call at night. Gram took the phone while I was in the living room watching *Dukes of Hazzard.* I heard her wail "Oh God, no!" I ran in and saw her collapse onto the floor. I was eleven years old.

Later we found out that Barza had tried to outrun a trooper in Alabama and skidded off the highway into a split-rail fence. He survived. Mom did not.

It shook me in a way I could not understand at eleven. But I would always feel a punch in the stomach whenever I saw a rainbow after that.

Gram did her best with me. But not having a father or mother in my life, or even a grandfather, was not the best thing that could have happened to the spawn of LSD-induced passion.

I started shoplifting, smoking, hanging out with the people I thought would help get me in the most trouble. If you were to look at me at twelve, you would see a poster boy for Future Skinheads of America. I stayed away from the house as much as I could. I loved Gram and did not want to see her hurt.

But the cops dragging me home after I stole beer from a 7–Eleven did that well enough. And so did the vice principal at school who suspended me for selling cigarettes on campus. Gram cried a lot over both of those things and I hated myself for that. But I didn't stop doing what I could to catch the slow train to state prison.

It was baseball that saved my life. Literally. I believe that to this day.

I'd always been good at the game, never taking it seriously. Mom put me in Little League for one season when I was ten and I ripped up the opposition. I was wild with the bat but usually made contact. Hard. My average was .782 for the season.

I also had a cannon for an arm. I was usually put in right field, because my glove work was not the best. Yet. But there was many a time when a hard one to the deep corner turned into a spectacular out as I gunned the guy down trying to stretch a double into a triple.

I was named to the All-Stars and had a great postseason, too.

The next year Mom died and I lost interest in Little League.

But one of the dads from that Little League year remembered me. He coached at Chatsworth High, and when I got there he sought me out. Got tough with me, got me back into baseball. My life got a little straighter after that. Much to Gram's relief.

I rose through the ranks, and by the time I was a twelfth grader I was among the top prospects in LA. I was named first team All-City.

The Red Sox offered me a contract. I had an agent and everything. Off to the minors I went, ready to embark on a glorious and highly paid future.

Then, in a game in Omaha, I blew out my arm. I was trying to make another legendary throw from deep right. The players were much faster up there than I was used to. I gave the throw everything I had and could almost hear the tearing of muscle and cartilage. It was like someone had napalmed my shoulder.

Coupled with the fact that I was still a wild swinger and could not catch up with a professional curveball, my baseball career came to a sudden and inglorious end.

At the age of nineteen I was out of baseball, out of work, out of options. Alcohol seemed like the traditional way to dull the misery. I went for it. That was the start, too, of what they now call *anger issues.*

At least I gave up drinking when I found out Paula was going to have our baby.

The anger, though, was about to have a field day.

– 5 –

We had a game, Maddie and I, that was her all-time favorite. I called it Maddie's Buried Treasure.

I did not simply give her gifts, or candy, or something fun. I put it in a little box or bag and hid it somewhere in the apartment. Then I'd tell her, in my best Long John Silver voice, "Treasure is hid, ahhrrrr, and ye best be lookin' for it."

Which would make her giggle and scurry all over the apartment. I had to get more and more clever about finding good hiding spots.

One time I bought a box of Nerds, her favorite candy, and a little squish ball and left them in the Rite-Aid bag along with the receipt. I just rolled the bag up and put it on the middle bookshelf, behind a copy of *Respect for Acting* by Uta Hagen and John Grisham's *The Pelican Brief.*

And promptly forgot all about it.

Three days later Maddie let out a scream while I was in the kitchen burning some toast. I ran to her, thinking she'd cut herself or something.

But she was jumping up and down, delighted. Holding the Rite-Aid bag in her hand.

"I found it!" she yelped. "And you didn't even tell me it was buried!"

"Ahhrrr!" I said. "Ye must be the smartest pirate on the seven seas!"

"Silly," Maddie said. "I'm a ballerina!"

The other ritual we had was when I gave Maddie a bath. I loved doing that. When I shampooed her hair with Johnson's Baby Shampoo (she could do this herself but I always wanted to, and she'd let me), I would lean her back in the water to rinse and her face got this beatific look. She'd close her eyes and smile. It was complete trust in me and pure enjoyment of the moment. Her hair would float like kelp in a calm sea, and I'd be thinking that I was really doing something here—making my daughter clean and fresh. I loved the smell of Maddie after a bath.

Our ritual was this: Maddie could ask me any question she wanted to.

So, one evening, she came up out of the water and said, "Do you like God?"

I laughed. "Yes, I like God."

"What does he look like?"

This was just a bath, but all of a sudden we were in deep theological waters. When your daughter starts asking questions about God, even if you're fuzzy on the concept, you tread lightly, because you think one wrong answer could start her down some strange path. You see your child, twenty years hence, hanging out in some waterfront dive as the piano plays, cigarette dangling from her mouth, telling sailors the funny story about what her dad said God looked like.

"I don't think God really looks like anything," I said. Good. Introduce a concept she won't understand and you cannot explain. Not look like anything? How can anything not look like something?

"I think God looks like you," Maddie said.

Perhaps I ought to take this more seriously, I thought, though I did appreciate the compliment.

So I told her the only Bible story I knew about God. I didn't have a Bible background, so I was running on fumes. I tried to make it exciting.

"One day," I told Maddie, "there was this big war going on and one side had a giant named Goliath fighting for them. It was really unfair."

"How big was he?" Maddie asked.

"Oh, I'd say about one hundred feet tall."

"How big is that?"

"Like a telephone pole."

"Wow."

"Yeah. And he would growl at the other army, which happened to believe in God, by the way."

"Cool."

"But they were all afraid of this giant, see? But there was a boy named David who was not a soldier, just a kid."

"What did he look like?"

Richard Gere? Nah. No way. "He was good looking, let's put it that way."

"I don't like boys."

"That's a conversation for another time, okay? Listen. This kid David doesn't have any armor or swords or anything like that. All he has is a slingshot."

"Like in cartoons?"

"It was more of a thing that you whirl around your head with a rock in it, and it throws rocks real hard."

"That's dangerous."

"You're telling me? But this big giant Goliath has a big old sword and spear."

"And a gun?"

"Maybe he's hiding a gun in his pocket, who knows? But he marches out and starts making fun of the army of God, calling them names and laughing at them. But no one wants to go out and fight this guy."

"He was too big."

"You got it. But David says he'll do it."

"Was he short?"

"Yeah."

"Was he scared?"

"Nah. He believed in God, see? And he knew God was stronger than any old giant any day. So David marches right out there with his slingshot, see, and some rocks. And that big old Goliath starts laughing at him. And David puts a rock in his slingshot and zips it and *BAM!*"

Maddie yelped, then giggled.

"Right in Goliath's head."

"Owie."

"Big-time owie. It killed him."

Maddie's eyes got big with wonder.

"So David became a hero and a king and got to have his own castle and everything, because he believed in God."

"Wow."

"Big-time wow."

I kissed her freshly shampooed head and knew that I needed some boning up on God. Because if I knew Maddie, she was going to ask for more stories just like this one.

After getting Maddie to bed I went to the computer to check out an industry website. It was my way of keeping up on the business I had my little toe in. While I was scrolling around I saw a link to an item that mentioned Antonio Troncatti and some "wild times" in Rome during the shooting of *Conquered.* Naturally I headed right for it.

As I did, I could feel my heart pulsing in my chest, like I knew what I would find. It had the feel of something inevitable and bad.

Here's what I read.

La Dolce Vida Redux

Fireworks are apparently breaking out on the set of *Conquered*, the new Antonio Troncatti opus starring Blake Patterson and Paula Montgomery. Shooting on the set has featured some outrageous behavior by Patterson, well known for his rather unconventional approach to life, the universe, and everything.

Cast and crew were seen drinking it up at a hot Rome nightspot. Meanwhile, Troncatti and Montgomery were cheek to cheek on the dance floor until the wee hours, according to reports, until heading off together for parts unknown.

A helpless, hot, grinding suction set to work on my guts. My hands and arms almost felt numb. And pictures formed in my mind, Paula and Troncatti. Couldn't help it. I imagined the worst.

Shaking, I got up, looked at the clock. Figuring as best I could, I made it nine in the morning in Rome. I grabbed the kitchen phone and called the contact number I had for the set. I got the voice-mail message of Sting Ray Stephens, the PR person. I didn't leave a message.

I called Paula's hotel. The guy at the desk barely understood English. I said I was Paula Montgomery's husband.

He said something in Italian and hung up.

I wanted to start an international incident right then.

I went to the computer and e-mailed Paula. *I need to talk to you right away. Can you call me on the cell ASAP?*

That was it.

Then I sat staring at the monitor for I don't know how long, chewing my thumbnail. It even bled, but I kept right on chewing.

No call.

I think I fell asleep around three A.M., watching an old Barbara Stanwyck movie on AMC.

– 6 –

Maddie knew something was up as I drove her to her day camp.

"Why aren't you talking, Daddy?"

Because your mother is eating my heart, honey. Because Mommy is probably in bed with a sleazy Italian director while I'm here taking care of you. Wanna Happy Meal?

"Sorry, cupcake."

"Your eyes look scrunchy."

I tried to unscrunch them, but it didn't work.

With Maddie safely at camp I drove around the corner from the park (somehow having Maddie close by, even though she couldn't see me, helped). I called the hotel in Rome again and had to leave another message.

I tried to keep the anger out of it. Maybe there was an explanation to all this. Imagination can be a terrible thing.

Looking at myself in the rearview mirror, I thought I'd be ripe for a remake of *The Picture of Dorian Gray.* The bags under my eyes were like suitcases. There would be no need for makeup.

A star in the making.

"You look tired," Nancy said.

"Ya think?" I said, trying to sound like I had some energy left for acting.

"Darling, you have an audition at two."

"Is it a vampire role? I'm ready."

Nancy Radford, my auburn-haired, middle-aged agent, pursed her lips. She was not in the mood for jocularity. She wanted to get me work.

Nancy herself worked for Talent Across the Board, a boutique agency in Encino. I was not a big-agency guy (as Paula soon would be—*Variety* said that Phyl was going over to AEA and bringing Paula with her).

Nancy had taken me on when I was hardly more than an ex-jock with all my teeth. She apparently saw something in me, enough to suggest acting lessons from a guy, Marty North, who has a studio in the Valley.

It was a good move, and I learned my stuff from Marty, who was a graduate of the American Academy of Dramatic Arts. I got some things going after that, some commercials, some income. The rest of my income came from waitering jobs, the best at Josephina's in Santa Monica, where Roland worked. He got me the gig.

"Listen, kiddo," Nancy said, "this is for a Showtime Movie, a great supporting role, and they're not insisting on a name."

Most casting lists for good parts insisted on "name only." In other words, an actor who wasn't me. An actor people had heard of.

"What kind of role?"

"Cop," Nancy said. "Here's the description."

She handed me a copy of a fax. On the sheet it gave a one-paragraph sketch of a guy named Dex Wainright—thirty-two, burned-out cop, alcoholic, dealing with family stress.

"I can play this part," I said, as if the casting fairy had dropped the perfect role in my lap.

"That's why I'm sending you up."

Just before I left, Nancy said, "How are things at home?"

Had she been reading the same gossip pages about Paula? Was this story all over town? Was I being whispered about in cafés and behind closed doors?

I looked at her with a cocked head. "Why?"

"Just asking. I haven't seen Maddie in a while."

"Maddie is Maddie. She's a survivor."

"Who's watching her?"

"She's at camp."

"What about after? Will that ever be a prob?"

"Prob?"

"Reason I'm asking, it's got to be hard, with Paula gone. You managing all right?"

Don't I look it? Don't I look like the bloom of youth?

"Sure."

"You know," Nancy said, "maybe now's a good time for you to think about what you really want to do."

"What's that supposed to mean?"

Nancy shrugged. "The business is tough enough. You have to really want it, more than anything."

Putting my fists on her desk and leaning over, I said, "Nancy, I want this. I need this. I am an actor. That's what I do. I'm not going to stop."

She smiled. "Just what I wanted to hear. Go and make me proud."

The call finally came at 1:12 P.M.

I remember looking at the time on the phone, as if I needed to get it exactly, as if Jack Webb would come out of the grave as the *Dragnet* guy and ask me for the facts. I was in Starbucks on Franklin because my audition was just down the street at a studio on La Brea. I took the phone outside so it wouldn't cut out. Also so I could yell if I needed to.

"I'm so sorry," Paula said, her voice sounding remarkably clear. "We were shooting in the country for a few days and the whole crew was out there."

"How'd it go?" I was keeping my voice as placid as possible. I wanted to get verbal cues from *her.*

"Oh, fine," she said. The verbal cue I got was *discomfort.* Something was definitely up.

"Great," I said.

"You don't sound too excited."

"Neither do you."

"Mark, it's late. I'm really tired."

"That makes two of us. I didn't get much sleep last night."

"How's Maddie?"

Slick change. "Maddie's great. Maddie's wonderful. I've been spending a lot of time with her, as you may well know."

"Mark, what is going on?"

Should I let it all out now? In one big torrent? Here outside a Hollywood coffeehouse so the ratty-looking guy at the bus stop could hear me?

"You know, the Internet's great," I said. "I can't be there with you, but it's the next best thing. I get reports on the movie, how it's going."

Long silence. "You saw it."

"Of course I saw it. What, were you going to keep it a secret from me?"

"No, Mark. This is so stupid."

"What's stupid?"

"This whole thing. We should both be happy, shouldn't we?"

That seemed like a pretty loaded question. She was preparing me.

"Tell me straight up," I said.

"Tell you what?"

"What's going on with you and Troncatti?"

She whispered a curse, the kind that signals defeat. Or getting caught.

"We shouldn't do this over the phone," she said.

The guy at the bus stop was looking at me, like he could overhear the conversation. He couldn't, of course, but it seemed like there was a spotlight on me and all the cars were not stopped because of the red light, but because they wanted to watch me lose control.

"No, let's," I said. "Let's do it right now. Did you sleep with him?"

The silence was my answer.

"How many times?"

"Mark, please. For Maddie's sake, for our sakes, let's just wait until I get back. We need to talk."

The Mayans, I once read, used to cut the hearts out of their human sacrifices while they were still alive. That way, the high priest could hold up the heart while it was still beating, showing the people the power of life and death at the same time.

I punched the End button and powered off the cell. I had an audition. It was time for my big break.

– 7 –

There are times when an actor sees something in the eyes of the casting people. A mixture of scorn and pity. A look of absolute amazement that here is a person who thought he could act, who thought he might have a future in this business. The room becomes an orchestra of forced smiles and coughs behind closed fists.

"Thanks for coming in, Mark," the director said. But it sounded like some guy saying, *Abandon all hope.*

Funny thing was I didn't really care. All I could think about was Paula. Losing her. Feeling like a prize chump. Wanting to kill Troncatti. Wanting to die myself.

Fighting traffic back into the Valley I almost got in a couple of road-rage confrontations. It wasn't me driving; it was some version of Mr. Hyde. Only the thought of Maddie, waiting to be picked up, kept me from totally freaking out.

I was half an hour late to the park.

"We do not appreciate this, Mr. Gillen," the matronly gestapo agent with the Camp Sunshine T-shirt said to me through the car window.

"I'm sorry," I said. "Traffic."

"We're not being paid to babysit, you know." *You vill obey!*

"Yes, again, very sorry." My voice was vacant, far away, like one of the pod people in *Invasion of the Body Snatchers*.

Maddie was getting into her car seat in the back. She did not look pleased.

"Where were you, Daddy?"

"I'm sorry. Let's go home and eat."

"I want to go to Wendy's."

"We had Wendy's yesterday. How about I cook us up something nice at home?"

"I want to go to Wendy's."

We were pulling onto Laurel Canyon now, into traffic. A black Cadillac Esplanade, regal and shiny in the late afternoon sun, cut in front of my Accord without signaling. I honked. Hard. The driver, some yoohoo with a cell phone to his ear, momentarily pulled the device from his head so he could give me a one-fingered salute.

"I said Wendy's, Daddy."

"No."

"Yes!"

There is a famous newsreel clip of Benito Mussolini, fascist dictator over Italy during World War II, looking at a cheering crowd. He folds his arms, juts out his chin, and protrudes his lower lip. *I am your master*, he seems to be thinking. *Bow down to me.*

I mention this only because that is the pose Madeleine Erica Gillen took whenever she wanted her way. Like now.

"We are going home," I said.

This time Maddie screamed, as loudly as she could. "NOOOOOO!"

I almost hit a kid on a bike when she did that. Adrenaline blasted through my body, mixing with all the anger and hurt and lack of sleep that had been pooling up in me for hours.

Without a thought between scream and act, I half turned and slapped my child's arm. Hard. It made a crisp popping sound, like a gunshot.

The pause that followed was the worst part. In that silence I could feel Maddie's shock, her sense of betrayal. Never had I struck Maddie, not even the time when she was three and refused to use the potty and deliberately peed on the floor in front of me.

In that long, haunting pause I thought I had lost the last thing on earth that loved me.

And then she wailed. She cried like I'd never heard her before.

Our apartment was on the second floor of a building on Archwood, around the corner from the Department of Water and Power building. It had a reasonable rent for the space, and was close to the freeway. That made it convenient for Paula to get to Burbank for her soap and me to get to auditions in various parts of the city. I could reach Hollywood in seven minutes, the west side in fifteen to thirty, depending on traffic.

As soon as we walked in, Maddie ran to her room, slamming the door. I waited a minute, then poked my head in her room.

"Maddie?"

She did not look up from the floor, where she was working on a coloring book.

"Maddie?" I knelt down.

"I'm coloring."

"Can I talk to you?"

"I'm coloring."

"I see that. What are you coloring?"

"This." Still not looking up.

"I did something terribly wrong," I said.

Half a look.

"I was angry and I hit you."

"It hurt, Daddy."

"I know. I was so wrong. And I'm so sorry. Do you think you can forgive me?"

Now she looked full on, confused.

Forgive. Something her little five-year-old brain had not yet taken in as a lasting concept. A word, I realized, I had not used around her or Paula. Now I was asking her to understand it.

"When somebody does something wrong or bad to you and wants you not to hate him, you can forgive that person. That means you sort of decide not to be mad about it and pretend everything is okay again."

Pretend? Was that the right word?

"I don't hate you, Daddy," Maddie said, looking at the coloring book and the sienna crayon in her hand. "But it really hurt."

Enough reasoning. I picked her up and held her close. She let me. I tried not to let her see my tears. Her arms were tight around my neck.

I walked her to our sliding door, and onto our little balcony. It was too early for the moon, too late for the sun. So I swayed with her in the dusk, and that was enough.

Demons

– 1 –

When the urge to drink hit me, it was always like a Randy Johnson fastball to the ribs. It would take the breath out of me, crush some bone, leave me staggering toward first. If you're a problem drinker, you never really get rid of all the urges.

But it seemed I was getting hit more and more by the urges, knowing about Paula and Troncatti. And Maddie. The hitting incident really knocked me flat. Nor did it help that Steve Monet was the one who got the Colgate commercial. He called me up to tell me, and I wanted not just to drink a whole bottle of vodka but actually eat the bottle.

Though Maddie seemed to have forgotten all about it, I couldn't. I kept seeing myself in the newspaper as some awful dad, nabbed by the police before I did more harm.

Drinking seemed a great alternative to the demons. I almost did it, too. I almost left Maddie with Mrs. Williams so I could go out to a bar and get soaked.

It hit me hard Sunday morning and that scared me. The morning? This was bad.

Without much thought, I knew I had to do something drastic. And when Maddie walked into the kitchen, rubbing her eyes, I knew what it was.

I took her to the same big church in Hollywood where Paula and I got married. Part of my thinking was that this would be a goodwill gesture to God on my part.

Hey, God, I'm here, see me? Remember the wedding that was right up this aisle five years ago? That was me, and here I am and you can do that miracle thing they say you're always doing.

For Maddie, there was a full-on Sunday school program, which she did not want to go to at first. I couldn't blame her. All these kids who were not her kindergarten class, who were not her day camp troop. Strangers. Threats.

She held on to my leg like I was the last life preserver on the *Titanic.*

"I don't wanna go in there," she said. I had managed to get her this far, to the church building. She'd even seemed somewhat excited about a new place to play.

But now that we were here, and all these kids she didn't know were walking by, she didn't want to leave me.

Then Mrs. Hancock came.

There are some people who really deserve the word *saint* attached to themselves. Mrs. Joyce Hancock was one of those people. She had a smile that made her eyes crinkle, so you knew it was genuine.

After introducing herself to me—I must have had a neon sign around my neck that flashed *Lost Father: Help Wanted*—she bent down and said, "And who are you?"

Mussolini stuck her lip out. "Madeleine Erica Gillen," she said, tightening her grip on my leg.

"That is a fantastic name," Mrs. Hancock said. "Do you know where it comes from?"

"No," I said. Maddie whipped a disapproving look at me for answering the question.

"Magdala was a village on the sea of Galilee in Bible times. It means *tower* in Hebrew. Mary Magdalene was a woman from Jesus' time who was called that because she was from Magdala. And guess what?"

"What?" Maddie said, loosening her grip on me a little.

"She became a great friend of Jesus."

Maddie broke into a big smile.

"I'm going to tell some more Bible stories today," Mrs. Hancock said. "Would you like to come hear them? Your daddy will be close by if you want him."

And then my little Mussolini became as soft as new snow. She let go of my leg. "Bye, Daddy."

The church service felt weird to me.

Maybe it was the surroundings. Stained glass windows and polished wooden pews and a choir with robes and everything.

When people sang, they stood up.

The minister was a trim guy with slate-colored hair and a great speaking voice. Looked like he could have been an actor at one time. Maybe he was. This was a Hollywood church, after all.

"This morning," he began, "I'd like to continue our series on prayer. Specifically, how God hears and answers prayer."

That got my attention. *I could use a direct line to God right now,* I thought. *I'm all ears.*

The preacher read from a Bible. "'Ask and it will be given to you; seek and you will find; knock and the door will be opened to you. For everyone who asks receives; he who seeks finds; and to him who knocks, the door will be opened.'"

I'd heard that before, somewhere. It always seemed a little like mumbo jumbo.

"Now people will do all kinds of things to gain God's favor and receive his blessings, especially when they are in great need or in extreme danger. You know: *God, I'll do anything if you'll just save me from this.* They make all sorts of promises. But while people are often willing to do great things in return for God's blessing, things God has not asked for and does not want, they are unwilling to do the one small thing that he actually requires, which is to pray."

Made sense. *Duh.*

"So how do we receive God's blessings?"

Bring it on, preacher dude.

"We ask in faith. We cannot come to God with an attitude of, *Well, I'll try praying to God, and if that doesn't work, I'll try something else.* That isn't faith. That's just covering your bases. God is not willing to be just one option among many. He will not be satisfied with a piece of our love, a piece of our devotion, a piece of our trust. He wants all of it. He claims his rightful place at the center of our lives. He demands that we trust in him, and him alone."

Now I started to squirm around a little bit. I think my mind was telling my body that God was certainly not in the center of my life, not the very center.

"God is not willing to be put on the shelf with all of the other deities, to be installed as part of our personal pantheon of gods. Maybe I'll try praying to God to meet my needs, and if that doesn't work, I'll try a little Zen Buddhism, and if that doesn't work, I'll try wealth and power, maybe some self-actualization. It's like asking five women to marry you, and then waiting to see which one says yes."

Paula had said yes. Once.

"It's an insult. On the contrary, we must place our faith and trust in God alone, with no backup and no contingency plan. The key to answered prayer is not the amount or strength of our faith, but the object of our faith. 'I tell you the truth, if you have faith as small as a mustard seed, you can say to this mountain, "Move from here to there" and it will move. Nothing will be impossible for you.' The power doesn't come from our faith; the power comes from the One in whom we have faith."

I didn't quite get that yet, but the thing about the mountain got me curious.

He finished off the sermon by talking about praying in Jesus' name. Frankly, that sounded a little like a magic formula. And I couldn't quite connect it all up. But when it was over, I felt like I was glad I came.

And Maddie didn't want to leave, she'd had such a good time.

Why couldn't it have lasted? Why didn't I just take her home? Did the thing in the park have to happen? What would the preacher man say about that?

– 2 –

Serrania Park is in the Woodland Hills area of the Valley, next to a development of some of the most expensive homes in town. It's a place you get a better class of parent and kid, not to mention dog. Maddie liked the swings at Serrania, because you could go so high.

A daredevil, Maddie.

We—Paula, Maddie, and I—had come here three or four times. I remember trying to teach Maddie how to throw a Frisbee here, when she was four. She got the hang of it real quick, as Paula applauded my efforts from a bench under a tree. Best applause I'd had in years.

Today there was some good activity in the sandbox, like a toddlers' convention, along with some kids Maddie's age taking to the slides and swings. Since the good high swings were taken, Maddie headed to the digging part of the convention. She is a natural conversationalist and immediately invited herself to join a boy's shoveling near the stone camel.

I took my flip-flops off, sat on the far edge of the box, and wiggled my toes in the sand.

And started to think about what Maddie would be when she grew up. I didn't see her going into acting, like her parents. Too unstable a profession—unless an Antonio Troncatti picks you out of thin air for a major flick.

I thought Maddie would make a good lawyer. She knew how to argue, could dig in her heels when she had to, and was already gaining a fine appreciation of the art of charging outrageous sums of money for her efforts. One day she asked me for a twenty-dollar bill.

"Twenty dollars? What for?"

"I cleaned my room."

I laughed. "But you're supposed to do that."

"Okay." She thought a moment. "Then give me ten dollars."

Smiling at the thought, I watched my daughter negotiate the plastic shovel out of the boy's hand.

"Yours?"

It was an attractive woman about my age. She was looking at Maddie and the boy.

"Yes," I said. "She's five."

"Mine's four," the woman said. "But big for his age."

"Yeah, he is. A middle linebacker, I'd say."

"His father was. Played in college. Really."

"Mark Gillen," I said, standing.

"Kay Millard. You live around here?"

"No, I'm from the land of the studios. Maddie just likes this park."

"Maddie? Short for Madeleine?"

"Yeah."

"I always liked that name."

"What's your boy's name?"

"Duncan."

"Scottish, isn't it?"

Kay Millard smiled. "Very good."

"I know that from the Scottish play."

"Ah, *Macbeth*."

"Shh!" I said. We were having fun. Not many people know the actor's superstition about Shakespeare's most notorious play. You're never supposed to mention the title, so the belief goes, or something will go wrong during the production. Like a set falling on an actor.

"You must be an actor," Kay said.

"I've been accused of that."

"You seem too nice to be an actor." She sat on the concrete next to me, her Reeboks in the sand.

"I don't know if that's a compliment or not."

"It is. I know a lot of actors. My husband's a director."

"Oh really?" I tried to keep my voice calm and nonthreatening, even as my actor's insides began to quiver, like a hungry dog hearing the supper dish being pulled off the shelf. Out-of-work actors are trained to pick up every possible vibe that might mean a *connection* to a *job.*

On the other hand, you can't jump all over every person you meet who has some foot in the business. The two unbreakable rules for actors are *Don't be dull* and *Don't be desperate.*

Even though I was feeling desperate, I was not going to show it. But I sure wasn't going to let this one go, either. Breaks come every which way, but never in a predictable fashion. Lana Turner, they tell us, was sitting in a tight sweater in Schwab's Drug Store in Hollywood when a talent scout went gaga for her. All my sweaters were at home.

But I had Maddie. The point of reference. The chip. She had opened the door for me to talk to this woman, whose husband was—

"Would I know any of his films?" I said.

"He's done some independent work, and now for cable."

"Hey, some of the best stuff is on cable."

"He had a movie on earlier, *The Tin.*"

"The cop movie?" I let the excitement grow in my voice. "That was really good." I hadn't seen it, but I'd heard of it. Heard it *was* very good. And knew that this is a guy I would love to work for sometime.

"Thank you," Kay Millard said. "We're proud of it."

"And you should be." *Okay, enough of the schmooze juice. Just play it loose.*

"He working on anything new?" I said.

"He's in preproduction now."

Preproduction! Casting decision! Loose, baby, but not too loose.

"Very cool," I said. "Good to have something going on."

Idiot, you sound like you've got NOTHING going on. Desperate!

"It's a crazy business," she said, in a transitional voice, indicating she was ready to change the subject.

No, not yet, not yet.

"Yeah," I said, homing in on her. "I keep getting calls from Spielberg."

"Spielberg?" Sounding impressed, if just a tad skeptical.

"Milt Spielberg, down at the deli. He wants me to settle the account."

She gave me a (polite?) laugh, but I was still in the ballgame. A little joke to keep the industry talk rolling. Maybe she'd think I was funny and charming enough to introduce to her husband, whoever he was.

"Where's she going?" Kay Millard said. I remember that clearly. She said it, looking past my shoulder. But it was like the voice came from across the street somewhere—white noise, inconsequential—because I had already formed my follow-up question and asked it the moment she stopped talking.

"Actually, I'm sort of connected to Antonio Troncatti. You'll think this is funny, but—"

Kay's eyes widened and she shouted, *"Look out!"*

I turned just in time to see it.

Maddie was running through the sand, head down, full of purpose. She was two steps from the front of the swings.

She was oblivious to the boy on the first swing, who was already beginning his descent from a huge arc.

Two steps . . . and I could barely open my mouth before it happened. The outstretched legs with the red tennis shoes—something else I will never forget—rammed into the side of Maddie's head.

The impact was like a tennis racket smacking a ball. The physics of it were unequal, unforgiving.

Maddie lifted from the ground, her body turning like a flipped baseball bat.

I was on my feet, not knowing how I got there, as Maddie hit the sand.

She did not move—my eyes were locked on her as I raced forward. In my peripheral vision I was aware of other adults closing in, while children stood by in silent watching.

A woman was already kneeling by Maddie when I got there. I heard a boy's voice saying, "I didn't mean to!" and a chorus of other voices muttering expressions of shock and sympathy.

"She's mine," I told the kneeling woman, partly as confession, and in part, I think now, to keep anyone from taking her away from such a negligent father.

"I'll call emergency," the woman said. "Don't move her."

Don't move her? Because her neck might be broken? Because she might not ever move again?

A sweat came over me as I dropped down in the sand and put my hand on Maddie.

"Don't move her," the woman commanded, fishing in her purse for a cell phone.

Maddie's pink overalls over a lighter pink T-shirt weren't moving at all, and I wondered if she was breathing. An ugly, red stamp was deepening on the left side of her face, the imprint of a tennis shoe becoming clearer.

"Maddie Maddie Maddie," I repeated in a whisper, my lips close to her ear. "You'll be all right you'll be all right." And then she moaned, low and soft. And I almost cried out with relief.

Someone else, a man, put a towel over Maddie, and then the waiting began. All the activity in the park had ceased, the crowd gathering. Even people walking dogs stopped for a look.

"It hurts," Maddie groaned.

Oh God, give that hurt to me! Take it away from Maddie and let me take it instead, please please.

I stroked her hair and told her to lie still.

"I want to dig," she said.

"We will. Later. We'll go to the ocean and dig up the whole beach, would you like that?"

"Yes."

And we stayed like that for about ten minutes until the ambulance came. A nice paramedic checked her out, and decided Maddie could be driven to the hospital—there was one about a mile away—and she wouldn't have to be taken in the ambulance.

I picked Maddie up and carried her out of the park, sure that the eyes of every parent there were on me. *There goes the guy who was so into trying to schmooze a gig that he lost track of his daughter. There goes a guy who doesn't deserve to be a father.*

The drive to the hospital was bad, Maddie moaning all the way, tears falling. But the waiting in the emergency room for a doctor was worse. I had to go muck around with the desk over insurance, Maddie screaming at me not to leave her alone.

When I got back to her bed, a doctor was there. He looked like a humorless Bob Newhart. He spoke in a monotone and only registered an expression when I told him what happened. The expression was a raising of the eyebrows.

He asked Maddie some questions, looked in her eyes with a light, touched her head in a couple of places. Maddie, my little trooper, hung in there, and I was proud of her.

"Mild concussion," the doctor told me. "Should be okay. Watch her for a couple of days—" like I wouldn't—"limit TV and reading. If she gets nauseous or vomits or gets numbness in her arms or legs, bring her back in. And no physical activity for at least two days. Any questions?"

Yeah, where do I go to get flogged?

"No. Thanks."

When we got back to the apartment I told Maddie to lie down, but she wanted me with her. Truth to tell, I wanted to be with her just as much. I flopped on the sofa and she got on top of me, resting her head on the soft spot underneath my shoulder. I stroked her hair. And as I did, I silently thanked God that it hadn't been any worse.

Even as I did, though, I had the strangest feeling, really weird, that *worse* was about to make a great, big entrance.

Homecoming

– 1 –

Paula came back on August 3, my birthday.

She did not come home.

Over the previous month I had tried everything to remain sane. I had developed the sweats. My pits and hands would break out in little moist bursts when I thought of seeing her again.

Paula and I had talked on the phone, and she said she wanted to get together as soon as possible. I asked her if she wanted to see Maddie. She said, "After the meeting."

Meeting. It sounded like a Hollywood deal. I knew it was going to be bad. Just how bad I couldn't have known.

She chose a sidewalk café in Beverly Hills, just off Rodeo Drive no less. Why here? Probably many reasons. It was public, so I couldn't make a spectacle of myself. It was social, to soften the blow she was no doubt going to deliver. And it was Beverly Hills. Paula's new stomping ground, after her meteoric rise to stardom.

Feeling out of place, I parked my Accord in a lot next to a Bentley and a Mercedes and walked to the place.

Paula was already there.

Sitting outside, she had sunglasses on and wore a red and gold scarf around her neck that complemented perfectly her coat and blouse. She looked like a catalog model, only better because she breathed.

What hit me then, like a doctor telling me I had only three months to live, was this thought: *She is out of your league now. She has left you behind.*

"Mark." Paula waved her hand at me like I was a waiter.

I entered through the black, iron gate that separated the pedestrians from the diners. As I did I saw Goldie Hawn at a table, yakking it up with another woman. Beverly Hills indeed.

There was a lily in a vase on the table where Paula sat. Aren't those what the cartoons always have on dead people?

Paula did not smile as I sat in the other chair, also made of iron.

"You look good," Paula said. It was a lie. I didn't look anything like good.

"You look great." That was *not* a lie.

She did not remove her sunglasses. "It's good to be back. It was a tough shoot."

"But worth it, I guess, huh?"

"The dailies were spectacular. Tony is such a—" She let her voice trail off in a self-conscious Doppler effect.

"Yeah," I said. "He sure is."

A waiter younger than myself, and twice as good looking, presented his million-dollar teeth to us and asked if he could bring us a drink. I almost ordered a double shot of tequila, but in keeping with the atmosphere made it a San Pellegrino. Paula ordered chai tea.

"I don't think I'll be eating anything," I said. "But you go ahead."

"No, I don't think so either."

"Your stomach bothering you too?"

"This isn't easy for me."

"Why should it be?" I let more acid drip from my words than I'd intended.

Paula took a deep breath. "I thought it might be a little easier than this. I didn't intend this to happen."

As if that made everything okay. "Well, it did. So what are you going to do now?"

"I think we have to start talking about divorce."

"You *think?*"

"Mark, please, I'm trying to be very even about this."

"So that's it? The decision's been made?"

Paula nodded slowly.

"Don't I get a say in this?" I said.

"I wish it hadn't happened the way it did."

There's a famous scene in the old James Cagney movie *The Public Enemy*, where his girlfriend wishes something. Cagney looks at her the way only he can and says, "I wish you was a wishin' well. Then I could tie a bucket to ya and sink ya."

Then he pushes a half a grapefruit in her face.

That scene came to me in a flash, and I knew I could have played the Cagney role to the max right then.

The waiter returned with our drinks and asked if we would like to hear about the specials.

"No," I said.

I didn't like doing that to a fellow waiter, but there it was. He took the hint and said he'd check back with us in a few minutes.

"I don't want a divorce," I said. "I want you to get over this thing with Troncatti and come home to Maddie and me. I don't like what you did and I want to have ten minutes alone with Troncatti. But I'm willing to forget the whole thing."

Could I ever forget it?

"I've already made the decision," Paula said.

"I'm trying to talk you out of it."

"Don't try."

"Why shouldn't I?" My voice was loud enough to make the couple at the next table glare at me.

"Because it will just make it harder."

"I want it to be hard. I want it to be hard on *you*."

"This is not helping."

"I don't want to help, either."

"I was afraid you'd do this."

I started to feel prickly heat on my neck, like a noose made of coarse rope had been thrown around it. Paula reached for her purse, which was hanging on the back of her chair.

"You're leaving?" I said.

"I have a lawyer," she said. "He told me not to talk to you, but I thought we could be nice about it."

She stood up and, with a certain flair, dropped a ten-dollar bill on the table. It was crisp and new, just like Paula. And it sent me over the edge.

"Sit down!" I pounded my fists on the table.

Goldie Hawn looked at me, as did everyone else in the place.

"Don't yell at me." Paula slung the purse over her shoulder. "Don't *ever* yell at me. I'll be coming over to pick up Maddie tonight."

She turned her back and walked out. I was so blinded by rage I couldn't formulate any words. Picking up Maddie?

The San Pellegrino bottle sat openmouthed on the table. My hand grabbed it, lifted, and threw it down on the sidewalk where Paula was now walking. It shattered. Paula screamed.

In acting class, they teach you to go for the emotional moment. It's safe to do in class, because there are no wrong answers. You go for it.

Sometimes actors forget they live in the real world and end up doing stupid things. Like I just did.

Paula's look said to me that any hopes I had of stopping her from divorce were now shattered, just like the bottle on the sidewalk.

— 2 —

I found it hard to breathe on the way back to the Valley. It was like the car was one of those crushing chambers in the old horror movies, the walls slowly closing in. My chest felt knotted and hot.

When I got home and rounded up Maddie from Mrs. Williams, I knew I wasn't going to let Paula waltz in and snatch Maddie away from me.

"How would you like to go to the beach for a few days?" I asked Maddie.

"Oh yeah! Can I wear my new swimsuit?"

Paula had bought Maddie this nice little blue-and-red suit right before she'd left for Europe.

"Yeah," I said. "New swimsuit and everything."

"Is Mommy coming?"

Maddie knew Paula was supposed to be home soon. She'd been pestering me about it for days. But I had mastered the art of being vague.

"Mommy won't be coming just yet."

"When will she?" Her little voice was pleading.

"Let's pack," I said.

Roland's folks had a beach house in Ventura, about a forty-five minute drive north of LA. They used it as a vacation place. Roland liked to go up and pound the keys on the weekends.

I called and begged him to let me use it for a couple of days. I told him I'd explain when I got back. Roland, my buddy and pal, said okay. The only other thing I had to do was sweet-talk Shelly, the manager at Josephina's, to give me the weekend off. Fortunately, one of the newer waiters wanted in for the weekend, and that was that.

We got up there by four o'clock, before sunset, in time to play a little on the beach.

Maddie shrieked with delight as she ran down toward the ocean. She loved the ocean. Loved to stand with her feet in the wet sand as the waves came up around her ankles then ebbed, sucking some of the sand with it. It tickled her feet. She would always laugh.

We played in the water. At one point I picked her up and waded out to chest level. Maddie held on to my neck tightly. She laughed every time a swell swept past us. When a wave came I'd jump up as it broke. It would splash us, and Maddie would laugh some more.

We built a sand castle. Maddie got sticks and beached kelp and did all the design work. I was the brawn, scooping up piles of wet sand and forming it into walls and turrets.

Must have been an hour that we worked on it. Maddie carefully placed her sticks in the mounds, making sure they were evenly spaced.

When it was all done both of us stood back and looked at it. Maddie took my hand.

"That's the best castle ever," she said.

And soon it would be washed away. Just like the marriage I once thought was the best ever.

"How about ice cream?" I said.

"Yes!" Maddie said, pumping her little fist.

We got some at a little snack cart by the public parking lot. We sat on a bench looking out at the blue Pacific. Way off in the distance we could see the outline of one of the Channel Islands.

"Pumpkin?"

Maddie looked at me, her mouth around an Eskimo Pie.

"Can I tell you something?"

She nodded.

"You know your friend Jenna?" Jenna lived in an apartment in our building. Maddie had been to her birthday parties for the last two years.

"Jenna's six."

"Yes, she is. Her mommy and daddy are divorced, aren't they?"

Maddie shrugged.

"You know what divorce means?"

"Where a mommy and daddy don't live in the same house."

"Right. That's what Jenna's parents are, divorced. But Jenna gets to see them both, just not at the same time."

"That's weird."

I had been rehearsing this little speech in my mind for the last five hours. The words were like heavy chunks of concrete in me.

"But Jenna is pretty happy, isn't she?"

"She has five Barbies."

"Yeah." My own Eskimo Pie was melting on my hand. I took a big bite of the soft ice cream. Half of it fell on the ground.

"Oh, Daddy!" Maddie rebuked. Then she softened. "You can get another one if you want."

I got up and threw what was left in a trash can. Then I sat down with her again.

"Maddie, if Mommy and I ever got a divorce, you'd be able to see us both, too."

Her eyes clouded. If I'd thought I could soft-pedal this, I was sorely mistaken.

"Don't do that, Daddy."

"But sometimes it happens."

"Uh-uh."

"*If* it happened, is all I'm saying. If it did, you'd be okay. You'd be with both of us." The irony of my being here to keep her away from Paula was not lost on me. If we were going to share custody, it would be on my terms, not hers. She was the adulterer here, not me.

"No, Daddy. Promise me you won't do it."

"You've got to be okay if it happens."

"No."

How I hated Paula at that moment. For making me have to spoil the innocence of a five-year-old child. How I hated and longed for her at the same time.

I looked out at the ocean then. A pelican was skimming across the water, looking for lunch. When I turned to Maddie again she was starting to cry.

"Baby," I said, picking her up and setting her on my lap. "Baby." I held her close.

– 3 –

Somebody knocked on the front door. My heart slammed. *Who could that possibly be?*

It was our third day. Afternoon. Maddie and I had done some beach time, and now she was taking a nap.

I'd been reading a David Morrell thriller, the perfect beach book, allowing myself escape from the nightmare down south.

The knock again, more insistent.

I got up and looked out the window.

A young man in a uniform looked right back at me. He was about twenty-five years old. His hair was short, like a Marine's.

I unlatched the chain and opened the door.

"Mr. Gillen?"

"That's me."

"I'm Deputy Tim Wise of the Ventura County Sheriff's office. We got a report of a missing child."

Stay cool. She's your daughter.

"Nobody's missing," I said. "Maddie is right here taking a nap."

"She's with you?"

"Of course she's with me. We came up here to spend some time at the beach. Who sent you?"

He pulled a folded document out of his rear pocket. "I have an order here demanding that you produce Madeleine Erica Gillen at ten o'clock tomorrow morning. In Los Angeles."

My hands were shaking like leaves in the wind. The document was coldly official looking.

"This," I said, "is unbelievable."

"I'm sorry, Mr. Gillen."

"How did she find me?"

Deputy Wise started to turn around.

"I'm her *father*," I said. "She can't *do* this." I threw the order on the ground.

"I'd advise you to cooperate, Mr. Gillen."

I kicked the document, sending it sliding off the front porch. The deputy closed the gate behind him.

"What's the matter, Daddy?" Maddie was rubbing her eyes.

I looked at her, wanted to whisk her up in my arms and run away with her. Take off in a boat or something, sail to Iceland where Paula couldn't find us, and I'd raise sheep and . . .

"I guess maybe it's time for you to see Mommy," I said.

"Cool!" Her face lit up and my body shook.

– 4 –

I drove Maddie to Brentwood the next day. The address where I was to go was on the court order.

Hold the anger, I kept telling myself. For Maddie's sake. You're an actor. You are supposed to be able to turn emotions on and off. Do it. Don't let her see that things are blowing up all around her.

Maddie was singing a little song to herself. *Mommy, Mommy. Gonna see Mommy.*

I gripped the steering wheel so tightly my wrist muscles started to hurt.

Add to that the traffic on the 405. I knew I should have left earlier, but something held me back. A fight for some sort of control maybe. This court order thing was making me jump through a hoop, like a trained dog. Well, this dog was going to make a little noise.

I still held onto this crazy hope that everything would clear up. Like a Valley fog, it would soon melt away, letting in the sun again.

You think a lot of stupid things while driving in LA traffic. So I decided to switch to something else. I started thinking about God.

Just a little bit, but enough to make it more than a passing thought. If there was justice in the world, then God had to be in charge of it, right? When you got into deep water, you were supposed to call out to God, right? No atheists in foxholes, that sort of thing.

Well, if I wasn't in a foxhole yet, I was sure sinking. So maybe I'd send up a real flag to God soon. I'd been going to church with Maddie. Wasn't I supposed to get some benefits?

I got off at Sunset, hit more traffic, then reached the address in Brentwood at 10:37.

It was a huge place. I could see some of it through the iron gates that protected the premises. I didn't need a neon sign to know this was Troncatti's southland residence.

A black limousine with darkened glass was parked in front of the gate. I pulled my Accord to a stop on the street.

The limo door opened on the driver's side and an olive-skinned man with a shaved head and goatee got out. He had a white shirt and black pants. He opened a rear door. Paula got out.

She looked like an international movie star. Dressed, once again, to the nines.

Maddie jumped out of the Accord and ran to her. "Mommy! Mommy! Mommy!"

I watched them like some prisoner on Devil's Island looking at the mainland.

Paula lifted Maddie and hugged her, spinning her around.

The driver glared at me, his eyes saying *This is Brentwood. Get that hunk of junk off the street.*

Instead, I walked toward Paula. The driver stepped in between us.

"Come on," I said to Paula. "This is ridiculous."

Paula was unmoved. The driver had muscles. I could see them under his tight shirt.

"Do you mind?" I said to the driver, who I called *Igor* in my mind.

"Is far enough," Igor said. He had some sort of Middle Eastern accent. Maybe he had been one of Saddam's bodyguards.

"I want to talk to my wife." I took another step, but Igor got chest to chest with me.

"That's Daddy," I heard Maddie say. She was trying to help.

"Farid, it's okay," Paula said.

Grudgingly, Igor (I was not about to give him the dignity of a real name) allowed me to pass.

Paula put Maddie down and bent over to talk to her. "Honey, I want to talk to Daddy a minute. Why don't you hop in the big car? We're going to go for a ride."

"Really?" Maddie said.

"Shopping," Paula said. "For toys."

Oh, how smooth. Maddie turned to me, waved with a big smile, and practically dived into the back of the limo. Igor walked a few feet away, his version of giving us privacy.

"What are you doing?" I said.

"Don't fly off the handle, like you did at the restaurant." Paula's tone was clipped and cool.

"A court order? You tracked me down?"

"You knew I wanted to see Maddie, but you took off with her."

"What gives you the right to order me around?"

"I'm her *mother,* remember?"

"You sure work quick." I was fighting my feelings like crazy. I wanted to choke her. I wanted her to fall into my arms. "What'd you do? Call Roland to find out where I was?"

"My lawyer did."

"Oh. Right. Silly me. I thought you and Roland were friends."

Paula sighed and shook her head. "This isn't accomplishing anything."

She was right. I tried to calm down. "We have to talk about this."

"I tried, remember? You threw a bottle at me."

"I threw it at the *sidewalk.* I'm not stupid." The breeze must have switched then because suddenly I could smell Paula's hair. Honey and cinnamon. And then my whole body changed. From anger and anxiousness to a sense of falling, away from light and hope, into some pit. In a few seconds I was going to bust out in tears. But I didn't want Igor to see that, or Paula. I clenched my teeth and took a deep breath to keep it from happening.

I had felt this way before, and knew immediately when it was. Back when the call came about my mom. She was dead and suddenly everything was wrong and ripped up and bad. And would never be the same again.

"Can we try again?" I said. "Can we maybe get some counseling?" That was supposed to be the thing to do, wasn't it? Find some professional and the broken pieces would be put back together again?

"We have to talk about what's best for Maddie," Paula said. "If we can do that in a way that doesn't upset her, then let's."

"What about the two of us?" I said, feeling like a movie cliché. Feeling like the guy who loses the girl to Clark Gable.

"I'll call you." Paula turned toward the limo.

"Wait. When? When do I get Maddie back?"

Paula's head was disappearing into the limo. "I'll call you."

That wasn't good enough. I stepped toward the door as it closed. Igor took the cue and got back into character.

"No more," he said. He had his hand in the air like a traffic cop.

I stood there as he got in the limo, fired it up, and pulled out of the driveway. I wondered if Maddie was looking at me out of the darkened windows.

– 5 –

"You *told him?*"

"Hey, man, I didn't want to. But he was a *cop*."

Roland seemed genuinely sorry. And who could blame him for being wary of cops? As an African-American in LA, he'd been pulled over more than once for DWB—"driving while black."

"I didn't know they'd send somebody up there," Roland said. "The cop just said you could be in a lot of trouble, and all I gave him was the phone number."

"They got the address from that." I threw myself on his couch. Roland rented a little house in Silver Lake. "Paula is playing for keeps."

"Come on, man. Let me play you a little Brubeck." Roland sat at the piano. "A little 'Blue Rondo a la Turk.'" His fingers started to fly over the ivories. It was delicious.

I'd met Roland Turner at a place in the Valley about ten years ago. When I found out Roland loved baseball like I did, we hit it off. Turns out we liked the same player best—Frank Thomas.

And we had the same sense of humor. *The Simpsons* was funny. *Roseanne* was not.

Roland played more Brubeck ("Kathy's Waltz") for me. I stared at his ceiling. Suddenly he stopped.

"You need to see a lawyer," he said.

When he said *lawyer*, something went off inside me. The reality of it. I saw the pictures in my mind again, the memories I had on that movie reel. Maddie as a baby, growing up; Paula beautiful, loving me.

I couldn't help it. I started crying and covered my face with a sofa pillow.

Next think I knew Roland was sitting there on the edge of the sofa. "Hey, man, I know."

That's all he said. He squeezed my shoulder. I was glad he was there.

My cell phone bleeped. That brought me to a sitting position as I quickly wiped my eyes. I had this crazy hope it was Paula, ready to come home.

It was Nancy, my agent.

"You ready for some good news?" she said.

I almost laughed out loud. "You have no idea."

"They want you for a callback on *Number Seven.*"

It took me a moment to sort this out. *Number Seven* was a major new dramatic series about firefighters, being developed at NBC.

John Hoyt, the veteran actor, was already attached, playing the chief.

In other words, this series had major hit written all over it, and anybody in the ensemble had an almost guaranteed shot at a major career boost. I'd read for it a month ago, along with every other actor my age in town, and thought nothing more of it.

"Are you serious?" I said.

"As a heart attack at Disney," Nancy said. "Your call is at 10:30 in the morning, tomorrow. Make me proud."

When I got off the phone and looked at Roland, I felt like I'd been put through several spin cycles.

"Life truly stinks," I said.

Next morning, Monday, Paula still hadn't called me about Maddie. Though I knew Maddie was happy to be with Mommy, I also knew I didn't want her staying up there while Mommy and Troncatti played house.

A callus was starting to form in me with regard to Paula. Maybe it was a natural defense mechanism, but I was sort of glad it was there. Especially since I had to concentrate on the biggest news my acting career had ever received.

I had a real opportunity for television stardom. Emmy Award city. On the couch with Jay or Dave. Cover of *People*. Real money rolling in for the first time in my life.

All through the morning I psyched myself up. In the shower, I *became* Vance, the macho firefighter with a heart. That was the part I was up for.

I did some of my acting exercises, the ones Marty North had drummed into me. How would Vance take a shower? How would he move? Marty disdained pure Method acting, which was only concerned with feelings. The outside was just as important.

So I showered like Vance, toweled off like Vance, drank coffee like Vance. I remembered what I could of his background. There wasn't much in the script, but I'd done another Marty thing and invented a whole past for Vance for my own use.

Driving to the studio in Burbank, I began to talk like Vance. Out loud. To myself. It did not matter that people in the other lanes were looking at me. This was LA. That's what people do here. Stand on the corner and talk. Ride in cars and talk. Talk, even if no one else is around.

I had a parking pass waiting for me at the gate, and when I walked into reception, it was like I was royalty. This was no cattle call. The office wasn't stuffed with dozens of versions of myself. I was here because they were *really* interested. In *me*.

The receptionist, I was happy to see, was Lisa Hobbes. We'd done a showcase scene together a few years back, something from a Mamet play.

"What are you doing here?" I asked.

Lisa smiled. "I gave up the acting thing. I'm going for the producing thing."

"That's a good thing."

"As things go. Hey, you want anything? Cappuccino?"

This was almost too good to be true. "Water's fine. Thanks."

Lisa came back with a bottled water and a few pages of a script to read. I was the only one in the reception area. A framed poster from *On the Waterfront* faced me. One of my all-time favorite movies. I looked at the big picture of Marlon Brando and nodded at him. *You and me, Marlon.*

Lisa and I talked about old times for a while, and then her phone buzzed. She walked me down a hall and suddenly I found myself in a conference room with six other people—and John Hoyt.

I was about to read with an Oscar-winning actor, a man with one of the great careers in Hollywood. I tried not to shake.

I am Vance. I am Vance.

The producer, Barbara DiBova, made some small talk, introduced me to everybody. Their names went in one ear and out the other. She explained the scene to me. Vance was confronting the chief for reprimanding him over an incident where Vance had rushed back into a burning house to save a little girl's pet iguana.

Whenever I was ready, she said, I could read with Mr. Hoyt.

In baseball, I learned there were days when I just didn't have it, no matter how hard I tried. The ball would look like a white pea coming at me at two hundred miles an hour. My legs felt like they had sledgehammers in them. And all my mental tricks couldn't get me out of it.

And then there are days when everything falls into place. Players call that being in The Zone. Everything seems effortless. The ball is as big as a watermelon, and you get the fat part of the bat on it every time.

Most of baseball, and life, is spent somewhere in between these two places. But when you have the most important audition of your life, you pray that you are not in the pits but in The Zone.

As soon as I started reading with Hoyt, I knew where I was. All my training and desires and hopes came together, and everything else disappeared for a few amazing minutes as I read that scene for all it was worth.

When it was over, Hoyt smiled and extended his hand. "That was fantastic," he said.

Everyone else in the room said something to the same effect.

All I could think was *Wow*. And I didn't want to leave. I wanted to keep reading with Hoyt. I wanted to start work on the show.

Barbara DiBova walked me outside. "I wasn't going to say this until later, but you were our number one choice on the callback list. We have more people to see today, but I just wanted to tell you that was one great reading you gave in there."

"Thank you."

"Stay by your phone," she said.

– 6 –

I sailed through work at Josephina's, smiling at everybody. Got good tips as a result, even from the lunch crowd.

And I wanted to celebrate. So that evening I went over to hear Roland play some jazz at Club Cobalt in North Hollywood. NOHO had become something of an artists' quarter in recent years. There were small theaters, art galleries, cafés, clubs.

I sat in a little booth and drank Coke, with a plate of jalapeño poppers as my meal. Very bad for the stomach, but it tasted oh-so-good. And with Roland wailing on the ivories, I was feeling better than I had in months.

The whole Maddie mess was still there, of course, sitting inside me like a ball of deep-fried grease. But at that moment I had hope. My trend line was heading up. Maybe the momentum would carry over into my dealings with Paula.

After his first set, Roland joined me, as did Milo Ayres. Mr. Ayres owned the club, and I'd met him before. He was an affable guy of unknown ethnicity, at least to me. He might have been Greek or Italian or some mix in between. He wore a goatee and always dressed sharp. He had assorted rings on his fingers and gold chains around his neck. Very old school, if by old you mean the 1970s.

"Good to see you again," Ayers said in his accent of unknown origin. His handshake was strong and sure.

"Likewise," I said.

"Mark here just got some good news," Roland said. "Big part on a new series coming up at NBC."

"Not final yet," I said. "But it's very close."

Milo Ayers rubbed one hand on his lapel. "Very nice. Congratulations."

"Mark needs a good lawyer," Roland said.

I looked at him like he'd mentioned I wore Barney underwear.

"Oh?" Ayers said.

"It's nothing," I said.

Roland put his hand on my arm. "Mr. Ayers knows some of the best attorneys in town. You need a referral."

"What's the problem?" Milo Ayers sat down. Now I had to come clean. I would break Roland's fingers later.

"I may have a family matter coming up," I said. My words told me I was still clinging to that thin reed of hope.

"Divorce?" Ayers asked.

"Yeah."

"You go see Gregory Arsenault. He's the best."

Not wanting to get more into this, I said, "It really hasn't reached that stage yet."

Milo Ayers took on the look of an understanding uncle. "Mark, you listen to me, eh? Speaking as one who has been through the mill myself. Divorce can get ugly very fast, and if you don't have somebody looking out for you, your ex will have the shirt off your back before you know it. You gotta know she'll be doing everything she can to squash you."

I couldn't believe that about Paula. Yeah, she had a lawyer and she had Maddie and she was serious. But squash me? No way. For one thing, she loved Maddie and wouldn't do that to the daddy our daughter adored.

"I still have a shot to talk things out," I said.

But Milo Ayers shook his head. "That's naive, my friend. You got any kids?"

"A daughter."

"How old?"

"Five. Almost six."

He reached inside his coat for a business card and pen. He wrote something on the back of the card. "You call Arsenault. It can't hurt to talk to him. Tell him I sent you his way, he'll give you a free consultation."

Ayers finished writing and slid the card across the table to me.

"Believe me," Milo Ayers said, "you need protection."

At the apartment I just could not shake the whole lawyer thing. I hated lawyers. All of them out for a buck, only making life worse for everybody. The thought that Paula would try to bury me with a lawyer was inconceivable.

Okay, maybe she'd had an affair, maybe she was going to divorce me. But that didn't mean all that we'd had together was squat, did it? How could she possibly look at her daughter's father as someone to *crush?*

The cliché popped into my head: *If only she'd listen to reason.*

Or her mother, I thought.

Erica Stanton Montgomery was not my biggest fan, but maybe that was the way to get to Paula. Her number was programmed in my cell phone.

I should have checked the time. It was ten thirty on the West Coast, one thirty back East.

Erica's voice was groggy. "What on earth?"

"It's Mark," I said. "Sorry, but this is important."

"What could possibly—"

"Do you know what's going on?"

Pause. I imagined Paula's mother in her huge bedroom in Darian, Connecticut. Her house was as big as a soundstage. "In what way?"

"Come on, Erica. What has Paula told you?"

"She has told me there is going to be a change in her circumstance."

Change in her circumstance? Cold as ice, Erica was.

"Is that all you can say?" I was pacing around the apartment, going by my bedroom and Maddie's, willing someone to be there.

"What is it you wish me to say, Mark?" Her voice was gaining its normal tone—haughty indifference toward her only son-in-law.

"Something besides her marriage to me being a circumstance," I said.

"That is between you and Paula."

"Oh, come off it. You're her mother. You can give her your opinion."

"My opinion is that she is doing the right thing."

"By divorcing me?"

"Yes."

No beating around the bush by this woman. If I thought I would get her to talk Paula out of her impending decision, I was dreaming.

"You approve of her sleeping around?" I wanted to hit Erica with the biggest guns I had.

"That is not what happened," Erica said like some eyewitness.

"How can you say that? Were you there? Are you even aware?"

"Don't take that tone with me."

"I'll sing opera if I have to, to get you to listen."

"I don't care for—"

"We got married in church, remember? Because you wanted a Christian wedding, right? So now that your daughter starts sleeping with a man not her husband, what's your answer? That she should go ahead and divorce me? Is that your idea of Christianity?"

"I will not go on with this—"

"And what about Maddie? Have you thought about her?"

"Maddie is a survivor."

"She's five years old!"

"She has her mother in her. And me."

"Now there's a horror story for you." I shouldn't have said that. But there was no sock around to stuff in my mouth.

"You will not call me again," Erica said.

"That's it? Forever?"

"As far as I'm concerned, yes."

That hurt, even though no love was lost between us. But I tried my best to be civil to Erica Stanton Montgomery. She was Maddie's grandmother, the only one she had. For that alone I did try.

"Why didn't you ever like me?" I said.

"Because you're a child, and you don't have it in you to grow up."

My instinct toward self-defense flew out of me. I was speechless.

Erica filled the void. "And you coerced my daughter to marry you, against my wishes."

"Coerced? How?"

"You got her pregnant and then took advantage of the situation."

My chin was shaking. "Paula *wanted* to get married."

"That's what you think."

My breath left me. Did Paula really feel that way?

"Thanks, Erica. You've been a great comfort."

I threw the cell phone across the room.

I couldn't fall asleep that night. Not until about two in the morning. Instead, I just lay in the dark, remembering voices, remembering when Paula and Maddie used to live here.

In the darkness of our bedroom I ask Paula, "What is the greatest movie scene you ever saw?"

"Greatest movie scene? From any movie of all time?"

"Yes. Silent, modern, whatever you want. What scene was it that moved you the most or is stuck in your head?"

She thinks a long time.

"If I had to choose just one," she says, "I think it would have to be the party scene in All About Eve.*"*

"Oh yeah. Where Marilyn Monroe shows up?"

"Yeah, but of course the best line in the whole thing is where Bette Davis goes up the stairs, stops, looks at everybody with those

big eyes, and says, 'Fasten your seat belts. It's going to be a bumpy night.'"

I crack up. Paula does a great Bette Davis.

"So what about you?" she says.

"My favorite scene of all time? That's a tough one, but I think I've got it."

"So?"

"It's got to be from Shane.*"*

"I haven't seen Shane.*"*

"You never saw Shane*?"*

"Keep your voice down."

"You never saw Shane*?"*

"No, I never saw Shane.*"*

"And I let you marry me?"

"So what's so great about Shane*?"*

"Shane, man! He's rides into this valley from some mysterious past, see?"

"Okay."

"And he's got no home, but he happens on this homestead, where Van Heflin lives with his wife and son."

"Van Heflin?"

"Will you listen? Heflin is chopping at this big old stump in the ground, and he lets Shane have a drink of water. Then the bad guys ride up and he thinks Shane is one of them, so Heflin tells Shane to get lost."

"Makes sense."

"Be quiet. But then Heflin sees Shane isn't one of them, and he's sorry and asks Shane to stay for dinner."

"This is your favorite scene?"

"Listen! So Shane gets the first good, home-cooked meal he's had in who knows how long, right? When it's over, he stands up and walks outside."

"He eats and runs?"

"I'm gonna clock you one if you don't be quiet."

Paula giggles.

"Now listen, please," I say. "This is really important to me. Shane goes outside and picks up an ax and starts chopping away at the stump. See, that's his way of saying thank you. Van Heflin grabs an ax and the two of them go to work on the stump together. By evening they're almost through. They're both pushing the stump, but it's not coming out easy. The wife comes over and says, 'Hey, why don't you hitch up the horses and pull it out.'"

"Seems reasonable."

"But Heflin says no way. He's been battling that stump for two years. If he gives in now, the stump could say it beat him."

"He really says that?"

"He says sometimes nothing'll work for a man but his own sweat and muscle. So he and Shane go at it again and together they push out the stump."

"That's your favorite scene?"

"That's it."

"You are such a guy."

I prop myself up on one elbow in the dark. "But see, they came together, and they got the job done. And then they have to get together again later in the movie to fight the bad guys who want to take over the valley. It's like the guys who fought World War II. It's like what made America great. Can't you see that?"

"Why don't we rent it?"

"You want to see it?"

"Of course," Paula says, leaning over to kiss me. "If that's your favorite scene, I'd like to see it, too."

"You got a date."

A shaft of light falls across the bed then, and the door is opening. It's Maddie, all of four years old.

"I could hear you," she says.

"Sorry, honey," Paula says. "Come here."

Maddie, in her fluffy pajamas, crawls up on the bed and gets under the covers between us.

"I'm really sorry," I say, kissing Maddie's hair. "Daddy was getting excited about movies."

"I like movies," Maddie says in a sleepy voice. "I like The Little Mermaid."

"The Little Mermaid *is good," Paula says.*

"Great," I say.

We lay there in silence for a long time. I'm feeling the warmth of Maddie's body and smelling the Johnson's Shampoo in her hair and holding Paula's hand outside the covers.

And then Paula whispers, "I think she's asleep."

I listen to Maddie's breathing, slow and rhythmic, like soft waves lapping on a distant beach.

"I was wrong," I say.

"Wrong?"

"This is my favorite scene."

Lawyers

– 1 –

"Hello, Daddy."

Maddie's voice sounded quiet over the phone, almost formal. A horrible thought hit me. She sounded like a little version of Erica Stanton Montgomery from last night's conversation. Maybe it was just the weirdness of the situation for her. But it chilled me.

Paula had accepted my call and given Maddie over to me immediately. I took that as a positive step.

"How are you, pumpkin?"

"Fine."

"Great. Whatcha doin'?"

"Watching TV."

"Uh-huh. Cool." Why was it so hard to make small talk with my own daughter? Because I wanted her in my arms, not in Troncatti's house. And I did not want to upset her.

"Are you coming over here?" Maddie said.

"I don't think so."

"How come? Tony has a big house."

The name, the familiar way she said it, was a hot knife.

"Wow, great," I said. "Hey, you want to go to the ballgame with me?"

"And get a Dodger Dog?"

"You betcha."

"Okay. When?"

"Soon. Let me talk to Mommy, will you?"

"Okay."

"I love you," I said, but I guess she didn't hear me. Paula came on.

"So?" she said.

"When will you bring Maddie back?"

"I'm not sure," she said.

"Well, that doesn't help me," I said, trying not to snap. "You don't have the right to keep her from me, if that's what you're thinking."

"We have to work all that out."

"Fine. Let's start by you telling me when she's coming home."

"Stop trying to force me into things, Mark."

A tongue of flame lit inside me. "Like I forced you to sleep with Troncatti? Come on, Paula, stop this right now. Come home and let's work this thing out."

In the short silence I indulged a vision—of Paula in torment about her actions and a real inner struggle. But for the good of Maddie, she'd see it my way and come home. At least to talk. At least to bring Maddie back.

That vision quickly vaporized. "I can't talk to you anymore," Paula said. "Talk to my lawyer. His name is Bryce Jennings and he's in Century City."

"Wait."

The line went dead.

My heart went dead, too, like someone had flipped a switch and cut the life out of it.

It was really happening. Milo Ayers was right. She was going to try to take everything, including Maddie. I started to sweat.

I fished out the card Milo had given me. I didn't want to do this. This was a bad soap opera story line. Wife runs off with Italian movie director. Hires lawyer. Dumb husband is standing there, phone in hand, as the music goes up and the camera closes in on his perplexed face.

I must have stood like that for ten minutes, waiting for someone to yell *Cut.* No one did. Instead, I dialed the number on the card.

The law offices of Gregory Arsenault were in the largest building in the Valley, on Ventura Boulevard. Spacious and done up in dark wood and brass, with expensive-looking leather-bound books in perfect order on floor-to-ceiling shelves, the office had the feel of money. Not chump change, either.

The receptionist was a tall, sleek woman who asked me to please be seated. There were some magazines on a glass table. I picked up *Forbes*. Maybe I could find a tip on how to make enough money to afford Mr. Gregory Arsenault.

A few minutes later a tall, angular man with penetrating blue eyes opened the big door next to the reception desk.

"Mr. Gillen? I'm Greg Arsenault."

I stood up and shook his hand. His grip was firm, like a Brinks guard holding the cash bag.

"Thank you for seeing me on such short notice," I said.

"Anything for Milo."

I followed him down a long corridor, past some workstations and inner reception areas, file cabinets and a kitchenette, to the very last office. It was in the corner of the building (we were on the thirtieth floor) and it had a breathtaking view of the San Fernando Valley.

"Have a seat," Arsenault said.

The chairs in his office were made of leather and wood, with arms and legs that had fancy curlicues. Arsenault's desk was large and organized. Absolutely nothing on it looked out of place.

Arsenault sat himself in a big executive chair and leaned back. He wore a crisp white shirt and patterned tie with a dark blue vest. A gold watch chain made its way out of his vest pocket and a watch fob—looking like a gold nugget—dangled from a vest button in the middle of his torso.

"So your wife wants a divorce," he said.

I'd told him a few preliminary things over the phone. "Right."

"What do *you* want?"

"I don't want the divorce."

"You want money?"

"No."

Arsenault blinked a couple of times. "Interesting. Children?"

"A daughter. Madeleine. She's five."

"You want custody?"

"Of course."

"Don't say of course," Arsenault counseled. "Not just yet. Does your wife have a lawyer?"

"Yes. Jennings something."

"Bryce Jennings?"

"Yeah."

Gregory Arsenault put his head back and laughed. I did not like the sound of that. When he looked at me again he said, "She is quite serious. Do you know anything about Jennings?"

I shook my head.

"Jennings is known as The Destroyer to the Stars. He has made a name for himself, and millions of dollars I might add, representing celebrities in divorce and palimony cases. He is ruthless."

My chest was beginning to tighten as my mind formed images of a lawyer I'd never seen.

"You are definitely going to need representation," Arsenault continued. "Otherwise Jennings will rip your head off and spit down your neck."

For a long moment I sat there, shaking my head slowly. "Why can't Paula and I just settle this thing?"

"There are alternatives. Have you tried marriage counseling?"

"Not yet, but I don't know if she'd go for it."

"Hiring Jennings is not a good sign, no. There is something called Family Conciliation Court. It's informal, confidential, and *free*. It's mediation, is what it is, and to work it requires that the two parties try to reach solutions without the blood of litigation. Again, the hiring of Jennings is a sign that your wife wants this to be handled with drawn swords. That's where your lawyer comes in."

"Why does it have to be that way? It seems so stupid."

"You're not the only one who thinks so," Arsenault said. "The whole purpose of the Family Code, if you look at the intent of the legislature, is to foster cooperation between the parties, to actually reduce the adversarial nature of the proceedings."

"You're kidding."

The lawyer shook his head. "But there is no area of the law that is nastier, meaner, as full of brass knuckles and raw hatred as family law. Defending child molesters is a walk in the park by comparison."

"But Paula and I were in love."

Arsenault nodded with understanding. No doubt he'd heard variations on this theme countless times. "Why don't you tell me exactly what happened. Don't hold back. Everything you say to me is held in confidence."

"Where should I start?"

"Why does your wife want a divorce?"

"Oldest reason in the world, I guess."

"Another man?"

"You ever heard of Antonio Troncatti?"

Arsenault's chin dropped just a little. "That's the other man?"

I nodded.

"No wonder Jennings is involved," Arsenault said. "When did all this happen?"

"Over the last few months," I said. "She got a part in his new movie and went over to Europe to shoot."

"You never went over there?"

"No. I was taking care of Maddie."

Reaching into a drawer, Arsenault took out a new yellow legal pad. He jotted something on it.

"All the time your wife was in Europe, you stayed home and took care of the daughter?"

"That's right."

"What type of work do you do?"

"I wait on tables, try to get acting work."

"Two actors in the family? How's that going?"

"Better," I said. "I just landed a great part in a series."

"Did you?" Arsenault brightened and wrote some more. "That's very good news. It pays well, I'm assuming."

"You can assume that, yes. John Hoyt is in it."

He scribbled. He asked me a series of questions, probing into more areas of the marriage. It was like having a dentist drilling me. Not much pleasure in it, but it had to be done.

Finally there was a long pause while Arsenault surveyed the notes he'd made. Five pages of legal paper. He flipped them back and forth a couple of times. "The only thing left to discuss," he said, "is the fee arrangement."

I tried to swallow. My throat constricted. "Sure," I said, waiting for him to give me the bad news.

"I will need twenty thousand up front."

"Twenty thousand? As in dollars?"

"It is a retainer," he explained. "If things are settled the final bill won't be that much. But if they aren't—"

"I haven't got anywhere near that much."

"Perhaps you have some resources."

"I don't own any property, if that's what you mean."

"Friends or family?"

"Can't we work out some sort of payment plan?"

Gregory Arsenault's face changed from understanding to hard reality. "You have to understand that Bryce Jennings is a $600 an hour man, and that's exactly what your wife—or your wife's lover—is paying for. If this thing proceeds, we can move the court for attorney's fees, but we can't count on that. My hourly rate is $450. As a friend of Milo's."

Suddenly the disparity of the situation hit me. I was still in the same economic shape I was when Paula left for Europe. But in the meantime, she had hooked up with a multimillionaire director; she would have no problem paying The Destroyer.

"I'll, um, see what I can do," I said.

"That'll be fine. My assistant will give you a client agreement form, and we can talk later. Meantime, you have some homework."

"Homework?"

"I have an information form for you to fill out. All sorts of questions on assets, your child, your work, your references, all that. It's self-explanatory. I also want you to make a list of positives and negatives. First, your positives. Then her negatives."

"Why?"

"That will be important when it comes to custody."

I shook my head. "I don't want to do that."

Arsenault's eyes got serious. "Do you want joint physical custody of your daughter or not? Because Bryce Jennings is going to do everything he can, with your wife's help, to get her sole custody. Of that you can be sure. And to do that, he's going to try to make you look bad."

"But I'm not. I mean, I'm not perfect, but—"

"Which is why I want to know your negatives, too."

"What for?"

"So I can anticipate what Jennings will be using."

I felt sick. Arsenault looked at his watch and stood up. The signal our time was at an end. "Last thing," he said. "Do not discuss these matters with anyone. If you do, the other side may claim that you have waived the confidentiality privilege. *Capice?*"

"Oh. Yeah. Right." Zombielike, I got to my feet. "She has Maddie," I said. "Can she keep her from me?"

"We can file an Order to Show Cause if there's a problem." He opened the door to his office. "I'll give Bryce a call, as soon as all this is official."

As I staggered by he said, "And try not to worry, Mark. We'll get this thing straightened out."

Sure. No worries. This was going to be a walk in the roses. For a mere twenty grand.

~ 2 ~

I called Nancy from the car. "When will the contract for *Number Seven* be here?"

"Whoa there, Lightning," Nancy said. "They haven't even made a formal offer yet, but I understand your reading was a killer."

Practically panting now, but trying not to sound desperate, I said, "Is there any way to speed the process along?"

"Hey, I'm just as anxious as you are, but this is not something we need to worry about. I'm sure it's going to be a great offer, and I'll do the agent thing and see how much higher we might be able—"

"I'm not concerned with the amount, but the *timing.* I need some money."

Silence on Nancy's end. Then: "Why?"

"You don't want to know."

"Loan sharks? Mark, tell me you're not into gambling."

"No, Nancy." I was on the freeway and realized I'd missed my off ramp. Not caring, I just drove. "It's Paula. She's hired a lawyer."

"Oh no."

"I went to a guy today and he wants twenty grand, up front."

"Twenty! My lawyer only charged five when I divorced Frank."

"Paula's apparently hired some big lawyer."

"Not Bryce Jennings, I hope."

"Ding ding ding."

Nancy cursed. "Look, my advice is to get out of this thing as quickly and quietly as possible. Maybe you can find a less expensive attorney, someone young and hungry who'll—"

"Roll over and play dead?"

"Not what I meant."

"Can I get some sort of advance on the money—from the agency maybe?"

"A loan? I wish you hadn't asked me that. We just can't—"

"I'm desperate here." Oops.

"I know, I know. Look, let me give a call over to Barbara DiBova and see what the time frame is. But the way this works, don't count on it. Meantime, take it easy. Try to relax. If Bryce Jennings is on this thing we don't want to upset him. That would mean negative publicity."

Her warning was well taken. I was not name enough to survive negative pub.

"You still there?" Nancy said.

"Yeah."

"You hear what I said?"

"Sure."

"Good. I'll call you."

Traffic had slowed to a crawl, and I saw why. A major car wreck on the side of the freeway. A silver Mercedes looked like an accordion and a Ford pickup was overturned. There were CHP cars and an ambulance there, lights flashing and all.

And on the ground, attended by paramedics, a man was sprawled, looking dead.

I don't know why I decided to get off at Gower. Maybe, looking back on all that's happened, it was God directing me. I sure didn't make any conscious decision.

The Presbyterian church where I was married, where I'd attended with Maddie, was staring me right in the face.

Was it a sign? I realized I was looking for one.

I parked on the little street by the freeway, adjacent to the back of the church grounds. It had a security gate, which was understandable. This was Hollywood, after all. But for some reason the gate was not fully closed.

Another sign?

I walked in.

No one was around, as far as I could tell. There was a complex of rooms, some offices, a stairwell. It was quiet. I kept listening for a voice.

Hearing none, I wandered toward the big church building. Someone looking like a maintenance worker came out of the side door. He nodded at me, like my presence didn't surprise him.

I nodded back and entered the door. I was in a corridor, again with no one around. Turning down a hallway, following my instincts, I saw another doorway and went through.

And found myself in the empty church.

The lights were off, but enough sun came through the stained glass windows that I could see just fine. The big pipes of the organ gleamed.

I don't know exactly when I knew I was praying. I wasn't down on my knees. My head wasn't bowed, my eyes were open. But I was talking in my mind.

There's a play called *The Ruling Class,* where the lead character becomes convinced he's God. When asked why, he says that when he prayed, he found he was talking to himself.

That bit occurred to me as I sat there. But I did not at any time feel I was talking to myself. There was a sense that a presence was there. And I laid it all out.

Can you cut me a break on this one? All I want is my family to be together again. I want Paula and I want Maddie and I want to live in the apartment and I want to buy a house with the money I'll be making on the show—which by the way thank you for—and Paula's going to be a big star and I want to enjoy it with her, together. Can you do something please? I'll do whatever you tell me to do, but I'm asking for this. I want to be with Paula and I want my daughter and whatever you want from me, you've got it.

I stopped when I realized I was crying. Not anything big, but a steady, warm pouring out of the soul. God was there, I believed that much. And the preacher said prayer worked. Well, it was time.

I stayed for a few more minutes, just to show God I didn't pray and run, then slipped quietly out the back.

– 3 –

"There was a guy asking about you," Julio said. He did work around the apartment building, landscaping, some handyman stuff.

"What guy?"

"Don't know. Ask when you be home."

"He didn't give you his name?"

Julio shook his head. "And I didn't say nothing. Didn't feel good."

"What'd he look like?"

Julio shrugged.

"How old?"

"Fifty maybe."

That would have ruled out my immediate circle of friends.

"Did he say he was going to come back?"

"Didn't say nothing. Just walk away."

Creepy. A guy asking about me, not leaving a name. Anger flaming up, I charged up to my apartment and called Paula. Surprisingly, she answered. I'd expected her voice message.

"What is it?" She sounded tired.

"Can I ask you a question please?"

"If it's about Maddie, I told you—"

"No, not about Maddie. Yet. Just between you and me." I was struggling to keep my anger in check. My theory might not even be right, so I had to give her the benefit of the doubt. Also, I was hoping—again—that we could talk about things.

On the other hand, my rage was something I could not fully control. "Did you hire a private investigator?"

No immediate answer.

"Did you?"

"You are supposed to get a lawyer," Paula said.

"That's not an answer."

"My lawyer says I'm not supposed to talk to you, Mark."

"Are you a puppet on a string?" Another thought hit me. How much was Troncatti involved in this? Was he telling Paula what to do as well?

"I just have to do what's right."

"This *isn't* right, Paula. This is so wrong. Maddie needs both of us. She needs us together. I don't care what people think they can do when they divorce. The best thing is to have us together under one roof."

"No."

"Please. Will you just call this thing off for a while? We can get counseling, or we can try something my lawyer suggested—"

"So you do have a lawyer."

I sighed. "We don't need to do it this way. There's a free service we can try. Why bring lawyers into it?"

"I have to do what's best for Maddie."

"What are you talking about? How is this good for her?"

"I can't talk to you right now, Mark. I was told—"

"Come on!" I was ready to yank the phone cord from the jack. "Don't turn this into a thing with investigators and lawyers and all that. We can work this out."

There was no answer, but some fuzzy sound. "Paula?"

The next voice I heard was male. With an accent. "Don't you call her again!" it said. Then the line cut out.

Troncatti. The great Antonio Troncatti himself. Ordering me around. Had to be.

I did rip the cord out.

Next morning I walked to the bank, a couple of blocks away, to see what I could possibly borrow. The very nice woman at the desk tried not to sound completely disheartening, but I had nothing to secure the kind of loan I needed to get my lawyer his retainer.

I called my life insurance company. They reminded me I had term insurance. Nothing to borrow against.

Duh, they must have thought.

Credit cards. I had a Visa and MasterCard. Or, rather, I shared them with Paula. Digging out our last bills I saw that there was roughly $8,000 available on the Visa and $4,500 on the MasterCard.

So back to the bank lady I went. I asked her if I could get a cash advance of $12,000. She told me to wait. When she came back she had that same look on her face from before.

"No available funds," she said.

"What? How can that be?"

"You have a joint account on both cards. There's been some sort of activity to stop advances. This sometimes happens."

"Why?"

She shrugged. "In divorce cases."

Must have been written all over me.

I walked out of the bank into a bright, hot afternoon. It had now been three days since I'd seen Maddie, and I could feel it. We'd not been apart for more than a matter of hours in a long time. As I walked down Ventura Boulevard, feeling a little sick, I remembered the time a few weeks ago when Maddie got sick herself.

We'd been to the movies. I took her to see the new Disney animated feature and splurged on candy. We made it through the movie and into the car.

But as soon as we were in traffic Maddie said, "Daddy, I don't feel good."

She looked so little in her car seat. "What's the matter?"

"My tummy."

Right. Good old Dad had done it again with the diet. "Hang on, pumpkin, we'll be home in a—"

At which point my lovely daughter spewed all over the back seat. It was no small act; it was operatic in its scope.

She started crying.

"Oh, pumpkin, I'm sorry—" Then the smell hit and I knew that I would have to get about fifty air fresheners for my car mirror.

I carried her up to the apartment and promptly got her into a bath. She was subdued. No talk about Bible characters or cartoon shows or the latest kindergarten scandal. All she wanted was to feel better.

After she was in her pj's I gave her what Gram used to give me when I had a similar ailment—a little 7 UP. Then I put her in bed and read her a Dr. Seuss.

With that done I turned out her light and started preparing for an industrial cleanup job on my car.

"Don't go," she said.

"You want me to stay awhile?"

"I want you to sleep in here." She put her hand out and touched my arm.

"There's no bed," I said.

"You can sleep on the floor," Maddie replied, and then with sudden concern for my well-being, she added, "with a pillow."

"But I have to—" I stopped myself. The car could wait. I'd make it a hundred air fresheners if I had to. "I'll get a pillow and blanket," I said.

And so I had a little slumber party with my daughter. We talked for about an hour, on all sorts of things. She especially wanted to hear about some of the trouble I got in when I was little, which is a vast reservoir to draw from.

When I realized she wasn't talking anymore, but breathing rhythmically, I switched off the lamp. I stayed there a long time, listening to her breath. No amount of money could have coaxed me out of that room at that moment. Eventually I fell asleep.

Now, walking down the street without aim, I kept that picture of Maddie and me in mind. *No amount of money*—Now money was very much what I needed.

At the corner I stopped by the bus stop and casually looked back behind me.

That's when I saw him.

He was dressed in jeans and a blue Hawaiian shirt. His hair was grayish and long. Behind his sunglasses I imagined two eyes looking directly at me.

There was a good distance between us, maybe fifty yards or so, but I had no doubt this was the guy Julio had mentioned.

Now what? Should I go up and confront the guy? Get in his face and tell him to leave me alone?

Maybe that's what Vance, my character on *Number Seven,* would do. But I quickly reminded myself this was life, not TV. I'd never had anyone tailing me before (at least not that I knew of).

And what if I was just paranoid? This could be some guy just looking up the street, waiting for a ride.

One way to find out. I continued on up to the corner and turned right, picking up my pace past the little strip mall on the right. The twenty-four-hour laundry, where I'd spent some time in the past, was doing a good business. As I looked past the laundry to the sidewalk, I noticed the guy was not in view.

All this was my overactive imagination, I told myself. But I'd started this little game and might as well play it to the limit.

I walked down the side street, past the Taco Bell, and turned down an alley, heading back toward my building. On my left was a block wall, behind which was a residential area. On my right were the backs of buildings—offices, a Thai restaurant, Jiffy Lube. It was like being in a concrete canyon.

Behind me, no sign of the guy. I laughed a little. Urban paranoia, nothing else. It showed me just how much I was on edge.

Which left the question open, who was asking about me at the building? By the time I reached the end of the alley, my mind was full of sneaking suspicions again. The only thing I was sure of was that it had to be someone Paula had hired. Or The Destroyer.

When I turned down my own street I was not anywhere nearer the money I needed than I had been before. My thoughts were just a merry-go-round of repetitions, with no new revenue sources turning up. I must have been pretty deep in my own mind because I actually let out a yelp when I saw him again.

The guy in the Hawaiian shirt stepped off the front steps of the apartment building and smiled at me.

"You ditched me," he said.

I took a step back and glared at him. "Why are you following me?"

"Mark," he said, "don't you recognize your old man?"

– 4 –

Of course not. How could I recognize someone I had never known?

Still, there was a resemblance. Or maybe it was just a projection on my part. I only knew I didn't want this to be my father. One major upheaval in my life at a time, please.

"Come on, who are you really?" I said.

"I really am," he said.

"No way."

He took off his shades. I almost gasped. I could see my eyes in his. "Your mom's name was Estelle. When I knew her she liked being called Rainbow."

My heart almost kicked its way out of me.

"I know this must seem bizarre." He had an easy smile. "How about I buy you a cup of coffee and we talk?"

Every corner in LA now has a Starbucks. In a daze I let this gray-haired, smiling stranger buy me an upscale cup of joe. We sat outside under a green umbrella.

"I know it's weird," he said.

"You got that right. What's your name, anyway?"

"Ron Reid."

That was the right name. Mom had talked about him a few times to me before her death.

"So why are you showing up now?" My body felt like a sack of wet laundry, weighted down by the liquid of mental strain. I had no idea how to deal with this. Part of me wanted to lash out.

When you grow up without a father, you're always aware other kids have something you don't. Not that all kids had dads at home, but all of my friends at school had dads somewhere and got to see them.

And when Mom died, I put some of the blame on my father, wherever and whoever he was. If he had been around, things might have been different. And maybe there wouldn't have been this hole right in the middle of me.

"It took me a long time to work up the courage." Reid looked down at the white lid of his coffee cup. "I wasn't exactly a dad for you."

"Did you ever try to see me?"

He shook his head. "Your mom made it clear she wanted me out of both of your lives."

"So what happened to you?"

Reid leaned back in a little. "I did some serious federal time at Terminal Island. I'm an ex-con, just so you know."

"I knew that."

"Which follows you around the rest of your life. Hasn't been a smooth ride for me. I've been all over the place, done a lot of different things. Welder. Carney. I was even a DJ in Tuscaloosa for a while."

"Looks like you have trouble holding a job." My tone was not warm, understanding, or talk-showy. What I wanted to do was grill him. A churning of resentment was roiling around inside me.

"Boy howdy," he said. "Part of it was just getting bored. If I'm not engaged, I can't stay with something."

"Engaged?"

"With the Wheel." He smiled at my perplexed look. "Have you heard of Mahayana?"

"Is that a resort or something?"

"No, it's a form of mysticism."

"Then the answer is no."

"I was a religious studies major at Berkeley. I don't know if you knew that."

"Nope."

"That never left me. I went to India for a while."

"Didn't the Beatles do that? I read it in a history book."

"Ouch, man." He laughed. There was something laid-back and easy about him. He might have been a typical Southern California surfer, but one who hadn't grown up. His body was lean.

"But of all the world religions, Buddha was the one who got it right. You ever read *Siddhartha*?"

"No. *Variety.*"

He blinked, then nodded with understanding. "Right. You're an actor. You should be into this. Mahayana is a form of Buddhism that is positive, not negative. Instead of saying that one finds salvation by escape from Samsara, which is an endless series of rebirths, you find it the other way, in the Wheel of Becoming."

"This sounds seriously weird."

"Only because you're of a Western mind-set. If you experience it, you know it makes perfect sense. Nirvana, see, is not found through the extinction of desire, as in older Buddhism. Nirvana is found in the self to be *attained,* not the self to be *stamped out.* This is how you can make each day a divine experience."

What was I doing here, I suddenly thought, listening to an ancient hippie and his riff about wheels and Nirvana? That he could be my father was disturbing.

"Why were you following me around?" I said.

"Good question," Ron Reid said. "I'm not sure I have a good answer from your perspective."

"Then give me a good answer from any perspective."

"I guess I wanted to know you a little first without you knowing me. I was nervous."

"How did you find out where I lived?"

"Not hard to do these days," he said. "Computers and all. Did I mention that I was a private investigator for a while?"

"Apparently not."

"Unlicensed, because of the felony thing. It didn't last long. But I've always been a good student."

So far, nothing he said seemed real. But it didn't seem entirely far out, either.

"So where do we go from here?" I said.

For a long moment he sat in silence. "I just thought maybe we could try to reconnect."

"Why?" It sounded cold, but I was still defensive.

"Because," he said, "I found out I have a granddaughter."

He was staying at a cheap motel not far from me. He didn't have much money (never had, since prison, he explained) and didn't have a job. He'd come down here as an act of faith, "faith in the Wheel."

So I told him he could stay a while at my apartment.

My thinking was this. If he was my father (and I was going to check it out further), then I guess I owed it to myself to find out about him. I didn't feel like I owed *him* anything. He was the one who'd run out on me.

But if I could understand him a little, maybe I could understand some things about myself. Like the sudden rages. Or the urge to drink.

And there was another reason, too. He was Maddie's grandfather, and that gave me an added arrow in my quiver. Paula had Erica on her side. This was a grandparent for my side. Even though he appeared to be stuck in the sixties and had a criminal record to boot, he'd done his time. Maybe I was hoping a court would eventually take that into account, though I wasn't naive enough to consider this a great bargaining chip. I was just grasping for anything that might help me.

Since I'd gotten into acting, I was always observing people, trying to pick up on what they were about. I did the same with Ron—I wasn't going to be calling him "Dad," that was too strange—as we moved his stuff from the Wagon Wheel, with its free HBO, to my apartment, with its free macaroni and cheese.

Ron seemed genuinely grateful. And mellow, that old Southern California word for all-around peaceful and laid-back. Whatever his beliefs about religion, he appeared to have found some sort of respite from the bad road he'd been down over the past thirty years or so.

"So when do I get to meet Maddie?" Ron said when we'd moved him in, which consisted of throwing his duffel bag next to the sofa.

"That's a question that can't be answered just yet," I said.

He looked at me, confused.

"Paula has not been cooperative regarding Maddie. And I've got to get a lawyer to help straighten things out. Problem is, I haven't got the money to pay for one."

"Lawyers are slime," Ron said. His eyes reflected bitter experience.

"Maybe, but I need some slime right now."

"What's the beef?"

I shrugged. "It all comes down to Paula hooking up with another man. She won't talk to me. Maybe that's understandable."

"Why?"

"I threw a bottle at her."

Ron laughed. "That seems like regular domestic bliss."

"I was out of control. I blew it. Now she won't talk to me."

"Hey, don't take this all on yourself." He made a circle in the air with his index finger. "All you have to do is connect with the Wheel."

"Look," I said, "you can stay here for a while and we can talk. But I'm not interested in your mojo."

"That's cool. Just trying to help."

"When I want help, I'll ask."

"Right on. You're not religious at all?"

"I believe in God."

"The Christian God?"

"Something wrong with that?"

Reid shook his head. "Nah, Jesus was cool. He was one of the enlightened ones."

He was really interested in Maddie, so I got out the photo album.

Bad idea, it turned out.

Going back to when Maddie was a baby, every photo was like sharp glass jabbing me. I'd see Paula in there, smiling. Or the two of us with Maddie, when somebody else took the shot. Arms around each other. Group hugs.

Ron would stop every now and then and ask about a picture.

There was Maddie, clomping around in her mom's shoes.

At the beach, Maddie's two-year-old buns to the wind.

Disneyland. Just outside Pirates of the Caribbean, Maddie wearing a pirate hat from the expensive gift shop. She's glaring at the camera, like a real pirate.

"In her non-girly phase," I said.

Maddie in the kitchen, making her favorite food, buttered toast, all by herself.

And then the one that made me clutch: Maddie right in the middle of Paula and me, arm around both our necks and a determined look on her face. It looked like she was trying to pull her mommy and daddy together. It was taken at a surprise birthday party I threw for Paula.

"You know what I see here?" Ron said.

I shook my head.

"Hope. I see hope here. It's gonna work out, my man. Don't ever give up."

I did not know this man who was my father. Truth be told, I still felt very strange about his being here. But that was a nice thing he said and, considering the day I'd had, I was appreciative.

– 5 –

The receptionist's eyes were wide and impatient.

"Mr. Jennings does not see anyone without an appointment," she said, as if this rule were inscribed on a stone tablet. It was Thursday morning, and in my mind a perfect time to interrupt a hot LA lawyer.

"Tell him anyway. My name is Mark Gillen and I'm not leaving until I see him."

The office was on the fortieth floor of a gleaming building in Century City. The minimum rent had to be on par with the gross national product of Paraguay.

"Will you excuse me?" the receptionist said with stiff formality. She looked like a model.

I scoped the reception area. It was about three levels above Gregory Arsenault's office in terms of snootiness. Some sort of African artwork was the theme of the place, with ebony statuettes and exotic plants taking up most of the space.

An ornately carved spear hung on one wall. I wondered if that was what The Destroyer used in court.

The receptionist returned, an angry look on her face. "Mr. Jennings will see you, but you'll have to wait."

"No prob," I said. "I'll just hang here in the jungle."

Turns out I waited an hour and a half. I was sure he kept me waiting in order to tick me off. It worked. But I wasn't going to let him know it.

The receptionist finally walked me to a corner office that was, once again, bigger and richer than my nonretained lawyer's. In the middle of the ministadium, standing stiffly like some general, was a fiftyish man with a full head of perfectly coiffed black hair. His white shirt had no wrinkles. His silk, burgundy tie was perfectly knotted. But he was shorter than I'd expected. I thought anyone named The Destroyer would have to be six feet at least. This man was just over jockey size.

He stood there for a moment, unsmiling. Sizing me up. In my Nikes, jeans, and Lakers T-shirt, I did not fit in his world.

But then his white teeth showed and he stepped forward to shake my hand. "Bryce Jennings," he said. "And before we say another word, do you have a lawyer?"

"Gregory Arsenault."

"Ah, Greg. Good man. He's the one I should be talking to. We can't—"

"All right," I said. "I haven't retained him yet because I haven't got any money."

His eyes narrowed a bit. "Sit down."

"Look," I said, "by now you know all about my assets, or lack thereof, and probably all my personal habits as well. Did you know I sometimes snort when I sleep?"

Jennings said nothing.

"Yep, sometimes, for no reason I can think of, I snort and wake myself up. Paula used to laugh about that."

Tapping his lower lip with his index fingers, Bryce Jennings waited for me to make a point.

"Anything else you want to know about me?" I said.

"Yes," Jennings said. "I'd like to know if you want to save an enormous amount of pain and time and money and help your little girl, too."

"What am I supposed to say to that? No?"

"Some people do."

"What's the catch?"

That got Bryce Jennings to smile. "No catch here, Mark. And despite what you may have heard, Satan is not a named partner in my firm. I know I have a reputation as being something of a—"

"Destroyer?"

"I detest that name, but what can you do? If pushed, I push back for my clients. But I would much rather settle a case without stress or strain. It's best all around."

"I only want what's best. I'd like to sit down with Paula and talk this out."

Jennings looked pained. "I'm sorry, but that's not going to be possible at this point. Paula has made it perfectly plain that—"

"Paula or Troncatti?"

"I'm not sure what you mean."

"Who's paying your bill?"

"I can't discuss that, of course."

"What can you discuss?"

"Terms."

Folding my arms, I waited for him to continue. No harm in listening, was there?

"What Paula would like is the least pain for you, believe me. These things happen. People fall in love, then fall out, we don't know why. But we can't change our feelings."

"Then I guess marriage vows don't mean anything."

"It's a different day and time," Jennings said. "Marriage used to be enforced by the church, but that institution's largely faded. We now recognize there's more torture in sticking to a bad marriage than there is in divorce."

"So my marriage was torture for Paula?"

"Sorry, Mark, that was just a metaphor. My point is, divorce is easier now, as it should be. We have to work to make sure it stays easy for all parties concerned."

"All right, here is how we can make it easy. I want to go to counseling with Paula. I want her to give this a chance. I don't know if she's willing to do that or not—"

"As I said—"

"Let me finish." I was feeling heat. "If she's still going to press this forward, then maybe there's nothing else I can do. I'll have to move on. But I want Maddie. I want her living with me, not Paula and that jerk Troncatti."

Jennings put one hand in the air. "Let's not let personal animosity ensue here."

That did it to me. "*Animosity ensue?* Why don't you talk like a human being? This is my daughter I'm talking about. I want Maddie living with me. If you want to write that up in a paper and have me sign it, fine."

Silence.

"Well?"

"Mark, I'm afraid that's not going to happen."

The chill in his voice was like something from the frozen north. The temperature in the office seemed to drop.

"Just what is that supposed to mean?" I said.

"It is Paula's desire that Maddie live with her. Physical and legal custody would be required. You would get to see Maddie, of course."

"Oh yeah? How often?"

"That's to be determined."

"And what if Paula and Troncatti decide to move to, say, Rome? What then?"

Jennings shrugged. "Relocation does happen, of course. People learn to deal with it."

I couldn't take this anymore. I stood up. "I'm not going to agree to that. You must think I'm nuts."

He gave no immediate response, which ticked me off all the more.

"This is ridiculous," I said. "If she thinks she's going to take my daughter from me—"

"Her daughter as well."

"—and live with Troncatti, it's not going to happen. I'll tell her that myself, right now."

As I started to go, Jennings said, "Don't call her."

Turning on him, I tried to keep myself from jumping across his desk. "I'll call her when I want to."

Now Jennings stood. "This is your notice, under Penal Code section 653, that any further phone contact by you with my client will be dealt with as a harassment offense by the office of the District Attorney."

When I finally got outside again, it felt like my arms and legs had been cut off. Like I was powerless to move, could not do anything.

God, I kept repeating in my mind. *God help me.*

On the street I found a phone with a phone book dangling and looked in the yellow pages under *Attorneys—Family Law.* I just had to get a lawyer, but one that would take this case without a whole lot up front. If that meant me calling every lawyer in the book, so be it.

I scanned a few of the ads and decided not to call these first. If they could afford to advertise, they probably charged the most.

Using my finger like a desperate guide dog, I scanned the page until something jumped out at me. *Father's Rights,* it said.

Gee, did I have rights? Not if I listened to Bryce Jennings. I put in two quarters and called the number. A guy with a Brooklyn accent answered the phone. I told him what was happening.

"Get in here," he said. "Now."

THE SYSTEM

– 1 –

They've tried to put a whole new face on Hollywood. At the corner of Hollywood Boulevard and Highland they built this huge monstrosity of a shopping mall next to the famous Chinese Theater. The monstrosity also has a theater, The Kodak, where the Oscars are held.

To me, the whole thing is like a doily on a dung heap. There's just no covering up the truth. Hollywood still has the homeless and the hustlers, the beggars and the bag ladies. It is just a little bit cleaner on the sidewalk is all.

At least it was clean just outside the tiny walk-up near Cherokee. The Father's Advocacy Group office was a small, musty space with yellowed windows. About as far from the lofty status of Bryce Jennings as Beverly Hills is from South Central.

"You the guy on the phone?"

The New York voice was instantly recognizable. He was a small, sweaty man with a bad comb-over, maybe in his late forties. He spoke from behind a messy desk.

"That's me," I said.

"Sit down. Name's Joe Pfeffer. One *P*, a whole lot of *F*s."

"Mark Gillen."

We shook hands.

"Glad you came in. Coffee?"

"Sure."

"Came out of my car battery just this morning." Pfeffer spun around in his wooden chair, which seemed 1950s vintage. The ancient springs squeaked. He poured some coffee from a little maker into a Styrofoam cup.

"Take anything in it?" he asked.

"Black is fine."

"Good," Pfeffer said, handing me the cup. "Take it straight to the gut. Get used to it."

"Used to what?"

"Getting it straight to the gut. Your first divorce?"

"Yes," I said. "Though I'm hoping she won't go through with it."

"Then why are you here?"

"Because her lawyer said she wants full custody of our daughter."

"And she'll get it, most likely."

My breath left me in a rush.

"Sorry for the jolt," Pfeffer said. "But I'm from New York. You know what New York CPR is, don't you?"

I shook my head.

Pfeffer looked down at an imaginary victim. "GET UP OR YOU'RE GONNA DIE!"

When Pfeffer laughed, I forced a little chuckle. Was this gallows humor?

"Look," he said. "Here's the harsh reality. Eighty-five percent of the time, the mother is awarded physical custody of the child."

"Eighty-five?"

Pfeffer nodded. "Now I ask you, are 85 percent of the fathers out there bad? The way the courts go about it, it seems so. Judges must have a rubber stamp marked MOM on the bench."

"Isn't there something anybody can do?"

"We're trying. Trying for legislation in the courts to get rid of the prejudice against fathers."

"Any luck?

"It's tough. You got some very powerful groups opposed to changing the system."

"Like who?"

"National Organization for Women, various trial lawyers' associations. I can see why the lawyers don't want to change it. Child custody fights are a cash cow. You know what happens if a mother keeps a child away from a father with visitation rights?"

"What?"

"Zip. Nada. Unless the father goes back to court. Cops don't care. Social services don't care. Dad has to shell out thousands more bucks to a lawyer, wait for a court date. So yeah, the lawyers always win in the end, don't they?"

"Great system."

"What I don't get is NOW's opposition. I mean, whenever you stick it to a father, you're also sticking it to other women."

"How?"

"Grandma. Aunts. Sisters. All people the child has formed relationships with. They're gone from the child's life. How is that good?"

"This sounds like a horror story."

"You don't know the half of it. Ever heard of a guy named Derrick Brainard?"

"No."

"Shot himself outside the San Diego courthouse earlier this year. He shouted his last words, 'You did this to me.' In his hand he had an order denying custody."

"Sounds like he wasn't too stable."

The wooden chair creaked as Joe Pfeffer leaned forward and put his elbows on the desk. "Tip of the iceberg, my friend. Surgeon General says suicide is the eighth leading cause of death in America."

"But what does that have to do with—"

"Men are now four times more likely to kill themselves."

"Why is that?"

"Guy at U.C. Riverside did a study. The rise coincides with the increase in divorce and the discrimination of family law courts against dads."

"There's a study on this?"

"Oh yeah. And the stories we get." Pfeffer dug around in the papers on his desk, pulled out a sheet. "Guy in the Valley gassed himself because he was denied access to his kids. A cop in New York hanged himself because his ex-wife charged him with child abuse, and the court bought it. After the guy died they found out the ex-wife was lying all along."

"Man—" My gut, which Pfeffer had warned me about, was feeling punched.

"See, not only are fathers being denied custody, they also have to pony up alimony, even if the wife lives with someone and is being supported."

Even if the wife has some rich, powerful director paying for her every whim?

"There's even a group on Yahoo," Pfeffer said, "called Ex-husband Is Now My Slave. All sorts of advice from ex-wives on how they stuck it to their former spouse and get away with it."

"You're kidding."

"My friend, about this I do not kid."

I rubbed my forehead. "My wife has this big-time divorce lawyer, and I can hardly afford to pay for gas. My daughter is five. They want to take her away from me." The hand on my forehead was trembling. In fact, my whole body shook.

"I know how it is, Mark," Pfeffer said softly. "Believe me, I know, having been through the wringer myself. First thing you got to do is take care of yourself, you hear what I'm saying?"

My eyes met his.

"Everybody thinks the man should have it all together," he said. "Not true. I want you to talk to somebody, a lawyer. No charge up front. How's that sound?"

I hoped the lawyer—Alex Bedrosian, the card said—was an ex-soldier from the Armenian Army or something. Someone who would not be intimidated by the fancy attorney Paula had hired. And someone who would take his time getting his money.

I parked in front of the small office building on Cahuenga, which backed up against the 101 Freeway. A car dealership with all sorts of balloons flying was next door. Across the freeway, the giant presence of Universal Studios reminded me of the old saying: You look under the façade in Hollywood, and you find more façade.

I walked into an office that was small but neat. A pleasant-looking woman of sixty or so was dusting in the tiny reception area. She looked like someone's nanny. My heart sank a little. I was so used to high-powered lawyers with beautiful receptionists.

"Hello," the woman said.

"Hi," I said.

"Are you Mark?"

I blinked. "Yeah."

"Joe told me you were coming over."

"Great."

She offered her hand. "I'm Alex Bedrosian."

There is a fake smile one puts on when faced with shattering disappointment. That was what I plastered between my cheeks as I shook her hand. Some soldier.

"My receptionist is home with a sick dog," she said. "Come on in."

She led me past the reception area, down a little hallway. We passed a bathroom-sized room that wasn't a bathroom. It had a shelf of books and a computer terminal. The world's smallest law library, I gathered.

We got to the back office. Small but homey. The faint strains of classical music—something Mozarty—gave the room a pleasant feel. But I did not want a pleasant feel. I wanted war marches.

"Can I get you a cup of coffee?" Alex Bedrosian asked.

Thinking back to Joe Pfeffer's brew, I declined.

She sat at her desk. A small, potted flower adorned one corner, like a dainty Good Housekeeping seal of approval. "Joe didn't tell you I was a woman, did he?"

"Uh, no."

"That stinker. He's always doing that. New Yorker, you know. What are you going to do?"

What indeed? Bolt out of there was one option. But that left me with exactly zero alternatives.

"Now, Joe gave me a little of your story over the phone. Suppose you—"

"Look, Ms. Bedrosian, I have to tell you this up front. I'm not rolling in bucks at the moment. To be fair, you should know that."

She smiled, and it was warm. I could not for the life of me picture this woman in a court of law battling the likes of Bryce Jennings.

"If I take your case," she said, "I will ask for a retainer. The rest of the payment I will take as awarded by the court. Under California law, the family court judge may assign payment if he sees inequality in the parties."

"Well, how much of a retainer?"

"Can you come up with $1,200?"

I almost burst out laughing. Before she could take it back I blurted, "Yes!"

"Then why don't you tell me your story?"

So I did. For the next half hour I poured it all out, feeling it gush forth like water from behind a broken dam. In the middle of it I realized I felt more comfortable with this woman than I had with the much higher priced Gregory Arsenault. And it wasn't just because of the money aspect. I felt like she was listening to me, almost as if I were her only client.

Maybe I was.

When I finished, she looked briefly at her notes. "I will file for an immediate adjustment of the *ex parte* order, so you can see Maddie. It may or may not happen. But we'll push hard toward the hearing, on the Order to Show Cause, and I'll do what I can to speed things along. I don't believe Paula is going to give in on any point."

"But why?" I said. "How can she do that to her own daughter?"

"Because she has hired Bryce Jennings," Alex explained. "Jennings practices family law the way Colombian drug lords practice kidnapping. No mercy."

At that point I started to have some doubts. Could I fight for Maddie by paying $1,200 to a lawyer who looked more like a favorite grandmother than a lawyer?

"Could I ask you a question?" I said.

"Of course."

"How did you get into this line of work?"

The knowing smile told me this wasn't the first time she'd been asked that question. "Because I went through the nightmare of it myself."

"Would you mind telling me?"

She seemed to sense that I was looking for some sort of comfort in my choice of lawyer. She began fiddling with a rubber band on her desk. "I suffered for many years from bulimia. What I know now, that I didn't know then, was that a huge psychological hole inside me drove me to men who were wrong for me and finally into an abusive marriage. At the time, of course, I thought I had found the perfect man. We had two kids. The bulimia did not go away. I got a Ph.D. in behavior psychology, and I was more messed up than ever."

Alex told all of this in a matter-of-fact way. No sign of self-pity at all.

"When my husband filed for divorce it was because he'd fallen for another woman, whom he eventually married. But in the divorce fight, his lawyer made me the villain."

She looked at me, as if in warning. "All the secrets I had about my behavioral problems became public record as I was dragged through the meat grinder of the family court. Of course, my fitness as a mother was issue number one. I was portrayed as a combination of Lizzie Borden and the Bride of Frankenstein. This was in Miami. I was grilled by Miami human resource agents, by psychotherapists who knew less than I did about everything, by a judge who was clearly biased, and by local reporters who couldn't get enough of this juicy story. My lawyer fought hard, but we lost. It was a slaughter. My ex-husband got everything he asked for, including full custody of the kids."

"Did you get to see them at all?"

"He moved them out here, partly out of spite, I think. I saw them only rarely. It turned out well, though. I now have a good relationship with both my sons, who have, unfortunately, grown to resent their father. I wish that hadn't happened."

"Why not?" It seemed just to me.

"Because children should have both parents in their lives, unless it's clearly destructive. Matt, my ex-husband, was not an evil man. But he got caught up in an evil system."

"So you went to law school?"

Alex nodded. "Came out here to be closer to my boys and went to night school. I've been doing this now for ten years."

"How?" I said, shaking my head. "It would drive me crazy."

Alex nodded. "You have to have something inside that gets you through it."

"What is that for you?"

"Since you asked, I'll tell you. It's the same thing that got me through the bulimia. I have a strong religious faith."

Please don't let it be the Wheel.

"Mind if I ask you what it is?" I said.

"Christian."

"I believe in God, too."

"I'm glad, Mark. That will help."

– 2 –

To blow off steam I went to an acting class at Marty's. He was thrilled about my *Number Seven* part and announced it to the class. I got the usual tight smiles of affirmation—tight because actors' envy induces a certain lockjaw that can't be completely hidden.

After a couple of hours and some improv work, I actually felt refreshed. So much so that I decided to defy Jennings' threat and called Paula. I left this message:

"I'm not supposed to be calling you, according to your lawyer. So I won't do this anymore. I just wanted to have one last shot at asking if we can't sit down together again and try to talk this out. I know that didn't go so well last time and I'm sorry. I really am. I don't want this thing to drag out and be bad for everybody. You should know something pretty mind-boggling. My dad showed up. After all these years. Can you believe it? He saw something about us on the Internet and tracked me down. It's very strange, but he seems to have mellowed out with age, and he is very interested in seeing his granddaughter. Might that be possible sometime soon? I miss Maddie. When can I see her again? Call me if you want, I won't make a scene. Thanks."

When I walked into my apartment I was assaulted by a familiar odor, one I hadn't been around in years.

Out on the balcony, his feet up on the rail, Ron Reid was smoking a joint.

I practically tore the screen door off its rail.

"What are you doing!"

My voice startled him into an upright position on the chair. He held the marijuana cigarette daintily, like a lady at tea.

"You scared me," Ron said.

"You're smoking weed in my apartment?"

"I came outside."

"That's not the point!" I slapped my hips, making a popping sound. "I'm in a custody fight for my daughter here! I don't need you doing this! And where'd you get the money for dope?"

Ron remained terminally laid-back. "I had this with me. You want some?"

"No, I don't want some. You want to stay here, you get rid of it. Can you imagine what'll happen if I got busted for this?"

"Will you relax?"

There was a scratching sound from the balcony next door. Mrs. Williams, my very pleasant neighbor and Maddie's sometime babysitter, stuck her head out. "Everything okay out here?"

I stepped in front of Ron, to block him from being seen. "Fine, Mrs. Williams. Sorry I got a little loud."

"You having a party?"

"No, nothing like that. I'll keep it down."

"You tell Maddie I said hello now, you hear?"

"Yes, Mrs. Williams."

"You bring her on over sometime real soon."

"You got it."

She went back inside. I looked at Ron with fire in my eyes. "Listen, this is my place, okay? My rules. You want to stay here, you do what I say."

With raised hand, Reid said, "Okay, okay." He licked his fingertips and dampened the end of the joint. Then he popped the whole thing in his mouth and swallowed it. "Enough said?"

"Just don't do it again," I said.

Before he could respond, my cell went off.

It was, surprise of surprises, Paula.

"I got your message," she said. "Is your father really there?"

"Right here," I said.

"Unbelievable. What's he like?"

"Maybe I should go into that another time."

Pause. "There probably won't be another time. I really can't talk to you. My lawyer just called me. I guess you hired another lawyer, huh?"

"News travels fast."

"She called Bryce, to see what was up."

"And what *is* up?" I asked.

"You can't see Maddie right now, not until a court rules. You are going to be served. I'm sorry."

She sounded stiff and formal. It was almost worse than having her angry at me.

"So it's come down to this, huh?" I said.

"I have to go now."

"I'm not going to let you have Maddie."

The line clicked.

"Everything okay?" Ron said.

"Don't talk to me," I said.

– 3 –

"So much depends on the judge," Alex said. "If we get a bad one, a pro-Mommy judge, or someone who just doesn't trust men, it will be very bad."

"There's nothing we can do?" I had come into Alex's office on Friday to show her the papers that had been served on me. It was three days after my last phone conversation with Paula. I had seen little of Ron. He was out looking for work, he said.

"We have one peremptory," Alex said.

"What's that?"

"It's a 170.6 motion. Either party can reject a judge, one time, and the judge has to step down from that case. He can't inquire as to the reason. It's automatic. Problem is you might get one who's worse. The presiding judge, who makes the assignments, might try to figure out why you made the move, and get you to a judge who's just like the last one. We won't do this except as a last resort."

"It's pretty much a crapshoot then? The judge?"

"Pretty much."

"I'm so thrilled. So what's going to happen at the hearing?"

"Jennings will try to convince the judge you are not the right parent for Maddie to be with, pending an evaluation."

"Evaluation?"

"A mental health evaluator will be assigned to make a recommendation to the judge."

"Mental health? Am I going to have my head shrunk or something?"

"If he or she wants to shrink your head, you let them. The judge almost always follows the recommendation of the evaluator."

"Who are these people?"

"It varies. You have Ph.D.s in psychology, social workers, licensed evaluators fresh out of grad school. But they're people above all. Some have great judgment and insight into what kids need. Others are houseplants in shoes. Some are good-hearted, some are little Darth Vaders."

"Man."

"Exactly. We will cooperate with these people. You will treat them very nicely. You will not get angry, or you will not pass Go and collect your daughter."

"What else can I do?"

"Pray."

"That's not a very comforting thought."

She narrowed her eyes. "If you look at it right, it's the most comforting thought of all."

MEMORIES

– 1 –

That evening I went to a Mexican restaurant with Ron. My treat. He'd landed a job with a car repair shop on Vineland. Good news. I was going to tell him to move out. I just didn't know how to relate to him. And after the smoking incident, I didn't think it was a good thing to have him around. But where did that leave us?

"Good news about the job," I said as we went at a basket of tortilla chips.

"Yeah," Ron said. "I'm a productive citizen again."

"I'm glad."

"Thanks for not throwing me out."

"You thinking of getting a place?"

He nodded. "Soon. I promise."

"You have any friends out here you can stay with?"

"Not really. Maybe some guys I could look up." He crunched a couple of chips. If that can be done thoughtfully, that's the way he did it. "Listen, is there anything I can do for you, Mark? I mean, I feel like I owe you."

"Nah, you don't."

"But I do. I made some bad choices."

"We all do."

"Yeah, but you were my . . . you are my son."

I still didn't know how to take that. "That's all past, Ron. I mean, I don't think of you as my father. How can I? I don't hold any bitterness toward you."

He looked skeptical.

"All right," I said. "Maybe I do. I didn't have a dad around and that bothered me. It bothered me that you never wrote. But maybe I was better off."

"How so?"

"You're a pot-smoking ex-con."

For an instant Ron looked stunned, then suddenly laughed. "I guess I deserve that."

But now I wanted more. "What *are* you like?"

"What do you mean?"

"I mean, what makes you up? What was your own father like?"

"Dad? He was a World War II vet, Navy. Man in the gray flannel suit type. Ran our house like a tight ship."

"Where was this?"

"Indianapolis. I couldn't get out of there fast enough. Got to San Francisco in time for the summer of love in '67. It was some scene."

"You did the whole drug deal?"

"It wasn't like that," Ron said, leaning forward. "It wasn't ever drugs for drugs' sake. We were looking for a higher reality to tune in to. It was like waking up from a deep sleep, which is what the fifties was like. We didn't want to grow up to be Ward Cleaver or Ozzie Nelson. Would you?"

I shrugged. "When you have a child, your ideas about that change."

"But it was an amazing time," Ron said.

"A lot of brains got fried, didn't they?" My mom, I remembered, had trouble holding a job. Gram always spoke about Mom with sadness, like Rainbow had been lost to her years before her actual death.

"Tell me about Paula."

"What about her?"

"What's she like?"

For a long moment I thought about it. "I don't know anymore. I thought I knew her. I loved her. I thought she loved me. Then she heads off to Europe. Maybe I was being naive."

"Stuff happens."

"That's very profound."

"The Wheel goes round and round. You have to accept that, just accept it."

"No," I said. "I'm not going to sit back while this happens. I have to fight."

"For Paula?"

"For Maddie."

"You still love Paula?"

"I don't know anymore." And at that moment I honestly didn't. You don't have the kind of love I had for Paula and just kick it out of your system.

"Hang in there," Ron said. "Just remember, the—"

"If you say anything about that stupid Wheel again, I'm going to throw the salsa at you."

At night, when alone in bed, memories of Maddie swirled around like gnats. I couldn't ignore them or get rid of them, so I let them come, even though they keep me awake.

I am sitting in the living room of the apartment, practicing some lines for an audition the next day. I'm supposed to be a young father with a kid. Typecasting. I can nail this.

Back and forth I walk, spouting line after line. ("Now don't you go out in the water unless I'm watching you!" my character dad says. "You stay where I can see you!")

And then I hear a CLOMP CLOMP.

Did Maddie drop something on the floor?

I stop and turn.

CLOMP CLOMP.

Maddie clomps in wearing a pair of my dress shoes. And a pair of pink underwear.

As I stand there trying to make sense of this new performance artist, Maddie holds her head up proudly.

"I am Queen of the Underwear," she announces.

Which cracks me up. I almost fall on the floor laughing, all the while wondering where on earth that had come from.

Maddie CLOMPS around some more and sings, "I'm Queen of the Underwearrrr."

That's when my dad voice kicks in and tells me to get some control. "That's a very funny song. Now what would you think about becoming Queen of the Clothes?"

"But I'm Queen of the Underwear."

"All right. I'm King of the Apartment. So I get to tell you to put on some clothes now."

Her Mussolini lip sticks out. "Do you have a duhjen?"

"You mean a dungeon?"

"You know, where you can put people."

"No, I don't have a dungeon."

She folds her arms. "Then I can still be Queen of the Underwear!"

I kneel. "Your highness, if Daddy really, really wanted you to put some clothes on, would you do it?"

Maddie considers this a moment, smiles, nods. "I am a good queen." She CLOMPS off to her room.

A short time later she comes out, having dressed herself in a shorts and a SpongeBob T-shirt. She puts her arms around my neck and kisses me.

"That was a fun game," she says. "What else can we play?"

– 2 –

I called Nancy at home the next morning. Technically, I shouldn't have. It was Saturday. But I didn't care from technically.

And I was suddenly *hot.* Or maybe warm enough to break a sweat. That meant Nancy wouldn't be bothered so much to hear from me. I hoped.

"Any word on the contracts?" I asked.

"Working out some details," Nancy said. "You're going to be pleased."

"When?"

"A couple of days, no more. Then we'll get you a big fat check to cash. How's that?"

"That would be great."

"And what about you?"

"Me?"

"How you doing?"

"Fine."

"I mean really."

Really? I was not so good. I'd gone to the market earlier and saw something that almost flattened me. A father and his daughter holding hands, walking along the cookie aisle. The girl was about Maddie's age. The father was a young guy, younger than me, and he was having a conversation with the girl.

"Where was I before I was born?" I heard the girl ask.

"You were inside Mommy," the father said matter-of-factly.

"Before that where was I?"

The father thought a moment. Fascinated, I followed them. "You were a little egg and a little . . ." He stopped himself. "You just weren't here yet."

"Where was I?" the girl insisted.

"You were in God's mind," the father said, pointing to his head.

And I felt a crushing inside me. It was the kind of conversation I used to have with Maddie. We'd had a bunch of them. She was so full of curiosity about things, always asking me questions. Now I realized the big silent void in my life was there because Maddie wasn't with me, asking questions.

To Nancy, who was my agent and not my psychotherapist, I said, "Really, I'm fine. I'll be just fine. Just show me the money."

She laughed. "Spoken like a true star in the making."

– 3 –

Two days later, Monday, I was in the courtroom of a judge named Harold J. Winger.

"Fair man," Alex had told me, which offered just a modicum of relief.

But any good feeling I had got sucked away when Paula entered the courtroom in the company of Bryce Jennings. Nor did it help that a train of reporters flowed in behind her. Paula was good copy now. I was just a subplot in her ongoing story.

Paula did not look at me. She wore sunglasses into the courtroom and was dressed like a star.

Bryce Jennings was dressed in a dark blue suit and a double-edged smile. He nodded at Alex. Alex nodded at him. Choose your weapons.

Paula sat down at the table near the jury box. I was seated at the other table, looking at her. She kept her face forward. She took off her sunglasses. Her beauty was breathtaking.

Alex patted my arm. Today was supposed to get me some time with Maddie. According to Alex, there was little chance I'd be denied it. Even if it meant being supervised, I'd get some sort of bone thrown my way. Then we could prepare for the big fight over custody to come later.

Fight. Just what I didn't want. But Alex said Jennings and Paula were taking a hard line, and we would have to do the same. And let the court sort it out.

Judge Winger walked in at precisely nine o'clock. He looked experienced. At least the lines in his face and gray hair indicated that. I hoped Alex was right, that he was a fair man.

He called our case immediately. Alex and Jennings stated their appearances for the record.

"We're here on a motion to modify the *ex parte* order entered by this court on August 5," Winger said. "The mother apparently has the daughter living with her, is that correct, Mr. Jennings?"

"Yes, Your Honor."

"All right. The issue is immediate sharing of custody, pending a final disposition. The father wants to see his daughter. Is that it, Ms. Bedrosian?"

"It is, Your Honor," Alex said.

"According to your moving papers," the judge shuffled something in front of him, "the last contact the father had with the daughter was on . . . August 6?"

"Correct. Eight days ago."

"Any phone contact with the child?"

"None. And Mr. Jennings threatened my client with a harassment charge under the penal code, of all things, for any phone calling."

The judge looked at Jennings for a response.

"Mr. Gillen was calling my client constantly," Jennings said, "and she is feeling threatened."

Threatened? That was absurd! I may have let my voice get a little heated, but Paula knew I would never try to hurt her.

Winger pressed his little finger to his lip. "Is that really an accurate characterization? The word *threat* is pretty loaded."

Go judge, I was thinking. *Tell him. Lay him out. Give me my daughter.*

Bryce Jennings looked as cool as a Brioni-suited cucumber. "And we do not use that term lightly. This is all in the context of Mr. Gillen's assault on my client."

There was an audible gasp in the courtroom. And then I realized it came from me. Maybe Alex joined in, because she flashed a look my way that was both surprised and accusatory.

"You're alleging an assault?" Winger said.

"I can have my client testify if need be," Alex said.

"Maybe you'd better."

Alex said, "Your Honor, may I have a moment to confer with my client?"

"Go ahead."

Leaning over like an angry mother, Alex whispered, "What is this all about?"

"I guess I didn't mention it." My face was flushing. I was sure the reporters could see this.

"No, you didn't. Is it true?"

"I didn't throw the bottle at—"

"Bottle? You threw a bottle?"

"It was only water."

"At Paula?"

"No, at the ground. I was frustrated. It got out of hand."

"Why didn't you tell me?"

There was no good answer. Maybe I was just too embarrassed. Maybe I thought it would just go away. "I'm sorry."

"Is there anything else you want to add?" Alex said. "Any other skeletons rattling around?"

"No, honest."

Alex sighed and turned toward the judge. "May we approach the bench?"

The judge waved her up, along with Jennings. There was no jury, of course, but I think Alex wanted to keep something from the reporters. There was some spirited discussion, then the lawyers returned to their respective corners. I could tell from the look on Alex's face that she had come out on the short end.

Which meant Paula took the stand.

After she was sworn, Jennings started to walk her through the testimony. It was very clear to me that he had set this up, that he was planning to have Paula get on the stand and testify all along. It would make great copy.

"You met with Mr. Gillen on the afternoon of August 3, is that correct?" Jennings began.

"Yes," Paula said.

"At a restaurant in Beverly Hills?"

"Yes."

"And at the time, Mr. Gillen met you and—"

"Objection," Alex said. "Leading."

"Preliminary matters," Judge Winger said. "Overruled."

"Mr. Gillen met you and you sat at an outside table?"

"That's right."

"Can you tell us briefly what you discussed?"

Paula, looking both beautiful and vulnerable, said, "I suggested that, for Maddie's sake, we should discuss the divorce in a friendly way."

"What was Mr. Gillen's emotional reaction?"

"Objection," Alex said. "Speculation."

"Overruled," Judge Winger said. "The witness's state of mind is the issue."

"Angry," Paula said. "He was in denial and very antagonistic."

I almost jumped out of my chair. Finally I understood the meaning of the phrase *raked over the coals.* I started writing some notes on a legal pad.

"What led you to believe he was antagonistic?"

"Well, first he said he didn't want anything to be easy for me. He said he wanted to make things hard on me. When I finally saw there was no reasoning with him, I got up to go and he slammed his fists on the table and screamed at me."

Paula paused and Jennings said nothing. Letting it all sink in, I thought. The judge looked intensely interested.

"And then," Paula added, "he threw a bottle at me as I walked out."

Another dramatic pause. Like it had been rehearsed.

"What sort of bottle?" Jennings asked.

"I think it was a bottle of sparkling water."

"Did it hit you?"

"No, thankfully. It hit the ground and shattered."

"Were you hit by glass?"

"Some, yes. But mostly I was terrified."

Jennings nodded. "That's all, Your Honor."

"You may question the witness," the judge told Alex.

My lawyer rose, took my meager notes, and walked to the podium between the counsel tables.

"Ms. Gillen—"

"Excuse me, Your Honor," Jennings said. "My client's professional name is Montgomery. We request counsel to address her accordingly."

At that moment, for some reason, Paula looked at me. I couldn't quite read her face. But my eyes cried out to her. *Why are you doing this?*

She looked away.

"Proceed," Winger said.

"Ms. Montgomery," Alex said, "the bottle you say was thrown at you was actually thrown at the ground, was it not?"

"I didn't know that."

"That's not my question. The bottle hit the ground, not you, isn't that correct?"

"Technically."

"What does that mean, *technically?*"

"He threw the bottle toward me."

"That's a little different than *at* you, isn't it?"

"I don't know."

"You know your husband was once a star baseball player, don't you?"

Paula looked as surprised as I was. "Yes, of course I know that."

"Don't you think if he was going to throw a bottle at you he would have hit you with it?"

For a moment Paula was silent. She shrugged.

"Please answer out loud for the court reporter," Judge Winger said.

"I don't know," Paula said.

"Well, if you don't know," said Alex, "then you can't make this accusation about Mark throwing the bottle at you, can you?"

"The bottle shattered at my feet."

"Please answer the question."

"I have."

"Yes," Alex said. "Perhaps you have. I will leave that to Judge Winger." She turned to the judge. "No further questions, Your Honor. This has been a bald-faced attempt to sway you in your decision. I trust you will see through it."

"The court appreciates the trust of counsel," Winger said.

Jennings smiled. A couple of reporters in the gallery laughed. Everyone, it seemed, was amused. Except Alex and me.

— 4 —

During the recess Alex took me down the stairs to the cafeteria on the second floor of the courthouse. We bought coffee and she took me to a corner table where we could talk without a reporter listening in.

"Is there anything else you need to tell me?" Alex said. "Think hard."

"Honestly, I don't think so," I said. "I'm really sorry about the bottle thing. I just wanted it to go away."

"Instead, it sticks. If I'd known about it, I could have brought it up first and lessened the impact. But they did, and the judge looks at it as something we were trying to keep from him. Honesty, even if it hurts, is the best policy when you talk to your lawyer."

I was suddenly aware of someone standing next to the table. It was a young woman with short, styled hair and glasses with black frames.

"Excuse me," she said. "I'm Jan Solomon, *LA Times.* Mind if I—"

"I'm sorry," Alex said. "I'm in conference with my client."

"If I could just get a statement."

"No statements at this time."

The reporter looked at me. "Don't you want to tell your side?"

"He is telling his side in court," Alex said.

"About the bottle-throwing incident?"

"We really have nothing to say."

"Because it looked pretty bad in there."

My chest tightened. Alex got a look in her eyes like a tiger. That heartened me. What I needed was someone to fight for me, in and out of court.

"No statements, Ms. Solomon. Now if you'll excuse us?"

Alex's expression worked wonders. The reporter, without another word, walked away.

"Thanks," I said.

"You will not talk to reporters without my say, understood?"

"Understood."

"Back to business. The judge seemed impressed with the abuse allegation. Throwing the bottle made the difference."

"Can I get on the stand and explain?"

"It won't do any good. We agree you threw the bottle, even though not at her. What we're going to ask for is an emergency screening."

"What's that?"

"When one party is withholding custody the judge can order an evaluation to take place immediately. Within twenty-four hours. The evaluator will interview you, Paula, and most likely Maddie."

"Then what?"

"He or she makes a recommendation to the judge, who will more than likely follow it. It can be anything from full custody to no contact at all, pending a complete evaluation."

"And how long can *that* take?"

"A month, sometimes more."

"More? You mean I might not see Maddie for over a month?"

"It's possible."

"I want to know how possible." I could feel my face flush as I tried to process the thought of not seeing or hugging my daughter for that amount of time. How could they do this? I was beginning to understand what was behind some of the things Joe Pfeffer told me. Dads going a little nuts.

"It all depends on you and the evaluator," Alex said, "and I want you to be very aware of that fact. You are to be truthful and calm. Hostility is something they are going to look for in you. Do not show it. We'll talk more later when—" Alex's look swept past me. "Who is this?"

I turned around and saw Ron Reid, all smiles in his Hawaiian shirt, jeans, and sandals, striding towards us.

"The clerk upstairs said I might find you here," Ron said. He put his hand out to Alex. "I'm Ron Reid, Mark's father."

"I'm Alex Bedrosian, his lawyer."

There was no doubt at all who was the more important person in my life.

"I just wanted to show up and be a support," Ron said.

"Thank you," Alex said. "That was very nice."

She was sincere. But I also heard an edge in her voice that was meant to be a subtle signal.

"Anything to help," Ron said.

"Mr. Reid, I need to talk to Mark about a few more things."

"Mind if I?" He grabbed a chair from a neighboring table and slid it to ours.

"Ron," I said quickly, "this needs to be private."

"Oh," he said in mid squat. "Sorry. Sure. Hey. I'll see you later then, huh?"

"Right."

Looking embarrassed, Ron Reid left us. *All part of the Wheel,* I wanted to say.

Alex brought us back to the moment at hand, laying out what would happen when court resumed, preparing me.

I assured her I got it, that I was ready. And for a small moment in time, sitting at that table, I thought maybe things would start to turn my way a little bit. Get this screening over with, get to see Maddie again, maybe in a couple of days.

But I wasn't ready. How do you get ready for a landslide that buries you?

– 5 –

The first boulder knocked me down the next morning.

Ron was snoring away on the sofa when I went downstairs to get my *LA Times.* The front page had a headline about a speech by the president the night before. His picture was there with the American flag in the background.

I flipped the front page over to see what was below the fold. Something about an earthquake in Guatemala killing a few thousand people. A possible medical breakthrough for balding men.

Same old, same old.

But then, just before I started back up the stairs, I saw it.

On the bottom of the front page the *Times* runs some highlights of what's inside. Paula's name jumped out at me like a neon sign. A gossip bit about the child custody fight. And a father going berserk.

My hands started sweating as I pulled out the Metro section. Page two. And there it was, for all the world to see.

Like Father Like Son?

Paula Montgomery, who is hotter than hot after nabbing a role in the latest Antonio Troncatti film (and Troncatti himself, we might add!), was in court yesterday, trying to convince a judge to let her keep custody of her daughter, Madeleine, pending divorce proceedings. She is repped by none other than Bryce Jennings, which is not good news for the father, sometime actor Mark Gillen. Add this to the plotline: Gillen's own father, Ronald Reid, is an ex-con who has suddenly turned up on the scene. We don't know if this complicates matters or not, but it may explain one thing, the bottle Gillen threw at Montgomery in Beverly Hills. During what was supposed to be a civil meal to discuss Madeleine, Gillen threw a bottle of sparkling water at Montgomery. The bottle shattered on the sidewalk, injuring no one, but putting Montgomery in fear for her well-being—and that of her child. Gillen and his attorney, Alex Bedrosian, refused comment. But Reid had his own opinion: "Mark's going through a tough time right now. I'm just trying to help him through it, keep him from erupting." Maybe Gillen's next role will be that of volcano.

Stunned is too weak a word for what I felt. And like it or not I couldn't keep down a very real eruption bubbling up in me.

My face was burning by the time I slammed back into the apartment.

"Wake up!"

Ron was groggy under the blanket on the sofa. I yanked off the blanket. Ron was in boxer shorts. "Huh?"

"You talked to a reporter?"

"Oh." He rubbed his eyes. "Yeah."

"And told them I'm going to erupt?"

"Huh?"

I shoved the paper at him. "Look at that!"

He took the paper and sat up. I gave him time to read it, thinking I could get my breathing back down to normal range.

Finally he said, "It's not that bad."

With an angry swipe I ripped the paper out of his hands. "Not that bad? The judge is going to think I'm a walking time bomb or something."

"Well, aren't you?"

I gawked at him.

"I mean," Ron said, scratching himself, "you've been uptight ever since I've known you. I was just hoping . . ."

"Hoping what?"

"I could help a little, you know?"

"By flapping your yapper?"

"No, by being a father for once in my life."

He looked down at the floor. And my anger started to subside a little. What was I looking at, anyway? A man whose life had pretty much gone down the toilet and maybe was looking for some self-respect. Problem was, it was at my expense. The way the cards were dealt, I just happened to be his son. That was nobody's fault.

One thing you don't want to do is take away a man's last shred of dignity. I saw that happen to a friend of mine, a forty-year-old character actor, who got ripped one day by a producer, a twenty-five-year-old New Yorker. The kid told my friend he was not a has-been but a never-was and a never-would-be. And I stood there and watched it. Nothing I could do consoled my friend, who later tried to kill himself with sleeping pills. He recovered, but left town for parts unknown. I don't know what happened to him.

So I stopped short of telling Ron Reid he was a boil on the backside of my existence.

"Look, I appreciate the attempt," I said. "But it didn't help. I don't want you talking to reporters, or showing up to court hearings, okay? Or living here. You've got a job now, maybe you can go out and get a place today."

There was a look of hurt on his face for a second. Then he said, "I'll try."

I sighed. "Let me give you some money to tide you over."

"You don't have to."

"You'll pay me back. If you need somebody to cosign for a place, I'll do that, too. But Ron . . ."

He looked at me.

"No more trying to help on the custody thing. Okay?"

– 6 –

The bad part was I did not get a call from Nancy.

Usually, following good news or bad, I get a quick call from my agent. That's the good part of Nancy Radford. Unlike a lot of Hollywood agents, she keeps in touch with clients even if they're not "hot." There were times I had been in the ice tray and she still called me.

She always read the *Times*—both LA and New York—in the morning, and then the trades. She would have spotted the item about Paula and me. She should have called to buck me up a little.

Maybe she was sick. Maybe she had some emergency.

Or maybe she was really upset with me.

An actor's mind plays all sorts of tricks when his agent doesn't call. Mine did.

So I was not exactly in the best frame of mind when I arrived for my meeting with the court-appointed evaluator.

Her name was Sheila Bonner and she looked about thirteen. Her office was in a bank building in Encino. She was one of four names on a door on the third floor. Marriage and Family Counseling was the designation.

She did not smile once during our meeting.

"We're here for an emergency screening," she said. I thought of that Monty Python skit, *I'm here for an argument,* but kept my mouth shut as she closed the door to her small, inner office.

There were a couple of diplomas on her wall which, I trusted, meant she knew what she was doing.

"I'll ask you some questions, Mr. Gillen," Sheila Bonner said. "But I'd like to encourage you to open up as much as possible. Give me any information you deem relevant."

"Sure."

"Now, the court has asked me to discuss the relative merits of the two, distinct living situations. There is a slight burden upon you to justify a return of the child pending final disposition. Is that clear to you?"

"I guess."

"You guess?"

"What I mean is, I'm not sure why that should be, but I'll answer any questions you have as best I can."

She went for it without a flinch. "What assurances can you give me about your relationship with your daughter?"

I told myself to relax, feeling my jaw tense as I did. "Well, my relationship with my daughter, when I had it, was great."

"In what way?"

"Every way."

"Isn't that a bit of an overstatement?"

"I don't think . . ." I stopped. Quick analysis. Alex had told me to be honest and objective. Yeah, of course I was overstating it. Making myself look good.

"You don't think what, Mr. Gillen?"

"I don't think there was any big negative with Maddie. There was the normal stuff a kid does that irritates the parent."

"Can you give me an example?"

I thought a moment. "A month or so ago she decided the funniest thing in the world was to make a fart sound on her arm."

Sheila Bonner said nothing.

"You know," I explained. "Putting her lips right here—" indicating the elbow crook—"and *blat.*"

"This was an irritant to you?"

"After about the hundredth time."

"You didn't view this as the child's exercise of expression?"

"Yeah, of course I did."

"But you didn't say that."

I felt my right hand clenching. "You asked me about something that irritated me."

"Yes, and that's what we're exploring."

Who are you? Lewis and Clark? "I mean, if it keeps going on and on, you tell her to knock it off. And when she doesn't, you get a little ticked."

"Were those your words? 'Knock it off'?"

"I don't remember my words exactly. No, I don't think I said that to her. I was saying that to you." And whatever I was saying was coming out wrong. Not the way I wanted it to sound.

"Do you get irritated easily?" Sheila Bonner said.

Like now? "I don't think of myself that way."

"What about the bottle-throwing incident?"

"I didn't get a chance to explain in court."

"Go ahead."

"Yeah, I lost my temper there. I just wanted to get through to Paula. She's my wife. She left me for another man. She wouldn't listen."

"So you threw the bottle at her?"

"No. That wasn't it. I threw it at the ground. I just wanted to be heard. Like now."

"Do you think I'm not listening to you, Mr. Gillen?"

What was she doing? Trying to bait me? Then it occurred to me that's exactly what she was trying to do.

"I'm sorry," I said. "I'm just a little upset at this whole thing. You would be too if someone wanted to . . . do you have kids?"

Wrong question. I could tell by the look on her face she didn't, and resented my asking.

"Let's keep the focus where it needs to be, Mr. Gillen."

"Sorry."

"Are you sorry? Or are you saying that just to please me?"

Oh man! "All I'm trying to say is that I love my daughter, I would never hurt her, and I want to be with her."

"Do you want to be with her because it's a way of getting her away from your wife?"

"No, that's not it at all."

She pushed her glasses up on her nose.

"Tell me about your father," she said.

"My father has not been part of my life."

"Why is that?"

"He was never around. He went to prison."

"What for?"

"I'm not sure. Something drug related."

"But he's back now?"

"A surprise to me."

"Is he living with you?"

"Was. He's out getting a place even as we speak."

"His status is a bit unfortunate for this case."

"He seems to be okay now," I said. Funny, but I was jumping to his defense without qualm. "I mean, he did his time. He's looking for work."

Sheila Bonner scribbled a note to herself. I wanted desperately to see what it was.

"Please," I said. "Please let me see my daughter. With everything in me I'm telling you I am not going to do anything wrong. I just want to hold her again. I miss her . . ." My voice choked. I felt embarrassed.

"Let's take a short break," she said.

– 7 –

Powerlessness. That's how I felt when I finally got out of the wringer that was Sheila Bonner.

The rest of the grilling had gone pretty much the same way. Now Ms. Bonner held my immediate future in her hands. A future with or without Maddie.

I could hardly stand the wait until tomorrow, when we'd be back in court.

I drove over to Jerry's Famous Deli, where industry types like to eat. It boosted my ego a little. As an out-of-work actor I'd come here and eat the pickles. Now I was, at least, going to have a regular part on a series. I could afford a sandwich.

I ordered a pastrami on rye and looked at a copy of *Variety*. Couldn't focus on anything. My mind was playing a movie.

Fade in: Troncatti's massive home. Maddie wakes up in a big, fluffy bed, surrounded by a whole bunch of new stuffed animals.

She goes down for breakfast in the huge dining room, overlooking a pool in the backyard.

"Can I swim today?" she asks Antonio Troncatti. "Tony" is reading *Variety* and sipping espresso.

"Of course-a you can, *bambina*," he says (my movie has clichés and Troncatti's voice sounds like he's from *The Godfather)*.

Paula wanders in, kisses Troncatti. "Maybe we can take Maddie to Disneyland today, huh?"

"You want-a Disneyland?"

"Yes!" Maddie says.

"You got-a Disneyland!"

After Troncatti goes off to do his hair and nails, Maddie looks at Paula. "When will I see Daddy again?"

Paula gets very serious. "Honey, Daddy doesn't want to see us anymore."

"Huh?"

"Daddy tried to hurt me, you see. And he might do the same to you."

"But Daddy wouldn't ever—"

"Daddy's not the same person he was. That's why I brought you here, to live with Tony and me. You're safe here, and you'll have everything you want."

"But won't Daddy be lonely?"

"No, honey. Daddy doesn't like us anymore. He told me so."

Lies! I almost shout it out right there in Jerry's. Am I going crazy now? Is that the way it's going to be? Will I . . .

"Are you okay?"

I looked up and saw a woman, about twenty-five, with silky blond hair.

"What?"

"You looked like you had a pain there," she said. "I'm sorry, I just wanted to say hi to you."

She looked vaguely familiar.

"I'm Nikki McNamara," she said. "From Gower Presbyterian."

I did recognize her. We'd passed each other the last time I was at church. I asked her to have a seat.

"I'm supposed to meet someone," she said. "So don't think me rude if I get up."

"Hey," I said, "at this point rude would be a step up."

She looked at me quizzically, but then she smiled. It was a great smile, too.

"You're an actress," I said.

"Is it that obvious?"

"Just a hunch. You could throw a dart in here and odds are you'll hit an actor or a screenwriter."

"I'm in the theater company at the church. Actors Cooperative. Heard of it?"

"Yeah. You get some great reviews."

"We have good people."

"Are all of you members of the church?"

"Not all of us. We're all Christians, though."

"Christian actors? You don't hear that term much in this town. Sort of like *honest lawyer.*"

She laughed. "Before I do any more confessing, you didn't tell me your name."

"Mark Gillen."

"Nice to meet you."

"Likewise."

My sandwich arrived.

"Can I buy you lunch?" I said.

"Oh, thanks. I'm meeting someone."

"Right." I found myself hoping it wasn't a man.

"Are you getting involved at Gower Pres?"

"Well, I sort of go sometimes. I'm leaning in that direction."

"Going to church?"

"God and things."

"That's good. God is a very good thing."

"I'm hoping."

Nikki cocked her head, waiting for me to explain.

"Just for personal reasons," I said.

"You an actor?"

"My SAG card says I am."

"Cool. Why don't you come by and hang with us?"

"Really? When?"

"We have a Wednesday night Bible study and play reading. Down at the church. Hey, tomorrow. Come by about seven."

"Yeah," I said. "Maybe I will."

"I hope you do."

"Hey, Nikki." A dark-haired woman, a little older than Nikki, came over to the table.

"Here she is," Nikki said. "This is Cheline Lester. Another of the gang. Cheline, this is Mark."

We exchanged pleasantries. Nikki stood up. "Thanks for the chat."

"Sure."

Off they went. And I found myself surprised at how glad I was Nikki had not met a man.

At 2:30 I called Nancy and got her assistant.

"She's in a meeting, Mark," Rachel said.

"Can you have her give me a call on my cell?"

"Sure thing."

I drove over to Tower Records and spent a little time listening to sound tracks. Movie scores are my favorite kind of music. I love the classic Maurice Jarre scores to movies like *Doctor Zhivago* and *Witness.* And Bernard Herrmann, who made the Hitchcock experience so much more memorable. I also like the haunting, lyrical quality of some of the new ones, like Mark Isham, who did *October Sky* and *A River Runs Through It.*

It's the sort of music that can transport you.

Around four I went to the newsstand at Van Nuys and Ventura and got a *USA Today.* My attention span could only take in nugget-sized chunks. McNewspaper was perfect.

I was reading about a bombing in Tel Aviv when my phone went off.

"Sorry I couldn't get back to you sooner," Nancy said.

"A busy agent is a good agent."

Silence.

"You there?" I said.

"Mark, can you swing by?"

"Now?"

"Yes."

"I suppose I can. Why?"

"Just come in."

I knew then it was bad news. An agent always tells you the good stuff over the phone.

"What is it, Nancy? Tell me now."

"Mark—"

"Please."

"I'd rather you come in."

"Is it about *Number Seven*?"

"Yes."

"Tell me. Tell me now."

Pause. "They dropped you, Mark."

VISIONS

~ 1 ~

Of course I knew it was not a good thing to curse at God. Did I care?

No.

My curse took the form of tears at first. I cried hard, for the first time in a long time. I sat in my car so people on the street couldn't see me unless they looked real hard. No one did.

Offing myself entered my head for a moment, making an appearance like a ham actor with two lines. That scared me a little. But the thought didn't hang around, and I chalked it up to the stress of the moment and yelled at myself for being such a wimp.

The next option seemed better. I drove down Ventura looking for a LIQUOR sign. No way I was going in to see Nancy. Not in the mood I was in. Changing my mood is why I wanted a liquor store. I found one a few blocks away and pulled into the parking lot.

And sat there for about fifteen minutes. My legs wanted to walk in and buy a bottle of Jack Daniel's. My throat thought it was a great idea, too. But I fought it. For some reason I was thinking of that old movie, *The Lost Weekend,* where Ray Milland does a great job showing the horrors of drink. He goes a little nuts, sees terrible visions.

An argument started in my head, like when the little angel and the little devil sit on opposite shoulders in a cartoon. The devil was saying this would be a one-time thing, and where was the harm if you're alone and responsible? The angel kept saying Maddie's name, over and over.

I didn't buy the booze. And I was mad about that, so I screeched into a Jack in the Box and ordered four—count 'em, four—spicy chicken sandwiches. I wolfed one down as I got on the freeway, so I could drive fast. I wolfed down another one as I tore down the Santa Monica freeway and then up the 405.

My stomach was full but I managed to stuff a third belly bomb down my throat, not caring if it came back up.

At 6:45 I saw I was coming up on Universal Studios. The big black tower where the suits make all the decisions hovered over the freeway like some glass King Kong. Up on the hill, Universal City Walk, a neon jungle of overpriced tourist stores and restaurants, was getting ready for the evening rush. Colored lights would be evident soon, turning the sky into some sort of artificial impressionist canvas—the color of LA hip.

And for one second I almost felt better. Despite all the crud that happens here every day, I actually like Los Angeles. It's my home, where I grew up, and I know it well. I've had dark days when everything seemed pointless turn into warm, pleasant memories in various places in the city—going with friends to the Hollywood Bowl; sloshing in the surf at Zuma Beach; kickin' it with Roland and some cool jazz.

All of that hit me at once under the shadow of Universal, and I was just about to let all the bad stuff melt away.

That's when the kid in the truck cut me off.

Weaving in and out of lanes is almost a sport in LA, especially if you're a punk with a pickup. More and more of these testosterone-laced, backward-baseball-hat-wearing dweebs are being handed trucks by Mommy and Daddy so they can race around at ninety miles per hour and show how macho they are.

Any pleasant change got yanked away from my spirits, as if chained to the guy's bumper. And anger flared.

So I chased him. Flashing my lights. Honking.

Road rage. Another urban sport.

What was I doing? People get shot over this stuff. I didn't care. There was no justice in the world, so I was going to bring a little to the blacktop.

I changed lanes without a signal, cutting off a guy in a Toyota. He honked at me, and that added more fuel to the chase.

Traffic slowed, and the truckster got pinned up ahead, giving me the chance to really lay it on his backside with my horn. He cut over a lane, almost nicking a Mercedes.

I followed, gunning the gas. No thoughts at all in my mind, just a blind desire to make life miserable for someone besides myself.

It felt good to be mad. It felt good to have all other thoughts run away and hide in fear of my all-consuming rage.

The pickup found an opening that let him get a good lead. I was hemmed in for the moment, but it wouldn't be for long.

I changed lanes again, in front of a Ryder truck, the driver of which added to the fun by blaring his horn at me.

A little VW got in my way, slowing for no good reason, so I gave it a good rebuke from my horn. The driver, an Asian woman, looked back at me, confusion on her face. I honked again.

On I went, keeping the truck in sight. Not knowing—not caring—what I'd do if I ever followed it off the freeway. Crazy time.

Then I noticed the flashing lights behind me.

My nerve endings erupted. That couldn't be for me. No way was I being told to pull over by the California Highway Patrol.

No, no, no, no, no, no!

Yes. He was on my tail. And the jerk in the truck was getting away.

Come on!

The Chippie blared his siren. I was toast.

I took the next off ramp, driving as carefully as I could. Staying within the lines. Maybe I could act my way out of this one. After all, how bad could this be? I hadn't hurt anyone. It was not my fault!

I pulled to a stop across from a tire store.

The CHP officer was not a *he*. It was a woman. Tough looking. But somehow this gave me hope. Call me a chauvinist, but I was sure I'd get through this okay.

"May I see your driver's license please?" Her chest pin said MEADOWS.

"Was I speeding?" A cliché was all I could come up with.

"License, please."

Right. And after countless cop encounters on TV, I knew I had to remove it from my wallet. I tried to keep my hands from shaking too badly. So far so good.

Officer Meadows glanced at my license. "Mr. Gillen, did you know you were weaving on the freeway for about three miles?"

"Weaving?"

"Yes, sir."

"Oh, I may have been a little distracted."

"Distracted?"

"Did you see that guy ahead of me?"

"All I saw was you changing lanes without signaling, weaving in and out. That's reckless driving."

"Wait." I put my hands out like a kid caught in the kitchen before dinner. "There was a guy who cut me off and I . . ."

"Wanted to teach him a lesson?"

"Officer, come on."

"Have you had anything to drink?"

"What? No!"

"Do you mind stepping out of the car?"

Stepping out? What was this?

"Am I under arrest? Don't I get to talk to an attorney?"

"Please step out of the car, sir."

Something happen, please. An earthquake would be good. A nice California 6.9 shaker . . .

I got out, on solid ground.

"I am going to ask you to perform a test," Officer Meadows said.

"I am not drunk! I have had nothing to drink!" The injustice of the accusation really hit me, especially after I'd talked myself out of the Jack Daniel's.

"Listen to my instructions, sir." Meadows removed a pen from her pocket. "I am going to ask you to keep your head straight and follow the movement of this pen with your eyes. Is that clear?"

"This is ridiculous."

"Are you refusing?"

"Let me level with you," I said. "I need a break here. I'm in a big-time battle for custody for my daughter. She's only five, and I think she is getting hurt, and I'm getting hurt, and this doesn't make one bit of difference to you, does it?"

Officer Meadows shook her head.

"Then give me a test," I said. "I want you to take me in and have me pee in a cup. I want to see your face when the test results come back. Just do it, Officer Meadows."

What she did was write me up for reckless driving, right on the spot.

Then she actually said, "Have a nice day." Sometimes Los Angeles is a sprawling city of clichés.

Ron was watching TV when I walked through the door.

"Good news, Mark. I found a place."

"Great."

"Yeah. Little studio. Not the nicest, but I think I can make it work."

"When do you move in?"

"Tomorrow. That cool?"

"Groovy," I said, tossing out a word he might appreciate. Truth be told, I was getting annoyed at the sight and sound of him. He was a graying longhair who seemed to have missed the reality boat. He was still living in the age of Hendrix, whose music I could do without.

Ron looked at me. "Only . . ."

"Only what?"

"I hate to ask."

"Money?"

Ron Reid shrugged.

"I just gave you a hundred," I said. "Where did it go?"

"I didn't spend it."

"You didn't score some dope, did you?"

"Hey, man."

"Hey nothing."

"Whoo. Something happen today?"

"Forget about it."

"Come on. Let me help you get out of this reality."

"Ron, do me a favor."

"Yeah?"

"Put a cork in it."

– 2 –

The next day I was in a daze so thick it was like I had a brain disease. This did not help my tips at Josephina's. I worked lunch and messed up just about every order. I dropped a tray of linguine on the floor; I knocked a lemonade onto the dress of a businesswoman who had the sense of humor of Dr. Kevorkian.

All the while I kept thinking about the time Maddie took care of me.

It was a day I was fighting a horrific cold. I'd been out on an audition, for Pepsi, and just couldn't give it anything. When I rounded up Maddie from Mrs. Wilson's, I was pretty much thrashed.

I'd promised Maddie we'd have hamburgers, the way I make them. I put little bits of onion in the meat, and Maddie likes that. But all I could do was plop down on the sofa.

Instead of talking to me, Maddie went into the bathroom and wet a washcloth, came out, and put it on my forehead. Even though I didn't have a fever, it felt right. And Maddie sat by me and stroked my hair.

She wanted to make me feel better, she said.

If only she could have made me feel better about working the lunch crowd. But my shift was ruined. Afterward I called Alex. We were due back in court tomorrow, and she said there was nothing else I needed to do—except not get arrested.

Funny.

I called Nancy, partly out of a wish to see if this was all just a bad dream. Maybe yesterday never happened. Maybe I was going to wake up like Dorothy, back in Kansas, looking at Barbara DiBova standing there with my contract. *I had this terrible dream, and you were there . . .*

But I didn't wake up in Kansas. Nancy was sympathetic, but something cool had drifted into her voice. You learn to pick that up with agents. It was the sort of chill that announces a client is about to become too much trouble.

With nothing to lose, I plowed right through it. "Did you ask DiBova why they dropped me?"

"Best to leave it alone, Mark."

"Don't we deserve some sort of answer?"

"It's their show."

"I want to know."

"Leave it alone."

"I'll call her myself."

"Mark," Nancy warned, "don't do that. You had a setback, but you don't need to stir up more trouble."

"Why not? Maybe that's just what I need to do."

"I'm telling you. Don't."

"Whose side are you on?"

"Cool off, Mark."

Click.

And suddenly, here I was again. About to blow up. Not what I needed to do with Maddie's future on the line.

I remembered it was Wednesday.

Nikki McNamara.

Bible group.

But mostly, Nikki McNamara.

When I got there, she was the first one I saw. She rushed over, welcoming me with a big smile. "You made it!"

"I'm here." I felt like the new kid in school.

"I'll introduce you around."

There were about forty people there, mostly actors. I didn't know there were that many Christian actors in LA. A couple of them I recognized from auditions. One of them, Tom Starkey, was pretty big now. He had a great ongoing role in an ABC drama. He also led the Bible study.

Which was out of Romans. We sat in a big circle on folding chairs. The room was large but warm. A big portrait of an older woman—looking like anyone's favorite grandmother—beamed down at us. I found out later it was a woman named Henrietta Mears, a famous Bible teacher from some time back.

Starkey had people open their Bibles (I shared with Nikki). And we read from chapter 8.

"Therefore, there is now no condemnation for those who are in Christ Jesus, because through Christ Jesus the law of the Spirit of life set me free from the law of sin and death. For what the law was powerless to do in that it was weakened by the sinful nature, God did by sending his own Son in the likeness of sinful man to be a sin offering. And so he condemned sin in sinful man, in order that the righteous requirements of the law might be fully met in us, who do not live according to the sinful nature but according to the Spirit."

Whoosh. That just blew right by me. I had no idea what this all meant. Sin offering? Condemning sin in sinful man? It sounded weird.

Starkey, though, was good at explaining things. His voice was easy and his enthusiasm obvious. He wasn't acting. He really was into this stuff.

Bottom line, he said, Jesus was indeed a sacrifice in the Old Testament sense, when they used to sacrifice animals all the time. Jesus was different. His sacrifice was for everyone. Once and for all.

I still didn't get it all, but it sounded better by the time Starkey was finished. It made me want to come back for more.

Afterward, several in the study went for coffee at a little café on Franklin. Nikki asked me if I wanted to tag along.

It was fun. For the first time in a long time, it was actually fun to hang out with some people. They were into movies and theater and music. Topics flew around like birds. I laughed and let the troubles drift to the back of my mind for a while.

When I talked to Nikki, they went away almost completely.

She was from San Diego, had been a theater major at the University of California down there. "Got to LA about three years ago," she told me. "Been knocking on doors ever since."

"How's it going?"

"I've been up for a few things, nothing big yet. Doing theater with the co-op has been a godsend."

"Too bad it doesn't pay."

"It does in other ways." She took a sip of coffee. "Acting for the soul can save your life."

"How so?"

She smiled. "I'm a preacher's kid. You know what happens to them?"

I shook my head.

"We usually start rebelling around fourteen, fifteen. Smoking after school. Hanging out with the wrong boys. I put my dad through what must have been a meat grinder for him. One reason I went to UCSD was to party. Actually didn't talk to Dad for three years."

She said all this with a certain sadness and took a breath. "Came up here more or less lost. Knew I was running away from God. Also knew I wanted to be an actor. Didn't care how or what. It was rough for the first six months. I didn't get a single thing. And then I was looking through *Back Stage West* and saw Actors Cooperative was having auditions for *The Hasty Heart.*"

"Great play."

"You know it?"

"Sure. Great movie, too. With Ronald Reagan and Richard Todd."

"Yes!" Nikki smiled. "I got the Patricia Neal role. And that's what did it for me."

"Did what?" I was intensely interested.

"My friend, Cheline, you met her at Jerry's? She has this saying about great art. It doesn't preach at you, but it makes you homesick for heaven. There's that part in all of us that seeks God, even if we choose to ignore it. The play opened up that part of me again. It brought me back to God. And that's how acting saved me."

We sat in silence for a moment. Nikki looked momentarily embarrassed that she had opened up so much. Without thinking about it, I put my hand on her arm.

"Thanks," I said.

She looked at me and I melted into her eyes.

"I needed to hear something like that," I said. "I got dropped from a new TV show that I was supposed to get."

"Oh no."

"Old story, different tune. I just need to regroup, figure out why I'm an actor." I took a sip of coffee. "I wonder if I could join," I said. "The theater group and the church."

"Really?"

"Think I can?"

"Church, of course. There's a new member class. And we have auditions every quarter for the company. If you want, I can set one up."

"You would do that?"

Nikki smiled again. "All you have to do is prepare a scene."

My mind clicked like a well-oiled machine. "Would you do one with me?"

"Me?"

"Only if you have time."

She looked at my left hand. "What would your wife think?"

It was like an ocean wave hitting me square in the face.

"That's kind of a difficult question right now," I said.

"I'm sorry."

"No, you're right to ask. She's living with another man. She wants a divorce."

Nikki's face reflected sympathy. She didn't have to say anything.

"I'm just trying to lead a normal life," I said, "in the midst of all this. Which means trying to be an actor."

There was a long silence. "Okay," Nikki said.

"Okay?"

"I'll do a scene with you. As a favor to a fellow actor."

I could not have begun to tell her how good that made me feel. We spent another hour or so chatting it up, laughing with the others, talking movies and theater and the bottomless pit of TV.

I left feeling good. It was a feeling that would last exactly nine hours.

– 3 –

"The court has taken into consideration the report of the evaluator," Judge Winger said the next morning, an unseasonably cold Thursday. "I have also considered the testimony offered in this matter, and the court rules that the respondent, Ms. Montgomery, shall retain physical custody of the child, pending final resolution. The court will allow two supervised visits by the father, Mr. Gillen, on the following two Tuesdays, for two hours each, with a third party present . . ."

His words faded in and out of my brain. Paula had custody? But I was going to see Maddie?

" . . . as appointed by the court. Costs for the monitor to be paid by Mr. Gillen. We'll set this matter for hearing September 25 if that is acceptable to both parties."

And just like that it was over. Head swirling, I followed Alex out of the courtroom. (Paula didn't appear at the session. At least I was spared that.)

"So I get to see Maddie?" I felt like a kid asking about going to Disneyland.

"Yes, supervised," Alex said.

"Why? The judge thinks I might do something?"

"He went along with the evaluator."

"That thirteen-year-old? Bonner?"

"This is just temporary. Now we go to work on the formal custody hearing."

"When do I get to see my daughter?"

"I'll call you."

"Alex, please."

She grabbed my shoulders, looking at me as much like a parent as a lawyer. "Mark, this is the first round. I told you to be prepared for a tough fight. Here is the good news. You will get to see Maddie again. And soon. It's a matter of setting things up—"

"Supervised visit. He said supervised."

"That's not unusual. Focus on this. You will be holding your daughter in your arms soon. Think about that, will you?"

I was more than happy to.

There are, they say, five stages in an actor's life.

In stage one, the casting director says, "Who is Mark Gillen?"

Stage two: "Get me Mark Gillen."

Stage three: "Get me a young Mark Gillen."

Stage four: "Get me a Mark Gillen type."

Stage five: "Who is Mark Gillen?"

The great fear of actors is that they'll go from stage one to stage five without those other steps in between. What's that line from the Dionne Warwick song about San Jose? Years pass so quickly, and the actors who thought they'd be stars are parking cars or pumping gas.

That fear is a little ferret in the belly of actors, and the only way to keep it quiet is to do something.

Well, I did something, all in the grip of this elation over Maddie. That emotion does funny things to your mind, especially after you've been hammered. You start to feel that the momentum is changing, like in a basketball game. Not something you can measure, but you have the feeling you're about to go on a roll, can't be stopped.

Sure it was only a small victory, getting supervised visits, but it was huge to me. I wanted to see Maddie again, hold her, laugh with her, more than anything in my life. And soon I would get to.

But this sort of mind-set can create a false sense of confidence, too. So I took my giddiness, mixed it with the fear of failing as an actor, and went out and did something really stupid.

I drove from the courthouse over to the Burbank Studios. I told the guard it was Mark Gillen to see Lisa Hobbes. He made a call, then gave me a temporary parking pass.

I was in.

Lisa met me outside the office of DiBova Productions. She did not look happy. "What are you doing here?"

"I came to see Barbara."

Lisa's nostrils flared in what was her characteristic gesture of disbelief. "Without an appointment?"

"I need an appointment?" I said with mock surprise.

"Idiot," Lisa said. "What do you want?"

"Really. I just want to ask her a question."

"But you can't."

"Why not?"

"She's in a meeting."

I folded my arms. "That's the oldest one in the book."

"She really is in a meeting, Mark."

"I can wait."

"I shouldn't have let you on the lot," Lisa said. "This is about *Number Seven,* isn't it?"

"*Ding ding ding.*"

"You can't change that, Mark."

"I just want to know *why.* Is that so unfair? I had the thing and then it's pulled out from under me. Maybe you can you tell me."

Lisa shrugged. "Things happen. Decisions get made. You know the drill."

"But I *killed* the reading." I tried not to let desperation make my voice all squeaky. "Barbara was hot to get me, my agent says. I want to know what changed."

"You know how this business is. Sometimes it just doesn't make sense. I'm really sorry—"

"What happened, Lisa? You know, don't you?"

She did not answer.

"You do know why." I almost jumped down her throat.

"Mark, don't." She put up her hands and took a step back.

"Why, Lisa?"

"Just let it go, Mark. You'll have other chances."

"I want to know about this one."

"I need to get back—"

She started to turn but I grabbed her arm. She jerked it away. "Don't."

"Please," I said.

"I can't tell you anything." But from her look I knew she could. There was more here and she wasn't letting me in on it. Which only made me crazy.

"You can't do this!" I shouted.

"I'm not doing anything."

"I thought you were a friend."

"Mark, don't put that on me."

"Why shouldn't I?"

Before Lisa could say another word a security guard with a shaved head seemed to appear out of thin air. He looked like he chewed bones.

"Problem?" he said, glaring at me.

"No," Lisa said. "He was just leaving."

I told myself it had to be the publicity angle. Barbara DiBova and the powers that be decided my profile in the papers made me too, what, unstable to work with?

But part of me argued that in a world full of Sean Penns and Russell Crowes, having negative publicity didn't really matter. In fact, it might even raise ratings.

At the same time, I knew that wasn't really it. There was something else going on, beneath the surface.

Or maybe I was just losing it, becoming another paranoid actor who ends up old and unemployed, muttering lines to himself on the corner of Hollywood and Vine.

The bone-chewing security guard made sure I found my way to my car, and watched me drive off the lot. I sort of lost track of time after that.

– 4 –

Maddie had a spell there where she had frequent nightmares. She'd wake up screaming. I'd jolt out of my sleep like someone getting a cattle prod in the back and run to her room to calm her down.

One time, when Paula was off shooting her movie, Maddie screamed for me around midnight. I ran into her room and she made me get in bed with her. She buried her head in my arm.

"He's in the closet," she said.

"Who?"

"The bad man."

"What bad man? Was he in your dream?"

She nodded, keeping her head buried.

"Why is he in the closet?"

"He wants all our Cheerios," Maddie said.

That made me crack up.

"It's not funny," Maddie insisted.

"Why does he want our Cheerios?"

"I don't know. He wants to eat them all up."

"Do you want me to get rid of him?"

Nod.

"Wait here," I said. I slipped out of the bed. Maddie put the pillow over her head as I went and opened her closet. A little part of me wondered if there really might be a Cheerio bandit inside. "You have to leave now," I said to the little dresses. "And don't ever come back again."

"No, Daddy," Maddie said in a muffled voice. "He's in the *hall* closet."

"Oh, sorry."

I tromped out to the hall, opened the closet, and picked a mean-looking jacket. "You hear me? Get out! Don't come back, ever!"

Maddie was out of the pillow when I got back.

"Was there really a man in there?" she asked.

"What do you think?"

She thought for a long moment. "If he wasn't, who were you talking to?"

I cradled her in my arms. "I was showing you what I'd do if

there ever really was a man who wanted our Cheerios. Or anybody else who tries to scare you. I'll always protect you, okay?"

Her little head went up and down on my chest, happily. I loved that.

I was thinking about that moment eating my own bowl of Cheerios the next morning. Ron Reid called to tell me his new address. I wrote it down, though I still didn't know what to do about this guy. He did not seem like my father, and I was sure he never would. That hole in me was going to stay.

After breakfast I walked to Samuel French to pick up a couple of fresh paperbacks of *Hamlet,* the scene I decided to do with Nikki. It was good to be in there, surrounded by plays. Made me feel like I was still an actor. Out of work, without pay. Still hurting from betrayal. But hey, I could still say lines. I could still act.

Around noon I got a call. From Lisa Hobbes.

"This is a surprise," I said.

"You free to meet?"

"What are we doing in the back of a used bookstore?"

"Looking for *The Complete Idiot's Guide to Being an Idiot,*" Lisa said. "By Mark Gillen."

"Thank you."

"Don't mention it."

Lisa had asked me to meet her at Book Central in North Hollywood, a big used-book store that does a heavy trade. It was housed in a two-story building off Lankershim, near Blockbuster Video. Inside it was all wood and musty smell. So the meeting with Lisa seemed clandestine and mysterious, something out of a forties film noir.

I found her in the back corner of the first floor, actually wearing dark glasses.

The first thing she said when she saw me was, "You almost got me canned."

"Nice to see you, too."

"You hear what I'm saying?"

"What did I do?"

"Barbara saw you."

"DiBova?"

"No, Bush. Of course DiBova."

I slapped a shelf of books, hitting, I think, a volume of Victor Hugo. "I'm sorry. All I was looking for was a reason."

"Yeah, with this big chip on your shoulder. So Barbara asks me what you wanted. More to the point, she asked me what I was doing out there talking to you."

"What, did she think I was packing heat or something? Going in to shoot up the place?"

"You never know. You're the actor. You're one of the crazy people."

"So what did you tell her?"

"I told her you'd left your SAG card with me and came to pick it up."

"Why did you do that?"

Lisa put her hands on her hips. "To save your sorry butt, that's why. You are on thin ice right now. You can't afford to make things worse."

"What do you mean *thin ice?*"

"The whole Paula thing. You're not exactly smelling like a rose."

"Is that the reason they decided to stab me in the back? They were so afraid of bad publicity?"

"That's part of it."

"Excuse me. Didn't Barbara DiBova do time at Betty Ford? That didn't seem to hurt her any."

"She's a name. She's a player. Drug rehab can be a career boost if you've got game. But who are you?"

"Thanks again."

Lisa sighed. "Look, sorry. I'm blunt. You know me. I always have been. But I like you, Mark. Would I be here if I didn't?"

"You said that was only part of it, the publicity. What else?"

Lisa ran her finger along the spines of some books. "Don't say anything about this, okay? Don't tell anybody, ever, we had this conversation."

"This is starting to sound very *All the President's Men.*"

"If this ever gets back to Barbara, I'm toast."

"You're really serious."

"Yeah, genius, I am."

"What's wrong?"

An old man with a crooked, wooden cane and smelling of Old Spice and older wool, shuffled to the shelf next to us. He put his nose near the titles and started scanning. He was obviously going to be awhile.

Lisa motioned for me to follow her to the staircase at the back of the store. They creaked like a haunted house as we went up. We were in paperback fiction now, mysteries. Which seemed appropriate.

I was busting at the seams. "So what is going on?"

Lisa spoke in a low voice. "I hard-copy Barbara's e-mails, the ones she marks. And then file them by date. Other ones she marks for trash. Usually, she trashes them herself. Sometimes not. It depends. I'm supposed to go through the trash at the end of the day and make sure nothing was put in that wasn't marked for it. Doesn't take long. Just a quick scan. Last Monday I did that and saw one in the trash with the subject line *Seven.* Which obviously meant *Number Seven.*"

"And?"

"I read it. Barbara has a special file for *Number Seven,* and I thought she'd put this in by mistake. Turns out this e-mail was about you."

My throat started to close. "From who?"

"Leonard Remey."

No way. Remey was a big-time agent at AEA, one of the top three agencies in town. Paula's new agency, in fact. "Remey was talking about *me?*"

"I have to assume."

"So what was in the message?"

"All it said was, 'Re: our conversation. Yes, has to go. Non-negotiable.'"

"How do you know that was about me?"

"Who else from *Number Seven* was let go?"

The sea of books around us actually started to undulate in my vision, like some old movie effect where a guy's about to pass out. "But why? Why would Leonard Remey be sticking his nose in my life?"

"I have a theory."

"Tell me."

Lisa sighed. "You know who he represents?"

"Yeah, Paula and a lot of big names."

"Including Antonio Troncatti."

Boom. I felt like I'd been jabbed in the face by a heavyweight. "You think Troncatti is behind my getting axed?"

"Look at the way it's worded," Lisa said. "It sounds like DiBova checked with Remey on whether you really had to go."

"And he said yes, nonnegotiable. And DiBova caved." My voice slammed into the shelves.

"Of course she caved. It goes back to what I've been saying. In the pecking order, Remey is up here—" Lisa put her hand up high—"and Barbara is here." She put her hand about shoulder level. Then she dropped it to her side. "And you're here. Remey has a lot of people Barbara wants to work with, so she's not going to fight him when it comes to an actor who has yet to break into the big time."

Emotions flared around inside me, like random fireworks. If this was all true, and it sounded too smarmy not to be, it was Antonio Troncatti himself who had cut the legs out from my career. My head started to feel real tight.

"I had to tell you." Lisa put her hand on my arm. "I think it stinks. But I wanted to tell you so you knew what you're up against. If you want to keep acting, you need to walk away from this thing with Paula as quietly as you can."

– 5 –

"*Calm down,*" Alex said.

"Don't I look calm to you?" I held two fists up in the air.

"I want you to practice keeping that anger in check. You're going to be sitting in front of another evaluator and the judge, and I don't want you to come off as Genghis Khan on steroids."

"At least he had the satisfaction of killing his enemies."

"You don't know for sure what happened."

"It all makes sense." Pacing up and down in front of her desk, I felt like a panther or some other beast of prey—say, a Hollywood agent? I wanted some raw meat to tear apart.

"You got some secondhand report that is easily deniable," Alex said. "It's not going to do us any good."

"I can't believe you're saying that! Troncatti calls up his agent and has the agent sabotage my career. What are we talking about here?"

"We're talking about a very rotten deal, but one that the court is not going to consider."

"How can that be?"

"Because unless you have some evidence to back it up, this will fall under the category of depraved vituperation."

I just stared at her.

"What that means," Alex explained, "is that so often in divorce proceedings one side accuses the other side of some big, nasty thing in order to gain the upper hand. Much of the time it's just made up, and judges know that. They don't want to sit up there and listen to accusations flying back and forth unless they can be backed up somehow."

"What if Lisa testified?"

Alex shook her head. "She doesn't want to lose her career, does she? Even if we force her on the stand, she might deny the whole thing. And even if she didn't, you know what Bryce Jennings will do to her on cross?"

My mind conjured pictures of Lisa sobbing uncontrollably, in true TV-lawyer-show fashion.

"What I'll do is shoot off a letter to Jennings," Alex said, "that tells him in perfectly vague legalese that we know something's been going on and it better stop. Yakkety yakkety yak. No threats, just a little wake-up reminder. And it'll become part of the file. Meantime, you concentrate on being a model citizen and be ready to stay perfectly calm when you see Maddie on Tuesday, and the evaluator sometime next week."

"It won't be the same one, will it?"

"It might."

"She looks like a teenager. How can I talk to her without thinking about zits?"

"Like the cool, calm, rational person I see before me now." She looked at my hands. "Unclench your fists, please."

I had to keep visions of my hands around Troncatti's neck from consuming me. Once more, acting was my way out.

Nikki met me at the church, where we could rehearse in the little theater. She came in looking like she'd just had makeup put on by the staff at Max Factor. Beautiful.

"I was reading for a mascara commercial," she explained.

"Looks like you got the part."

"We'll see. You know how it goes."

Did I ever.

We sat in the audience seats and I threw her a fresh copy of *Hamlet.* She smiled. "Boy, you are ambitious. Why Shakespeare?"

Because I fell in love with my wife talking Shakespeare.

"They don't do much Bill Shakespeare around here anymore," I said.

"We do," Nikki said. "We're planning a production of *As You Like It* for next season."

"No way."

"Way." She laughed. "Why is that so astounding?"

"It's not. It's just sort of a coincidence." I didn't explain that that was the very play Paula and I talked about on our first date. Some things are better left unsaid.

I flipped open my copy of the play. "I thought we could do the 'Get thee to a nunnery' scene."

"Ah yes. So you think Hamlet's insane?"

"The way I play him? Definitely yes. Typecasting."

Again she laughed and opened her book. "Where are we starting?"

"I promise I won't do 'To be or not to be.'"

"What a silly question."

"Right. Page 35. Start with 'Soft you now! The fair Ophelia! Nymph, in thy orisons be all my sins remembered.'"

And off we went, reading the scene. No acting, just the lines. That's always how you start. Let scene and character come to you gradually.

All went well until I got to Hamlet's line, "I say, we will have no more marriages." My face must have changed like a traffic light.

"You doing okay?" Nikki asked.

"Yeah. No. Hanging in there."

"You didn't want the divorce?" She said it so simply I was not at all offended. It did not seem like prying. It was more like a friend asking me to talk it out. Actors tend to do that. Peel away the emotional layers to get at something real inside.

"No." I shifted in my seat. "I wanted to stay married. I wanted us to be a family and all that. I keep looking for something I may have done, or not done, that ruined things. Honestly, I can't. But now it's happening. I hate the whole thing."

"You're on the right side," Nikki said. "God hates it, too."

"Excuse me?"

"Hates divorce."

"So what does that mean? Does he hate me?"

"Of course not. Although some churches might make you feel that way."

I shrugged.

"Divorce is sometimes treated as the unforgivable sin. I'm a preacher's kid, remember? Though my dad didn't do it, some people over the years managed to elevate divorce to the level of murder and child molesting."

"Are you kidding?"

Nikki shook her head. "What was so sad about that is since there is no-fault divorce law, a party can be perfectly innocent and still get the scarlet letter—in this case a *D*—stitched on his shirt."

"Great. Get the tar and feathers ready."

"You're not that far off. Many Christians would actually say you are just as guilty as your wife. That's so stupid it's not funny."

Her mind seemed crisp and alive, like she'd thought this all through deeply and it meant something to her. "So you're really a preacher's kid, huh?"

"Yep."

"Know your Bible pretty well?"

"Oh yeah. You want me to tell you the names of the Bible books, in order?"

"Some other time, maybe." I paused, feeling like she and I were together for a reason more than just doing a scene. "So what would you, as a Christian, advise me to do now?"

Nikki paused for a long moment, treating the question seriously. Then she said, "Forgive."

The word blasted out at me like mace spray. "Forgive? Paula? For having an affair?"

"I know it sounds crazy."

"Yeah, it does."

"But God has a reason for it."

"And that would be?"

She patted her chest. "To keep you from being eaten up inside."

I shook my head. "That does not make sense to me."

"Me neither," Nikki said. "But I finally figured out it's better to obey God than wait until you've got it all straight in your mind. Remember what Jesus did on the cross? He asked God to forgive those who were executing him."

"Let's get back to the scene," I said.

VISIT

– 1 –

Thursday finally came, and with it a new player in my little drama. His full name was Renard J. Harper, and he was a robust African-American social worker assigned to monitor my visit with Maddie. Middle-fifties, I guessed. We sat on a bench at a Studio City park. At least I got to choose the location for the visit.

"This is very uncomfortable for me," I said.

"I can relate," Harper said.

"I mean, this whole security thing." I waved my hands around. "Like I'm going to do something to my daughter."

"Happens all the time." Harper had a deep voice, kind of soothing. Like somebody's favorite uncle. "Doesn't mean there's anything to it, but we have to walk carefully when a child's involved."

"Yeah, but what about the parents?"

"What about them?"

"Don't they have rights, too?"

"That's what court is all about. Better if the two of them can get together and talk it out."

"Right." Bitterness dripped off my tongue. "What if the other party doesn't want to talk?"

"Then you end up with me." Harper smiled. At least he was trying to be pleasant.

"What gets me is that anybody can say anything, and we end up with you. I mean, this whole thing is so stupid. Paula knows I love Maddie and I'd never try anything."

"What about the beach thing?"

"You mean when I took Maddie to Ventura?"

Harper nodded.

"You know about that?"

"I got the whole file, of course. All I'm saying is, the littlest things can come back at you."

I looked him right in the eye. "You think I'd ever do anything to my daughter?"

"Not for me to say. I'm just doing what the court tells me to do."

"And I get to pay you for the privilege. That's another thing that bites."

"Mr. Gillen, you want some free advice?"

"Sure." I slapped my thighs. "How much will it cost me?"

"My football coach in high school used to gather us around before a big game and say, 'Gentlemen, show me what you're made of.' And we'd all go out and pound heads for him. Well, this is a big game for you, seeing your daughter. Show her what you're made of. I'll see it. And when I report back to the court I'll be able to say something good about you. I'd like to, you see."

"Thanks for that." I almost choked up. Somebody in the system was showing a little humanity. I needed that.

"No problem. You played baseball, right?"

I nodded.

"Who's your team?" Harper asked.

"Dodgers."

"Too bad."

"Why?"

"I'm from the Bay Area."

"Oh no, you're not a Giants fan."

"Going back to Willie Mays, my friend."

"Oh great!"

Harper let out a big laugh. "Now, let's see. How many times did you steal the pennant from us?"

And I couldn't help laughing, too. I knew what he was doing. Trying to get me relaxed, get my mind off things until Maddie got here. A good man, Harper.

We talked baseball for another ten minutes or so. Harper told me he'd once tried to sell a country song about baseball called "You'd Be So Nice to Slide Home To," but it never made it. He even sang a verse or two. What I remember was the line, "I've been in right field so long, missin' you, I feel like The Babe's old mitt."

Then the limo pulled up.

All the relaxing I'd been doing shot out of my head, replaced by a twisting of nerves and a stomach doing flips.

The same driver I'd seen up at Troncatti's—the one I called Igor—exited and opened the rear door.

And Madeleine Erica Gillen got out.

My heart started pumping something fierce. A sweat drop came out of my armpit and slid down my side.

"Game time," Haper said, encouragingly.

That helped only a little, because I immediately saw something that turned my stomach into warm clay. The limo driver was holding Maddie's hand as they walked toward us. Her hand in his. Like it belonged there. Still, I stuffed my feelings down as deep as I could and put on a smile.

"Maddie!" I jumped up and started toward her.

The driver stopped, putting up his hand. And Maddie slid behind his leg, like he was a protective fence and I was some sort of animal.

The move froze me.

"You Mr. Harper?" Igor looked right past me.

"Yes, sir," Renard J. Harper said.

"Can I have a word with you, please?"

Harper gave me a glance.

"What's going on?" I asked him.

"Hold on, Mr. Gillen. I'll find out." Harper went over to Igor and Maddie and started talking. I stood there like the stupid statue on the Island of Idiots.

A minute or two later, Harper walked back to me. "There's been a request for no physical contact."

"What?"

"This happens. The mother has requested that you not touch your daughter."

Heat ran up my face. "No way! If they think I'm going to just sit here and not touch Maddie—"

"Mr. Gillen, listen to me. If there's a request like this, I have to honor that, unless you want to go back to court and convince the judge to allow it."

"This is unreal."

"It seems the child is a little upset about this visit," Harper said.

"Please, you can't let them do this to me."

Harper spoke calmly, a veteran of many battles like this. "I understand what you're going through, I really do. Some advice again?"

"What?"

"Talk to Maddie. If she makes a move toward you at any time, wants to hold your hand, anything, I'll allow that. If she doesn't, just remember this is all only temporary. You'll have your day in court soon enough."

Maddie was peeking from behind Igor's leg.

"This is killing me," I told Harper. "How could she be afraid of me?"

"I can't answer that," Harper said. "So come on and sit down and we'll do this thing."

I sat on one side of the picnic table. The bench was cold and hard. Igor coaxed Maddie to come along and sit down opposite me. She did, but her eyes avoided mine.

What was going on?

"Hey," I said to my daughter.

"Hi," she said, still not looking at me. I had my hands on top of the table, hoping she'd put hers out and touch me, so it would be all right. But her hands were in her lap.

"How's it going?" It was like talking to a stranger. I could hardly stand it. It felt like Maddie was on drugs or something. I sensed Igor glaring at me from several feet away, and it was all I could do not to scream at him to get out of my face. But I fought for control. I knew I had to, for Maddie's sake.

Maddie shrugged in answer to my question.

"What have you been doing?"

She shrugged again, still not looking at me.

"Maddie?"

She kept her gaze on the tabletop.

I looked at Harper for some help, knowing there was not a thing he could do. He nodded at me to try again.

"I've missed you," I said. "I miss story time."

"Tony reads me stories."

If an ice pick had been jammed in my heart it wouldn't have hurt more.

"Do you miss me?" I said.

Maddie didn't answer.

"I sure miss you, pumpkin."

Suddenly, I felt like a prisoner, getting a visit from a reluctant relative. Nothing much to say. Small talk that goes nowhere. And a big screen between us. No human contact.

I looked at Harper. "Something's not right here."

Igor huffed.

"Starting with him." I pointed my finger at Igor's face. He didn't like that. I didn't care. If I hadn't been sitting down I don't know what I might have done.

"Go ahead," Harper said. "We'll stand over here." He got up and motioned to Igor.

"No," Igor said.

"Come along," Harper said, his voice with just the right amount of official insistence.

Igor shook his head.

Maddie looked at her hands.

"You don't want to be here, do you?" I said.

Maddie shook her head.

"All right, baby," I said, my voice wavering. "You don't have to."

Without any hesitation Maddie slipped off the bench and ran to Igor. Out of everything that had happened in this nightmare, that was the worst part. It reminded me of the time Maddie was four and I took her to a birthday party. There were some older kids there as well, and one of them jumped out from a corner and screamed, scaring the little kids. Maddie was one of them, and she turned and ran directly for me, throwing herself at my legs. I was her protector.

Not anymore. And it killed me.

– 2 –

I was desperate with Alex over the phone as I told her about Maddie's behavior at the visit.

Alex tried to calm me. "This is not uncommon."

"You've got to be kidding me."

"Kids Maddie's age are very susceptible to influence from the custodial parent."

I thought about that a moment. "You mean Paula's messing with her head about me?"

"Like I said, not uncommon. I've seen cases where in a matter of days a child has been turned around."

"But Maddie and me." My voice was hollow. "She loved me."

"I know."

"She wouldn't even look at me."

"Mark, I'll put this in the file—"

"File? We've got to get Maddie out of there."

"We're working on that."

"Meanwhile, Maddie's stuck up there? With Troncatti and Paula? And they're feeding her lies about me? And we can't do anything about it?"

"We *are* doing something about it. We have to do it the legal way."

"Not enough. I can't just sit here."

"Mark, don't do anything—"

"Good-bye, Alex."

I disconnected and turned off the phone. Then I burned rubber onto the San Diego Freeway.

The offices of AEA, American Entertainment Artists, Inc., were in a new glass building on Wilshire in what was known as the Power Corridor of Beverly Hills. It was halfway between CAA and William Morris. Fully 90 percent of the big players in the movie and television industry had their reps in these buildings, all within a half mile of each other.

I was not even in the other 10 percent. But that didn't stop me from walking up and down Wilshire, across the street from the place, waiting for someone to emerge.

That someone was Leonard Remey, and he loved sushi for lunch. You pick up those facts by reading the industry trades and assorted media. Most of the time it's about actors. But Remey was a superstar agent, the biggest kahuna since Ovitz ruled the roost, and he was news.

He liked Ito Sushi, a very upscale place within walking distance of the AEA building. I'd been in there once, with a small group after an acting class. The sushi was good and expensive, the atmosphere alive with power talk. How many stars had been made or broken there over a plate of raw fish?

What I was about to do was a high-wire risk, but I didn't care. I was beyond caring about my reputation. This was about protecting Maddie, and whatever might happen to me came in a distant second.

It was shortly after twelve when Remey finally came out. He was coatless, but in a crisp white shirt and blue tie. A couple of other men in similar attire were with him. I thought to myself, if a car hit all three of them, the town would probably have to shut down for a month while they figured out what to do with all the A-list stars who suddenly had no agents.

The trio strolled to the corner, waited for the light, crossed. They yakked it up, but as they got closer I saw that they were not speaking to each other. All three of them had cell phone earpieces inserted in their heads and were talking into the little mikes.

Perfect, I thought. *All human contact cut off. Business as usual.*

The three power mongers walked and talked another block or so, me strolling along behind. They turned left at the next corner and, as predictable as the night, entered the gold and burnished walnut doors of Ito Sushi.

I waited a minute or so, then walked in.

The place was already doing a brisk trade. A few young turks—black shirts, short goatees, earrings—sat at the bar, talking to each other and a couple of impossibly blond women in dresses that hugged their silicone. An older couple, probably citizens of Beverly Hills since the Lucy-Desi era, seemed out of place in the corner. It was as if they had been stuck there purposely, so as not to intrude on the important schmoozing now under way in the prime sushi-bar seats.

A hostess asked if I had a reservation, and I said no, I'd sit at the bar, and there was a chair open. As I made for the chair—between one of the turks and a guy who looked like his jaw had been chiseled by Michelangelo—I spotted the three agents at a table near the back.

Still talking into their little wires. To be hip in LA you have to have a busier-than-thou attitude. You have to believe there is simply not enough time in the day, and so on the eighth day God created cell phones and PDAs to prove your indispensability to the universe. Staying hip is almost a full-time job for Angelenos. And the three major cheeses at the back table were in frantic pursuit of their calling.

A nice-looking waitress handed me a warm, damp cloth and asked if I'd like anything to drink. I asked for a very un-hip glass of ice water and continued to watch the three stooges.

Was I nuts? My thought had been to just walk over to Remey with a surprise attack. An in-your-face to tell him I knew exactly what was going on.

Too public, too desperate, I decided.

Which meant I could accidentally-on-purpose follow him into the men's room and let him have it with a threatening cool.

But to what purpose? Did I really think one of Hollywood's most powerful agents was going to care what I had to say?

This was beginning to feel like another of my fool's errands.

A sushi chef with a bright bandana on his head asked me what I'd like to start with, so I ordered shrimp.

I remembered Maddie liked sushi. We couldn't afford it very often, but every now and then, for a treat, I would take her out. Shrimp was her favorite.

And thinking of that only made me angry. Maybe I would go over to Remey right now, while the feeling was with me.

What stopped me was the sight of one person I never expected to see.

Paula's mother, Erica Stanton Montgomery, was making a beeline for Remey's table.

I almost choked on some ginger root.

Erica was tall, statuesque, perfectly groomed, and dressed to the nines. She looked like old money and new surgery.

Yet here she was, in the land of warm beaches.

Remey stood up to greet her. They shook hands like old friends.

She did not sit down. She spoke to Remey for a couple of minutes—as the other two agents spoke into their wires—and then she turned to walk out.

Without a thought I got up, tossed a ten on the counter, and followed her.

Erica was strolling down the street, casually looking in windows. She could have been going anywhere. There were tons of upscale stores in the vicinity. I followed her.

She did not go far before ducking into a place called Maria's, which was, from the look of it, a woman's apparel place.

I waited a moment, then went in.

The place looked like it was designed in gold. Maybe it was. All I knew was that I was a fish out of water in there.

Erica was looking at a dress display near the window. It was some sort of strapless number. I made my way to her side.

"Not your style," I said.

Her look was startled at first, then furious. When the Montgomerys get mad, it's like something out of *Nature's Savage Fury* on The Discovery Channel.

"What. On. Earth."

"Hi, Erica. Longtime."

Suddenly she looked around, as if afraid someone would see her talking to me. "How did you—"

"Find you? Serendipity. Sometimes things are just meant to be." I slapped my hands together. "So, what are you doing out here on the coast?"

"I don't have anything to say to you, Mark."

"Maybe you'd like to explain to the judge what you're doing meeting with Leonard Remey?"

I wondered if her heart was beating as fast as mine. Certainly blood was pumping to her face. I could even see it through the industrial layer of makeup.

"You were *spying?*"

"I was sitting in a public place, is what I was doing. Leonard Remey has taken a bit of an interest in my career, though not in a way that's very flattering. You know anything about that?"

"I am not going to stand here and let—"

"Chill, Erica. You owe me."

"I owe you nothing."

"Oh really? Let me hazard a guess then. Meeting with Remey has something to do with Paula, obviously. Why else would he give you the time of day? I figure you're getting some money, maybe you're managing her career. What's that, fifteen percent?"

Erica stiffened, and I knew I had her on the run. "I don't have to stand here and—"

"Your daughter and her boyfriend are trying to keep my daughter away from me. You all right with that? You think that's right?"

Erica said nothing.

"And Remey's part of the plan. You probably know all about it. You know he made sure I didn't get the role that was going to save my sorry acting career." The outrage was still fresh in me, and my voice was getting higher. "He called up and—"

"Is there anything I can help you with?" A saleswoman—all pearls and stiff hair—was behind us.

"The gentleman is leaving," Erica said.

"I'm just browsing," I said, nodding toward the dress on display. "Do you think it's my color?"

Apparently, the sense-of-humor fairy had flown over Beverly Hills without stopping.

"Is this man annoying you?" the saleswoman said.

Erica looked me up and down. "As a matter of fact, yes."

"Sir, I'll have to ask you to leave."

"Are you the one who put Remey up to it?" I leveled my eyes at Erica.

"Sir," the saleswoman said.

I ignored her. "You the one who's pulling the strings?"

"Sir!"

"Answer me, Erica."

"I'll call the police." The saleswoman marched toward the counter.

"See what you've done now?" Erica said.

"I'll find out," I said. "I will."

"You're a pitiful man. It's a good thing you won't have Madeleine anymore."

My chest spasmed, like I'd been given a shock from a live wire. "How do you know that?"

She looked sheepish all of a sudden and completely turned away. I grabbed her arm and spun her back.

Her chin dropped like a stone. "Don't you touch me!"

"What do you know? What sort of scam is going on?"

There were about half a dozen women in the shop, all looking at us.

"What you're doing," I said, "is wrong." That's all I could think of to say. It was wrong, but did that matter to her? Had it ever, her whole life?

Erica said nothing. She looked behind me. Before I could turn I felt a hand like a bear trap clamp down on my shoulder.

Igor. He had me and was pulling me toward the door.

"Hey man!" I tried to whirl out of his grip but couldn't.

So, with all my might, I jammed my elbow into his stomach. It was like hitting a wall. The guy was in shape.

My blow, such as it was, did nothing but make him mad.

Igor threw me out the door of the shop.

I went sprawling on the hot sidewalk, head hitting hard.

Something took hold of me then, and I knew what I would do if they ever tried to keep Maddie away from me.

God forgive me, I knew.

– 3 –

Next day I was in Nancy's office. She'd called me in. More bad news.

"Are you seeing anyone?" she asked me, almost before I was in the chair.

"Seeing someone?"

"A shrink."

"No."

"Maybe you should reconsider."

"That why you called me in here?"

"No, but it's a good idea, don't you think?"

"Why did you call me, Nancy?"

"You have some decisions to make. I have some decisions."

"Such as?"

"Such as whether to keep you on as a client." Her face was as cool as November. Gone was any of the warmth she used to toss my way when I faced troubles.

"You're actually saying . . . Are you dropping me?"

"That's what we're here to discuss, yes."

I could see a thin layer of Valley smog outside her window—a dull, grayish haze that kept the mountains from view. Nothing was clear out there. Or in here, for that matter.

"Why would you do that?" My palms were starting to sweat.

"There comes a time, that's all. A time when it looks like it might be in the best interests of both parties to pursue other avenues."

"But why now? I got on a big series. Until Leonard Remey got involved."

"Are you sticking with that story?"

"Story? It happened."

"You can't go around town telling people Len Remey sabotaged your career. You know what that'll do to you? Ever hear the expression 'You'll never eat lunch in this town again'?"

"What about truth?"

"Truth is not the currency of the moment, Mark."

"Great. What is it then?"

"Relationships. People returning your phone calls. That's what this business runs on. When that's jeopardized, you're finished. I don't want to see that happen to you, or to me."

"Are you saying having me as your client is harmful to your career?"

Nancy said nothing, letting her silence answer for her.

"So that's it? You want me out of here? Never darken your door again?"

Finally, a little thaw showed through. "Here's what I'm saying, bottom line. You have to decide something, Mark. Once and for all. You have to decide if you want to make it as an actor. I know you have the talent. But you have to have the *want to.* It has to be the most important thing in the world, and you have to be willing to put everything else aside. You have to be willing to shut up if it's hurting you to talk. There is no other way to do it, my friend. You know that. And those are the terms for our future together. If you can assure me that you're going to put your career on the front burner, then we can move on. That's what I want to hear from you."

For a long time I sat there, a swirling in my belly. And I knew she was right. It was the only way to make it in the business. You had to make it A-number one on your life list. I gazed out her window as I thought about it. The smog was still there, but I thought I could see, way off in the distance, the peak of one of our local mountains, just barely visible in the muck. Once, a couple of years ago, we got some rare snow on the tops of those mountains, and I'd taken a day to drive Maddie up there. It was like Wonderland to her.

I stood up. "That price is too high, Nancy. I can't do it."

She seemed shocked. "You're giving up?"

"No," I said. "I just figured out what I want to be more than anything else."

"And what's that?"

"Maddie's father."

Paula is stroking my hair as we sit entwined on the sofa, her legs over mine, watching Maddie perform her dance.

Maddie has taken ribbons and wrapped them around her ankles. She has used Scotch tape to hold the ribbons in place. The ribbons go round and round until they disappear into her slippers, which are fuzzy and have rubber puppy-dog faces.

These, Maddie announces, are her ballet slippers.

And now she dances, arms swirling in the air as she spins, then stops and leaps. It is not an abridged dance. It is the long, uncut version. It seems like she will dance forever.

"She has talent," Paula whispers to me, not wanting to disturb the genius.

"Gets it from me," I whisper back.

"Not."

"You haven't seen me in tights?"

"Nice image." Paula hits a phantom computer keyboard with her fingers. "Deleted."

"No, watch me!" Maddie twirls.

– 4 –

Sutton Hallard was his name. He was a licensed psychotherapist and avid golfer. At least that's what his office made it look like.

There was a huge, framed photo of a gorgeous golf hole on one wall. It had an oceanscape and clear blue skies.

"Pebble," Hallard said when he saw me staring at it. "You ever play Pebble?"

I shook my head. "Don't play golf."

"Too bad." Hallard chuckled, but it sounded forced—like a man who thought anyone who didn't play golf could not possibly be a fit human being, let alone father.

Hallard sat behind his desk—a mini-golfbag held his pens and pencils—and regarded me. He was trim, about fifty, with perfect, steel-colored hair.

"This is your time," he said. "I want to be clear on that. I'm here to listen, maybe ask a few questions. But the most important thing for me is to get to know you. I have to make a recommendation to the court about custody for your daughter. That's a hard thing to do, I want you to know."

Hard for him? What about me?

"Sure," I said.

"So why don't you start. Just tell me anything that's on your mind." He leaned back in his leather chair.

I reminded myself to keep calm. I didn't want a repeat of the Sheila Bonner interview. Hallard seemed a little more human, and maybe the fact that he was a man was a good thing.

"Well, I love my daughter. That's pure and simple. Since she was born I've been a different person. I didn't realize just how different until she was taken away from me."

"That hasn't happened yet."

"But it has. I mean, that's why we're sitting here. I gave Maddie to Paula in good faith, and she refused to return her to me. In my book, that's a taking. And it hurts. It hurts bad."

"But you've had a visit with her—" he looked at a paper on his desk—"on the twenty-second, isn't that right?"

"Hardly a visit. They brought her to a park, and I had to pay for a social worker to be there with me."

"As per the order of the court."

"That wasn't the bad thing, though. It was Maddie. She didn't want to be there at all."

"She is, after all, five years old."

"Yeah, but this was something else. When she was with me, she loved me. We had a great relationship. Somebody has been messing with her."

"Are you accusing your wife of that?"

"I don't know who, I only know that Maddie wasn't herself, and that concerns me. What if they're trying to poison her against me?"

"If they are, they will be in deep trouble."

"Meantime Maddie suffers. And I suffer. And who knows how bad it is?"

"But you haven't any actual proof."

Calm. Stay calm. "It comes from years of knowing my daughter. I mean, living with her and doing all of the things a father does. You get to know a person."

"How well do you know your wife?"

"I thought I knew her pretty well. I guess that was naive."

"You're saying, then, you don't know her?"

I shrugged. "It's all messed up now."

"Do you really think she would do something to hurt your daughter like this?"

Did I? I did not want to. But hatred was starting to well up in me and I didn't care to deal with it. "There are all sorts of things people do when this sort of thing is going on. Divorce and child custody. It's not unheard of for a mother to try to keep kids from the father."

"Nor the other way around."

"I don't know. It seems as if most of the time it's the fathers who get the shaft."

Sutton Hallard tapped his lower lip with the eraser on his pencil. "Are you a sociologist, Mr. Gillen?"

"No, but—"

"Where have you been getting this information?"

"I just came across it."

"Did someone share this with you?"

He sounded like a man homing in on me. I suddenly felt I had to hide the fact I talked to Joe Pfeffer of the fathers' rights group. I also felt like Sutton Hallard knew I was hiding something. And that my next response was crucial.

"When I was looking for a lawyer," I said, "I did some talking to people, yes. Do I need to go into details?"

"It's entirely up to you."

"I don't know what it will accomplish. All I'm saying is that I don't have Maddie with me, and it's possible she's being influenced. I don't think that's right."

"It is not right, Mr. Gillen, but again, facts are the only things that matter. Otherwise, we would be flying back and forth with accusations alone. My concern, if I may, is that if you think this way, then if you were to get custody of Maddie, you might try doing something similar, out of spite. That would not be a good situation either."

Stay calm!

"Mr. Hallard, I don't know what else I can tell you except that I've never done anything to harm my daughter, or even put her in a place where harm would come to her. I mean, willingly. I would never do that. And doesn't a child need both parents around? For the best shot in life, I mean?"

Hallard lightly sucked on the eraser. "Are you saying a mother who brings up a child alone can't do a good job?"

"No, I wasn't saying that at all. Just that all things being equal, both parents should be involved."

"Yes, that's the ideal, and the courts seek to do that when there are no circumstances that militate against it. That's part of this evaluation process."

"Is she being evaluated?"

"Excuse me?"

"Paula. Is she going to have to go through this same deal?"

"Of course. I will be interviewing her, just as I am interviewing you. And I will talk to Maddie as well."

"Alone?"

"Yes. For part of the time, anyway."

This excited me. "Then would you do one thing for me?"

"What would that be?"

"Would you ask her a question?"

"Maybe."

"Ask her about the moon dance."

"What is the moon dance?"

"She'll know. Ask her if she remembers dancing with me, by the light of the moon. Just ask her that and look in her eyes. Please."

Sutton Hallard jotted something on his pad.

I decided Hamlet was crazy-in-love.

Nikki thought so, too. But his obsession with avenging his father's murder makes everything else pale. Even Ophelia. And so he has to drive her away. Because he loves her so much.

"I think that lends a lot of colors to the scene," Nikki said. We were rehearsing at the house in the Hollywood Hills she was renting with two other actresses. There wasn't much furniture in the place, in keeping with the actors' life. But potted plants and some funky artwork made the house feel homey.

Nikki was wearing a sweatshirt with UCSD on it and light blue jeans. She offered me a soda, and we sat across from each other and read the scene together.

Then we decided to try it on our feet, to see what emerged.

What did emerge neither one of us was prepared for.

Hamlet begins by teasing Ophelia, and I did that by remembering the times I used to tease Paula—she didn't like it, but usually I could make her laugh after a while.

"Are you honest?" I—Hamlet—said.

"My lord?" Nikki answered in character.

"Are you fair?"

"What means your lordship?"

I began to circle her. "That if you be honest and fair, your honesty should admit no discourse to your beauty."

Nikki stood still, as Ophelia might, wondering what Hamlet was up to. "Could beauty, my lord, have better commerce than with honesty?"

"Ay, truly; for the power of beauty will sooner transform honesty from what it is to a bawd than the force of honesty can translate beauty into his likeness." I looked at Nikki/Ophelia as if she were a statue. "This was sometime a paradox, but now the time gives it proof. I did love you once."

"Indeed, my lord, you made me believe so." Nikki/Ophelia had eyes wide with sadness, confusion.

"You should not have believed me," I/Hamlet said, but I did not move away. "For virtue cannot so inoculate our old stock but we shall relish of it. I loved you not."

Nikki's eyes began to mist. She was crying already! Totally into the scene. Amazing.

"I was the more deceived," she said.

Following our improvisational format, I felt moved to grab her by the shoulders. Nikki went with it. Her eyes were filled with fear.

The feel of her shoulders was soft and warm. She was delicate, as I imagined Ophelia would be. And smelled like orange blossoms.

That's when I kissed her.

Was it part of the scene? I, as Hamlet, doing what the moment demanded? Or was it something I just wanted to do?

She went with it again. Was she just an actress?

When I pulled back and looked at her I knew neither one of us was acting.

Her face got red. There was a long pause. She looked at the hardwood floor.

"Interesting choice for Hamlet," I said.

She laughed defensively but did not look up.

"Do you want to start from the top?" I said.

Before she could answer her roommate, Deborah, walked in carrying an *Entertainment Weekly* and eating a peach.

"Hey guys," she said. She stopped, getting that sense of interrupting something secret. "Oh, sorry."

"No, Deb, it's okay." Nikki waved her in. "This is Mark Gillen, an actor friend."

"Oh, hey," Deb said. She wiped her hand on her shirt and shook mine. She had short curly hair and a lithe body.

"Nice to meet you," I said.

"You guys doing a scene?"

"*Hamlet,*" Nikki said.

"Cool," Deb said. "Which scene?"

"Get thee to a nunnery," Nikki said.

Deb laughed. "That's exactly what I was thinking today. Nunnery. Beats Hollywood, don't it? You dudes go ahead." She whisked out of the room.

Leaving Nikki and me in an awkward silence.

Finally, I said, "If we do the scene again, it's going to go the same way."

Nikki nodded. "I think it will. Maybe that's why we shouldn't do it."

"You want to postpone until tomorrow?"

"I mean, maybe we shouldn't do it at all."

"No," I said, "I want to do it."

She shook her head. "Let me call you tomorrow."

"Hey, I'm sorry. I was out of line. I shouldn't have—"

"No," she said. "I wanted you to."

"What?"

"Can we talk later? I'm feeling a little irrational at the moment."

Go ahead, I wanted to say. Be irrational! Irrational is good! But it's bad, too! What was I doing?

"All right," I said. "I'll call you tomorrow."

"Thanks," she said.

I exited, like Hamlet leaving Act III—confused, needing to do something to keep the ghosts away.

I almost yelped when I saw Ron Reid sitting outside my apartment building.

"What are you doing here?"

"Came to see my son, man." He was dressed in jeans and sandals.

"I'm not into seeing anybody right now."

His face got a hangdog look. He was my father. I didn't want him to be.

"All right, all right." I started to unlock the front door. "You want to come up for a minute?" Ron followed me in.

I made up some instant coffee, and we sat at the dining-room table.

"So how's the job working out?" I said.

"Ah." Ron waved his hand. "It'll do for now."

"You have to work. You have to settle down now. Don't blow this thing."

"I don't know, it's just not a good fit."

"You're drawing pay, right?"

"Well, yeah."

"Then it's a good fit. You're a convicted felon. You don't have a lot of choices."

Ron shook his head. "Enough about me. How are you doing?"

I shrugged. "Getting by."

"What's the latest on Maddie?"

"There's an evaluator dude looking at me, at Paula. He makes up a report and gives it to the judge. Then we'll see."

"How do you think it's going?"

"I don't know." I ran my thumb along the rim of the coffee cup. "They can't think I'm a bad father. No way."

"No way," Ron echoed. At least he was trying to sound supportive. "So where you been?"

"Huh?"

"I was out there a long time."

"Oh, rehearsing. Doing a scene."

"The old acting thing."

"I can pretend."

"What kind of a gig?"

"Not a gig, just a scene. To try and get into an acting company."

"Oh yeah? Very cool."

It was still unnerving to hear my father, now in his fifties, talking hip. But it was a mild diversion.

"So what's the scene?" Ron said.

"You really interested?" If he was, I wouldn't mind talking about it. Acting discussions were fun for me.

"Yeah, really."

"I'm doing a scene from *Hamlet*, where he confronts Ophelia."

"*Hamlet*, huh? Cool guy in tights?"

"Funny. Maybe I'll look as good as Mel Gibson did."

Ron laughed. "Who's the chick?"

"Chick? Did you really say *chick?*"

"Babe?"

"Ron, the *woman* is named Nikki, and she's very nice."

"How nice?" His eyebrows bobbed.

"Come on."

"You like this . . . young lady?"

"Like I said—"

"No, I mean really like?"

It almost seemed like I was fifteen and Dad was asking about my first crush. "I don't know."

"But maybe?"

"Maybe. Who knows? My life is a little unsettled right now."

"But if the opportunity came up, would you . . . ?"

His eyebrows danced again. I didn't like it. "Would I *what?*"

"You know."

"Sleep with her? Is that what you meant?"

"Don't get bent about it."

"First, what business is it of yours? Second, the thought hadn't crossed my mind."

Ron squinted at me.

"Other than what's normal," I said. "She's a Christian girl, I'm not going to try and get her into bed."

"Why not?"

That snapped it. I put my cup down so hard it splashed all over the place. "Shut up, Ron, just shut up."

He put his hands up. "Whoa—"

"Grow up, will you?" That sounded odd coming from me, but I went with it. "Quit acting like some teenager. Quit talking about not working. Get your life together, man."

"Look who's talking," he said, with an edge.

"What's that mean?"

"You can't even keep your family together."

I recognized the familiar grip of rage inside me. It was almost as if I was standing outside, looking in, watching myself lose control. The outside part was passive, didn't even try to intervene. Didn't want to.

In my mind I saw my fists driving into Ron Reid's face. I don't know what stopped me, but looking back it seems a voice was whispering to me. *Don't don't don't.* Was it the voice of God? I think now it was.

If only I had continued to listen for it.

– 5 –

I woke up the next morning thinking of Nikki McNamara.

She was there in the fading landscape of my dreams, hanging on despite the onrush of consciousness. As I showered and shaved, I kept replaying the scene from *Hamlet* and wondering what she was thinking today.

I wanted to call her. Now. But I sensed she needed room to breathe, so I put it off until later.

What I needed to do now was salvage the rest of my life.

Acting had been everything to me for the past ten years. Becoming a star was what I was about. Every year I'd watch the Oscars and see myself up there someday. *I thank the Academy for this honor, and all the people who helped me along the way.*

There would be dinners at Spago and interviews on E! network and major movie deals the rest of my life.

Somewhere in there was a real love of acting, too. Because you could assume a role, play somebody else. For some reason, I found that appealing.

But now I wanted nothing more than Maddie in my life. And I knew that being a struggling actor was not the best profile for a soon-to-be single father.

So where did that leave me?

As I sipped morning coffee, I made a mental list of options. Baseball coach maybe, at some high school. Not real glamorous, but it could get me back in touch with the game. Maybe I could look up the coach at Cleveland High and offer my services as an assistant.

Or maybe I could reach higher. What about being a lawyer? Do what Alex did. Help fathers with their custody battles.

Only problem. I needed to go to law school. And to do that, I needed to go to college. I'd gone straight into baseball after high school. I was not a great student to begin with. From where I sat now, at thirty-four years old, actually doing the whole college thing seemed like a huge mountain to climb.

But challenges were part of sports, and I'd never backed away from those.

So I finished my coffee and drove over to Cal State Northridge and picked up some admissions information. What the hey? The journey of a thousand miles begins with a single step. I'd made it half a step anyway.

Shortly before noon I called Nikki's cell phone.

"Hi, Hamlet here." Trying to sound as positive as I could.

"Oh hi. How are you?"

Very much in limbo. "Fine. You want to have lunch?"

Pause. "I would like to see you, but you don't have to—"

"Done. Let's pick a spot."

"I really don't think lunch is a good idea."

The air was suddenly heavy with intrigue. "You have to eat."

"Can we maybe meet at 1:30 at the church?"

Not the place I had in mind, but . . . "Sure."

"Thanks."

I arrived at 1:15, and waited in the courtyard. A gardener was cutting some shrubs with big clippers. *Shick shick shick.* Made me think of the death of a thousand cuts. The only other sound was the 101 Freeway and the traffic rushing by the church grounds. Sunlight dappled the courtyard through the tree leaves. The church seemed to be straining to be an oasis in the city wilderness.

Nikki arrived looking so good I almost fell off the bench.

"Sorry I'm late," she said.

"Are you?" I had lost all track of time.

"A little. Been waiting long?"

"No, just watching the clipper do his work."

She gave a quick glance at the gardener, then sat down on the bench. "Thanks for coming out here."

"No prob. I've been thinking a lot about what happened last night."

"Me too."

"Want me to start?"

"Maybe I should."

"Okay."

She paused a moment, took in a deep breath. "Mark, I don't think it's a good idea to do the scene together."

My stomach knotted a little bit. "Why not?"

"We got a little too involved in it."

"That's Method acting!"

My attempt at humor brought only a polite smile from Nikki. "It was more than that."

You're a man, you try to read a woman's face. You try to pick up signals in voice and tone. Sometimes you just plow on through, doing what you want to do, hoping it's the right thing.

I took her hand. "I know it was more."

She gently but firmly pulled her hand back. "Wait. This is like a train, things are going so fast."

"Hey, let's enjoy the ride."

"I can't. We can't."

Shick shick shick. The sound of the clippers filled the silence.

"Why can't we?" I said.

"You're married." She looked at me as if that were bad but undeniable news.

"But my wife is divorcing me."

"It doesn't matter," Nikki said. "You are still married."

"Not for long."

"It isn't right for us to get involved."

"Why not?"

"I just told you."

"That doesn't make sense to me. You like me, I know it."

"Yes, that's what's hard about this."

"It doesn't have to be."

She shook her head. "Mark, God looks at marriage as sacred. You're married, we just can't see each other."

"Not even to do a lousy scene?"

"It won't be for just the scene. We both know that."

Boy did I. "I want to keep seeing you."

"I know. But we can't."

"What if I won't stop?"

"Please, Mark."

"I mean it."

"What do you mean not stop? Even if I want you to stop?"

Shick shick shick.

"I'm sorry," I said. "I'm being a real jerk here."

"No."

"Can I still come to church and the Bible study?"

"Of course. I'd like us to stay friends."

For a short moment, the sound of the clippers stopped.

"Why do you have to be so mature?" I said.

She laughed.

THE SETUP

~ 1 ~

"Let's talk about your anger for a while," Sutton Hallard said.

Great. It was Friday, and I was in for another interview with him—I felt like the proverbial dog jumping through hoops—and now we were on my weakest point. What I was busting to ask him was whether he'd talked to Paula or Maddie. I knew he had. I also knew he wouldn't tell me boo about it.

"I know I have a problem with anger," I said, being up front and confessional. I was going to be so even tempered that Sutton Hallard would want to put me up for a humanitarian award when we were finished. "But I feel I know about it and can manage it."

"What makes you say that?"

"Just what I've seen in myself the last few weeks."

"Can you give me an example?"

"Sure." I tried to think of one and ran with the first thing that popped into my mind. "The other night I was talking to my father."

Hallard looked at the paper in front of him. "That would be Mr. Reid?"

"Right. He came over, wanted to talk or something, so he came up to my apartment and I made some coffee. We talked for a while, then he said some things that I thought were out of line. We got into sort of an argument, and I told him he needed to get his act together."

"In what way?"

"Just plain old growing up. He's still acting like a kid. Not being responsible about his job and stuff like that. Well, I told him that, then he says to me, 'Look who's talking.' And I start to get hot and ask him what he means. He says I can't even hold my own family together. That was below the belt, and my first thought was to take a punch at him. But I didn't. And that's what I'm saying."

"Why don't you think you took a punch at him?"

Should I tell him about the voice? Or would that put me in a whole new category in Sutton Hallard's eyes? *N* for nutcase.

"I just didn't. I held back. I could feel myself holding back, not wanting to do it."

"And you have no idea why you didn't?"

For some reason I'll never fully understand, the next voice I used was Peter Lorre's. "Who knows the depths of the human mind?"

Sutton Hallard stared at me like I was, in fact, a nutcase.

"That's my Peter Lorre imitation," I explained. "Just to show you my acting side."

"Very amusing." Hallard tapped his pencil on the fleshy part of his palm.

"No, but seriously," I said, using the familiar segue, "I truly think I'm becoming a better person. I'm not just lashing out."

"People don't simply change, out of the blue. There is some sort of stimulus and, if you look hard enough, you can usually find it. If we can do that now, it may play an important role in this aspect of the case."

Important role? I wondered what he meant. It sounded like a verbal clue, almost like he was prompting me to give him something he could work with. Maybe like he was on my side a little bit. Feeling sorry for me? I didn't care. I'd take any bone Sutton Hallard wanted to throw my way.

"Maybe there is something," I said.

"Please."

"Church. I've joined a church. I'm really trying to look at things from that perspective."

"A Christian perspective?"

"Yeah. I mean, the Bible and all that. I'm in a Bible study group; we meet on Wednesday nights, a lot of actors in it. Good people. I feel like I can talk about anything with them."

"What church is this?"

"Gower Presbyterian, in Hollywood."

Hallard jotted a note. "Tell me more."

That had to mean I was on the right track with him. Good. Ride this train to the end. "For instance, the other night we're all talking about how frustrating the acting business is. And I say, 'Amen, brother.' And the guy leading the study, who is doing pretty well I might add, says, 'How do you handle it?' And I say I have no clue. And then he opens the Bible and reads about not having any anxiety, but by praying to God and being thankful for what you *do* have, you can have peace. That really helped me a lot."

"You pray regularly?"

"I'm trying to get in the habit."

Hallard scribbled another note. I wanted to see what he was writing so badly I almost snatched the paper.

"Are you seeing anyone?" Hallard asked when he was finished.

"What?"

"Anyone romantically?"

That was a bolt out of the blue. But I guess he had the right to ask, and I had to wag my tail and jump through the hoop. "No," I said.

"No dating?"

I thought of Nikki McNamara and was glad now we hadn't gotten into anything. I felt it was better for me if I played the role of spurned husband, wanting to keep the marriage together.

Did I? If Paula suddenly called it quits with Troncatti, would I even want her back? I didn't know at this point.

"Do you have any plans in that area?" Hallard said.

"No," I said, truthfully. "What I want is my daughter. And it was my wife who started fooling around with another man. I didn't do a thing."

"Not anything? You are claiming this is all a one-sided situation?"

"All I know is things seemed pretty good until Paula left to do that movie. Meanwhile, I stayed back here and took care of Maddie while she got to go and make herself into a movie star."

"Let's talk about that part of it for a moment. Your wife has done exceedingly well in the last few months, has she not?"

"Yeah, she has. She's being made into this major star."

"While your career has not exactly gone upward."

What a great psychologist this guy was. Knew how to make me feel like absolute dirt.

"No," I said. "But that's another thing."

He raised his eyebrows in a signal to continue.

Should I tell him what I knew? Or what I thought I knew?

"You were about to say?" Hallard blinked at me.

"Just that my career was set to have a major boost. I got cast in a new show with John Hoyt, on NBC. But then it was yanked out from under me. And I know why."

Sutton Hallard waited.

"The producer got pressure to drop me," I said, trying to sound as objective as possible. "I found out about it through a friend who works at the company. I did a little snooping and found out it was Antonio Troncatti's agent who put the pressure on. Coincidence? I don't think so. Especially after I saw Paula's mother meeting with him."

"Meeting with whom?"

"The agent, a guy named Leonard Remey."

Hallard tapped the end of his pencil on the desk, making dull *thud thud* sounds. "Do you have any corroboration of this?"

"I only know what I saw and heard."

"What *you* saw and heard?"

He wasn't buying this. And I knew what it must have sounded like. The paranoid ravings of a spurned husband. Grasping at straws. Flinging mud at my wife.

"No, there's Lisa, my friend at the production company. She . . ." I stopped. I had promised her I wouldn't say anything.

"Can you get a letter from her, addressed to me, setting forth these facts?"

"I just don't know. I told her I'd keep it confidential. She has a job . . ."

Sutton Hallard's face became vaguely skeptical.

"I'll do what I can," I said weakly.

"Please. Until then, I can't consider this in my report. What I need are facts and supporting documentation. You understand that, I'm sure."

"Yeah. Sure."

"But getting back to your acting career—"

"Look, I've been doing a lot of thinking about that lately, and I want to tell you that my number one concern is Maddie, being able to be a good father and support for her. I've been looking into going back to school, getting my degree, getting something more stable going."

"You're thinking of leaving the acting profession?"

"If that's what it takes to be a good father, then yes. I don't care about acting more than I do my own daughter."

"If you go back to school, money will be tight, will it not?"

How was I going to deny that? "But people do it all the time."

"Who would watch the child when you're in class?"

"I'd work that out, like other people work it out."

"You would need money to pay for daycare then, wouldn't you?"

"Yeah, I suppose."

Hallard wrote something on his paper.

I couldn't stand it anymore. "Dr. Hallard, did you talk to Maddie yet? Did you ask her about the moon dance?"

He stopped writing. "You know I cannot answer that."

"You can't tell me anything?"

"It will all be in my report."

"When is this going to end?"

"Soon."

– 2 –

I went home and decided to get a little more acquainted with my friend, Antonio Troncatti. Having no idea what Hallard was getting on him, I thought I'd better do my own research project.

Starting with Google, I did a search for anything with his name in it. I got over a thousand hits. So I added the words "career" and "biography." That narrowed it down some, but I still had a ton of material.

After a couple of hours, I'd cut and pasted a nice dossier on Troncatti. What I had made me hate him all the more.

He'd been the protégé of Bertolucci and Lina Wertmuller, working on several of their films. His first film, as a twenty-six-year-old wunderkind, featured Giancarlo Giannini as an aging hit man who has an encounter with a small child that changes his life. I never saw it, but it captured an award at the Cannes Film Festival, and Troncatti's career was launched.

His next film was the one that set him up as an international directing star. It was a remake of *The Count of Monte Cristo*, only this time done as a modern tale of corporate greed. It starred, of all people, John Hoyt, and really reactivated his career.

What got the attention of the critical set was the fact that Italian cinema is not generally known for its action. Most of the time, in fact, it's like watching paint dry. But Troncatti became the "Italian John Woo" and soon moved to the U.S. for his directing chores.

Three major hits followed in succession. The guy was a movie god.

Also, from what I read between the lines, quite the ladies' man. Have to admit, from the pictures of the guy, that he was good looking. A Roman nose above thin lips and a jaw that might have been chiseled marble; olive skin that grew naturally darker in the Southern

California sun; long black hair of shoulder length. I mean, he could have been the cover boy on some romance novel.

Which didn't do a lot for the old self-esteem.

He'd had affairs with three actresses, all of whom you'd know. One, who was somewhat older than Troncatti but still considered a queen of glamour, almost got him to the altar.

What kept them all away, apparently, was Troncatti's volcanic temper.

There were stories of Troncatti tearing up hotel rooms, wrecking cars, beating up people in bars, and generally carrying on like a large, petulant child. (I was thinking all this time how I'd love to be the one to give him a whipping with the thing they used in *Mutiny on the Bounty*. What did they call that? The cat-o'-nine-tails? Perfect.)

I found one item of particular interest. Back in the nineties, around the time of the O. J. Simpson murder trial, there had been a domestic violence incident. One of the actresses whom he'd been living with had summoned the cops. The case went to the D.A.'s office, which was particularly sensitive to these things in the wake of Simpson, and was close to being filed.

But the actress withdrew her complaint. She said it had all been a mistake, that she'd just been mad at him for making eyes at some other woman.

It was all swept under the rug. I thought it would be a good thing to whip that rug away at the custody hearing.

I felt a new wave of disgust. And fear. This was the man who was around Maddie. What might happen to her sometime if he lost it? What sort of example of adult behavior would he be? (I admit I was not thinking of my own anger. It was all focused on Troncatti.)

Then I decided to do a search for pages with both Troncatti's name and Paula's. That brought up thirty-one hits. Most of them were references to the movie they'd shot. But one item was from a gossip page in an online entertainment site:

Taming the Bad Boy of Cinema?

Has Antonio Troncatti finally met his match? The former wild child of the film business seems to have settled into a bit of domestic bliss, sources tell us. Falling head over Amore shoes for Paula Montgomery during the shooting of *Conquest*, Troncatti is becoming a real homebody. He's particularly fond of Montgomery's daughter, Madeleine, who has had an almost hypnotic effect on the Italian auteur.

Montgomery, who is engaged in a custody battle with her soon-to-be ex, sometime actor Mark Gillen, has settled into home life with the director. Maybe his next film will be a paean to wedded bliss, rather than another blow-'em-up. But don't bet on it!

That was the last thing I read. I couldn't take any more after that. Funny thing was, I didn't mind the part about being a "sometime actor." Maybe a year ago that would have been the hard part.

Now, I was somewhat surprised to learn, that didn't matter a bit. What mattered was that Maddie was apparently bonding with the jerk who had stolen my wife.

Why was Paula with him, if he was such a jerk? Well, he was major league powerful for sure, and such Hollywood power was a turn on. No doubt the guy was charming and magnetic and all of that. And maybe there was a part of Paula that was drawn to the wild thing in order to tame him.

And I was powerless to stop her from trying.

I said that was the last thing I read. I meant about Troncatti and Paula. Feeling like I was about to rip my computer out of the socket and throw it out the window, I went back into Google and searched for a Bible.

Jesus said something about asking and getting, I remembered. A couple of search terms later, I found what I was looking for in the New International Version, Matthew, chapter 7:

> *Ask and it will be given to you; seek and you will find; knock and the door will be opened to you. For everyone who asks receives; he who seeks finds; and to him who knocks, the door will be opened.*

I looked for a loophole in there and couldn't find it. I decided to check another version, the King James, for the same passage.

> *Ask, and it shall be given you; seek, and ye shall find; knock, and it shall be opened unto you: For every one that asketh receiveth; and he that seeketh findeth; and to him that knocketh it shall be opened.*

My tongue twistethed as I read it out loud, but the effect was the same. Jesus really did say it, and I was being taught to trust the Bible.

So I asked.

God, give Maddie back to me. Please.

~ 3 ~

I went to church on Sunday, hoping to see Nikki there.

She wasn't.

Which made the service a little lonely to me. I tried to do my duty though and mouthed the songs along with the words on the screen. I even tried to believe all of what they said—about the glory of God and the love of Jesus being all we need.

The pastor, Scott Stephens, was in his forties and gave a good sermon. Only today I found myself answering him in my mind. I kept saying, *No way, José.*

Pastor Scott—as he insisted on being called—was preaching on the subject "The Heart's Radical Makeover." Basically, he said, living the Christian life begins with a surrender of the heart, the will, to God.

"When Jesus said you must be born again," Pastor Scott explained, "he did not mean that you become some sort of baby, although in a spiritual sense that is true. Rather, what he means is that your heart must be changed, cleansed of all the muck that's grown around it over the years. Muck that this society keeps throwing on it."

Muck is right, I thought. *Try the family law system sometime!*

"The Bible says in 2 Corinthians 5, 'Therefore, if anyone is in Christ, he is a new creation; the old has gone, the new has come!' This is a radical makeover. It is a complete change in our nature. But the strange thing, the unfortunate thing is this—many Christians don't live any differently in their day-to-day lives than they did before they were saved.

"You remember that bumper sticker many years ago? It said, *I'm not perfect, just forgiven.* Well, the theology may be correct, but the message to the world is lost when the car carrying that bumper sticker cuts somebody off in traffic. Or honks in anger. Or when the driver bends the truth, or acts out of self-interest only."

The image of the kid in the truck—and my road-rage reaction—came charging into my mind. *He deserved worse than I gave him,* I thought. And realized I was arguing with the preacher.

"To become a Christian who walks the way Jesus did requires more than good intentions. It requires a decision, followed by action. Listen to the words of Paul from Romans, chapter twelve. 'I *urge* you, brothers, in view of God's mercy, to offer your bodies as living sacrifices, holy and pleasing to God—this is your spiritual act of worship.' Do you hear that? Unless you are willing to offer all of your life to God, you are not worshiping him.

"And further, 'Do not conform any longer to the pattern of this world . . .' We live by habits, and most of us have grown up with the habits of the world pounded into us: Do your own thing. Get all you can. Look out for number one. Do it to him *before* he does it to you."

If I could do it to Troncatti and Paula, I sure would.

"But the Bible tells us to cultivate habits different from the world and only then will we begin to actually be salt and light."

Salt? Light? What's up with that?

"Where do you start? May I suggest one place that hits very close to home in all of us. If you will do this one thing, I believe it will do more to cleanse your heart of the muck we've been talking about than just about anything else."

Okay, doctor, give it to me.

"We find it in Ephesians, chapter four, beginning at verse thirty-one. 'Get rid of all bitterness, rage and anger, brawling and slander, along with every form of malice. Be kind and compassionate to one another, forgiving each other, just as in Christ God forgave you.'"

In the morning *LA Times* they had a picture of a possum on a residential wall with an arrow sticking through it. The homeowner was tired of the creatures around his house and shot him with a crossbow.

I felt like that possum. The arrow was this stuff about anger and forgiveness and there was no way I was going to be able—

"Friends, if you have anything against anyone, you must learn to forgive, or a root of bitterness will take hold in you and block your fellowship, not just with each other, but with the Father. The Bible is very clear about this. You have been forgiven in Christ, therefore you must forgive . . ."

Forgive Paula? Troncatti? No, José, there is no way. They don't deserve it. You don't go around forgiving people unless they deserve it.

" . . . even if you don't think they deserve it."

I almost slid off the pew. But not before remembering that Nikki had said something to me about forgiveness, too. It was getting to feel like a conspiracy around here.

"Because you did not deserve the mercy of God. I say, forgive, and you will feel a burden lifted from your spirit. And you will feel what it is like to become new."

I waited around after the service to see if I could catch Nikki. Maybe she was coming to the next service.

But I didn't see her.

I did, however, see Mrs. Hancock.

"How is that little girl of yours?" she asked.

"As far as I know, fine."

She looked confused.

"It's a bad situation right now," I explained. "My wife wants a divorce."

"Oh, I'm sorry—"

"And Maddie. She wants full custody of Maddie."

Mrs. Hancock put her hand on my arm. "If there's anything I can do."

"Thanks, but . . . You know, maybe there is. Would you be willing to write a letter? I need every friend I can get."

She said she would.

I hung around a little while longer. Still no Nikki. So I went to Tommy's for a burger and thought about what Pastor Scott had said. I thought about trying to forgive Paula and Troncatti, but it didn't make sense.

They were in the wrong, not me. They were up in Brentwood, laughing it up, with Maddie around.

No, I couldn't let go of my anger and hatred. It was about the only thing I had going for me.

– 4 –

Maddie had this thing when she was four. All kisses had to be rubbed in.

I couldn't just take a little peck on the cheek from her. She'd kiss me and then say, "Rub it in."

The first time I sort of laughed and said, "What?" Then she put her hand on my cheek and rubbed it, hard.

"It has to stick," she said.

And when Paula or I kissed her, Maddie would rub that in herself.

I started wondering if Maddie remembered when I kissed her, and how she rubbed it in.

I wondered about that for the next two weeks of my life, which came and went with numbing routine.

I worked Josephina's.

I went home.

I went to church on Sunday. Saw Nikki and waved, said hello, but that was about it. At least Ron Reid wasn't coming around.

The person I saw the most, in fact, was Sutton Hallard. Two more follow-up visits went just like dentist appointments, only less fun. Hallard was as easy to read as the Washington Monument. I had no idea what his report was going to be like.

Then came the day Alex called me and said I should come in. She had the report.

"Better for you to see it with me," she said.

Bad to Worse

– 1 –

Alex was subdued. I was like a terrier puppy hearing the dinner bowl sound. *Tell me tell me tell me!*

"Sit down," Alex said.

"What did he say?"

"Please sit down, Mark." She went behind her desk and waited until I parked myself in a chair.

"I'm going to give you a copy to read along with me," Alex said. "I want to go through this with you."

You know what this sounded like to me? A doctor about to discuss the various options for treatment of brain cancer.

That's why my hands were shaking as I took the thick report from her. I guessed it to be about sixty pages. I looked down at the cover page.

Sutton J. Hallard, Ph.D.
Clinical and Forensic Psychology

Declaration of Sutton J. Hallard, Ph.D.

I, SUTTON J. HALLARD, PH.D., a Psychological Child Custody Evaluator, hereby declare as follows:

I have completed a sixteen (16) hour Advanced Domestic Violence Training Program as required under Section 3111 of the California Family Code, as described in Section 1816.

I have also completed a four (4) hour Domestic Violence Update Program for the current calendar year, as required under Rule 1257.7.

I declare under penalty of perjury under the laws of the State of California that the foregoing is true and correct.

It was dated and signed.

I looked up at Alex. "Meaning basically the guy knows whereof he speaks?"

"Just read," Alex said.

I turned to the next page and saw this:

CONFIDENTIAL. DO NOT DUPLICATE FOR DISTRIBUTION. ALL INFORMATION CONTAINED HEREIN SHOULD BE KEPT FROM CHILDREN.

"This sounds horrible," I said.

"The page you're reading is boilerplate. Turn to the summary section, which starts—" Alex shuffled through the report—"on page forty-eight."

I did as ordered and started to read.

Pursuant to Stipulation of the parties and the court order, I have conducted a Psychological Evaluation in the custody and visitation matter of Madeleine Gillen, aged five years, the daughter of Mark Gillen and Paula Montgomery.

I received and reviewed from counsel and the parties numerous documents, including, but not necessarily limited to, Letters, Pleadings, Declarations, Court Orders, and the report of Sheila Bonner, Marriage and Family Counselor, as per previous order of this court.

DISCUSSION

This case presents a situation where the court ordered monitored contact between Mr. Gillen and Madeleine, and the results thereof. Mr. Gillen also has a previous history of abusive behavior.

"History!" My eyes were stinging with outrage. "Of abuse?"

"We'll get into that," Alex said. "I want you to read the rest of the section."

I tried, my face boiling all the way.

Mr. Gillen represents that he has been unfairly denied visitation with Madeleine, and further that the monitored visit on August 17 was deliberately sabotaged, a charge not supported by documentation received by this evaluator.

He denies all accusations of abuse, either physical or verbal.

There appears to be an envy factor at play as well. Mr. Gillen's career as an actor has been on the opposite trajectory as that of Ms. Montgomery. Mr. Gillen made certain allegations to this evaluator suggesting a bit of paranoia at the circumstances against him.

"Paranoia! Alex, this is so unfair."

"Tell me about it."

"I don't want to read any more."

"Read it, because you need to help me understand it."

"I'll help you understand it. It's all a lie."

"All of it?"

I threw the report on the ground. "Whose side are you on?"

Alex kept cool. "If you react this way in court, the judge is going to conclude that the report is all true. Can you see that?"

Ms. Montgomery represents that she is fearful of Mr. Gillen's anger, and what that might mean for her safety and that of Madeleine. While Mr. Gillen has expressed an interest in religion as a way to deal with his anger, he has not as yet taken any specific steps toward anger management. He does appear aware that he needs such counseling.

"Wow," I said. "He threw me a bone."

Alex said nothing.

Madeleine has been reluctant in her responses concerning her father. She expresses that she does not wish to visit with him unattended by a monitor, but that she would prefer there be no visitation.

My heart, broken in half, was now shattering into smaller bits. Tears came to my eyes. I tried to stop them, but there was no way.

I threw the report on Alex's desk. "I can't read anymore."

Alex said, "Mark, I need you to—"

"No! Not now." I turned toward the door.

"Mark—"

"Please. In God's name. Do something."

I left before she could say another word.

– 2 –

"You look bad," Roland said.

"Thanks."

"No, I mean Freddy Krueger bad. Ugly bad."

"Thanks again."

"Meaning what's up?"

I was at Roland's NOHO club again, sitting at a table with my piano-playing friend, trying to get out of myself. I told him about the report issued by Sutton Hallard.

"Bad," Roland opined.

"It's like I'm in this nightmare I can't wake up from." I was working on a Coke, wishing it had a heavy dose of rum in it. But no, I was determined not to get back into the drinking thing.

"What's next?" Roland said.

"The hearing. Comes up in a week."

"What happens there?"

I shrugged. "The lawyers duke it out."

"So will Maddie be there?"

"Probably not."

"Paula?"

"For sure."

"Troncatti?"

I lifted a glare. "If he is, I may do something I'll regret."

"Don't talk that way."

"I mean, it's all slipping away from me."

"Your lawyer okay?"

"She's not in the same league as the other guy. Money buys you certain things."

"It'll work out." Roland patted my arm. "You'll see."

But I didn't see. "What makes you such an optimist?"

"He's watching."

"Who?"

Roland pointed upward.

"God?"

Roland nodded.

"His eyesight isn't so good."

"God plays jazz."

"Right."

"No, think about it. God's the ultimate jazz man. Bible says the universe was chaos till God starting playing. A riff on light, and there it was. Light! Plays a little with the ocean—fish! I mean, where'd that come from? Fish? Jazz. So he gets hot, keeps jamming, makes a man."

"Big finish, huh?"

"Only he's not finished. Man keeps messing up, doing bad things, hitting all the wrong notes. But God still plays so man can hear the music. And the great thing is, we can jam with him if we want to." His face brightened. "This is good stuff. You writing this down?"

"Sorry."

"Thanks a lot, man. I'm tossing out genius and you just sit there."

"I heard you."

"I hope so." Roland stood up. "I gotta go play. Wait around, huh?"

I had another Coke as Roland got ready to play. Then Milo Ayers, the owner, came over to my booth. "Hey, good to see you, my friend."

I shook his hand. "You too, Mr. Ayers."

"How's things?"

"Hanging in there."

"You ever get a lawyer, like we talked about?"

"It's been in all the papers," I said.

"Never read 'em. Too depressing."

"Yeah. I couldn't afford your friend, but I found another one. I'm in the middle of things right now."

Milo Ayers, like a concerned uncle, slid into the booth next to me. "She's not cooperating, your wife?"

"No."

"Going to court?"

"Soon."

"You let me know how it turns out, eh?"

I looked at him, wondering why he should be so concerned about my little problems.

"I mean it," he said. "Consider me a friend. Who can get things done." He winked, patted me on the shoulder, and left.

And then Roland started playing a nice rendition of the old Billie Holiday song, "Ain't Nobody's Business If I Do."

3.

When I got to the courthouse on the big day (without the benefit of a sound sleep for at least a week), I could see there was a media camp set up on the walkway between the two main buildings. Word had gotten around that Troncatti and Paula were going to show up at the hearing together. I'd seen that report on a cable program, as if it were the opening night of some rock concert. These two were the new darlings of the paparazzi.

I, on the other hand, was the news equivalent of chopped liver. None of the eager reporters recognized me as I made my way from an overpriced downtown parking lot toward the security doors of the Los Angeles Superior Courthouse. As anonymous as an unproduced screenwriter, I ambled past the reporters, who had the look of circling sharks in their eyes. I just wanted to get inside with the real sharks—the lawyers who would be doing battle for my future.

But along the way, I changed my mind. In Los Angeles, live media events are not to be avoided. I was half an hour early anyway. So I bought an *LA Times* from the machine and waited to catch the show like everyone else.

I also knew, but didn't want to admit, that I wanted to see Paula, live and in person. I wanted to watch her body language as she made her appearance. Maybe I was just a glutton for punishment.

There was no mention in the *Times* of the hearing, or Troncatti and Paula. Not that I could find, anyway. Instead there was the usual spate of bad news from the Middle East, our own inner city, along with today's special guest disaster area, Tennessee, which was experiencing massive flooding.

The world, in other words, was spiraling along as always, and for a fleeting moment I forgot about my troubles. Who was I, in the grand scheme of things? With people being slaughtered over barren strips of land, or losing their homes and, in some cases, lives, under the grinding forces of nature?

Who cared what happened to me?

The answer came like a cliché: God. God was supposed to care. That was what I was told in church, in Bible study, by friends. So maybe there would indeed be a party of One who gave a rip about what became of Mark Gillen after today.

Can you hear that, Lord? Consider it a prayer, will you?

I turned to the sports section. The Dodgers were in the wild card hunt, half a game behind the Giants. Then I noticed the reporters suddenly start to mill around like anxious sheep. Camera lights flicked on, making it seem like a small, artificial sun just erupted. People on the outside got the message something was up and angled in for a closer look. I was one of those people.

And suddenly, there they were.

Troncatti was taller than I thought he'd be. He wore the obligatory shades and had some sort of furry thing around his neck—either the carcass of a weasel or a fashionable item from some Italian men's store. His hair was longish and stylishly unstyled. His bearing was roguish and bad-little-boy. Along with plenty of money.

Paula was also in dark glasses along with a thousand pounds of jewelry. I could hardly believe it. She'd gone from being a good, working actress to some sort of Brentwood diva. I remembered reading about Elizabeth Taylor and Richard Burton back in the sixties. How they hooked up and became jet-set icons and "stars" more than real actors who cared about the craft.

Was that what I was observing now? The ruination of Paula Montgomery? We used to talk about how we wanted to be real actors, do Shakespeare together, maybe start a theater company someday. Dreams. Everything fades in the green light of money and the crush of media attention.

Troncatti started making some statement. Bryce Jennings, shorter than the director, was almost obscured by the thrusting microphones. He'd do his talking in court, of course, but right now he seemed more like a puppet master. Did he have his hand up Troncatti's back, controlling the whole deal?

I edged closer, trying to catch some of what Troncatti was saying. Like most Italians, he was doing a lot of talking with his hands. And I could tell, even from this distance, that this guy had a personal magnetism that would be hard to resist.

The reporters weren't resisting at all. They were eating up his every word. And I had a quick, stomach-churning thought that I wasn't in this guy's league, never would be, and no wonder Paula was attracted to him.

Paula was standing by his side, holding his arm, but looking subdued. No smile on her. I thought for a second she was going to turn and run toward the courthouse. That would have been news.

But she didn't move. She kept her lips pursed and her gaze forward while Troncatti kept flapping his yapper.

I strained to hear.

"—to all of our friends," he was saying in his accented voice, "and their support, we cannot say more. We are grateful for what is being shown to us. But we remember, always, this is not about the two of us alone, but of Maddie, beautiful Maddie, and what is best for her."

My heart was really pumping now and the air felt hot and sticky. I was starting to sweat under my arms. But still I couldn't turn away. It was like watching a car wreck; the car wreck was me.

Voices shouted more questions. Troncatti started to answer, but then Jennings stepped in and took over. He pulled Troncatti forward, parting the Red Sea of reporters. From where I was standing, near a brown trash can, the Israelite army would pass within a few yards.

I waited, hoping to get a closer look at the happy couple.

Paula glanced over and saw me, through a crack in the reporter mob. Very clearly and directly, her dark glasses looked at my face. I knew she saw me, because her mouth dropped open a little.

The power of surprise.

What surprised *me* was how I felt. I didn't know I was capable of such depths of hatred and rage. But the surprising thing, the shocking thing, the thing that almost sent me screaming into the street, was the other part of the feeling—longing.

You're so sunk. You still love her. Even while she and Italy Boy are sticking the spikes in you!

And then, just as quickly, she had her back turned to me. The reporters, amoeba-like, moved almost as one organism, after the couple du jour. And I almost lost my breakfast. I realized I was hugging the trash can to keep from doubling over.

– 4 –

"Remain seated and come to order," the bailiff said. "This court is now in session. The Honorable Harold J. Winger presiding."

The judge, his robe sweeping along with him, hotfooted it to the bench. He looked all business today. And like he'd already made up his mind.

My neck started to itch, in part because my shirt collar was too tight. I hadn't bought a new shirt in years, or worn a tie in months. Sweating outside during the little press conference didn't help. It was just past nine on a hot morning and stains were already appearing under my arms. The air conditioning in the courtroom was a little too cold. I'd probably come out with a case of pneumonia. But that was the least of my worries.

My biggest worries were sitting on the other side of the courtroom. Paula was enthroned, like a queen, next to Bryce Jennings. Troncatti was in the gallery section, near the slatted wood wall. He still had his dark glasses on. His limo driver, who I had somehow missed on the outside, was seated next to him, all brooding and Vin Diesel-like. Troncatti's bad boy bodyguard. There were a couple extra deputy sheriffs in the aisles, no doubt to keep autograph hunters and troublemakers at bay. A whole bunch of reporters, ready to scribble, were in the other seats.

"This is a custody hearing in the matter of Montgomery versus Gillen," the judge said. "State your appearances."

The reptile representing my wife stood up. His suit was perfect. Some men just are born to wear expensive clothes. Jennings was one of them. I wanted to stuff one of my nice T-shirts into his mouth.

"Good morning, Your Honor. Bryce Jennings for the petitioner, Paula Montgomery."

My lawyer, raring to go, got to her feet. "Alex Bedrosian for the respondent, Your Honor."

"Parties are present with counsel," Judge Winger said. "Very well. Mr. Jennings, call your first witness."

Jennings swept his arm toward the gallery. "Petitioner calls Dr. Sutton Hallard."

Like a rabbit appearing out of a hat, Sutton Hallard stood and ambled down the aisle. Reporters craned their necks and wrote in their little pads. The drama was about to begin.

Hallard stood like a bedpost as the clerk swore him in. Then he took his spot on the witness stand. He looked fresh and composed, as if he'd done this a thousand times before. Which he probably had.

"Good morning, Dr. Hallard," Jennings said, as if this were some tea party.

One lump or two? I thought.

"Good morning," Dr. Hallard said.

"You are the court certified evaluator in this matter?"

"I am."

Jennings snagged some papers from his table. "May I approach the witness, Your Honor?"

"You may," said the judge.

Jennings placed the papers on the rail of the witness box. "Is this the report you prepared and submitted to the court?"

Hallard gave it a quick glance. "Yes, it is."

"Is that your signature on the cover of the report?"

"It is."

"Thank you. I am not going to go over all of the ground you covered here, Doctor. The court has read the report. I would, however, like to have you expand upon a few matters."

"I'd be happy to."

I just bet you would, I thought. *In your completely objective and unbiased fashion, right? And what right do you have to be happy about it?*

"Dr. Hallard, on page seven of the report you reference Mr. Gillen's charge that his monitored visit with Madeleine on August 17 was *sabotaged.* You also state that the evidence for any interference with this visit was not forthcoming, and further that Ms. Montgomery denies any such charge. Do you recall that?"

"I do."

"Is it uncommon for one party in a custody dispute, such party being challenged on his or her parental competence, to react with charges against the other party that may, in fact, be completely fabricated?"

"Objection," Alex said. "Assumes facts not in evidence. The report of Dr. Hallard is only his opinion."

"It is merely a hypothetical, counsel," Bryce Jennings said with a condescending smirk. He looked at the judge. "I am entitled to ask a hypothetical question. This witness is an expert. The court has approved him in that regard. Further, the evidence code permits facts or data which are reasonably relied upon by experts in their particular field, to be considered in a hypothetical question. Such data is in the report."

"Whether this data is reasonable is what is at issue," Alex said. "Much of what is in this report is bogus."

"All right," Judge Winger said. "I'm going to overrule the objection. You will have the chance to cross-examine the witness, Ms. Bedrosian. Go ahead, Mr. Jennings."

Bryce Jennings repeated the hypothetical.

"No," Sutton Hallard said, "it is not uncommon for this to occur. It is, in fact, all too frequent. When one party perceives that evidence is mounting against him, resorting to false charges may be the last, desperate ploy."

The good doctor was calling me a liar, a desperate liar willing to say anything to win. Funny, but I thought that was what Bryce Jennings was. *Why don't you psychoanalyze him, Sutton? There's one for your medical journals.*

The assassination of the character of Mark Gillen continued. Jennings asked, "Does it sometimes happen that the party making the allegations actually comes to believe they are based on fact, when they are not?"

"Sometimes, yes."

"In which case, the party is somewhat delusional?"

"Or perhaps completely delusional. But, I must add, this is rare."

"But it does happen?"

"Yes."

"Do you have an opinion as to whether it has happened to Mr. Gillen?"

Sutton Hallard's beady eyes—at least that's how they looked to me, Mr. Delusional—bore in on me for a second.

"I would not like to speculate on that," he said.

How big of you, I thought. *But you'll speculate on everything else.*

The witness added, "Although . . ."

"Yes?" Bryce Jennings prodded.

"There is an aspect to Mr. Gillen's behavior that may point, in a small way, in that direction."

My hands were squeezing the sides of my chair now. Was I hearing right? Was he going to say I really was delusional, crazy, a wild-eyed danger to society? If he was, I thought I might prove him right by jumping into the witness box and pulling his tie extra tight.

"What aspect would that be?" Bryce Jenning asked.

"Mr. Gillen has made a sudden leap into religion," the good doctor explained. "This coincides with the timing of this custody dispute. Now, religion can be a perfectly healthy way for people to deal with problems in their lives. But under certain conditions, it can be an escape from reality."

I had this terrible feeling that Hallard had rehearsed this little speech, and he and Jennings had set it up to appear spontaneous. My anger was flaring, but if I was going to be painted as a religious nut, I thought it might be good for some Old Testament action to happen right here in court. Maybe a pillar of fire to consume Hallard and Bryce Jennings, right in front of everyone's eyes. *Is that admissible enough for you, Your Honor?*

Hallard continued. "In this instance, from what I have gathered from Mr. Gillen, he has gone rather quickly into a constricting form of Christianity. It offers him the sudden and comforting appearance of black and white, good and evil, and makes it easy for him to separate himself from Ms. Montgomery in this fashion. This, of course, raises concerns for—"

"Objection!" Alex's voice rang out, louder than I'd ever heard it. "Is this court seriously going to entertain the religious bigotry we are hearing from this witness?"

Winger drummed his fingers on the bench. "Do you have grounds for your objection?"

"Relevance to start with. Materiality. Competence. This witness is not an expert in the field of religion. Furthermore, we have First Amendment implications here. The right of free exercise. To make my client's religious affiliation grounds for denying custody is unconstitutional."

"If I may?" Bryce Jennings said.

Judge Winger nodded at him.

"Ms. Bedrosian's impassioned speech notwithstanding, there is a line of cases which makes religious affiliation one of several factors to consider in custody matters. The court must always seek the best interest of the child, and how religion may affect the child is of critical importance. It is quite true that religion alone has not been held dispositive. However, it has certainly been considered along with all other factors. If the court wishes, I can prepare points and authorities."

"I am aware of the cases," Judge Winger said. "What about Ms. Bedrosian's argument that Dr. Hallard is not an expert in the field of religion?"

"If Your Honor please, I can qualify him in that regard."

"Go ahead."

Jennings turned back to Hallard. "Doctor, what is your background with regard to religious studies and its psychological impacts?"

"As part of my doctoral program at Johns Hopkins, I took a seminar in comparative religion with Dr. Simon Stuart, of Princeton Theological Seminary. That resulted in a paper in which I compared the religious teachings of Judaism, Christianity, and Islam with regard to the mind's place in monotheistic moral systems."

If this was gobbledygook, it was sure impressive sounding. I could feel the heat emanating off Alex. She wanted to get at this guy. But did she have the weapons?

"I also contributed a paper to the *Journal of Theological Studies* on the impact of religion on various mental states."

"Is one of those mental states relevant to this case?"

"Yes. I have concluded that Mr. Gillen has a problem with anger, and that is one of the mental states I explored in this paper."

"Your Honor," Jennings said to Judge Winger, "I submit that Dr. Hallard is qualified to offer an expert opinion in the matter of religion, when it has a direct bearing on the question to be decided, namely, the competence of Mr. Gillen as a parent."

With hardly a second to think of it, Judge Winger said, "I agree."

Alex objected again, the judge denied it again, and Bryce Jennings smiled as he asked his next question.

"How do anger and religion play a role in the matters at issue?"

"It is quite common for the sudden adherence to a fundamental religion to result in the subject's attempt to sublimate, rather than deal openly with, perceived personality problems. In the case of anger, the subject may attempt for a time to keep from expressions of anger and may even be successful in the short term."

"What about the long term?"

"Inevitably, the suppression results in an explosion. A fit of rage may result with attendant violent manifestations. The subject, feeling massive guilt, may then go to the opposite extreme in his religious life."

"Expand on that, if you will."

"There will be a tendency to become something of a fanatic in religious exercise. And this is where I am most concerned about the child in this case."

"Tell the court."

Sutton Hallard, all professional dignity and with the calm of a professional hit man, half-smiled at the judge. "I am concerned that Madeleine would be subject to the more harmful effects of religious fundamentalism with Mr. Gillen. His religious sensibilities are still quite new, and until there is a record of his being able to deal with those, I fear harm may come to the child."

"What sort of harm?"

"It runs the gamut, from psychological harm in the form of thought control, to physical violence in the form of corporal punishment."

Alex couldn't contain herself any longer. "Your Honor, I object in the strongest terms possible to this testimony, ask that it be stricken, and that you do not consider it in any way in your decision. This is patently unconstitutional and outside the purview of this witness's alleged expertise."

The entire courtroom seemed to take a collective breath. The judge thought about it for about two seconds.

"Overruled."

I felt like I'd been socked in the mouth, and I know Alex felt the same. We were both reeling as Bryce Jennings finished with Sutton Hallard.

Alex requested a short recess.

– 5 –

"Can we rip his lungs out?" I asked Alex. "Is that legal?"

"Moral maybe," Alex said. "But I don't think the D.A. would look kindly on it."

We were on a bench outside the courthouse. We had half an hour before court started up again. Sitting in the shade of the municipal trees was actually pleasant. But my mind was too consumed with visions of Sutton Hallard buried up to his neck in sand to take any pleasure in it.

"How can he sit there and lie like that?" I was having trouble getting my breath to stay below hurricane level.

"He's Jennings's hired gun, is what he is. He wants to be used by Jennings in the future because he knows he will be well paid. And while it's not uncommon for evaluators to be biased, it is odd that Jennings would call him to the stand after a favorable report. He really wants to bury us in front of the judge."

"Is the judge buying it?"

Alex shrugged. "He's hard to read. I'm going to try and make sure the words are very plain when I cross-examine."

"What are you going to do?"

"Go for the jugular."

That brought the first smile of the day to my face. Maybe the first in a week. "You know, I love it when you talk like that."

"Shut up and finish your coffee."

As I took a sip I glanced to my left. What I saw made me almost spit my coffee out like a bad comedian.

Ron Reid, in an ill-fitting shirt and tie, was making his way toward the courthouse.

"What's he doing here?"

Alex gave a look. "Who?"

"My wayward father."

My lawyer watched Ron amble toward the doors. She shrugged. "Public's entitled to hear what's going on. Except . . . your father doesn't normally dress that way, does he?"

"No."

"Hmm."

"What do you mean, 'hmm'?"

"I mean he's dressed for court. Like a witness."

I looked at her. "You think Jennings is going to call him as a witness?"

"I wouldn't put anything past Bryce Jennings."

Ron was sitting in the hallway outside the courtroom. When he saw me he stood up and put his hands out, as if to say, *I'm as mystified as you are.*

Not likely.

"Hey," he said, "I got subpoenaed by the other guy."

"What for?" I asked. Alex was standing next to me, wanting to hear for herself.

"I don't know. I just—"

A young woman with tight blond hair and a dark blue suit tapped Ron on the shoulder. "Please don't talk to anyone, Mr. Reid. Come this way, please."

Sheepishly, Ron shrugged at me and then followed the woman down the hall.

"What is that all about?" I asked.

"She's an associate of Jennings's," Alex said. "They're going to put him on the stand if they need him."

"What's he going to say about me?"

"You don't know?"

I tried to think. "There's nothing he can say either way. He never saw me with Maddie. Maybe I got ticked off at him. It could be my anger."

Alex nodded thoughtfully.

"Will they put him on?" I asked.

"If they don't think Sutton Hallard makes enough of a case."

"He's doing pretty good so far," I said, the despair thick in my mouth.

"He hasn't gotten by me yet." Alex started for the courtroom.

Alex took her notes to the podium in the middle of the courtroom. This was it, the showdown at high noon—her cross-examination of Sutton Hallard. My best hope for a chance to get custody of Maddie.

And where was Maddie? I suddenly wondered. Who was she with at this very moment? Not Paula or Troncatti. Erica? That thought spilled ice cubes in my veins.

I pictured Maddie in that big house. Was she, even now, crying for some reason? Had she skinned her knee or stubbed her toe or lost Bonson, her stuffed ape? Why wasn't anyone there? Why wasn't I allowed to comfort her? Why wasn't—

"Dr. Hallard," I heard Alex say, "how long have you been a clinical psychologist?"

"Twelve years," Hallard said.

"And how long have you been giving evaluations in family law cases?"

"About seven years, give or take."

"Give or take what, sir?"

Hallard looked momentarily confused, like he'd misplaced his cuff links or something. "A few months, I suppose."

"Dr. Hallard, we are going to be covering very specific questions regarding a highly sensitive matter. Rather than supposition, I would like to—"

"Objection!" Bryce Jennings was on his feet. "Ms. Bedrosian's lecture, I am sure, is of little interest to this court. I would remind Ms. Bedrosian that there is no jury present to play to and that we are all here on a matter of much more—"

Judge Winger put his hand up. "All right, counsel. For the record I'll overrule the objection. We're just getting started here, so we all might as well take a deep breath. The witness is experienced, and I'm sure understands the need for specificity. I'm going to give Ms. Bedrosian some latitude, since she bears the burden of persuasion. Continue, Ms. Bedrosian."

Score a round to us, I thought. Or maybe it was just one punch. But I was willing to take anything at this point. At least Alex was showing both Jennings and the judge she was not going to back down one bit.

She took a white piece of paper out of a manila folder. "According to your *curriculum vitae*, Dr. Hallard, which is quite extensive, you were in partnership with two other doctors for five years?"

Hallard nodded. "That is correct."

"And you left the partnership in 1996?"

"Correct."

"What part of 1996? For specificity."

Sutton Hallard looked up at the ceiling a moment. "That would have been—the early spring, I believe."

"And then you opened your own office in that same year, is that correct?"

"Correct."

"What month was that?"

As I watched Sutton Hallard, the cool and collected clinical psych-dude, I thought I noticed his eyebrows twitch. Or maybe I was just hoping I saw it.

"I believe it was September," Hallard said. "Yes, September."

"Early, middle, or late?"

"Your honor," Bryce Jennings said, "how is this relevant?"

"Good question," Judge Winger said to Alex.

Alex said, "Indulge just a couple more questions on this, Your Honor?"

"A couple," said the judge. "But then let's move it along."

Alex looked at the witness. "Your answer?"

"Yes, I believe I was in the latter part of September. I remember because my lease began in the beginning of September and I was trying to get everything up in the new office, but things kept happening."

I threw a quick glance at Bryce Jennings, sitting at the other table. He had a concerned look on his face. What was Alex up to? Whatever it was, it was making Jennings sweat a little, and I loved it. Paula, on the other side of Jennings, was clasping and unclasping her hands.

"Things do happen, don't they?" Alex said.

Hallard seemed mystified.

My lawyer stepped to the side of the podium. "So between the spring of '96 and late September of the same year, you did not have an office, is that correct?"

"That is . . . true."

"Why not?"

The question rang out like a shot. The way Alex asked it, she was telling everybody in the courtroom, including the witness, that she very well knew the answer. And suddenly Sutton Hallard's poker face got a serious case of the jitters.

Bryce Jennings got the message. "How is this at all relevant, Your Honor? I must object. When Dr. Hallard took residence in his office? How he spent his summer vacation? I don't understand."

"You will," Alex said.

The courtroom was suddenly stone silent. The reporters seemed to lean forward as one.

"May we approach the bench?" Jennings said quickly.

The judge motioned them forward, which only heightened the tension in the room. And with both lawyers striding toward the bench, there was no human obstruction between Paula and me.

I looked toward her. She looked at me.

For one second our eyes locked. My breath left me. She was so beautiful, even with the exhausted look she had. For a split second I almost felt sorry for her, thought I'd let her off an embarrassed hook by looking away. But steel came back to me, and I knew I was not going to be the one to look away. In fact, I kept right on honing in with my stare until she looked down at her hands.

A minor victory. I felt hollow.

Jennings was motioning wildly in front of the judge. Alex stood by calmly, listening. When the huddle broke, I couldn't tell from the looks what had happened, who had come out on top.

"Back on the record," Judge Winger said.

"The question is," said Alex, "what happened between your leaving the partnership in the spring of 1996 and opening your own office in late September, that interrupted your professional life?"

Sutton Hallard breathed deeply. "I experienced some personal setbacks, and was taking steps to deal with them."

"By personal setbacks, what do you mean?"

Bryce Jennings was tight lipped. The judge had ruled in our favor. Had to be. Why else was Jennings sitting there like a dumb Buddha?

"I went through a divorce," Sutton Hallard said, "and was drinking more than I should."

"You sought treatment for the abuse of alcohol?"

"Yes. But may I add—"

"Thank you. You've answered the question."

"Your Honor, please," Jennings said. "The witness wishes to expand upon his answer."

"The question has been answered," Alex repeated.

"I'll allow the witness some latitude, just as I've allowed you, Ms. Bedrosian." The judge nodded to Hallard. "You may complete your answer, sir."

"Thank you." Hallard assumed a prouder pose. "I have never allowed anything in my personal life to interfere with my professional duties. I have never had any disciplinary action taken against me by the governing boards of my various associations, nor the state of California."

Good answer, I thought. But Alex had managed to make a good point, too. Was it enough to shoot down this guy's testimony? That remained to be seen.

– 6 –

Alex grilled Dr. Sutton Hallard for two hours. She attacked every part of his report. She bit into Hallard like a Doberman chomping a mailman's leg. She was magnificent.

But so was the witness. He fought back hard. It was like the Ali-Frazier fights. One fighter went down, got up, knocked the other guy into the ropes. For fifteen rounds.

Then, somehow, Alex kicked into a higher gear.

"Dr. Hallard, I want to read to you a portion of your report. This is from page twenty-seven if counsel wants to refer to it. You state: 'Madeleine has been reluctant in her responses concerning her father. She expresses that she does not wish to visit with him unattended by a monitor, but that she would prefer there be no visitation.' Did you write that, sir?"

"Yes, I did."

"You choose your words carefully, don't you?"

"Of course I do."

"Every word here is important, because this is a matter of the utmost importance, the future of people's lives, is it not?"

"I take this all very seriously."

"But there is a word in here that is not very specific. Negative, yes, but not specific. That word is *reluctant.* It is ambiguous, is it not?"

"Ambiguous?"

"Yes, that means it is open to several nuances of meaning."

"I know what ambiguous means." Sutton Hallard looked like the kid on the playground who just got teased for an answer he missed in class. "The word seems clear enough to me."

"Does it now?" Alex left the podium and approached Hallard. He stiffened. "Do you refuse to answer my questions, sir?"

"No, of course not."

"Would you rather be back in your office now?"

"I'm not sure I know what you mean?"

"Rather than testifying here in court."

"Well, certainly, all things being equal, who'd rather be grilled by an attorney?"

There was a ripple of laughter in the courtroom.

Alex nodded. "Then I take it there is a degree of reluctance here?"

Hallard narrowed his eyes. "I wouldn't say that."

"Did I use the word incorrectly? You just said you'd rather not be *grilled* by an attorney."

"If you're going to get technical, sure, you might use the word that way."

"So there are a number of ways to use that word. That makes its use in your report ambiguous, does it not?"

"I can explain what I meant."

"I'm not interested in what you mean *now*. You filed a report, you used this word, and you have no facts to back it up. You offer it as an opinion, but there is nothing in this report that explains the basis of that word, is there?"

"I think the report is clear."

"That's the problem, Doctor. Your definition of clearness is different than mine."

Bryce Jennings objected and the judge sustained it, but Alex did not even pause for a breath.

"There is nothing in your report on the basis for Madeleine's so-called *reluctance*, is there?"

"Her visits with her father," Hallard snapped back. "She doesn't want to see him."

"I asked you about the basis of that opinion, sir."

"It's what I picked up from her responses to my questions."

"Did you include any actual questions and any actual responses in this report?"

"I don't believe so."

"You don't know?"

"No, I did not."

Alex swept back to the podium and looked briefly at her notes. "Do you recall testifying on direct that it is a frequent occurrence for a party to resort to false charges as a desperate ploy?"

"I believe I said that is likely to happen when one party believes the evidence is mounting against him."

"And by *him*, you of course mean *him* or *her*, don't you?"

"Depending on the case. In this case—"

"Thank you. Isn't it also true that false charges may be made based upon ill feelings alone?"

"That can happen, yes."

"So if one side bears enough animosity toward another side, this ploy of false allegations may be resorted to."

"I've seen it done."

"And isn't it also true that this may be a trial tactic used by overzealous attorneys?"

Bryce Jennings lurched out of his chair. "This is an outrage, Your Honor! If Ms. Bedrosian is accusing me of unethical behavior then I demand the basis for the charge."

I think Alex's eyes twinkled. "It is merely a hypothetical, counsel."

Judge Winger almost laughed, like a parent would at two siblings fighting over the TV. "I'll allow the witness to answer."

Hallard seemed surprised. "I cannot speak to that. I don't interview the attorneys."

"Lucky for you," Alex said. "I have one more area I want to discuss with you, Doctor. You have held yourself out as an expert on religion as it relates to mental health, is that right?"

"That's a somewhat broad description, but yes."

"And on direct, I believe you used the term *constricting* form of Christianity. Do you recall that?"

"Yes."

"What did you mean by that word, *constricting?*"

"Well, I meant to say that Mr. Gillen has accepted the teachings of that wing of Christianity which is very harsh in its treatment of personal expression."

"Harsh?"

"Yes."

"Do they use whips?"

"Of course not. I mean they teach a very black-and-white doctrine of right and wrong."

"That's terrible," Alex said. "Imagine that."

"Objection," said Jennings. "Argumentative."

"Sustained."

Alex acted like she didn't even notice. "So your assessment of a religion which teaches right and wrong is that it is *harsh?*"

Sutton Hallard cleared his throat. "It can be, especially for a child. It can become a fearful experience."

"I see. Tell me, do you agree with the following statement: *The fear of the Lord is the beginning of knowledge.*"

"No, I don't believe that's an accurate statement. God should be an object of love, especially for a small child."

"If I told you that statement came directly from the Bible, what would you say?"

Again Bryce Jennings objected, but Alex was ready. "Your Honor, Mr. Jennings qualified Dr. Hallard as an expert in religious studies. If I wish to explore that subject, he can hardly bring about an objection."

"My only question would be relevance," Judge Winger said.

"If you'll allow me to continue, Your Honor, I expect to show an unprofessional bias in this witness, which calls into question his entire report."

If this had been a TV movie, the courtroom would have gasped at that point. The silence that followed had almost the same effect. It felt like a ticking bomb had just been placed in the middle of the courtroom.

After what seemed like a ten-minute breath, Winger said, "All right. I'll let this go a little further."

Jennings was steamed as he sat down. For the first time I thought he looked a little shaky. *Go Alex!*

My lawyer opened the briefcase on her table and took out a leather-bound Bible. She held it like a weapon. Opening it, the pages riffled like little gunshots.

Alex stopped turning the pages. "Please answer the question, Doctor. I just quoted a passage from the Bible for you, the book of wisdom, Proverbs. Chapter one, verse seven. Do you disagree with the statement that 'the fear of the Lord is the beginning of knowledge'?"

"I believe the Bible teaches that God is love," Hallard said.

"How about this passage?"

"I'd have to see it in its context."

"Do you believe the Bible teaches that it is a sin to have rage?"

"That may very well be."

"So if a person, let's say Mr. Gillen, believes the Bible to be the Word of God, and believes that rage is a sin, and devoutly tries to overcome that sin, wouldn't you say that's a good thing?"

"My opinion is that a person has to deal with who he or she is, and that attempts to sublimate parts of the personality may result in an explosion later on."

"I believe you said *sublimate* as opposed to *dealing openly with.* Is that right?"

"I don't recall saying that."

"Would you like me to have the reporter read the answer back to you?"

"Yes." Hallard was now openly defiant.

"Your Honor, may I have the reporter read that back?"

The judge said, "All right. The reporter will do a word search for *dealing openly with.*"

The reporter, a rotund woman with flying fingers, stood up from her transcribing machine and went to a computer terminal on a table near the judge's bench. She keyed something in, waited a moment, made a few clicks with a mouse. Then she hit a key and waited. She returned to her station with a piece of paper from a printer.

"The witness gave the following answer," the reporter said. "'It is quite common for the sudden adherence to a fundamental religion to result in the subject's attempt to sublimate, rather than deal openly with, perceived personality problems. In the case of anger, the subject may attempt for a time to keep from expressions of anger and may even be successful in the short term.'"

"Does that refresh your recollection, Dr. Hallard?" Alex asked.

"Yes."

"And is that still your opinion?"

"Yes, it is."

"Do you know what Christians mean by confession of sin?"

"Of course."

"It's something like when clients open up to you in your office, isn't it?"

I thought I saw Hallard's cheeks getting rosy. "In some ways, I suppose."

"Please don't suppose any more, Doctor. Yes or no?"

"Yes."

"And when people tell you intimate things, they are seeking to deal with them openly, aren't they?"

"Yes."

Alex flipped a few pages in her Bible. "Quoting now from the book of James, chapter five, verse sixteen. 'Therefore confess your sins to each other and pray for each other so that you may be healed.' Does that sound like failing to deal openly with problems, sir?"

"Ms. Bedrosian," Hallard said, "you can quote chapter and verse all day long. What I was concerned with is the actual outworking of this form of Christianity with regard to the child."

"Just what is that concern? Are you afraid Madeleine might actually come to believe in Christianity?"

"No, that's not it."

Alex answered with a shout. "Then just what is it, Doctor!"

The whole place seemed to rock back at the sound of her voice. Sutton Hallard looked like a man slapped. And when he jumped back at Alex, I knew she'd gotten him right where she wanted.

"It is the threat of physical harm," he said. "This type of Christianity believes in corporal punishment of children. I've seen it time and time again."

"Oh, you're one of the progressive doctors who knows that a spanking can never be good for a child, is that right?"

"Corporal punishment is antithetical to the best interests of the child."

Alex had a file sitting on the counsel table. She opened it and took out some papers, then put them on the podium. "Are you aware of the study conducted by Dr. Diana Baumrind, a psychologist at the University of California at Berkeley?"

"I have heard of Dr. Baumrind."

"Do you agree or disagree with her findings, which she summarizes as follows: 'Occasional spankings do not damage a child's social or emotional development. These results call into question claims that any physical punishment hurts children psychologically and damages society as a whole.'"

"I happen to disagree."

"Have you conducted any such study?"

"No. I've read several, however."

Alex looked at her notes. "Have you read 'Familial and Temperamental Determinants of Aggressive Behavior: A Causal Analysis'?"

"I don't recollect at this moment."

"Wherein it was concluded, 'Childhood aggressiveness has been more closely linked to parental permissiveness and negative criticism than to physical discipline'?"

"I would have to read it."

"Obviously."

Jennings's objection was sustained.

"It is inappropriate to hit a child!" Hallard said.

"Not in the opinion of the Ninth Circuit Court of Appeals," Alex said, pulling out another paper. "You are familiar with the *Calabretta* case, I'm sure."

"Which one was that?"

"A Christian family that dared to spank a child? And based on an anonymous tip, a social worker showed up with a policeman and forced the mother to pull down a three-year-old child's pants. Does that refresh your recollection?"

"I think so."

"What did the court hold, sir?"

"I don't remember."

"I'll read it. 'A social worker is not entitled to sacrifice a family's privacy and dignity to her own personal views on how parents ought to discipline their children.' Do you agree or disagree?"

"In that case, I would have to disagree."

"Let's see then. You disagree with the Bible, other psychologists, and the Ninth Circuit Court of Appeals, is that about it?"

"There are always areas of disagreement in my field."

"Precisely," Alex said. "And what you have presented is a one-sided, biased report which justifies your personal opinions."

"Object to the speech, Your Honor," Jennings said.

"Noted," the judge said.

Alex flipped to another part of Hallard's report. "You did not interview Antonio Troncatti, did you?"

The name hit like a balloon popping.

"No, I did not. He is not a party to this action."

"He is, however, Ms. Montgomery's live-in boyfriend, is he not?"

"Yes."

"That didn't factor into your opinion?"

"That Ms. Montgomery is living with Mr. Troncatti?"

"That Ms. Montgomery is an adulteress, yes."

Well, you could have set off the fire alarm in the building after that, and no one in the courtroom would have moved. The reporters acted like kids at a birthday party when the piñata erupts. Candy for everybody! Big ol' pieces, too.

Jennings, of course, put on a show of outrage. But it was Troncatti who became the perfect sideshow. His shout of what I took to be Italian wrath was both pitiful and theatric, sort of a Verdi aria as sung by Jackie Gleason on *The Honeymooners.* His arms were flapping around, like some landlocked crane honking at intruders. I almost laughed.

Judge Winger was not laughing. He was pounding his hand on the bench (he didn't have a gavel for some odd reason) and shouting, "Enough! Enough!"

Meanwhile, Alex leaned casually at the podium, her arms folded.

Finally, some order was restored. Judge Winger's face had a slight, crimson glow. "Ms. Bedrosian," he said, "your use of inflammatory language is not needed."

"Excuse me, Your Honor," Alex said, in a way that made me think *contempt of court.* "What word would you have me use? Paramour is a bit dated, don't you think?"

"You do not need to cast aspersions on the petitioner."

"Just so I'm clear, Your Honor. You are saying that the fact that Ms. Montgomery is engaged in a sexual relationship outside of her marriage is not of any relevance here?"

"It isn't to me," the judge said.

"I want that noted, on the record."

"It is already on the record. Now move on."

"Clarification. Does the fact that Ms. Montgomery's boyfriend has a violent temper have any relevance?"

"Object to that as well," Jennings said.

"Sustained."

Alex looked ready to jump up and literally hit the ceiling. "Your Honor, I take exception to that. I have numerous reports from news sources that point to Antonio Troncatti's own anger problems, and thus call into question his fitness to be around a young child and—"

"I have ruled, Ms. Bedrosian." The judge looked at Hallard. "Sir, do you think there is any danger, any at all, in the girl's living where she is, with her mother and the mother's boyfriend?"

Hallard didn't hesitate. "Not at all. In fact, the home and amenities provided are quite good. I did not witness anything to indicate any risks."

"Thank you," Judge Winger said. "That covers that, as far as I'm concerned. Do you have any other areas to go over, Ms. Bedrosian?"

"Your Honor, you are cutting off a relevant line of inquiry."

"I take it then your answer is no. We will take a recess."

– 7 –

The press was all over us outside the courtroom. Funny, now we were the stars. Alex's cross-examination and the fireworks over that word—*adulteress*—had met all the requirements of drama for the evening news.

Alex did the talking, and she was like an actor that handles the big moment in a play with a Tony award-winning performance.

"The report in this case is a bogus piece of psychobabble that is biased and unprofessional. When the best interests of a child are at stake, this simply cannot be allowed to go unchallenged. The attacks on Mr. Gillen's character are without foundation. I believe that was shown through the testimony of the other side's own witness."

"Will your client be testifying?" a reporter shouted.

"We'll see," Alex said.

"How has this affected him?"

"How do you think? His life is being trashed for no other reason than vindictiveness. But that's how some people practice law in this city."

As if on cue, Bryce Jennings walked out of the courthouse doors, Troncatti and Paula next to him. As soon as a couple of reporters saw them and scampered over, the rest followed suit.

Like hogs at feeding time.

Troncatti was livid. He was doing that same wild stuff with his hands. I hoped they got a good dose of that and would report it again.

"Let's get out of here," Alex said.

We drove a few miles away to a Quiznos. My stomach wasn't accepting food, so I sipped a Sprite while Alex munched a sandwich.

"You want to go on the stand?" she asked.

"Want to or need to?"

"I think Jennings is going to put on more witnesses. How they do will answer your question. Regardless, I don't want to do it if you think you'll . . ."

"I'll what?"

"Not be able to handle it." She looked me square in the eye. "I'm sorry to say it, but Jennings will do whatever he can to get you to lose your temper."

"So if I kick him until he's dead, that's a bad thing?"

"I mean it."

"I know. I can do it. I want to do it."

"Think long and hard," Alex warned.

"For Maddie," I said. "I can do this for Maddie."

Alex was right. Jennings called Ron Reid to the stand.

It was a surreal experience, seeing my biological father step up to testify for the other side. The big question was what possible relevance he was to Paula's case. It didn't take long to find out.

After a few preliminaries, Jennings asked Ron about his reasons for making contact with me after all these years.

"I just thought it was time," Ron explained. "And I found out I had a granddaughter."

When he said that I looked over at Paula. I wondered what she thought about that aspect of this whole thing. Ron Reid was not the sort of person she'd want seeing Maddie.

"How did you find that out, sir?"

"I saw something in a news story. About the divorce and custody thing and all."

"Which prompted you to contact Mr. Gillen?"

"Yes."

"And was that contact successful?"

"Sort of."

"What do you mean, *sort of?*"

"I mean it wasn't exactly a warm family reunion."

"Can you explain that?"

Ron shrugged. "I can understand. Father comes to you, after all this time, you're not exactly gonna take it like Christmas. But we talked it out, and he let me stay in his place."

"He invited you in?"

"Yeah."

"And what can you tell us about that experience?"

With a little twitch of the lip, Ron said, "It wasn't the greatest. We had a fight."

"What was the fight about?" Jennings asked.

I leaned forward.

"Do I have to say?" Ron Reid asked.

"You are under oath, sir," Jennings snapped.

"Well, I came in one night and he was doing something I thought wasn't a good idea, for him or for his daughter, if she ever came back to live with him."

Now I was coiled tight, like I might snap. What was he talking about?

Jennings knew already and asked with a calm voice, "What was this something you didn't think a good idea?"

Reid swallowed. "Smoking dope."

My voice exploded. Words came out by themselves, like horses from a flaming barn. "No way! That's a lie!"

It was one of those TV moments, where the innocent accused screams out just before the commercial break. Up to that point I always thought those moments a bit contrived. No more.

"Mr. Gillen!" The judge said. "You are not to talk in open court, is that understood?"

"He's a liar!"

Alex put her hand on my arm, trying to calm me. I jerked it away.

"That's all, Mr. Gillen." The judge's face was getting red.

"Do something!" I shouted at Alex.

Judge Winger pounded his fist on the bench. "Last warning, Mr. Gillen. Sit down and be quiet."

Alex took my arm again and pulled me down, generating laughter from some in the courtroom. "Be quiet," she whispered sternly.

"But Alex—"

"Be *quiet.*"

Finally, a modicum of sanity prevailed in my mind. I clammed up and let my hatred of Ron Reid warm my body.

Bryce Jennings, who had been smiling at the podium, continued as if nothing had happened.

"Mr. Reid, how did you know that Mr. Gillen was smoking a narcotic?"

"I'm not proud about it, but I know what grass—marijuana—smells like, because I used to do a lot of it."

"You have drugs in your background?"

"Like I said, I'm not proud about it. But I'm clean now."

"No longer use drugs?"

"No, sir."

"What did you tell Mr. Gillen, if anything, about the use of drugs?"

Ron Reid swallowed once, the liar. "I told him he shouldn't be doing that around his kid, my granddaughter. I told him that was about the worst thing he could do."

"And what was his reaction, if any?"

"Nothing. He told me to mind my own business if I wanted to stay around."

"What did you say to that?"

"I told him I was going to move out. And the next day, I did. I didn't need to be around that stuff."

With a nod, Bryce Jennings smiled at Alex. "No more questions."

I don't know what Alex was thinking when she got up to question my lying father. I did see the back of her neck, though. It was fire-engine red.

"Mr. Reid," she said, "you have a criminal record, isn't that right?"

"Objection," Bryce Jennings said. "Improper impeachment."

Judge Winger looked at Alex. "Only felony convictions can be considered for impeachment, Ms. Bedrosian. Do you have a foundation for this?"

"I do," Alex said.

"Then I'll allow it."

Alex turned back to Reid. "Sir, do you have a criminal record?"

"I'm not proud of that."

"Apparently you're not proud of a lot of things, are you?"

Bryce Jennings mouthed an objection, more for show, I think, than anything. It was like a halfhearted attempt to give his witness a few moments to think about things. But the judge sustained it, calling the question argumentative.

Big deal, I thought.

Alex didn't pause. "You served time for dealing drugs, right?"

"Yeah." The slightest bit of fear snuck into Ron Reid's eyes. He glanced over at Bryce Jennings. I got the feeling he wanted to say something like *Hey, I didn't sign up for this.*

"And you served how long for that?"

"Six years, give or take."

"What comes next on your menu of crime?"

Jennings objected again, calling the question argumentative again. *Of course,* I thought. *This is court, you jerk.*

Alex sighed. "Your Honor, I'm sorry that Mr. Jennings is so sensitive to the English language. But he is the one who put this witness on the stand, he is the one who brings Ron Reid's criminal record into this proceeding. If he does not care for the way I ask questions, tell him he is free to step outside. But allow me to cross-examine."

The judge said, "All right. The question is colorfully phrased, but there is nothing objectionable in it. Overruled."

"Tell us," Alex practically spat at Ron Reid.

Reid said something I couldn't hear. Neither could the court reporter, who said, "Please repeat that."

"A little louder, please, Mr. Reid," said Judge Winger.

"Battery," Reid said.

"Whom did you batter?"

"A guy who provoked me."

"Oh? Are you easily provoked?"

"I don't think so. I try to get along with everybody."

"But not this man you battered, is that right?"

"He was drunk. We were in a bar. He was coming at me."

"What did you use as a weapon?"

Ron Reid's chest went up and down in a cautious heave. "A glass."

"What kind of glass?"

"Beer glass."

"One of those heavy kind?"

"I guess."

"Don't guess while you're under oath, Mr. Reid."

"It was pretty heavy."

"Did you draw blood?"

"Yes."

"Mr. Reid, isn't it true that the police took a statement from you at the scene?"

As I watched Ron squirm I could see, out of the corner of my eye, Bryce Jennings lean forward. I leaned a little, too. How had Alex gotten all this information?

"Yeah," Ron Reid said. "Of course."

"And isn't it true that this report was admitted into evidence during your trial?"

Ron's eyes got a little wider. "Yeah."

I half expected Alex to whip out the police report right then and there, but she couldn't have. We hadn't known Ron was going to be put on the stand.

"And isn't it also true that the statement you gave to the police was contradicted by witnesses at the scene? Isn't that true, Mr. Reid?"

A flash of anger shot out from the mellow follower of the Wheel, which was crushing his toes at the moment. "So what? They were friends of this guy."

"The jury did not believe you, did they?"

"I didn't take the stand."

"They didn't believe your story in the report, did they, Mr. Reid?"

Bryce Jennings almost cried out in pain. "Objection to this line of questioning. How long are we going to have to go down memory lane here?"

As long as your witness, my loving dad, is bleeding in the corner.

"I think the point has been made," Judge Winger said. "Let's move on."

Alex did not even pause for a breath. "Mr. Reid, you have also lied in this proceeding, haven't you?"

"What?"

"Am I speaking too fast for you, Mr. Reid? I'll slow it down. You. Lied. Under. Oath. Right?"

"No!"

"You claim you found my client smoking dope?"

"That's what I said."

"It's a lie."

"No, it isn't."

"Anyone else see this?"

"I don't know."

"Anyone else report this?"

"Not that I know of, I only know—"

"So all we have is what you, a perjurer, tell us."

No surprise that Jennings objected and the judge sustained it. I didn't care. Alex was doing with words what I wanted to do with a sharp weapon. The sense of outrage and betrayal in me was almost more than I could stand. I'd taken this guy in, given him money . . .

Money.

I scribbled the word on a piece of yellow legal paper and slid it toward Alex. She saw the motion, came over and read it. Nodded, then returned to the podium.

"Mr. Reid, how much money are you getting for your testimony?"

That's when the place went crazy. Jennings started shouting, Alex started shouting, and Troncatti, his Italian hands waving in the air, shouted too. Just to join in the fun, some reporters started shouting questions, at who I don't know.

The judge started pounding on the bench with his gavel and when he finally got a word in he ordered a recess. And the lawyers to get their behinds into his chambers *now.*

– 8 –

"Why won't anybody help him?" Maddie asks me.

"Some of them are afraid," I explain. "Some of them are ungrateful."

We're watching High Noon *on TV. I'm trying to share some of my favorite movies with Maddie, but she's not old enough for a lot of them yet. She gets squirmy.*

But for some reason she likes this one. There's something about Gary Cooper's face, I guess. It's etched with a devotion to duty, but also a deepening sorrow. The killers are coming into town soon, and no one will sign on to help the marshal, played by Cooper.

Maddie's always had a soft spot in her heart for injustice. When she sees something that's unfair—like a big kid at preschool snatching a toy from someone—she gets very upset.

"What's 'ungrateful'?" she asks.

"Well, when somebody does something nice for you, you say thank you, right?"

"Right."

"That's being grateful. When you don't say thank you, that's being ungrateful. And in this town, see, the marshal did a lot of good things for the people. He helped make the town safe. But now that he needs help, nobody will help him."

"That's not fair!"

I am about to tell Maddie that life is not fair. But she is only five and that lesson can wait. Hopefully, for a long time.

"What is he gonna do?" Maddie says.

"Let's watch and find out."

"I'm scared for him. He's all alone."

I was alone on the corner, pacing behind a bus stop bench, when Alex found me.

"What are you doing out here?" she asked.

"Calming down. What happened with the judge?"

"He is plenty ticked off. Mostly at me."

"Why?"

"He thought my question about money was improper. He's probably right. There's no basis for it."

"It just makes sense," I said. "Why else would he lie like that?"

"Point is, the judge does not want this thing turning into a hockey game. My sense is that he wants to get it over as soon as possible. Which leaves us with a decision to make."

It sounded serious. "What is it?"

"Jennings said he has no more witnesses to present. He's made his case, in my opinion, even though we've tried our best to blow some holes in it. We went into this thing with the weight of evidence against us. So we have to decide whether to put you on the stand."

"I'll do it."

"Not so fast. You're very emotional right now. That can blow up in our face if it continues."

"No," I said. "Put me on. I won't blow it."

"You understand Jennings is going to hit you with everything he's got. He may well have held back some things he knows just to use them when you testify. It's called sandbagging."

"What else can he know? Everything's out there."

"You didn't know he'd call your father."

True. But that was his big weapon, it had to be. I could handle anything after that.

"I want to tell my side," I said. "I'll be good. I promise."

What an easy word to say, *promise.* What an easy thing to break into a million pieces.

– 9 –

"Mr. Gillen, please tell the court how you feel about your daughter."

The question was so simple, but it hit me like a 350-pound lineman. Where do you even begin? How do you get it out so it made sense? This was like my one moment, the big one, the only chance I'd get.

If I was too emotional I'd seem unbalanced. But the emotion was so strong in me I wanted to jump up on the bench and grab the judge by the robes and shake him until he understood.

But Alex had prepped me and told me to take a few deep breaths before answering.

Which is what I did. And it helped. For about two minutes.

I looked at the judge, who seemed like Thomas Jefferson on Mount Rushmore. Rock hard, expressionless. "Words can't really do justice to what I want to say, Your Honor. I could say I love my daughter, and that would be true, but it would also be something you've heard before, and it's just words. I don't know how to say that it's more than that, so much more than that."

I glanced at Paula. She was looking at the floor.

"I've pretty much been on my own ever since I was a kid, had to make my own way. And I thought I was pretty good at it. But when Maddie was born it was like—it was like being born myself, in a way. My life was just starting then. I felt like this was my life being born, because there she was, and then I had a reason for not being on my own, ever again."

The courtroom was dead silent, but my pulse was pounding in my ears. This was when I began to lose that fragile control the few, short breaths had given me. A heat was rising up from my chest and taking over like a wildfire in the hot, dry California hills.

"What I guess I mean, judge, Your Honor, is that Maddie is more important to me than anything, and that's coming from a guy who's only wanted two things in his whole life. To be a major league baseball player, and to be an actor."

When I said *actor* I looked, by reflex, out at Troncatti. He rolled his eyes. That's when it all left me, the self-control. The bad reality of it hit me then, the nightmare part, the worst part of the nightmare, right before your brain wakes you up.

The words literally stuck in my throat. I always thought that was a dumb cliché, but it's not after you feel it. My skin started tingling like I had a fever.

The next few seconds were like slow motion. There's that scene in Sam Peckinpah's *The Wild Bunch* where the entire population of Mexico is shot and dies in slow time, blood pouring out. That was the scene I was in.

I looked from the judge to Alex, who was starting to look concerned. She must have known I was in trouble.

I looked over at Bryce Jennings, weasel lawyer, sitting with what looked like a grin.

And then I saw Paula—smash cut to close up. Paula. The only woman I'd ever really wanted. Beautiful, but also somehow lost now.

I found my words. "Paula, don't do this. Why are you doing this? Paula, why? Don't, don't—"

"Mr. Gillen." It was the judge's voice, from a far-off place.

"Paula, please, you can't do this. Why—"

"Stop, Mr. Gil—"

I stood up. "Paula, look at me. Call this off, will you? Don't do this to Maddie—"

"Ms. Bedrosian, tell your client to—"

"Mark!" That was Alex.

I was in a tunnel now, just looking at Paula like she was at the other end. "Paula, look at me, will you?"

She didn't.

Next thing I knew this beefy deputy with a red face was at the side of the witness box, looking up at the judge like some obedient Doberman, waiting for the cue to bite.

The judge was slamming his hand on the bench and looking at me with all the understanding of Hannibal Lechter.

"That will be enough, Mr. Gillen!" He sounded like Moses, as played by Charlton Heston, rebuking the Israelites.

My face felt like it was going to melt right off me. It was Alex's face I couldn't bear to look at. She seemed at once to be full of pity for me and about to implode with professional embarrassment.

I clunked back down in my seat, like a condemned prisoner who just got turned down for a pardon from the governor.

"I'm not going to let this happen in my courtroom," Moses said to me. "Do you understand that, Mr. Gillen?"

"Yes," I said.

"I'm not sure that you do. I'm going to take a ten-minute break. Ten minutes exactly. You can confer with your lawyer and decide what you want to do. But if anything like this happens again, I'm going to disallow any further testimony from you. Are we clear on that?"

"Yes."

The judge left the bench.

"You've done enough," Alex said when we were alone in the hall.

"I couldn't help it. You want me to lie?"

"Calm down." She was gun-shy now, looking around for reporters. "There's nothing more we can do. Nothing you say is going to add or detract from what just happened in there. You can go back in and be contrite, and it will make your outburst look more like some out-of-control episode. Or you can go in and say nothing and look belligerent. What we're going to do is go in there, and I will make a statement of apology to the judge on your behalf. I don't think he wants you to say anything at this point, but if he does you get on your feet and say you're sorry. Right?"

"You know what a blimp feels like when it's deflated?"

"Mark, this was the Hindenburg. My only hope is that the judge will pick up your sincerity and not your instability."

"Thanks."

She put her hand on my shoulder. "We are long past the point where I patronize you, Mark. You are not doing well on this whole thing. We have no more evidence to put on. We leave this to Judge Winger."

"Throw ourselves on the mercy of the court?"

"If it helps to think of it that way, yes. And start praying now."

Making News

– 1 –

"Your Honor," Alex said, "my client is apologetic for his outburst on the stand and wants the court to know that he regrets his feelings for his daughter became so—obvious. We trust the court will take his testimony into account on its merits."

"You can trust the court, Ms. Bedrosian," the judge said. "Do you wish to question your client further?"

"No, Your Honor."

"Mr. Jennings, do you wish to cross-examine?"

The lawyer stood, like a man about to start demolition. "Most definitely."

"Mr. Gillen," Judge Winger said, "please retake the stand. I will remind you, you are still under oath."

My knees were doing a rumba as I walked back to the witness chair. I was, frankly, scared out of my shoes. Alex had said she'd do everything to protect me, if Jennings crossed the line. Whatever that meant.

But the look on his face was something between a surgeon's seriousness and the maniacal glee of a serial killer.

"How are you feeling, Mr. Gillen?" Jennings asked with fake concern. A nice way to remind everybody how I'd lost my cool half an hour ago.

"I'm fine," I said, and out of habit added, "thank you." It was like we were at a tea party.

"Good. We were a little concerned there."

I'm sure you were. Like an aardvark is concerned about ants.

"Mr. Gillen, you're an aspiring actor, are you not?"

What a great question, slipping that little word *aspiring* in there. But I was ready. “I’m a professional actor, yes.”

“Professional?”

“Yes.”

“How much did you make from acting last year?”

Not much. “I did all right.”

“Can’t recall a figure?”

“Not right now, no.” And that was true.

“Would it be fair to say that the majority of your household income came from Ms. Montgomery’s paychecks?”

“She had a recurring role on a soap.”

“Do you have a recurring role in anything?”

I saw Troncatti was smiling widely, the way a beer-guzzling gambler must smile at a cockfight when his bird is humiliating the opponent.

“Not at this time.”

“Have you ever had a recurring role?”

“I’ve done stage work.”

“Paying?”

“Minimum.”

“You also work as a waiter, is that right?”

“Yeah. I have a recurring role at Josephina’s.”

“You make more money as a waiter than as an actor, is that right?”

Alex objected. “Irrelevant.”

“Sustained,” the judge said, but it was clear Jennings was satisfied with his opening salvo. My right leg was jerking up and down, the way it gets when your nerves are snapping through it. I put my right hand on my thigh to stop it.

Jennings said, “Do you consider yourself a good actor, Mr. Gillen?”

Again Alex objected, but Jennings convinced the judge this was a different line of questioning. The judge gave him some room.

"Yes," I said.

"Feel like you're good enough for a series or movie role?"

"Yeah. If I didn't, I'd quit."

"Take acting classes and the like?"

"Sure. I work hard at the craft."

"So it wouldn't be hard for you to make a scene, say in a courtroom, to try and sway a judge?"

"Objection!" Alex almost blew papers off the counsel table with her voice.

"That's argumentative, counsel," Judge Winger said. "Sustain the objection."

But Jennings was unfazed. It seemed to me he was more than willing to ask the occasional improper question, just to get into my head. So if it was acting he wanted, I'd give it to him by acting as calm as I could. Only my right leg didn't want to cooperate.

"Let's turn to the matter of your church, Mr. Gillen."

Alex told me this was going to come up. How a parent intends to educate the child, what religion, if any, he wants the child to be raised in—these are all things a court will take into consideration. So I had to sweat it out.

"You attend this church, Gower Presbyterian, correct?"

"Yes."

"And you have taken your daughter to church there?"

"Of course. She likes it."

"They have a Sunday school, something of that nature, for children?"

"Yes."

"Are you aware of what they teach?"

"Yeah," I said. "The Bible."

"Their *interpretation* of the Bible, correct?"

"They teach Bible stories. Maddie loves Bible stories."

Jennings flipped to another page on his legal pad. "Are you aware this church has a program of child rearing called, I believe, Raising Godly Children?"

"Yeah, I've seen that."

"Ever attend any classes?"

"No."

"Intend to?"

"Maybe."

"Do you endorse this program?"

"I don't know much about it."

"You do know it is sponsored by your church, do you not?"

"Yeah."

"Do you know, for example, that this program, Raising Godly Children, advocates corporal punishment with a stick?"

"Objection," Alex said. "Foundation."

"I am only asking if the witness knows," Jennings said. "If counsel likes I can introduce into evidence a copy of the curriculum of this program, which we have obtained."

"I also object on grounds of relevance," Alex said. "As I mentioned during my cross-examination of Dr. Hallard, the Ninth Circuit Court of Appeals, in the *Calabretta* case, held that the use of a token rod for disciplinary purposes did not violate California law."

"It did no such thing," Jennings remarked.

Alex went to her briefcase and snatched some papers. "I took advantage of the break to make copies of *Calabretta*. I will hand one to Mr. Jennings and one to the court. The relevant language is as follows: 'The social worker plainly expressed the view to the mother that use of any object to spank a child, such as the "rod" (a nine-inch Lincoln log) was illegal, and she did have reason to believe that such an object was used, but appellants have cited no authority for the proposition she was right that California law prohibits use of any object to discipline a child. The statutes we have found prohibit "cruel" or "inhuman" corporal punishment or injury resulting in traumatic condition. While some punishment with some objects might necessarily amount to cruel or inhuman punishment, a token "rod" such as a nine-inch Lincoln log would not.'"

Judge Winger motioned for a copy of the case. Alex handed it to him. For what seemed like an hour, but was more like five minutes, the judge went through the copy. During the silence I kept my head down, not wanting to look at anyone. I think I was praying. Only once can I remember looking up, at Paula. She was not looking at me.

Finally the judge said, "In the best interest of the child, I am going to consider the curriculum Mr. Jennings has obtained. Regardless of what *Calabretta* holds, and it is a narrow holding, I believe I am duty bound to consider the consequences of a particular form of discipline on a particular child. Counsel's objection is overruled."

"Exception to that," Alex said, "on First Amendment grounds."

"Exception noted. Continue, Mr. Jennings."

Paula's lawyer, unflappable, in quiet and deadly tones, went on. "Would you describe yourself as a person who has to deal with anger, Mr. Gillen?"

"Deal with it?"

"Yes."

"I don't know what you mean by that."

"That's confusing to you?"

"I just don't know what you mean." *Easy. Easy.*

"Do you have an anger problem?"

Now what do I say? "I get angry sometimes, like everybody."

Jennings raised his eyebrows. "Not everybody throws glass bottles at people, do they?"

Someone cackled in the audience. I looked over. It was Troncatti.

"I threw a bottle of water on the sidewalk next to Paula," I said, keeping myself in check. "I lost my temper."

"Do you often lose your temper?"

Alex stood. "Objective. Vague as to *often.*"

"Sustained."

No stop from Jennings. "Have you lost your temper this week?"

"I don't know."

"Can't recall?"

"Right. Can't recall."

"Throw anything?"

"No."

"Stayed pretty calm?"

I shrugged. This wasn't getting any of us anywhere. "I'm not this out-of-control freak," I said. "I'm no danger to society."

"Pretty normal, you feel?"

"Sure."

"Have you ever hit your daughter in anger?"

The question was delivered softly, but it had the impact of a smart bomb—the kind that kills people but leaves buildings intact. Looking back, I'm sure Jennings had asked all of his previous questions just to set me up for this.

The setup worked. My body jerked and my face flushed. I was sure it was a neon sign to the courtroom, flashing *guilty guilty guilty.*

"I never . . . I only . . ." I stopped to regroup, catch a breath, which must have made me look even worse. "There was one time in the car, she was screaming and wouldn't stop. I hit her on the arm. Once."

"You dealt with her behavior by striking your daughter, isn't that correct?"

No getting around it, nowhere to hide. "One time."

"You did not spank her, did you?"

"No."

"You did not, with deliberation, lay her over your knee and use a Lincoln log to discipline her, did you?"

Alex was silent at counsel table, and I knew there was nothing she could do to stop the bleeding.

"No. But I was sorry I did it, I told her how sorry I was."

"Were you sorry when you let your daughter get kicked in the head at a park?"

I tried not to let my face light up with shock. How did Jennings get that information? It was like he had a video camera on my whole life.

"I did not let my daughter get kicked," I said. "It was an accident."

"She suffered a concussion, isn't that right?"

"Mild concussion. I brought her home."

"You were at a park, let her wander away—"

"She was *playing*. That's what kids do at parks. Ever heard of that?"

Jennings smiled slightly, and I knew he was doing this to get me to lose it again. With all my strength I calmed myself down.

"The fact is," Jennings said, "that your daughter was injured at a park while under your care, that is the truth, isn't it?"

"It was an accident."

"That's not what I asked you."

I just shook my head. "I'm telling you what happened."

"I think we have enough of an answer here." Jennings tugged at one of his cuffs. A gold cuff link glimmered in the harsh courtroom light.

"Do you have anger toward your wife?" Jennings said.

Another quick shift in the questions. I was starting to rock back and forth on the swivel witness chair. It squeaked. So did my voice.

"Paula?" I cleared my throat.

"Do you have another wife?" Before Alex could object, Jennings said, "Strike that last remark, Your Honor."

"Stricken," Winger said.

"Do you have anger toward your wife?"

His snide little remark had given me a moment to regroup. "No, I wouldn't say that. Maybe at first there was. Now it's just . . . hurt. I don't understand why she's doing this."

"Do you think your *hurt* might affect how you act around your daughter?"

"No."

"No chance of that?"

"No."

"What is it that *hurts* you, Mr. Gillen?"

Was he serious? Or setting me up again? I just stared at him.

"Did you understand the question, Mr. Gillen?"

"Sure." I paused. "Wouldn't you be hurt if your wife took up with another man?"

Jennings didn't flinch. "I'm not on the witness stand, sir. You are. So the fact that Ms. Montgomery fell in love with Antonio Troncatti is what *hurts* you?" Every time he said *hurt* he pounded it, like a boxer hitting a heavy bag.

I looked at Paula, who wouldn't make eye contact. "Of course it does."

"How does that *hurt* manifest itself?"

"You really want to know? I'll tell you. I wake up every day feeling like I've lost something I'll never get back. I wanted us to be a family, and now that's not going to happen."

Jennings paced a moment. "Does your *hurt* manifest itself by your involvement with other women?"

"What? Are you kidding me?"

Judge Winger said, "Please answer the question, Mr. Gillen."

"Of course not," I said.

"Do you know a woman named Nikki McNamara?"

Stunned, I stopped rocking. My face—must have been flashing neon again—felt hot.

Alex objected. "What is the relevance?"

"Veracity," Jennings said. "Catching the witness in a lie."

"I object to the characterization!"

"Hold on," the judge said. "Let's just take a step back here. The witness has asserted that he has a certain emotional state toward Ms. Montgomery—"

Emotional state? What was I, a lab rat?

"—and that included an assertion of fact that he was not, I think the word was *involved,* with other women, and now counsel has asked about a woman I assume he is going to link to Mr. Gillen. Doing so would have a bearing on Mr. Gillen's veracity. So I will overrule Ms. Bedrosian's objection."

I felt bad enough, but now Nikki's name was dragged into this thing. A complete innocent.

"That is unfair," I said. "Nikki McNamara is a friend, someone I know from church. That's it."

Jennings snatched something from the podium. He put it in front of me. It was an 8-by- 10-inch photograph, in full color. Taken with a telephoto lens. Me, embracing Nikki in the courtyard of Gower Pres.

My mind blew up in a million pieces. I glared at Jennings. His smug face glared back. "You slime," I said. "You hired some guy—"

"Mr. Gillen," the judge said. "No question has been asked."

"How can you allow this?" I said to him.

"Mr. Gillen, please wait for a question."

What a farce.

"Who is pictured in this photograph?" Jennings asked.

"How did they ever let you practice law?" I said.

Troncatti snorted in the gallery. That was, as they say, the final nail in the coffin. Or my heart. I was dead.

Jennings took the photograph away. "Your Honor, I don't think I can get anything more from the witness that will be of use to the court. We are ready to submit this matter to you."

"Anything else for this witness?" Judge Winger asked Alex.

"No, Your Honor," my lawyer said.

What more could there be? Every time my lips moved I dug a deeper hole.

"You may step down," Judge Winger told me.

My body moved out of the witness box. As I walked by Paula I thought she had a little look of sympathy there. The way a hunter looks at a wounded lion right before he finishes the job.

"Any further evidence?" Winger said.

"No, Your Honor," said Alex.

"It has been a long day for all of us," Judge Winger said. "I understand that, having been on this side of the legal fence for twenty years. I will take the matter under submission."

– 2 –

We are at the arcade in the mall because Maddie wants to see me shoot baskets.

It is not as easy as it looks, even to a former jock like me. The rim is smaller than regulation and balls are extra bouncy. So you have to put the ball perfectly through the hoop or else clunk it in off the backboard.

I choose clunk.

The balls come fast off the canvas that catches them. The unforgiving clock ticks down.

Maddie is cheering. "Come on, Daddy! You can do better! Come on!"

Her voice is practically begging me.

I drop about five bucks' worth of tokens into that stupid game, but manage to win enough tickets to get us something from the lower-end shelf.

Maddie doesn't care. I am her hero. Ticket man.

She presses her nose against the glass, quickly scanning the items. She finds no attraction in the Chinese finger trap, or the loudly colored plastic geckos, or the giant wax lips.

No, for some reason she chooses a red kazoo.

"You sure you want that?" I say.

"Yes! You can toot with it."

"What about a nice gecko?"

She looks at me like I'm weird.

"Okay," I say, "get the kazoo."

Which is a mistake. All the way home, it is kazoo time. Only Maddie is not playing any tunes. She's talking. Talking through the kazoo.

ZIZIZZMOBZZZZIZBUBZIZZIZWUBZIZIZIZ

"Maddie, take the—"

ZIZZYMUBOOOIZZYZABBOOZOOOY

"I can't understand—"

ZIZZYZOOOBOOIZZYOOO

All the way home, and into the apartment. And finally I lose myself in laughter, pick her up, turn her upside down, and say, "Oh yeah? Oh yeah? Then ZIZZYOBBYZIZZYOZIZZY to you, too!"

We fall on the sofa, laughing our heads off.

It was not a good night, beginning with the evening news.

Local channels 4 and 7 made me their lead story. Lead story! When they had several choice murders to choose from and a high-speed chase down the Harbor Freeway.

This town sure has its priorities straight.

I flipped back and forth, but watched channel 4 first. The talking head who was reading the news—Mr. Mousse, I called him, for his helmet of hair—had a smirk on his face when he announced the next story. Behind him, the pop-up graphic shows my own, undignified kisser in an attitude that is a mixture of bug-eyed rage and a sort of Kathy-Bates-in-*Misery* insanity.

"Some major testimony today in the Paula Montgomery custody dispute," Mr. Mousse said.

They pulled back to a two shot that includes the female portion of this tag team, a gorgeous blond who seemed to be having a great time in the studio tonight.

"We finally heard from Paula M's ex, didn't we?" she said.

"Oh boy, did we," Mousse chuckled.

I didn't expect they would get it right. Our divorce wasn't final yet. But as far as the news media was concerned, that was all over. This was a fight between the woman they were starting to call by her initials, and some crazy, angry former husband who couldn't contain himself.

I turned off the TV and tried to pray. But it wasn't happening. Maybe, in some small way, I didn't think I deserved to have God listen to me.

And I thought of Nikki. I had dragged her into this thing. I needed to call her. But weird thoughts kept intruding. Like maybe my phone was tapped. I was going bughouse.

It was seven o'clock when I realized it was Wednesday. The Bible study at church. She'd be there. I could do this thing face-to-face, and maybe that way she'd be in a more forgiving mood.

And I needed to be around some people. So at 7:30 I was there.

Nikki wasn't.

Which almost made me get up and get out. But Tom Starkey made a big deal out of welcoming me. He'd seen the news (who hadn't?) and was full of concern. He convinced me to stay.

He got everybody together—the group was about fifty or sixty people—and we sat. Then he opened up with a prayer. When that was over, he asked how people were doing, if anybody had anything they wanted to share with the group. He looked at me, and when he did I thought everybody else was looking, too.

So I jumped in. "I just have a question."

"Shoot," Starkey said.

"About prayer."

"Okay."

"It says ask and you'll receive?"

"Yes."

"Where does it say that?"

"In the Sermon on the Mount."

"Pretty big promise."

"It is."

"So how come I've been asking and not getting? What's up with that?"

Tom Starkey nodded, like some sage from a hilltop in India. I got irritated. I know it was wrong. These were good people. Maybe I wanted to be irritated. It helped dull everything else. But I was also really interested in the answer.

"There are times when what we ask for may not be good for us," Tom said. "We have to find out what that condition is."

"Why?"

"Because God's first concern isn't to give us things. It's to make us more like Christ."

"I don't want to be like Christ," I said. "I just want some answers. Isn't there something in the Bible about having faith, just a little bit, and you can throw a mountain into the ocean?"

"Yes."

"So?"

"There is also this, from the book of 1 John. 'This is the confidence we have in approaching God: that if we ask anything according to his will, he hears us.'"

"What's that mean?"

"It means that God's will comes first. Jesus even prayed a prayer that wasn't answered with a yes."

"Yeah?"

Tom flipped a few pages in his Bible and read. "'"Father, if you are willing, take this cup from me; yet not my will, but yours be done." An angel from heaven appeared to him and strengthened him. And being in anguish, he prayed more earnestly, and his sweat was like drops of blood falling to the ground.'"

"What's this about a cup?"

"Jesus was praying that he wouldn't have to go to the cross. The cup was figurative, meaning a cup of suffering."

"So what was going on? He prayed not to be killed?"

"But he says to God, not my will, but yours. That's the key to prayer. If it is not God's will, it's not good for us."

"That's very convenient."

"How do you mean?"

"Well, you ask and it's supposed to happen. If it doesn't happen, you can say, oh, not God's will. Sorry."

"It also says, in 1 John . . ." Tom flipped more pages. The guy was good with pages. "'Dear friends, if our hearts do not condemn us, we have confidence before God and receive from him anything we ask, because we obey his commands and do what pleases him.' So there's a condition there, about obedience. If we need to be taught something about what pleases God before our prayer requests are given to us, then we have to bite the bullet and learn that. Sometimes God has rough hands."

I frowned.

"A potter's hands are rough," Starkey added, "from working with all that clay. Loving and rough at the same time."

This time I shrugged. It wasn't coming through loud and clear. Or maybe I didn't want it to.

To Starkey's credit he didn't press me on this. The Bible study continued. I tried to listen but my mind was all over the place.

Until Nikki walked in. She took a chair on the opposite side of the circle. We locked eyes for a moment. I didn't move. She nodded at me. If I was a nod reader, I would have read that as being shocked or dismayed. But I wasn't, so I waited to see if she'd talk to me after the study was over.

She did. Walked across the room.

Her face was full of knowing and that much I *could* read.

"You look like you heard about it," I said.

"My dad called me. It was on the news in San Diego."

"I'm sorry."

"Not your fault."

"I don't want this to hurt your career."

"Such as it is?"

"I mean it."

"I'm not worried. What about you. How are you getting along?"

I shrugged.

"I'm glad you're here," she said.

"Yeah, it's fine. Everybody's been great."

"But?"

"There's some things you just have to work out for yourself."

"I don't believe that."

I put my hands up. "Nikki, don't tell me to pray or think about God right now. I know all that. I just—have to work it out."

She nodded. Smiled. And that's when I said, "Can you come outside a second?"

We went out into the night, near the same courtyard where a snake hired by Jennings had taken our picture. I didn't care now if they had a video camera on.

"I want to see you again," I said.

She looked at the ground, like this was bad news. "I knew you were going to say that."

"How did you know?"

"Because I was thinking it, too."

"I want to see you."

"I know. But nothing's changed."

I put my hands on her shoulders, wanting to kiss her. "But how do you *feel?*"

"Mark, please don't press this right now. Please."

I hesitated a moment, feeling suspended in midair. Then took my hands down. "Okay."

She breathed a sigh of relief. "Come on, let's go back inside."

"I need to go."

"Mark—"

"Keep praying for me."

– 3 –

No sleep.

There's a scene in the old Dick Powell film noir, *Murder, My Sweet,* where Powell, playing detective Philip Marlowe, is drugged by the bad guys. Hopped up, as they used to say. He can't see anything straight. The world is all webby and fuzzy and off-kilter. He starts to wonder if he's ever going to see things straight again. And he's alone.

That's what I felt like. Alone and in a fuzz. Didn't want to see anybody, talk to anybody.

Except one guy. And that became my obsession.

I drove over to Atlas Auto Body and walked into the first bay. Some guy with a shaved head and tattoo on the back of his neck—I think it was a fish or an eggplant—gave me a look.

"Ron Reid around?" I said.

"Not here," Fish Neck said.

"When's he coming back?"

"Never. If he does, I'll wrap some cable around his neck."

"I'd appreciate that."

Fish Neck stared at me. "Who are you?"

"Somebody who wants real bad to talk to him."

"You and me both. He left me doing double time."

"You have any idea where he might've gone?"

"None. Wait. You're his kid, right?"

"Yeah."

"He talked about you."

"Oh yeah?"

"Said he was gonna make some money off you."

A white light flashed behind my eyes.

"Wasn't he on parole or something?" Fish Neck said.

I left without answering, drove immediately to the federal building downtown. Ron had been in on a federal rap, so this was the place to start looking for him, I guessed. I wasn't going to tell them why I wanted to find him, of course. That was my business. But I could say I was his son and really needed to contact him. True.

My plan was all mucked up with red tape once I walked in. Guys in blue blazers with earphones gave me the twice-over even before I checked through the metal detectors. The suit at the front desk gave me a *Can I help you* that was larded with suspicion.

I explained my business as best I could. Long-lost son looking for paroled father and all that. The suit told me to wait and got on the phone. Then he told me someone would be right down.

That someone was a young-looking woman who introduced herself as Stephanie Wong, marshal. I got the immediate impression she was running interference for everybody else, maybe got the short straw when they said some guy looking for his father was downstairs.

I put my best face on. "My dad is on parole, I think he was in Terminal Island. I'm looking for him, but he's gone. I'm wondering if he's in trouble or something." He *was* in trouble. With me.

"If he is under our jurisdiction," Stephanie Wong said, "I'm afraid that information is not something we can give out."

"Even to a family member?"

She looked at me, making me wonder if she believed me. "I'm afraid so."

I wished she'd quit saying she was afraid.

"So there's no way you can help me?"

"You could fill out a JN–30 form."

"What's that?"

"Request for confidential information. You'd have to provide a justification, and then the matter would be reviewed. It happens sometimes."

"How often?"

Marshal Wong shook her head. "Not often."

"So what do I do?"

"You really want to find your father?"

"Oh yeah."

"Can I ask you why?"

I told myself to stay calm. "There are just some things I haven't had a chance to say to him yet."

"Have you thought about a private investigator?"

"No."

"Sometimes they have resources and contacts. I can't promise you anything and this is off the record, okay?"

"Sure."

"That's what I would do if I were you."

I wanted to say *You can thank your lucky stars you're not me.*

– 4 –

I didn't know any private investigators. It's not like the movies, where you can find them in an office building, and some guy looking like Bogart comes out to help you. I didn't know where to turn.

And then I did.

I headed out to Club Cobalt. But it wasn't to see Roland. He wasn't appearing tonight.

But Milo Ayers was there. Like always.

"Hey, Markie, how are you?" He gave me a firm handshake and a slap on the shoulder. "Rolie isn't here."

"I know. I just came by."

"You want a table? Sit at the bar?"

"Mr. Ayers, could I talk to you a minute?"

His eyes, rigid and warm at the same time (I imagined a hit man looking at a puppy), looked deeply into mine.

"Sure," he said. "Come on over, I'll get you a drink."

"Just water."

"Bottled," he said.

When we were settled at a table in the corner, me with my San Pellegrino and Milo Ayers with his scotch, Ayers rubbed his hands together. "Now what can I help you out with?"

"You gave me some good advice once," I said. "About finding a lawyer. You gave me a name."

"Gregory Arsenault."

"I couldn't afford him."

Ayers shrugged and stuck out his lower lip. "Not a problem. I hope you like who you got."

"I think she did her best."

"But that wasn't good enough?"

"Not when the other side got a lying witness."

"Who?"

"My father."

"Your father lied against you?" His tone was one of complete disbelief, like that wasn't a possibility in his world.

"The other side got to him somehow."

"And this lie hurt in court?"

"Big time."

Milo sat back, drumming his fingers on the table. His gold bracelet jangled. "Markie, I like you. You been a good kid, a good customer. I help you out, you keep it between us, huh? Like a favor I'm doing and you don't want to spread it around, hey?"

"Yes. Whatever help you can give, I'll take. I'm at the end here."

"I'll call you. Now what you do is, you go home. You do what you do and don't let anything anybody does to you get you. You know what I'm saying?"

"Yes, Mr. Ayers."

"Then you'll be okay."

Sure. Okay and alone.

– 5 –

There was a structure to my loneliness.

Like the arc in a good play, I went through the acts, wandering through what actors call the "through line." That's the thing that holds the drama together, the string that penetrates through each beat of the play.

Act one began when I woke up, wishing I hadn't, seeing the light and knowing there was a long act two to come, knowing I had to live through the day wondering if the court would let me see Maddie again.

Somehow I'd pull myself out of bed and begin the living of it. Moving forward was the hardest thing. I felt like I had on one of those lead aprons, the ones the dental assistants plop on you before they take the X-rays. It was like it was permanently attached, and that's how my life was going to feel from now on.

So I'd go through the motions of the day. Not helpful to anyone. Hearing people talk to me like they were disembodied ghosts. Life was a haunted house. Act two seemed interminable. The minutes, as they say, seemed like hours, and the hours go so slowly. Wasn't that from some song in *West Side Story*? I didn't care. This was my play, and it wasn't a musical.

Then I'd come on toward night, and act three. The curtain came down as I tried to go to sleep, sometimes crying, sometimes numb. And always in the back of my mind a little critic saying maybe we should close this show. Maybe tomorrow the theater could be dark, and that wouldn't be a bad thing.

And then I'd wake up again.

For a week I was like this.

Mrs. Williams tried to pull me out of myself. She stopped me once in the laundry room, where I wasn't doing any laundry. I was just listening to the machines.

"Don't do any good to stew," she said. "Come on and let me fix you a meal."

"Thanks, but I have plans."

"What? You gonna go down to the bus stop and listen to the traffic?"

"Passes the time."

"Time heals all wounds."

"Wounds all heels," I corrected. "Groucho Marx said that."

"Never liked Groucho Marx. Now Phyllis Diller, there was a funny lady."

Somehow, I went to church on Sunday. Maybe it was a life raft thing. I'd been having a recurring nightmare. It went like this:

I am on board a luxury liner making its way across the Atlantic. The Atlantic Ocean is the scarier ocean, of course. Pacific meaning "peaceful" and all. It is much too placid for a nightmare.

Also, the Atlantic seems colder. I grew up sloshing around in the Pacific on hot, Southern California days. It is the type of ocean that embraces you; the Atlantic couldn't care less.

Anyway, it's night on this cruise and everybody is dressed up in evening clothes, like Cary Grant and Deborah Kerr in *An Affair to Remember,* and there's a party going on. I seem to float through it, looking for someone. No one sees me.

I am like a ghost, and I am looking for my daughter.

She is not here among the guests. In my dream-mind I reason that, of course, she should be in bed. It is late at night, after all. And in the way you shift locations in dreams, I find I am going through the door to my stateroom, the stateroom I share with Maddie, sure that I will find her soft, brown hair and calm face on the pillow on the bed.

She is not there.

I begin to panic. Where is she? Has she just wandered off, sleepily? Or has something more sinister taken place? Has someone, in fact, stolen into this room and taken her?

My dream takes me through the stateroom corridors, up the steps, deck by deck, until I am outside in the chill, running a complete circle around the ship.

No one pays me any mind. There is light fog on the deck, and the upper-crust people strolling around—it always seems like a 1930s black-and-white movie at this point in the dream—give me rebuking looks.

I stop to ask a man, in top hat and tails like Fred Astaire, if he's seen a little girl tonight. He huffs, does not answer, and my panic expands.

Maybe she's fallen off!

I try to scream for help, but only manage a low moan (I am sure that is what comes out of my throat as I dream).

I run to the stern and look over into the dark, churning ocean. Leaning over, desperate to see something, anything, I fall off.

Down into the black nothing of the sea.

Flapping my arms, I scream. And now it is full-blooded, desperate, dying.

No one hears.

I scream again. Only the sound of the wake slapping at my ears comes back in answer.

The stern of the ship is getting farther and farther away.

Please! Somebody!

And then I see her.

Maddie.

She is looking over the stern, looking for something. Or someone. Me! She is looking for me. I am lost to her, and she is looking.

Maddie!

She does not hear, and then twin shadows appear next to her. I know one of them. Her mother. The other is a man, and it is not me. I know who it is.

The two of them enfold Maddie in their arms. She falls into them with comfort and joy.

The lights of the ship become pinpricks in the death shroud of night. Farther and farther away it goes, then disappears altogether.

Now all that is left is darkness and night and me treading water, and knowing that there is nothing to be done. I am lost in the middle of the freezing ocean, not a lifeboat in sight.

There is no one to save me, no one to hear me.

I had this dream five times in one week.

So I went to church.

I saw Nikki but didn't talk to her. I'm sure she took it as embarrassed silence. I took it as not wanting to have anything to do with anything human. The sermon that day droned on like commercials on the car radio during a long commute—you hear the noise but none of the message stays with you.

Then one night things changed.

I forget who it was who said if a story starts to drag, just bring in a guy with a gun. That means a sudden change in the plot.

In my own sorry story line the sudden change was a shoe box in the back of my closet. I was looking for an old pair of boots. I found them, dusty and black, in the rear corner. As I pulled them out I saw a pink shoe box. Clearly not mine or Paula's, because of the size.

Maddie's.

I grabbed it. When I got it out into the light, I saw it had a rubber band around it and something written in crayon. In the unmistakable hand of my daughter, it said: DADYS BEREED TRESER.

I did everything I could to keep my heart from bursting. I removed the rubber band carefully, so it wouldn't break, because I didn't want anything that Maddie had touched to break. Slowly, I removed the top of the shoe box.

The first thing I saw was a little kush ball, red and yellow rubber strings together in a sphere. She loved those things, so it was no small gift. I picked it up, smelled it, and rubbed it against my cheek.

There was a nickel in the box. Treasure indeed. I decided I would tape that nickel to the refrigerator.

Last of all was a paper, a piece ripped off a yellow legal pad. I turned it over and saw the crayon drawing. Three stick people. A man, a woman, a little girl. Holding stick hands. A building in the background, roughly the shape of our apartment complex.

And above the building, where the sun would have been, a heart. With light rays coming from it, down toward the three stick people holding hands.

I lost it then. I was thankful I was alone in a closet.

– 6 –

Even before she said anything, I knew Alex had bad news. It was the look in her eye, like her cat had been run over by a cement truck. I was the cat.

"Sit down, Mark." Alex looked trapped in her own office. She'd called me that morning and said I needed to come in. Try as I might I couldn't get her to talk to me over the phone.

"Give it to me." I made no move to sit or even move.

"Please, sit. We need to talk."

"She gets Maddie, right? All Maddie, all the time."

"Yes."

The word hit like one of those anvils that drops on Wile E. Coyote in the cartoons. Now I sat, pushed down by the weight of it. And then I got that feeling, the one that comes with my nightmare, when I'm in the sea at night as the ship pulls farther and farther away. Gets me in the pit of the stomach and stays there, even after I wake up.

"Why?" It sounded like a stupid question, considering how I'd messed up in court.

"That's the way the judge decided. We can appeal."

"What did it? What was the thing that did it?"

"He looked at the totality of the circumstances, which is what he's supposed to do. We both know it didn't look good."

"What about the lying witness? That didn't help."

"It was not emphasized in the decision, but certainly that hurt."

"And what if he admits he lied?"

"How is he going to do that?"

"I might convince him."

Alex cocked her head at me. "Are you not telling me something again?"

I put my hands up. "Relax. I don't know where he is. But I'm going to find him."

Sighing, Alex said, "Mark, listen. You have been through an ordeal, a bad one. There is still hope. There's still more we can do within the system. If you start doing dumb things, I won't be able to help you. And you may not get to see Maddie at all."

"At all?"

"If you'll just listen. You still get monitored visits, Mark."

"Oh yeah, and we know how great those things are."

"It's better than nothing."

"I don't know if it is. I couldn't stand it happening the same way again." I looked at the ceiling for a moment. "I'll take it."

"But there's a condition."

I looked back at Alex as if she were Torquemada ready to twist the rack again.

She said, "You are to enroll in an anger management program before you see Maddie again."

"Anger management?"

"That's right. There are programs that are court approved that—"

"I have to go through some stupid program to see my daughter?"

Alex closed her eyes, then opened them again. "The sooner you start, the sooner we can set up a visit."

Oh yeah, I was going to start all right. I was going to kick the life out of something before the night was through, and then I'd worry about managing the old anger.

I thought if God was in front of me, say like a burning bush, I'd kick that bush, too.

"You have not responded well to setbacks," Alex said.

"Thank you."

"You want it straight, or do you want it namby-pamby?"

"Namby-pamby."

"Sorry, you're not going to get it from me. I didn't get to this point, advising clients, by short-shrifting. You have got to get yourself together."

Her words reminded me of that scene from *Tootsie,* when Dustin Hoffman is told by his agent that he has to get some therapy because he's too difficult for anyone to work with. So Hoffman puts on a dress.

I considered that option, too.

MANAGING

– 1 –

Anger management. It sounded so eighties, so Richard Simmons. Get all touchy-feely and you're a model of calm. You come out wearing a leotard and passing out flowers at the airport.

But it was what I needed to get a shot at seeing Maddie. It took me a couple of days, but I finally accepted that. So I was going to do it. In fact, I was going to be the best manager of anger the world had ever seen, because nothing was going to keep me from my daughter. I was going to become the best father the world had ever seen, the kind of guy Maddie would love again, forever.

And I knew I had an anger problem. I wasn't anxious to dig too deep about it, but I'd take it as it came.

Turns out what came was some advice. Which hit me like a truck doing seventy.

The first class I went to met, wouldn't you know, at a church, a Methodist in North Hollywood.

There were ten of us that first night, not counting the facilitator. His name was Stanley; he was about fifty, and looked like a commercial for mellow. He had a salt-and-pepper mustache, and his voice was calm as a pond.

We sat in a circle in metal chairs. Stanley kicked off the evening with a welcome, then said, "We have a new member tonight. This is Mark."

Everybody said *Hi, Mark.*

"We don't make anybody talk here," Stanley said, "if they don't want to. If you want to share anything about yourself, Mark, we'd all be happy to hear it. What we say in here, stays here."

Fair enough. "Well, I'm here because I've been told I have an anger issue—isn't that the way you're supposed to put it? And a judge says I need to deal with it if I want to see my daughter. Custody fight and all that."

Several heads nodded. I was among friends.

One guy on my left, whose name I would later learn was Rick, said, "I'm trackin' ya, bud. Been through that sweatbox myself."

From the look on his face, it was a painful experience, but he seemed . . . resigned. Did I even want to feel resigned? Not at the moment, but I'd work my way into it. I just kept thinking about Maddie.

"The way we like to start," Stanley explained, "is to go around the circle and see how people handled situations this week, things that might have made them angry, or did in fact make them angry, and how they handled it. Our big saying here, Mark, is 'In your anger, do not sin.' Anger is an emotion, it comes of its own volition. It's what we do with the anger that counts."

And so around they went. Each of the guys was open about their struggles and victories, and by the time it got to me I was feeling pretty good about this crowd. It was like there was nothing phony about them.

So when it came back to me I let them know the whole story. Everything. And it felt good, like letting a big sack of rocks off my back.

When it was over, we helped ourselves to some Famous Amos chocolate chip cookies and coffee from a big urn. Stanley let me know that I'd just given a very promising first session and said I'd made good progress.

It all was positive, upbeat. Until I got outside the door.

Rick stopped me. "I'll walk to the parking lot with you."

He was a big guy, did construction work. Looked, in fact, like he could tear a mattress in half with his hands. Or teeth.

"You're here under court order?" he said.

"Yeah. You?"

"Oh yeah. My old lady dragged me in. Domestic violence. They let me off with a fine and community service, and this deal." He jerked his big thumb back toward the church.

"What do you think of it?" I said. "Stanley and the whole thing?"

Rick shrugged. "Good as anything, I guess. Won't do jack squat for your case, though."

"What?"

"Listen, my friend, once they've got you going to this, it's like admitting you're a child molester or something. No way a judge is going to change his mind on the custody deal. They're too afraid somebody like us is going to end up killing the kid or the spouse, and then they're up for reelection with that hanging over their heads. Nope, we're up a creek, pal."

"So what's the point?"

"There is no point, that's the whole thing. The system's set up to squash guys like you and me like bugs. We're here because the court makes us, and it's better than getting time in the cooler. But it's all over."

Suddenly, LA at night seemed like a giant vacuum, sucking my ribs out.

"No," I said. "This is going to work. I'm going to get to see my daughter."

He shrugged again.

"You believe in the God part of all this?" I said.

"Like the higher power deal? Nah."

"Well I do. I have to. It's got to work."

"Just keep telling yourself that, man."

I did keep telling myself that. Over and over, for the next several days.

I told myself that at Josephina's. I told Roland.

God was going to get me through this, because I was in the right. God was going to overrule the judge. I'd wait them all out, Paula and Troncatti and the judge—and Maddie, too. I'd earn her trust back, one visit at a time.

She'd have to remember the good times. The moon dance. The buried treasure. You couldn't just rip those out of a child's head, if that's what they were trying to do.

Even though a little voice, sounding like Linda Blair in *The Exorcist,* kept suggesting they could, oh they could. Day after day they could feed her whatever line they wanted about me and the acid of that would coat Maddie's mind, burning away all of the good things.

It was enough to drive a guy with an anger problem into kicking a baby seal. What kept me sane was knowing that a visit with Maddie would be coming soon.

Meanwhile, my only job was to keep it together, check in with my group, show the court proof of attendance and all that. *Ruff ruff.* See Mark jump. See Mark jump through hoops.

I didn't care if the hoops were on fire. Just as long as I got to see my daughter.

– 2 –

"Daddy, I can't sleep."

"What's the matter?"

"I miss Mommy."

"So do I."

"I'm scared for her."

"Scared?"

"What if she falls in the ocean?"

"She won't. And even if she does, she'll have a floatie."

"How do you know?"

"Because Mommy's smart, like you, and she'll think of that."

"You're smart, aren't you, Daddy?"

"Sure I am. I'm smart enough to be your daddy, aren't I?"

"Then if you're smart, tell me how to go to sleep."

"You crawl right up here with me. I'll sing to you until you sleep."

"Please don't sing, Daddy."

"All right, no singing. What would you like me to do?"

"Just be with me."

The day before the monitored visit I went to Ralph's and bought a bag of chocolate chips and all the ingredients needed to make cookies—butter, flour, eggs. I could have snagged Pillsbury pre-made dough and slapped them on a cookie sheet (which I also bought at the store), but that would have been cheating. In my mind at least.

I wanted to make these cookies from scratch, for Maddie, to be able to tell her I did it all by myself—what she used to say when she first tied her shoes or did her own braids.

No one will mistake me for some guy on the Food Network, but I whipped up some pretty good dough. I ate a couple of scoopfuls myself, and it tasted right. I preheated the oven, following the directions on the bag of chocolate chips, and spooned out the dough on to the sheet.

The first batch came out smelling as sweet as you please, a party in my nostrils. I couldn't wait and picked up one of the warm beauties before it was cool enough, and put the sloggy thing in my mouth, chasing it with milk. Heaven.

I made another batch, let them cool. I poured another glass of milk and had about six of them. Then I put the rest in a big baggie and secured it with a twist tie.

I was ready to meet my daughter.

But not ready to sleep.

I just couldn't, so I paced around the apartment, TV infomercials softly playing in the background. At various times I could have been a real estate millionaire, sculpted my body using a machine made mostly of rubber, become a master chicken chef with the touch of a button, or emerged wrinkle free after subjecting myself to weeks of some new goop from Sweden.

None of that appealed to me. Instead, I tried to appeal to God. I tried to pray, but the words kept failing me. My mind was all over. I think I know what it must be like to be in a cell in solitary confinement.

I needed help and knew who to call.

"Hi, Nikki."

There was a pause on the other end of the phone. "Mark?"

"Sorry it's late."

"That's okay. Is everything all right?"

"I'm going to see my daughter tomorrow."

"Oh, that's fantastic. So does that mean you have—"

"It's a monitored visit. I'm still on notice with the court. There's stuff my lawyer is working on. I thought you might pray. There's something wrong with Maddie."

"What is it?" Her voice was full of concern. I wanted to be with her. It was good I wasn't.

"I think Paula and Troncatti are getting into Maddie's head."

"How?"

"I don't know, but the last time Maddie was so different. I've heard stories about parents who try to turn their children against the spouse they're divorcing. When a kid is Maddie's age, it's easy, I understand. I need Maddie to see that I'm the same father she once couldn't get enough of."

"Of course I'll pray."

I didn't say anything for a couple of seconds. "I don't have many friends left in this town."

"You have a family. Here at church."

Family. Was that even possible?

"Thanks," I said.

"Try to get some sleep," Nikki said.

Fat chance.

When I got off the phone I went out on the balcony. The moon was almost full and I could feel the memory of Maddie in my arms. And I just looked up at the sky, and in my head some words flashed.

Okay, God, I don't want to be a star. I want Maddie. I want to be part of her life. I don't know why you let the Troncattis of the world have all the success and never take them down. I don't care anymore. I don't know why you took Paula away. I know I'm not supposed to hate anybody, but I do. But I'll give that all up if you'll just get me back with Maddie. Just please, please, give me my daughter back, and let her remember the way things were and make her want to be with me, God. Is that a deal? Just make it happen. Please, please, please.

– 3 –

Seeing Renard J. Harper again was like a family reunion. He greeted me with a warm handshake and a smile. Called me Mr. Gillen.

"How you doing?" I said.

"Better'n most, not as good as some," Harper said. "How you been?"

"Model citizen, baby."

Harper laughed, the way a friend does when he wants to encourage you. We were in the parking lot at Woodley Park, where they have a man-made lake and ducks. Maddie loved ducks.

I was anxious to tell Harper what I'd been up to. "Been doing anger management, cleaning up my act. No driving wild. No smashing bottles."

"All right!"

"I mean, you've got to look at the positive, right?"

"Always."

"And that's what I'm doing. I know it's not going to be easy, but I'm doing it for Maddie."

"That's the way."

"Going to let her take it slow with me, I won't force anything. Just sit and listen. Won't even say anything if that's the way she wants it. Just being with her, that's the first step, right?"

"You're gonna be all right, man. I know it."

I showed him the bag of chocolate chip cookies I'd made. Opened it up so he could smell them.

"Take one," I said.

"You sure?"

"Come on. See if I passed the test."

He smiled, took a cookie. A moment after the bite he nodded his approval. "Good job. Oh yes. My mama used to bake all the time. Cookies. Cakes. That's why I'm in such good shape." He patted his tummy, which was round in a comforting sort of way.

There was a little bit of wind today, making tiny whitecaps on the lake. A couple of paddleboats were out there. And the ducks, of course. Maddie and I would crumble up a cookie or two and feed them. Real duckie treats.

We took a bench near the parking lot. "You think it'll be better this time?" I said. He wouldn't know, but I had to hear somebody say it. I was so nervous my hands were shaking.

"I'm sure it'll be," Renard J. Harper said. "All you have to do is relax."

"Yeah. Right."

"Take a deep breath. Think about happier times."

"When were those?" I said with a laugh.

"Oh, I can remember." Harper smiled. "Radio days. Back before rock took over everything. I remember my mom listening to the radio, and the DJs saying simple things like, 'Here's Nat King Cole singing "Stardust."' And then you'd hear Nat King Cole, and then the DJ'd say, 'That was Nat King Cole and that great old number, "Stardust."' You're too young to remember."

"I've heard of Nat King Cole," I protested.

"You had real groups back then, too. Frankie Valli and the Four Seasons. Sally Jesse and the Raphaels—"

"Sally Jesse . . . you're messing with me!"

"Just wanted to see if you were listening."

And I was, and I wanted to kiss Renard J. Harper. He was playing with me, helping me forget my nerves, setting me at ease. The guy was a saint. He even sang me a little more of his country song, "You'd Be So Nice to Slide Home To."

When I looked at my watch, I was surprised to see twenty minutes had passed. It was now 11:40. Maddie was ten minutes late.

"What happens if she doesn't come?" I said.

"Don't worry. She'll be here. If they don't bring her, that'll look bad. You haven't done a thing, and I can see what it's doing to you. Just relax."

But I couldn't. I kept fiddling with the twist tie on the bag of cookies.

"Tell me about your acting," Harper said.

"I don't think acting's for me anymore," I said.

"No way."

"Yeah."

"What makes you say that?"

I shrugged. "The business, I guess. So much of it now is based on plugging in the right look. There's not much respect for acting anymore. I mean, actors who wanted to make it in Hollywood used to go to New York and train on the stage. Or the studio would make them take acting lessons. Now some guy who looks like he had his jaw cut for Mount Rushmore walks off a soap and into the movies because he's got some fan base made up of teenage girls."

"Not like you have an opinion or anything."

"Did I run off at the mouth there?"

"I like a man with opinions."

"Funny, when I was first with Paula, she said the same thing." I stopped a second, feeling transported. "I told her the same thing about acting and she agreed, and we used to talk about doing some stage work together, but of course realized there's no money in that. Pretty soon, it always comes down to money. And now she's got it."

The wind was all I heard for a long moment. Then I looked at my watch.

"Could be traffic," Harper said.

But the knot in my stomach was telling me it wasn't traffic. It was telling me Maddie wasn't going to be here. Period.

It was at 11:55 that Harper gave in. He took out his cell phone and made a call. I couldn't listen to that. I walked to the edge of the lake and started tossing a few cookie crumbs to the ducks. I became instantly popular. There was so much delighted quacking I didn't hear Harper walk up to me.

When I turned around and saw his face my soul dropped.

"Bad news," he said.

– 4 –

Alex's receptionist looked at me, eyes wide, and said, "She's with someone. If you can call—"

"Get her," I said. "Now."

The poor girl must have thought I was strapped with a bomb or something. She looked at me that way, got up, and sort of backed into Alex's office.

A moment later Alex herself came out, took one look at me, didn't say a word. She went back into her office and walked out a middle-aged woman who seemed confused but understanding.

"I'll call you with the details," Alex told the woman, who gave me a look before she went out the door. I could only wonder what she thought.

"Come in," Alex told me.

The moment I stepped in the office I couldn't stop shuddering—shaking wildly like a man caught in the Arctic in his underwear. The rage was so intense behind my eyes I couldn't focus. For a moment I couldn't even speak.

"I got a call from Jennings," she said.

"What—"

"Please have a seat, Mark."

"No way."

"Are you going to just stand there?"

"No, I might walk around a little."

"I know what you must be feeling, believe me."

"I don't think you do, Alex. I was sitting there waiting for Maddie. Waiting for her with all the ducks. You know what happened? I stepped in duck doo. It was perfect. I was standing there rubbing my shoe on the grass as Harper tells me they're not coming. They're not going to let me see Maddie anymore. They think they can pull this—"

"Mark, please—"

"I'm sick of this! What are they trying to do?"

"Wear you down."

Yes. Exactly. The words rang true. Wear me down emotionally and financially. They were certainly doing a great job.

"What can I do?" I said. "I'm running out of money to pay you, Alex, and I'm not going to be able to afford you from my tips."

"Don't worry about money. I can still petition the court."

"Petition?"

"They may award reasonable attorney's fees."

"And may not?"

"Maybe."

"I can't ask you to take that risk."

"Forget that for now." There was something in Alex's eyes that told me she was not being completely level with me. Not that she was deceptive, just not willing to give me the whole nine yards.

"Alex, what's going on? Did Jennings tell you—"

"Why don't we schedule a hearing date, then you and I can—"

"What aren't you telling me?" I hit the edge of her desk with my fist. It hurt but the pain didn't matter to me.

"If you sit down, I'll tell you."

The words were ominous in her mouth, like an executioner taking an order for a last meal. I threw myself into a chair.

Alex paused a moment and took a breath. "You've got to understand something, Mark. This happens in more cases than I care to think about. Most often it's a desperate lie."

"What is?"

"Paula is accusing you of sexually molesting your daughter."

– 5 –

There's a long stretch of asphalt in the rural part of Orange County called the Ortega Highway. It meanders along an old Indian trail, past dark green oaks and golden grasslands, up into the Santa Ana Mountains where you can still glimpse the occasional mountain lion or a red-tailed hawk circling around in the sky. As the highway climbs up into the hills you have rock walls on one side and steep canyon drop-offs on the other.

It's a narrow snake of road, and some say it's the most dangerous road in the state of California. Sections of it have catchy nicknames like Dead Man's Curve, Ricochet Rim, and Blood Alley.

That's where I drove after Alex gave me the news.

Alex told me this was a desperate ploy, this sexual molestation charge. That it wouldn't hold up, that we had remedies. But I no longer believed her. I no longer believed anything. If you couldn't trust God, if you could pray and not get anything in return, how could you trust a lawyer?

I drove. I had to drive, and I was drawn to the road where there are more accidents every year. It's one of only two main arteries connecting homes in Riverside County with jobs in Orange County, so the highway lures more and more lunatic commuters every year. They speed, drift over the center line, pass illegally—even on blind curves—to advance their place in the string of cars, trucks, and big rigs.

Sexually molesting my own daughter?

My insides were exploding as I gunned the Accord. Drive, drive, drive, figure out what to do.

I finally reached the crest in the grade and thought for a moment about plowing through the guardrail, over the side. Compromising, I stopped at a turnout, got out of my car, and looked over the side. Scrubby pines stuck up like spears. It didn't look like lovely nature.

I started to think thoughts that scared me. Would anybody care if they found my body, bloody and bruised, at the bottom of a gorge? What would it do to Maddie? It couldn't be any worse than what Paula and Troncatti were doing to her. No doubt they had her convinced she had been molested. And they probably had some quack doctor to say whatever Bryce Jennings wanted him to say.

I was history. The allegations would go out over the news, and whatever scrap of reputation I had left would be like gum on the bottom of a shoe.

Then I remembered something Nikki told me. It was the word *hope*. She'd said that the one thing Christians had that atheists didn't was hope. If you were convinced that the universe was a great big void, and when you died you became worm food, hope was a pipe dream, a deception, a ruse.

Yeah, I thought as I stared down at the gorge, but maybe hope was not enough to live on anymore.

What kept me from jumping was an old familiar feeling. Good old hatred. And a picture of Troncatti feeling satisfied, the great director directing his greatest scene: the death of a jerk.

I got back in my car and drove to the ocean. And that's where I gave God my ultimatum.

Standing in the sand, looking at the water that Maddie loved so much, I just cranked out a prayer.

I don't know what you want from me. I don't even know what to say to you. Why won't you make it stop? Why won't you give me some sign that you're there, that you'll help me out a little here? What's going on, I want to know—I have to know, so tell me. Or I'm just going to go on by myself and forget everything. It isn't worth it if I can't have Maddie. Is that clear enough? Then be clear back to me, will you? Finally?

I stayed at the beach till the sun went down. I didn't hear any voice from the sky. The only thing I felt was the wind, and it got cold out there.

But on the way back to the apartment I found myself behind a slow-moving car, an old Chrysler, one that had seen its best days when George Bush the elder was president. What caught my eye was the faded bumper sticker it had stuck on its old chrome:

I Still Miss My Ex—but My Aim Is Improving.

From some dark, dim corner of my mind, came this laugh. The only thing I can compare it to is that famous laugh from Boris Karloff's *The Mummy*, where Bramwell Fletcher goes screamingly, laughingly crazy at the sight of the walking dead. My laugh was just like that—maniacal, all consuming. For about one minute I laughed, until I realized cars were honking behind me. I sped up, knowing I'd crossed over some line I had never quite seen, never wanted to see.

And I started wondering, *Is that the sign, God? Is that it?*

The Edge

~ 1 ~

Alex called me the next morning, checking up on me, telling me to hang in there. And pray. I was way ahead of her, though I didn't tell her about my ultimatum to God.

I also didn't tell her that I hadn't slept all night and was, in fact, feeling like another person. Like some big part of me had been yanked out and twisted too much to get back in.

Roland knew something was wrong when I sleepwalked through the lunch shift at Josephina's. He tried to get me to talk but I wouldn't. It was like I didn't want *anybody* talking to me. No personal contact. Roland invited me to come hear him play that night and I think I only grunted.

After the shift, though, I got some contact I did want.

My cell phone chimed as I was driving home. The voice on the other end was smooth and dark, like black honey. "I'm the guy Mr. Ayers told you about."

"Mr. Ayers?" I said. "I don't recall—"

"Maybe he didn't tell you."

"Tell me what?"

"About me."

A Hummer nearly cut me off with a lane change. "Hold it," I said. "Who are you?"

"The guy Mr. Ayers hired."

"To do what?"

"Find things out."

My hand started to sweat as I held the phone to my ear. I remembered that Milo Ayers said he would help me out. I guess this was it. "Are you like a private investigator?"

"Like that," he said. "Yeah."

"And what have you found out?"

"A couple of things. You were looking for Ron Reid, right? Your old man?"

"Yes."

"Give me a couple of days on that. I might have an address for you."

The thought made me anxious, as if I wasn't that already.

"The other thing is that Italian and your wife."

Now I almost rear-ended the Hummer, which was still in front of me. "What about them?"

"His house is on Dakota up by—"

"I know where it is."

"I was watching the place last night. There's a big slope down the street, another guy's house but it's way back, I could scope the Italian's place from there." He pronounced it *Eye-talian*, which I found odd and amusing at the same time. "You can see right into the pool area and into a big window of the house."

"Did you see anything?"

"I'm getting to that. I think I saw your wife, or is she your ex-wife?"

"Ex, I guess, though it isn't official yet."

"Bummer. Anyway, I saw her sit in a chair and it was like she was talking to somebody. Then she stood up and clenched her fists and started screaming at whoever it was. That's all I could see."

"How could you see this?"

"Nightscope. No big deal. But it just looked to me like there was a little trouble in paradise."

A scene played out in my mind, of Paula screaming at Troncatti, and it was vivid. I could almost hear the voices shouting.

"Is that all?" I said.

"Yeah. I'll call you about your old man."

He cut out before I got his name. But that wasn't heavy on my mind at the moment. What was heavy was Paula. And Maddie. In a house with Troncatti. And something bad was going on, I was sure.

But what could be done about it? The police? Tell them to go out there because some PI had told me he was snooping and saw Paula upset about something?

Sure. In a case where I was being accused of sexually molesting my own daughter.

No. I had to do something. *The Lord helps those who help themselves* kept going through my mind. That's not in the Bible, I know that now. I should have known it then.

Instead of going home I drove down to Jamy's Optics and picked out the best scope they had. LN–24 Night Vision. Set me back $1,200. They took Visa.

A sweet scope, the LN–24. Computerized proximity sensor, digital control, long-range infrared illuminator. You can see a bug scratch itself in total darkness from three hundred yards away. The guy at the store gave me a half-hour seminar on how to use it. By the time he was through I was a black belt in light amplification and infrared magnitude.

"You doing some PI work?" the guy asked me.

"Just for myself."

"You could go into business with that thing."

"I just may do that."

I poured myself into my car and took the freeway to the 405, taking the loop toward the west side. I got off at Sunset just under the looming gaze of the Getty Museum. It was up there on its perch, looking down at the city, me especially. I wondered if there were other people there, taking a break from the masterpieces of European art, to care about what went on below.

The traffic on Sunset was backed up. The sun was beating down and made the car feel like a kid's lunchbox left on the playground. My air-conditioning wasn't working and the flow through the open windows was nothing more than hot breath. There was even an accident—a bumper thumper around Roxbury—that gave me no choice but to take my sweet time.

It also gave me the opportunity to think a little bit about what I was going to do once I got near Troncatti's house.

Like driving the car right through the gate. Ram that baby like it was those big battering rams they used to break down castle doors with. I'd smash in and drive through the front door, lay down some rubber in the living room, hop out and say, "Hey, guys, nice to see ya."

Then Maddie would come running through the living room, giggling loudly like she always did when I came home, and jump into my arms and say, "Daddy, let's go for a ride."

"Sure honey," I'd say. "But before we do I have a little business to attend to." I'd go over to Troncatti and I'd grab him by the lapels of his imported shirt and throw him through one of those big plate glass windows that surrounded his house like vanity mirrors.

And then I'd turn to Paula and I'd say, "Are you ready to forget all this and come home?"

And she would quietly nod her head, give me a kiss on the cheek, and then all of us would get back in the car and drive away from the Troncatti house once and for all.

That's the way you dream of revenge in LA, I guess. With real audience appeal and plenty of shattering glass.

Traffic opened up a little bit past Roxbury, but it was still a long, slow drive until I got to Dakota. As I turned the steering wheel, it slipped in my fingers. I could feel the sweat stains in my armpits. If a cop would have stopped me, I'm sure he would've thought I was some lunatic who'd forgotten to take his meds but had, somehow, stolen a car.

I continued to climb up the curving road. Every house I passed seemed to be an immaculate example of how perfect people live. I saw a gardener, a Latino, hunched over a clump of yellow flowers in front of a huge, Tudor mansion. He looked up at me when I passed, and his eyes seemed to say *I know you're an intruder but what am I going to do about it?*

When I got near Troncatti's house I almost slammed on the brakes. What if Paula and Troncatti and Maddie were outside the gate? What if they were in the limo with Igor at the wheel?

And what if my daughter saw me, her eyes meeting mine, and she turned away in disgust? I don't think I could've handled that.

But with my pulse pumping, I drove on. I had to. This was the only thing left for me to do. No exit, no turning back.

I heaved a little sigh of relief when I saw there was no one out on the driveway. Place was as closed up as a bankrupt theater. The gates were shut and some thick, visual barrier had been put up, keeping gawkers from being able to see inside.

I drove on, looking for that slope the guy had told me about. I found it at the bottom of another private driveway that coiled up a hill. There was a fancy mailbox at the bottom of this driveway—a smaller version of a mansion set atop a twisting chain.

Stopping my car, I got out to take a quick look. That's when a dog started barking.

I couldn't see the house where the sound was coming from, but it sounded like a house further up the road. It was a big dog, too, and from where we were in this canyon, his *woof* echoed around like a big, pounding Salvation Army drum.

I wondered if the dog barked all the time anyway, or if it was just me. Because if I got up the hill at night and no one saw me, but this dog kept beating the drum, there'd probably be a 9-1-1.

Hey God, I thought. *Maybe you can at least take care of a dog for me, huh?*

– 2 –

And what a night.

I drove up there again and it was like Oscar night at Troncatti's. Major party going on. Cars and limos driving up to the big gate where a couple of burly guys with earpieces would motion them in. There was even a paparazzo flashing pictures as fast as he could with no one making any effort to stop him. I figured this was part of Troncatti's publicity machine at work.

My Accord was definitely out of character, and I drove on by the gate, catching a quick peek of the inside. For a quick second I thought about jumping out and just running on in. Surprise.

Instead, I drove on, well down the street, then parked. If I kept my eyes open I could get to Checkpoint Charlie—my name for the hillside where I was going to watch the house—without being seen.

I was all made up in my ninja gear, which consisted of black tennis shoes, black Levi's, and a complementary black T-shirt I'd gotten from watching a taping of *That '70s Show*. I even wore a black knit hat, the kind OJ reportedly wore when he went out after his ex-wife. Yep, this was going to be a real Hollywood story.

The rest of the street was relatively quiet. But from Troncatti's I could hear the strains of classic rock. I think it was the Stones, who I never liked. Fitting.

The big dog wasn't woofing. I wondered if that was a sign from God.

Then, with my scope around my neck, I scurried up the hill.

From where I was positioned, headlights from oncoming cars would not illuminate me. The only thing that could find me would be an LA police helicopter shining its high beams down, not an unlikely scenario. That is, if someone reported something strange happening in their neighborhood.

I had a good view of the swimming pool that was lit up in a light blue shade. All around in the yard were torches set off with flame. It looked like the Tahiti set in *Mutiny on the Bounty*.

And all sorts of people were milling around. A bartender in a fancy red coat had a setup near the pool house. Guests were swilling booze and laughing it up. And why not? This was a Hollywood party. At the home of the hottest director in the world. Exclusive. No outsiders allowed. Except I got to watch everything.

There was no sign of Paula or Troncatti for the longest time. I was beginning to think they left the house to an army of lackeys for a weekend without them. And I kept wondering where Maddie was.

Please God, let me see Maddie.

Troncatti finally made an appearance, walking out of the main house and throwing his hands up in the air to every guest that approached him. It was like he was greeting some long-lost brothers. Or maybe it was more like the pope receiving supplicants crawling on their bellies to kiss the great man's ring.

For a few moments I fantasized that the scope I was looking through was attached to a high-powered rifle. I felt a chill. Had I really been reduced to thinking like this? Something like a voice in my head, whispery but strong, was telling me not to do this, to get out of there, to keep from slipping further into the hole I was digging. Was it the voice of God? I shook it off and just kept watching.

Paula came out a few minutes later. My throat clenched. It felt like she was five feet in front of me. She was in a form-fitting dress, bare shouldered in the warm night. Stunning.

But I noted she did not attach herself to Troncatti. That was surprising to me. I thought they were like trophies to each other, so it was strange they didn't make the rounds together. I thought they would be the perfect Hollywood couple, strolling arm in arm around a party greeting visitors.

But Paula and Troncatti did not come together. Not once.

Paula looked like she was in a good mood. Maybe too much of a good mood. She was laughing more than was normal for her, almost like she was putting on an act. But I thought I understood that. She was in a throng of real power brokers. That's what being

Troncatti's squeeze brought her. Who could fault her for trying to make an impression?

I could. Why wasn't she miserable, like me?

And where was Maddie? Was she inside that house right now? Alone, perhaps, watching TV? Could I slip in and quietly take her now?

My eyes started to feel heavy, so I turned my attention to Troncatti for a while. He was acting hyper, like he was on drugs or something. The guy never stopped moving. And another thing—he kept planting big old kisses on all the women. Not a friendly, nice-to-see-you kind. More like the hope-to-see-you-after-the-party variety. No wonder Paula wasn't hanging around with him. I almost felt bad for her.

Paula went back inside the house a couple of times. She also made several appearances at the bartender station. Paula had never been a big drinker, maybe a glass of wine with dinner sometimes. Now she was throwing the stuff down like Elizabeth Taylor in *Who's Afraid of Virginia Woolf?*

An hour and a half went by. I was feeling more than exhausted, but I willed myself to keep watching, because the party was in full swing. Some people fell into the swimming pool, fully clothed. That generated a great round of applause from the other guests. Yes, Hollywood is an entertaining town.

Some salsa dancing, very nineties, broke out. I could hear the music. And I could sure see Troncatti grinding against some shapely starlet types. Now I was not just tired; I started feeling sick.

I rolled on my back and tried to keep myself from crying out to the whole neighborhood.

The big dog barked.

I closed my eyes and just breathed. Breathed. And, at some point, I fell asleep.

I had no dreams.

When I woke up the dog wasn't barking anymore, and the moon had skipped over half the sky. And something was crawling on my face.

I sat up with a gasp and brushed whatever it was off. My neck was kinked and I was cold. And for a minute I didn't know where I was.

Then I grabbed my scope and looked down. The party was largely over. A few people were still scattered around, but the bartender was gone and the music was over.

No sign of Troncatti or Paula.

The guards were gone from the front gate, which I noted was slightly open now. Maybe they were around somewhere, but for a moment or two it felt like I could have walked right in.

Then I saw some movement in the house.

It was Paula. She had her back to the big front window. She stood, with fists clenched at her sides. And she was screaming something at somebody else in the room.

It was just like what the PI had described, happening all over again. My skin erupted in a million pinpricks.

Troncatti came into the picture, like an actor entering a scene. He grabbed Paula by the shoulders and shook her.

I squeezed the scope so hard my hands started hurting.

And then Antonio Troncatti slapped Paula across the face.

– 3 –

Even now I can't remember exactly how I managed to get in. My mind was like a volcano, one thought flowing into the next, a hot mess. I half remember charging through the gate and running past a man who was staggering near the pool. He may even have said something to me.

But everything came into focus when I opened the big white door and found myself standing in the same room with Paula and Troncatti.

I still had my expensive night scope around my neck. It kept thunking against my chest, stopping only when I did, a few feet from the happy couple.

Troncatti was speechless, his eyes filling with rage.

Paula was in shock. "Mark!"

Before I could say anything, Igor charged into the room. We made eye contact, and I reveled in his look. It was outraged, no doubt because I had managed to get into physical proximity with Troncatti.

He grabbed my arm. I yanked it away.

"It's all right, Farid." Troncatti waved his hand at Igor. "Leave him with us."

Igor looked almost injured, and he backed out of the room very reluctantly.

"Time we had a talk," Troncatti said. "One talk. You understand?" The last word sounded like *unnerstanna.*

I looked at Paula, who was now strangely silent. I say *strangely* because she was never one to back down—on screen or in real life. My nerves were crackling. For a moment we all stood there, like we were holding guns on each other.

Then Troncatti walked in a big semicircle around the room, looking at me, like he was sizing up a shot in one of his movies.

"You are not a pleasant man," he finally said. "Things go so much better if you are a pleasant one."

"You need a new writer," I said.

"You are in a lot of trouble, being here."

I looked over at Paula. "Am I in trouble?"

"You shouldn't have come here," she said.

"You are talking to me," Troncatti said. "Leave her out."

"You want to be left out, Paula?"

"Over here!" Troncatti hit his chest.

Paula looked a little scared. That made me angry. "I want to see my daughter."

Troncatti shook his head. "That has been decided already."

"You two can let me."

"No way," Troncatti said.

"I'm no threat to her. Paula, you know that."

"You shouldn't have come," she said.

"Why are you turning her against me? Why are you making up lies about abuse? What did I do, Paula?"

She didn't answer.

"There is no reason with you," Troncatti said. "I will call the police you don't get out."

I wasn't afraid of him. Foolish, yes. But there was nothing more anybody could do to me. I didn't care what happened. All I wanted was to say my piece to Paula. Even as Troncatti fished for his cell phone, I didn't move.

"He tell you what he did?" I said.

Paula was still silent, but this time she frowned.

"Or were you in on it?"

No answer. Troncatti was barking into his phone.

"You know about the part I was supposed to get?" I didn't take my eyes off Paula's. I didn't just see the beauty in them, I saw something else. A darkness. Like somebody had just shut off the lights.

"I was all set to get a lead on a new show at NBC." My voice was calm but strong. "They wanted me. They picked me. It was going to make me a star. And your lover had his agent get hold of the producer and ax me. He did that. Did you know?"

I couldn't tell from her face and dark eyes what she knew. All I knew was she was listening. But that wasn't enough for me. I took a step closer. "Did you know?"

There was a flicker in the eyes, like she might want to say something.

"Did you?" I was feeling tears stinging my eyes. "And you went along with it?"

We looked at each other. Her lower lip quivered a little, like there was a heavy word teetering on the edge.

And then Igor was back, grabbing me by the shirt.

"Farid will take you outside to wait for the police," Troncatti said.

I tried to jerk away, but the limo-driver–bodyguard held me fast. I was considering what to do next when I sensed someone else in the room.

Maddie.

She was standing on the upper level, looking down into the room. She had a robe on and her big eyes stared at us, like we were hyenas at the zoo.

"Maddie!" I screamed.

She turned quickly and ran away.

"Maddie!"

"Shut up," Troncatti said.

I put everything I could into an elbow to Igor's midsection. It was rock hard. But it got me loose for a split second.

I ran toward the stairs yelling, "Maddie! Maddie!"

I made it to the first step when my feet went out. Igor had me by the legs. My head thudded against the banister and my chest detonated in pain as I fell on the stairs with my scope under me.

For good measure, Igor let me have a fist to the left eye. Red opened up on my mind's screen like a special effect from a World War II movie. My head shot back to the hard edge of a step.

"Stop it!" Paula's voice came from across the room. "Let him go."

"Shut up!" Troncatti spouted.

"Just let him go," Paula pleaded.

"Farid, get him to the gate. Wait for the police."

As I was jerked to my feet, my head buzzing, I heard Paula say *Please* and Troncatti say *Shut up* again. What was left in me wanted to run over and grab the guy by the neck for talking to her like that, but what was left in me wasn't too strong. Igor had no trouble getting me out into the night.

"You try to run," he said, "I will break all your fingers."

– 4 –

"You want to tell me what you expected to do there?" the cop asked. He was a uniform, a sergeant, and we sat at his desk at the Santa Monica station. They'd given me Insta-Ice for the side of my face, which felt like a football after the extra point.

"Not particularly," I said.

"You want to be difficult?"

"Aren't you supposed to read me my Miranda rights or something?"

"You watch too much TV."

"What if I want a lawyer?"

"Do you?"

"No."

"Then why don't you tell me what you were doing in Troncatti's house."

"Trying to stop him from hitting my wife."

"You were trespassing."

The officer's name was Ruchlis. I wondered if he was a reasonable man.

"You have any children?" I asked.

He looked at me a little disappointed. "We're here to talk about you, not me."

"Look, I'm sorry I was on that scum's property. I didn't damage anything. In fact I'm the one with the black eye. But I'm not a criminal."

"What are you, Mr. Gillen?"

"Just a guy who's . . ."

"Go ahead." He seemed to want to listen.

"I just wanted to help her."

"Who?"

"My wife. And my daughter was in there, too."

"Is this a custody thing?"

"Yeah."

"You're supposed to go to court for that. You take things in your own hands it ends bad."

"It can't get any worse."

Another uniform walked over to the desk. "I need you for a second," he said.

"Just sit here," Ruchlis told me. He got up and walked a few steps away from the desk. I watched them talk and knew it had to do with me. Ruchlis looked over at me a couple of times while the other cop talked to him.

When he came back to the desk he sat down, looking almost upset. "You'd better call that lawyer after all," he said.

– 5 –

The Men's Central Jail in LA is not the place to plan a vacation. It's meat storage, a holding pen for as many accused as they can stuff into it. That results in more than a few disturbances among the inmates. But there's also a marketplace. Drugs are sold, deals made, even lives are occasionally traded.

I was booked, showered, garbed, and given a cell. It was the weekend, so I got to sit there for two days, waiting until Monday to go before a judge.

I did get my one phone call, and used it for Alex. She said she'd show up for the arraignment and bail hearing. But she did not sound happy about it. I couldn't blame her. It wasn't bad enough having a client who had permanent foot-in-mouth disease. Now he was a criminal.

I got the shakes getting shown to a cell. They got a little worse when I met my cell mate, a very large person named Ignacio. He had muscles in places where I don't even have places, and a face that had been on the business end of more than one fight. He told me he was in for beating up a guy in a bar who had dissed the Oakland Raiders, Ignacio's favorite team.

I decided to leave football out of our conversations. And we did have conversations. Or rather, Ignacio did. He loved to talk. He gave me an earful, especially when he found out why I was here.

"Trespass? You in here for that? Man, you getting the *dedo grande.*"

When I told him about Maddie, Ignacio actually got kind of brotherly. He said he had a daughter too, with his girlfriend. The girl's family took her back to Mexico to keep her away from Ignacio. Maybe just as well, he said, until he learned how to keep from hurting people who ticked him off.

"Got to get rid of the hate, man." Ignacio shook his very large head. "If I got hate, I use it. Got to get rid of it. So how'd you lose your daughter?"

Nervously, but then warming up, I gave him the story, warts and all, and he gave me another earful. "Man, you are stupid. You know how stupid you are? If there was a school for stupid people, you'd be the teacher, man."

I let him have his opinion.

"You let the system beat you up. You got to know how to play it." He went on to tell me all about how to beat an assault rap. Maybe that would come in handy if I ever came face-to-face with Troncatti.

That night I didn't get much sleep. There was a lot of noise in there, but mostly I couldn't sleep because I kept thinking about Maddie and Paula. And Troncatti.

And a lot about what Ignacio had said about hate. *Got to get rid of it.*

I didn't want to get rid of it. That was absolutely the last thing I had going for myself.

– 6 –

I woke up on Sunday with Ignacio talking to himself. Actually, I think he was singing, something about birds and guns. And he kept it up even while we were walking in the long line toward what they call breakfast in this place.

"You stay with me," Ignacio said. "I don't want you hurt."

That was a relief.

I was halfway through cold eggs and limp toast when they made the announcement that if anybody wanted to talk to a chaplain—and they had different kinds for different religious preferences—then you could sign up. And, after breakfast, I did.

Maybe I was halfway curious what a jail chaplain would have to say to somebody like me. Maybe I really wanted to hear some words of wisdom. Or maybe I just wanted to be relieved of Ignacio's rat-a-tat talk for a while.

Whatever the real reason, I was glad to get out of the cell and walked by a deputy down to an interview room. Inside I saw another inmate, only this one was dressed in civvies. I wondered how he'd gotten those clothes.

Then he introduced himself. "Chaplain Ray," he said.

He was the Christian chaplain? He was a muscular Latino, had a tattoo on his forearm and a shaved head.

"You're not the type we usually get in here," he said. "Mostly they look like me."

"How did you . . . ?"

He smiled. One of his front teeth was gold. "You believe a sweet face like this used to bust heads? When I got saved, I told God I was gonna do whatever it took to get back in here and talk to my people. Ten years ago. And now I'm talking. But like I said, you don't look like the type. So why don't you tell me how you find yourself in this place?"

For the second time in two days, the first being with my roommate in the cell, I told the story—of me and Paula and Maddie, of Troncatti, and everything I did about it. I sounded even more stupid this time around. I was glad Ignacio wasn't here. When I finished, I asked the chaplain, "So how stupid do you think I am?"

He shrugged. "About as stupid as David. Dude couldn't keep his eyes off the pretty girls. Brings one into the palace, gets her pregnant, tries to cover it up by killing her husband. And the guy is one of the heroes of the Bible. If God didn't use stupid people, he'd have a pretty tough choice about finding anybody."

"But I made a real mess of things, I mean, bad."

"Yeah, you did. Only question now is what're you gonna do about it?"

"What do you think I should do?"

"You told me you were going to a Bible study and church. What happened to that?"

"I tried it with God. I even prayed that he'd let me have my daughter. It didn't work out."

"So you walk away? Listen, you don't *try it* with God, like he's some cafeteria line and you don't get the dessert you wanted so you don't come back to the place. You got to grab hold with everything, like your life depends on it, which it does."

"But what does that even mean? I poured out my heart to God and got hammered."

"Pouring out your heart is a good thing, but it's not the only thing. It's not the place you stop. It's the place you start. You move on to where God wants you to be, which is in Jesus Christ."

"What do you mean, *in?*"

"It's what the Bible says. Listen." He reached for his leather Bible—which was as worn as any book I've ever seen with the cover still on—and flipped through it. I could see the pages marked up with different colored inks and highlighter pens. Every page was like a child's rainbow.

"'Therefore, if anyone is in Christ, he is a new creation; the old has gone, the new has come!' You see that? *In Christ.*"

I remembered that passage. Pastor Scott had used it in one of his sermons. Was this a telegram from God?

"Not outside," Chaplain Ray continued, "not looking in, not messing around, but making the big dive with your whole life into Christ. You give it up for him, and you don't look back, you don't keep things to yourself, you don't make it halfway. You spill out everything and admit that you can't make it on your own and that you want Jesus to be making it for you, and you don't mess around with sin anymore, which means trying to have everything your own way all the time and running around hating everybody, like your mother-in-law and this Italian dude. You make a decision and you ask Jesus to forgive you and make you right. And if you want to know how to do it, take a look at Psalm 51, which is the one David wrote after he murdered the guy and took his wife. And if you can say those words and mean them then you're going to be home free, understanding that Jesus is the one who died in your place on the cross."

"Whoa."

"I can keep talking, man. I'm just getting warmed up. But I don't want to talk to the wall. I want to know if you're gonna do anything about this."

My last line of defense flew up like a ragged cobweb. "I haven't got a Bible."

He reached for his coat, which was laid across a chair, and pulled out a brand new hand-sized Bible. "Now you do. Want to walk through it with me? I got time."

"I guess I'm not going anywhere, either."

I don't know how to explain what happened next. After we read a bunch of the Bible together, all of a sudden Chaplain Ray was praying over me and with me and I was praying to Jesus and it felt like a washing of my body, inside and out. And when we were done, I was still in jail, still in the jailhouse jumpsuit, I still didn't have Maddie, I still had a string of stupid things behind me—but I felt like there was a hand on me pulling me up from where I was to where I had to be.

Ray said, "When you get out of here, I want you to get your rear back in church. Got that?"

I nodded.

"You trust God. For everything. Your daughter. Your life. You ask him what to do. You get your face in the Bible. You trust God. You hearing me?"

"I'll try."

"No, man. You do it. I don't want to hear no excuse."

After all the ways I'd messed up, I knew I was full of excuses. And I knew the people I cared about, and who cared about me, could look at this and see only a thin jailhouse conversion.

But the trust thing hit me hardest. Chaplain Ray was right. I had to trust God this time, all the way, no matter what people thought.

And that's the way it was going to be, for Maddie's sake.

– 7 –

On Monday, Alex got me released O.R. after the arraignment, where she asked for a continuance. The deputy D.A. went right along with that, which seemed strange. Didn't they always fight for bail on *Law and Order*?

A few hours later, after I was officially sprung, I found out why.

Alex told me to come to her office, which I did.

"I've been talking to the D.A.'s office," Alex said. "They're ready to drop the filing."

Stunned but feeling a tiny glimmering of hope, I could only say, "Why?"

"Because there's a catch."

That brought me back to earth, but quick.

"I've got some papers here from Bryce Jennings," Alex explained. "I'm obligated to tell you about it. So I'll just come right out with it. Bottom line, there will be no complaint against you if you agree not to fight for custody of Maddie."

Suddenly it all made sense.

"You don't have to do it," Alex said. "We can still—"

"They've worked it pretty good, haven't they?"

"Mark, like I said, I'm willing—"

"You've been around this type of thing. Nasty people fighting over a kid. What's that do to the kid?"

Alex treated the question seriously. "It depends on the child, but most of the time it's not good, obviously. But Maddie—"

"And it can be worse if the kid's the emotional type."

"That depends, too, on a lot of—"

"Maddie's emotional."

Alex looked at her hands.

"If I sign the papers, she won't have to deal with this whole mess anymore, right?"

"You don't have to sign. I can still—"

"I know. But I'm saying, if I did, she wouldn't have to go through anything. I mean, we fight the abuse charge and she's going to have to go on the stand. You're going to have to question her."

"At some point."

"And doctors probing her."

"Yes."

I couldn't let that happen. There was this time when Maddie and I were out walking and went past a chain-link fence. Suddenly, this little dog appeared out of nowhere and ran toward us, barking its head off. Maddie got scared, grabbed my leg, held on tight.

I patted her head and said, "It's all right. Watch." I put my hand near the fence, letting the dog smell it. The pooch stopped barking and wagged its tail.

"See?" I told Maddie. "You want to say hi to the dog?"

Maddie, (I could still feel her trembling) peeked out from behind me and said, "Hi doggie."

I was there to protect her from the barking dog and to show her she didn't have to be scared. But now if I went forward in a fight over Maddie and child abuse, I wouldn't be able to protect her anymore. In fact, I would be the barking dog.

I looked at Alex. "Can I tell you something?"

"Of course."

I recounted my jail experience, then added, "It seems like climbing a mountain, and after all this struggle you get to a plateau and know that you're not going back again. You are higher and safer than you were just a little while ago. I want to stay here."

Alex listened closely.

"I can't give up fighting for her, Alex. But I can't see her hurt, either. What do I do?"

Alex waited a long time before answering. "I'll stall Jennings. Do you have any job opportunities?"

"I've been thinking of coaching baseball. Would it matter if it was in Arizona?"

"Why there?"

"I have a friend, a guy I played with in the minors, who coaches a high school team in Phoenix. About a year ago he said if I ever want to assist, give him a call. I want to get out anyway. I'm through with LA.

"You still get monitored vists—"

"I'll never miss one. I'll make the drive. Ride a bike. Crawl if I have to."

"Meantime, we get you a good criminal lawyer. I know a few."

"Whatever it takes."

"At the right time I'll go back to Jennings with our own offer. I can't promise anything will change but—"

"Go for it, Alex."

She nodded. "And you and I, we pray, right now. We pray for that trust you were talking about. Even lawyers need it. Maybe especially lawyers."

So we prayed. I gritted my teeth as we did. I kept seeing Maddie's face in my mind.

Findings

– 1 –

I gave notice at the apartment that afternoon. And started wrapping up my affairs, if thin threads left blowing in the wind can be called *affairs*.

The idea of moving to Arizona and starting all over again felt right. Any place that was not Los Angeles was fine with me.

I'd only be a six- or seven-hour drive away and could get back for the monitored visits with Maddie. It wouldn't seem like a bad drive if I knew she was on the other end. And my getting it together as a baseball coach or some other job would look good to the court down the line. The criminal case was hanging over my head, but I decided to believe it would work out. Somehow.

The first person I told about my move was Mrs. Williams. In many ways she'd been like a mother to me and a grandmother to Maddie. One of the last few decent people in LA, I say.

She almost cried when I told her, standing in front of her open door in the hallway.

"Will you call me from time to time?" she said.

I hugged her. "Count on it."

When evening came I went over to the Club Cobalt, to see Roland. How was I going to break it to him? Part of me sensed he already knew. I hadn't called him, I'd quit waitering with him, I'm sure he knew something was up.

Roland was in the middle of a set when I came in. Man, he could play. I'd miss that, but I had heard a rumor that jazz had made it to Arizona. There would be other venues.

I sipped a Coke in a booth while Roland played and for a little while felt musical relief. Roland finished off with a rousing update of "Take the A Train." It was like he had sixteen fingers. Piano doesn't get much better than that.

When he joined me I apologized for not having been in touch and told him I was moving out, good-bye.

"Can't believe it," he said. "There's no way."

"Way."

"You're just giving up?"

"Moving to a different location, that's all." I tapped a little tune on the table with my fingers. "You remember that thing you said, God playing jazz?"

He nodded.

"Well, I'm trying to listen for that now, see? I'm really trying to listen."

A long silence passed between us.

"You keep in touch," Roland said.

"Not just that. When I come back into town, maybe I can take up some room on your couch."

"If you shower first."

I put out my hand and we shook. "Deal."

Roland went to play another set and I ordered another Coke. Halfway through the first number, Milo Ayers came into the Cobalt. He made a few rounds, then came over to my booth.

"Markie! You don't answer your calls?"

"Hi, Mr. Ayers. I haven't listened to my messages today."

He sat down. "The guy, looking for your father?"

I'd almost forgotten about that. "What about him?"

"Wants to talk to you. I think he has something."

My skin pulled tight on the back of my neck. "Found him?"

"Don't know. Call him." He took out a pen and wrote something on a paper napkin, then handed it to me. It was a phone number. "You call, huh?" Milo said.

– 2 –

It was a Motel 6 off Highway 15, just outside of Barstow. That's where the guy said he was. Ron Reid, on his way to who knew where.

There was a Denny's next door, separated by a block wall and some dusty oleander. I parked in the Denny's lot and found a place near a couple of pea-green Dumpsters where I could look over the wall and watch the motel parking lot.

The Dumpsters gave off a lovely scent—industrial stink, rust, and rancid food. It blew toward me on a soft wind.

I ignored it, because I was focused on finding a way to get into room 107. That was the number the guy Milo hired gave me.

Your Motel 6's don't get the BMWs or the Benzes, the ones with the most sensitive alarm systems. My best guess for what I was about to do was a new Acura, which was only a few yards away from the door to 107.

Worked like a charm dipped in chocolate. All it took was me sitting hard on the hood, and the alarm—a real nasty one—tore up the quiet of the evening.

I ran down to the end of the row and waited.

Doors began opening, light from inside rooms flooding out on the walk. A husky voice cursed, shouting that the owner—whose legitimacy the shouter was questioning—better take care of this situation *now.*

My hope was that the owner of the Acura would be the last one to respond. In a bath or something, or maybe at Denny's grabbing a cup of coffee.

The alarm kept going. Room 107 stayed sealed.

I edged a little closer, right in front of the window of 108, which was dark. Sound sleepers.

The *WAW WAW WAW WAW* of the alarm was like an ax to the brain.

The shouter was out on the walk now, a hairy man in boxers and a T-shirt, holding a Dr. Pepper like a grenade.

And then a crack in 107.

I waited half a beat, then pushed it open.

Ron Reid shrieked, but the Acura worked its magic and no one could hear it.

"Mind if I come in?" I said over the noise.

"How'd you find me?"

"Are you going to leave me standing out here?"

"You don't understand—"

I pushed past him and walked inside the room. He closed the door quickly, as if someone outside might be spying on us. For all I know he could've been right.

The car alarm continued, though now we were able to talk in a more normal tone. He had on a Hawaiian shirt, red, with pictures of little surfers and fish.

"How did you find me?" he repeated.

"I just want to know one thing—how much did you get?"

"Mark, listen—"

"How much did Troncatti give you to lie in court?"

Ron Reid gave me a long look and sighed. "Ten," he said.

"Ten *thousand?*"

"Yeah."

"Who gave it to you? Who made the drop?"

"Look, they're gonna hurt me, I say anything. I gotta get out of here."

He looked like a lost and desperate mutt. Where I should have felt something hard and hot inside me, I now felt this black, cold hole. I sat down on the edge of the bed.

I looked at him. "You've got to come back and talk about this."

He paced toward the window. The alarm died outside. "Mark, maybe I wish I could, but I can't. I'm afraid of these people."

"You can be protected."

"You don't believe that."

He was right. "You're just going to leave then, take off?"

"I've been on the road most of my life now. I'll find a way to get along."

"You know I have to tell this to the police."

He nodded. "I don't think they'll believe it."

"They just might."

He cocked his head.

"Look, I'm going to be moving to Phoenix. If you want to talk, you can find me. I'll be listed."

He swallowed hard, like his throat was parched. "Why would you want me to do that?"

I wasn't sure myself, but I told him about being in jail and Chaplain Ray and what that all did to me. It must have gotten through a little because Ron Reid nodded and said, "Heavy duty."

I got up. "Just tell me one more thing. Who handed you the money?"

Ron Reid paused a moment, then said, "Troncatti's driver, I think his name's Farid. You know him?"

"Yeah, I do."

"Gave it to me in a gym bag and showed me the gun he said he'd use if I talked."

One more try. "Come back with me, please. Turn this over to the police. Let them—"

He shook his head. "I'm getting out." He looked at his feet. "I'm sorry, Mark. I know I messed things up pretty bad for you."

"You did."

"If it means anything, I'm pretty messed up, too."

"That Wheel isn't so hot, is it?"

He looked up at me and a small glint of realization flickered in his eyes. I went to the motel dresser, pulled out the top drawer, and there it was—a good old Gideon Bible. I took it out and tossed it on the bed. "Read that," I said. "Read that like your life depends on it, because it does."

I started for the door.

"Mark."

I turned back.

Ron Reid's voice quavered. "I wish things had been different. You know, between us."

"Me too, Dad."

I left the room. A desert breeze cooled my cheeks, because they were wet. I wiped them with the back of my hand. I was shaking a little when I got to my car, but managed to unbutton my shirt and take off the cassette recorder I'd strapped to my body with duct tape.

– 3 –

I had to wait an hour at the Santa Monica station before Ruchlis came in. From the look on his face he probably would have expected to see Winona Ryder with a bagful of stolen clothes before he saw me.

"I need you to hear something," I said.

Maybe it was the seeping desperation in my voice that convinced him. He didn't ask for any explanation but showed me to his desk where he took out a small cassette player. We loaded the tape and listened.

It was a pretty good recording with the usual muffles associated with a shirt over a torso. But the stuff I wanted him to hear came out clear.

Ruchlis sat back in his chair and folded his arms after it was finished. "You know this is not admissible evidence."

"I don't care what it is as long as you believe it and get the D.A. on it."

"Suppose I did believe it. The D.A.'s gonna say, what can I do with this? Unless the guy comes in and is willing to testify about what he knows, I can't use this."

"Can you go talk to him then? He's probably still at the motel, or if he isn't you can find him. I did."

"Then you're talking about resources," Ruchlis said. "I got to tell you I don't think this is going to fly. Who's to say this isn't a doctored tape? You're an actor, right?"

"What's that got to do with it?"

"You get one of your friends to play Daddy and out comes this little tape."

I just looked at him for a second. How could he think I would make up something like this? My hands were like claws as I touched my forehead. In my mind I was crying out to God for help.

"Look," Ruchlis said, "you've got to see it from my standpoint. I'm a cop and my feelings don't matter. I think you may be telling me the truth. But I also know you were spying on Troncatti's house, you broke in, you're desperate, and maybe even a little nuts. Who knows?"

"*I* know."

"Does anybody know if they're nuts or not? I may be a little squirrel food myself. Point is, I can't do anything for you, except maybe give you a lead."

I looked at him.

"You forget we had this conversation when it's finished, got it?"

I nodded.

"Call Harrison Ellis at channel 7. Say the stripes from Santa Monica sent you over. He'll listen to what you have to say, but from there I can't promise you anything. My advice, don't get your hopes up."

– 4 –

Harrison Ellis was well known to LA audiences. He'd broken quite a few stories, including one that brought down the head of a major studio. Ellis had the reputation of being a straight shooter and a good reporter.

We met at a little restaurant on Argyle. It was out of the way but sort of LA tony. That meant a lot of people who pretended like they didn't want to be seen ate there, hoping to be seen.

Ellis was about forty and didn't have an anchorman's good looks. That was a point in his favor. He was a guy who had to make it on his reporting skills and not on the fact that he could read a teleprompter with a straight face over a square chin.

The hostess knew him and showed him to what I took to be a regular table. It was near the kitchen out of the way. We were not among those who wished to be seen.

I told the story as quietly and objectively as I could. I didn't want him thinking that I was what everybody else seemed to think I was—a slightly off-kilter child abuser with an ax to grind. Fifteen minutes later I ended my tale, which was only interrupted a couple of times by the waiter who wanted to do his job.

Then I handed him the cassette and told him what was on it. His eyebrows went up at that. He seemed to be smelling a story.

"You have a copy?" he asked.

"Of course," I said.

"Don't say of course. I've seen smarter guys than you make the stupidest mistakes. Like this lawyer who liked to make videotapes of his, shall we say, conferences with female clients. He digitized the tapes and put them on a CD-ROM. Then one day he was in court presenting a final argument to a jury, and using the CD-ROM on his laptop to project some graphics about the evidence—"

"Don't tell me."

"That's right. Instead of a picture of the accident scene up came a nice shot from one of his private consultations. That was the end of his legal career. I hear he's making two hundred grand a year now making adult films. America, what a country."

He laughed.

"Personal note," he said. "Let's say all this is true, what you went through, which I'm judging it is, looking at you. How're you keeping it together?"

It was strange how quickly and surely the answer came. "I'm just hanging on to God, Jesus, hope."

Harrison Ellis smiled. "Throw in good ratings and I might just be with you on that."

– 5 –

That old cliché about the quiet before a storm is true. Aren't all clichés based on fact? In my case, it should be modified a little. Because what happened next was worse than a storm. A storm's something you've been through before, so you think you can handle it. What hit next was something I could never have been prepared for.

It happened three days after I left the tape with Ellis. I had a week left on the apartment and was cleaning it up, hoping to get back the security deposit. There was even a small beam of light at the end of my tunnel. Garner Charles, my coaching friend in Arizona, said there was a spot on his staff for me. It wasn't much money, but it was more than I was making now, which was zero.

I gave in and called Nikki. I felt like I could finally talk to her. I thanked her for all she'd done, for getting me into the Bible study, for being one of those people God uses to point someone in the right direction.

I also thanked her for reminding me what real acting was all about. "I hear there are some good regional theaters near Phoenix," I told her. "Maybe I'll give it a shot."

"You should," she said. "Because you're really good."

That meant a lot, coming from her. I said I'd keep in touch.

That evening I went down to the Cobalt to hang with Roland. In a way, it was like a going-away party. He played some of my favorite jazz, just for me. It made me feel happier than I had in a long, long time.

It was around nine and I was still at the club when my cell phone rang. It was Ruchlis on the other end. I almost fell off my chair.

"Paula's in the hospital," he said.

My heart froze. "What happened?"

"I'll tell you when you get here. We're at St. Stephen's, Santa Monica."

I made it in record time. At the desk they told me she was on the third floor.

As soon as I got out of the elevators I saw Erica Montgomery. She was pacing in the hall, as if she were waiting for me.

"Oh, Mark," she said, without any animosity in her voice. That in itself was strange. There was defeat about her. Every other time I'd seen Erica, she had this air of invincibility, like she was made of cold granite. Now there were chips and cracks, and a confusion in her eyes. The world she had tried to control was no longer under her influence.

She started, very slightly, to shake. Without a word I took her arm and pulled her into the waiting room and sat her down on one of the vinyl chairs. She did not resist me a bit.

"Where's Maddie?" I said. "Who has Maddie?"

"She's—" Erica cleared her throat—"with a woman, a social worker."

"Where? What happened?"

And then the granite shattered. Erica put her head in her hands and quaked with sobs. There was one other person in the room, an older gentleman on the other side. He looked at me with a sort of weary wisdom, as if he had been through this scenario countless times and was telling me what to do.

I did something I never thought I'd do in my life. I put my arm around Erica's shoulders. More amazingly, she did not pull away.

"He cut her with a knife," she said, into her hands, so it was muffled. But I knew what she said and felt paralyzed—I don't know, with fear of the awful implications. Was Paula hanging on to life by a thread?

"My beautiful Paula," Erica sobbed. "He cut her beautiful face."

That was more shocking, more horrible. I knew exactly what she meant. There was an infamous case out here some years ago, where an actress's face was scarred by a crazy stalker. He couldn't have her, so he was determined to punish her. And I knew that fit Troncatti's profile. He considered himself a god among men, an impression reinforced by all of the bootlickers that hang on to a good Hollywood ride. Paula must have threatened to leave him.

It fit with what I'd seen that night at Troncatti's, when he'd hit Paula. She was so much like Erica, not a woman to take anything lying down. Was this the result?

I kept my arm around Erica as she fought against her tears and lost. I just held her for a while.

"I'd like to see her, Erica," I said. "May I?"

I did not have to ask. I could have left her and gone straight to the room. But I asked anyway.

She stopped crying—well, stopped gushing—and looked up. Her eyes were red and wet and tired. She opened her mouth but did not speak. Then she nodded her head.

"Wait here for me," I said. I went outside the waiting room and found a water fountain with paper cups. I filled a cup and took it back to Erica, lifting her hand to put the cup in it.

"I'll be back," I said.

The nurse at the station told me Paula was in room 504. I followed the wall around until I found it. I went in the open door and saw Ruchlis.

He was standing midway in the room, which held two beds. The one nearest me was empty. A screen obscured the second bed, which held Paula.

Ruchlis put his finger to his lips and motioned me outside the door.

"I want to see her," I said.

Ruchlis put up his hand. "I know. You will. I just want to have you talk to me later."

"What happened up there?"

"Troncatti apparently sliced your wife's face."

"Apparently?"

"Well, that's what she says."

"Where is he? Did you get him?"

"Not yet."

That news made me want to jump out of my skin and scream. Troncatti was still out there. "And where's my daughter?"

"Down at the station with a very nice lady from child services."

"I want her."

"One step at a time."

I shook my head. "I want her, and I want her right after I talk to Paula."

"Don't fight me on this, huh? I'm going to have a man come up and keep the press away. There's going to be a circus when the news hits, and I'm going to try to keep it from hitting as long as I can. You blundering around isn't going to help."

He was right, of course. "Can't you get Paula to some secret location?" I said.

"I can't. Maybe she has friends, family. You."

The prospect of me having anything to do with Paula's future hadn't entered my brain. Ruchlis provided me an odd little jolt, like the snapping of static electricity.

"Why would he do that?" I said. "Cut her?"

Ruchlis shrugged. "Paula says she didn't know about the payoff to your father, that Harrison Ellis got to her by phone and asked her about it, played the tape over the phone. She says she confronted Troncatti and they had a blowout and she said she was leaving him, and that's when it happened. Troncatti may have been under the influence at the time. Drugs."

I nearly dropped to the floor. It was almost too much for my mind and body to handle.

"Come down to the station after you talk to her," Ruchlis said. "I'll see what I can do."

"Thanks."

As I walked into the hospital room, two waves of emotion hit me simultaneously, like I was some hapless surfer in storm-tossed waters. The first emotion was a growing elation that I was going to get to see Maddie soon, down at the police station.

The other emotion was a burning dread in my stomach as I got closer to the curtain and Paula's bed. It wasn't just what I thought I'd see, though the pictures in my mind were bad enough. What was I going to say to Paula? Or she to me?

What was I going to feel?

I stepped slowly around the curtain and there she was. Her eyes were closed but they were barely exposed anyway. Her face was wrapped in gauze. Two large bulges stuck out, one on each cheek. I could only imagine what was underneath the bandages.

For a full minute I stood there, just looking at her. I tried to imagine her face the way it was, and saw it—not the last time, at Troncatti's, when it was full of dark confusion. But the first time I saw her, at Roland's party, when I'd been knocked over by her beauty. The way she smiled when we ate peanut M&Ms together. That was the face I saw.

Some low sound came out of my throat, and she opened her eyes.

I took one step closer.

Her eyes got big and then she shut them again, turned her head toward the pillow. Then she shook it a little, like someone saying No with a tone of regret.

"I came as soon as I heard. The cop. I know him."

Paula didn't say anything, but her breath came out in a slow, labored way.

"I mean, he knows me. I won't go into it. He says Maddie is okay. Down at the station. Maybe you know that. I saw your mom out there, we actually talked a little. Can you believe that?"

Still not a response from Paula.

"You want me to go, I will," I said.

She did not turn her head. She put her hand over her face, like she wanted to hide from me.

"We don't have to say anything," I said. There was a chair near the bed. I sat in it and stayed there for a long time.

Sometime in there Paula fell asleep. She was peaceful finally, and I imagined it was the most peace she'd had since, well, since getting involved with Troncatti.

How could she have known all this awaited her? She'd gone to Rome for a big break, the thing that all actors hope for. You get into that whole whirlwind and don't think about much else. Don't think about a director who gets high on power and manipulation, and what he might do if you don't let him have power over *you.*

That he might go nuts and scar you.

In a way that made me sick, I thought about my own bouts of craziness. Throwing glass bottles. Losing control. Not caring what other people said.

Was I that different from Antonio Troncatti? Only by a miracle of grace was I going to be better than I was. And I wanted to be better. For Maddie. And for Paula.

I leaned over her and whispered, "I'm sorry."

A nurse swept in, all business.

"The police," she said. "They're not here?"

"Not right now."

That seemed to disturb her. "And you are?"

I didn't hesitate, the answer flowing out of my mouth without doubt or question.

"I'm her husband," I said.

SIGNS

– 1 –

Arizona is everything they say. The Grand Canyon State. Landscapes to take your breath away—mountain ranges, winding rivers, grasslands, sand dunes, and sunsets that stick to your heart.

It's also hot. Hell's stove. Especially right outside Phoenix.

How do people make it in the summers? I suppose I'll find out. I plan on sticking here for a long time.

The nights are what I love best about the place. Sometimes the moon is so big you can poke lunar dust with a stick. And the stars—well, let's just say the same sky doesn't flicker over LA.

Nights here are what give me hope, and what I hang on to with a grip that would make a bear trap weep with envy.

I hope a lot of things. I hope they'll catch up with Troncatti someday, hiding out in Europe, get him back here to stand trial. At least I won't be. The D.A. had to drop the criminal charge, their chief witness being a slasher on the run.

And I hope they nail Bryce Jennings as an accessory to fraud on the court. Ruchlis keeps me posted on this. The tape I made of Ron Reid was played on a TV news report and a legal firestorm broke loose in town. Alex called me a week ago to say that Ron had been located and might even be willing to cooperate.

In a strange way, I hope that Ron will do the right thing and that I'll actually talk to him again. That part of my life has yet to be written up.

There's also the chance that Paula and I will do some theater work together, if she ever gets the desire again. She'll always have two jagged white scars on her cheeks, but makeup will suffice for a theater performance. There are a couple good regional theaters here and one that does a lot of Shakespeare. With Paula's name recognition, she'd be a shoe-in to be cast as Rosalind in *As You Like It*. I'd be happy to be a spear carrier, so long as I got to be in the show with her.

We'll see. The fact that she's here with me is miracle enough for now. Even Erica seems to be for us. I guess we've all been through enough to see that none of us are made of granite.

But what I pray for constantly is that I get Maddie back.

Oh, Maddie is with us here, physically, in the new apartment just outside Phoenix. Getting her out of protective custody, even with Paula's consent, was a two-week nightmare. We did it, though the system wanted to keep putting the screws to us. Alex was a big help. It took an emergency court appearance and sworn testimony from an unexpected source—Renard J. Harper testified on my behalf.

The LA part of the nightmare was finally over.

But Maddie is not the same little girl I knew.

A very nice psychotherapist in Phoenix, someone we now go to church with as a matter of fact, is giving us a reasonable deal on therapy for Maddie. She was definitely messed with by Troncatti and Paula. Dr. Nelson deals with Paula's guilt, which is almost as bad as Maddie's distrust. But both of them are tough. They got that from Erica.

As for me, when we were alone, Dr. Nelson told me what I can do, and it's what I've already done a hundred times over—forgive and seek God's healing in all things. When I do, I can't help thinking of that thing Tom Starkey said one night, about how the most important thing we may need, before anything else, is to be shaped by God's rough hands. I still don't quite get it. I'm not a saint in the forgiving part. But then I'm beginning to realize you don't have to get everything before you trust.

Which helps with the guilt I sometimes feel. If I hadn't given the tape to Harrison Ellis, if he hadn't played it for Paula over the phone before he ran with the story, maybe Paula wouldn't have been cut up.

Paula told me what happened. When she heard the tape she confronted Troncatti. She said she'd tell everything to the police about what they'd done to Maddie unless he left her and Maddie alone and didn't do anything else to hurt my career. Troncatti had been drinking heavily that night, and the threat of exposure, coupled with the threat of a woman leaving *him*, made him snap. That's when he grabbed a knife and did it.

All I know now is that Paula and I are somehow finding our way back to each other, both of us broken, both of us helping each other glue pieces back together. Maddie does not trust me fully yet. But I think time will overcome that. I pray hard to God every day. And look for signs.

– 2 –

Last night I went out on the balcony of our apartment. The moon was big and silvery, like in the storybooks. I sat down on a plastic chair in the warm air and watched the sky for a while.

Then the sliding door opened. I thought it was Paula coming out. But it wasn't. It was Maddie.

This was a little shocking, as Maddie had not wanted to be alone with me since we'd all gotten back together. She would cling to Paula, of course. And as long as her mother was in the room I was welcome. I didn't push anything. Dr. Nelson said I should just let things happen naturally. Even though Paula had explained about the bad things she and Troncatti had made up about me, there was a wall between Maddie and me that had to be taken down a brick at a time. That project was only just beginning.

Maddie didn't say anything to me at first. She sat in the other plastic chair and looked at the sky, too. Her feet, dangling from the chair, did not quite reach the ground. She swung them back and forth slowly. Still so little.

Finally, I said, "Hi."

"Hi," Maddie said.

"You like it here in Arizona?"

She nodded.

"Where's Mommy?" I asked.

"Lying down."

"Good."

We shared a silence for a long moment. I wanted to be so careful.

"Maybe we could all go get some ice cream tomorrow," I said.

"Okay."

I looked back at the sky. "Big moon, huh?"

"Yeah." Maddie's eyes reflected the moonlight as she looked up. Then she started to hum something. I wasn't sure at first what it was, maybe just an embarrassed tune to fight the discomfort of our moment. But as it went on I could hear it clearly. She was humming "Buffalo Gals."

"You remember that song?" I said.

"Uh-huh."

I stood up, slowly, so as not to scare her. But there wasn't any stopping me. It was like I was being pulled up by a string from the sky. Facing my daughter then was like an actor's horrible moment, when the casting director is about to announce who made the cut and who didn't. Who would be called back for more auditions, and who would be sent home to lick their wounds and wonder whether they'd ever make it in the business.

What would Maddie tell me when I said what I just couldn't hold back?

"Would you let me pick you up, Maddie?"

It was pushing it, I know. But I couldn't stay silent.

Maddie looked into my eyes, like she was searching for a memory, one that was smudged and unclear but sitting back there in her mind as real as the dark hills off in the distance.

Then she stood up and came to me, raising her arms a little. I reached down and lifted her to me, being very careful not to squeeze too hard.

I shifted her so she was against my chest and she put her head on my shoulder, just like she used to. I smelled her hair. The scent of shampoo was on it and it was silky soft against my cheek.

And then we swayed, swayed, swayed. Time went completely away as we danced by the light of the moon.

ACKNOWLEDGMENTS

As usual, I owe thanks to several key people who helped in the writing of this book.

Ronald Gue, attorney-at-law, was wonderfully generous with his time. He shared his expertise in California family law with me and gave me helpful comments on the novel as a whole.

Dave Lambert, my editor, once again helped me shape a better book. Karen Ball was insightful and encouraging in so many ways. What a blessing it is to have them on my side.

Many thanks to Heather Wilke, Elaine Clubb, Lisa Samson, Colleen Coble; also to Alan Perkins of Journey Christian Church, Westlake, Ohio, for allowing me to reproduce a portion of his sermon, "A Commitment to Prayer," in these pages.

And to my wife, Cindy, my first editor and encourager throughout the writing process—I can't thank God enough that you're my partner in all things.

Deadlock

James Scott Bell

She is a Supreme Court justice.

She is an atheist.

And she is about to encounter the God of the truth and justice she has sworn to uphold.

For years, Millicent Hollander has been the consistent swing vote on abortion and other hot-button issues. Now she's poised to make history as the first female Chief Justice of the United States Supreme Court. But something is about to happen that no one has counted on, least of all Hollander: a near-death experience that will thrust her on a journey toward God.

Fighting every inch of the way, Hollander finds herself dragged toward belief in something she has never believed in—while others in Washington are watching her every step. Too much is at stake to let a Christian occupy the country's highest judicial office. Even as Hollander grapples with the interplay between faith and the demands of her position, and as she finds answers through her growing friendship with Pastor Jack Holden, a hidden web of lies, manipulation, and underworld connections is being woven around her. It could control her. It could destroy her reputation. Unless God intervenes, it could take her out of the picture permanently.

Softcover 0-310-24388-2
Microsoft Reader® ebook 0-310-25612-7
Adobe® Acrobat® ebook Reader® 0-310-25613-5
Palm™ Reader ebook 0-310-25615-1

Pick up a copy today at your favorite bookstore!

GRAND RAPIDS, MICHIGAN 49530 USA

WWW.ZONDERVAN.COM